dragon fire

dragon fire

Charles Ashton

WALKER BOOKS

AND SUBSIDIARIES

LONDON • BOSTON • SYDNEY

First published individually as
Jet Smoke and Dragon Fire (1991),
Into the Spiral (1992) and *The Shining Bridge* (1993)
by Walker Books Ltd
87 Vauxhall Walk, London SE11 5HJ

This edition published 2003

2 4 6 8 10 9 7 5 3 1

This book has been typeset in Bulmer

Printed and bound in Great Britain by Bookmarque Ltd, Croydon, Surrey

British Library Cataloguing in Publication Data:
a catalogue record for this book
is available from the British Library

ISBN 0-7445-9061-2

for rachel, anna and ben

CONTENTS

jet smoke and dragon fire

into the spiral

the shining bridge

jet smoke and dragon fire

the search for the stone

SPARROW COULD REMEMBER FIVE OCCASIONS WHEN Ms Minn had taken one of her "turns" and marched off into the mountains. The last time was when he had found Murie's milkstone. The next time it happened, his whole life changed.

Poor Ms Minn, poor old stick – that was what parents said; but as far as their children were concerned, her "turns" were something to look forward to, because they meant a holiday of weeks, or even months, before the old creature tottered back from wherever she had been and clanged the school bell once more.

"She's going," Sparrow whispered to Bull. "I can feel it. She's cracking."

Bull tapped his head. "This'll be a one-monther, at least," he whispered back.

On Sparrow's other side there was a crash as Gogs' tower of coins teetered and fell all over the floor. Gogs' curly red head went down as he scrambled for them. His nose came up over the edge of Sparrow's seat. "This'll be a one-monther," he whispered, grinning his biggest Gogs-grin.

Last time – the time when Sparrow found the milkstone – Ms Minn's departure had been quite dramatic. She had tipped over the desks and stamped on the calculators before storming off in floods of tears. The calculators had seemed undamaged – not that anyone would have known either way – but the carpenter had had to be called in to repair some of the desks. That had been a four-month holiday, the longest Sparrow could remember.

Today Ms Minn had them haul out the boxes of copper coins. First of all they had to sort out the ones with women's heads on them from the ones with men's heads. The girls took the women's-head coins and the boys took the men's-head ones, and then they had to make towers on their desks. Ms Minn went round the class admiring their teetering spires of money. Occasionally she poked one and sent it crashing to ruin on the floor.

Just before lunch, she suddenly asked, "Does anyone know how to tell the time?" There were a lot of strange looks as everyone tried to work out what she meant. "Very well," she went on, "I'll tell you. Everyone cover their eyes. Now –

> 'At the third stone
> The time has come…'"

Everyone waited. "That's it," said Ms Minn brightly. "Time for lunch."

But late in the afternoon she stopped and moaned and stood wringing her hands, like a bony old scarecrow in her dusty black dress. The paper-thin skin of her face puckered in an expression of unspeakable sorrow. "Oh," she groaned, "oh – oh – oh no, that's enough, that's quite enough…"

Everyone became very quiet. A far-away look came into the old teacher's mild face, while her pale brown eyes seemed to film over like tar in a puddle. "All right," she said decisively, "I'm coming." And she turned and left the classroom.

An excited buzz of talk broke out, and there was a scraping and a scrambling as chairs were pushed back and coats were fetched and holidays were thought about.

Soon afterwards, people saw Ms Minn clumping off in her big boots, a black scraggle under the autumn-golden trees by the road out of the village. Her wild white hair flamed in the sunset and her coat flapped like a washing-line of rags. No one who saw her thought much about it: Ms Minn had been the teacher at the village school for as long as anyone could remember, and for as long as anyone could remember she had been having her "turns". No one knew where she went, but as she always seemed to come back safely enough, no one was much worried about her.

Sparrow, Bull and Gogs followed her shortly afterwards. Their homes were outside the village, on three little rounded green hills that rose beside the Old Road: Gogs' first, then Bull's, and Sparrow's the last of the three. All the way up the steep, cobbled street that led out of the village, the three friends shuffled fallen leaves and argued about how long their holiday would be, and what they would do during it; but by the time they got to the foot of Gogs' path they had got no further than agreeing to meet on the railway track the next day.

In the light of the sunset of that last ordinary day of his life, Sparrow panted up the white-pebbled path to the top of his own hill, and came in sight of the thatched roof of his house. The great rounded mountain peak that loomed over the valley glowed gold-rose as the sun sank. Over the roof, the forest climbed towards the mountain's stony base in tangled folds and hummocks from the small, hilly fields where he and Murie had gathered the last of their harvest two weeks before. He trotted on down between the tall kale plants in the vegetable garden, stopped to tickle the tummy of a large ginger cat stretched on the seat outside the front door and passed into the wood-panelled hallway where his father's crossbow and quiver of bolts still hung, polished and greased, on the wall.

"Is that you, Sparrow?" Murie, his mother, called through to the living room, where Sparrow had paused in front of the television. "You'll need to get wood from the coalshed."

"School's stopped," Sparrow called back absently, gazing at the blank grey screen. "Ms Minn's off again."

"Poor old thing," Murie's voice came back. "I don't know how she keeps going."

Sparrow's eyes fell on the milkstone, glowing coolly from the shadows in its place on the top of the television, and a thought struck him.

The railway line was a favourite place for the boys. Over a good deal of its length lower down in the valley, the village people had lifted the rails from the sleepers and melted them down to make knives or ploughs or grates for their fires; but higher up, where the line climbed off into the mountains, it had been left untouched. The metal was rusted, and amongst the stones on the bed of the track skinny weeds poked up, and a strange, acrid smell always hung faintly in the air. It was a desolate, mysterious thing, stretching off through the rocky, green-grown land, and no adults ever came there.

Sparrow minced along the flat, rusty top of one of the rails, one foot in front of the other, holding out his arms to either side to balance himself. "Anyway, I do know what an aeroplane looks like," he said, continuing an argument they had been having before.

"Go on then, tell us," challenged Bull, whose grand-mother had told them there was no such thing.

"It's like a sort of tube with wings like birds' – only they don't flap – out to the sides like this," said Sparrow, flapping his hands up and down on the ends of his outstretched arms. "And people sit inside the tube."

"You said that their wings didn't flap," remarked Gogs.

"I was just showing you," Sparrow dropped his arms and immediately lost his balance and slipped off the rail. "Anyway, I know, because my grandad used to say he flew in one once, when he was very young."

Bull snorted. "If there was such a thing, my gran would know all about it. She says there're no stories about them at all."

"I didn't say they were a story. My grandad really flew in one."

"So why didn't my gran?" said Bull.

"Or mine," added Gogs.

In most things Sparrow would not have dared to suggest that anyone could ever have known more than Bull's grand-mother. For one thing, Bull's gran had brought Bull up because both his mother and father were dead, and neither

17

Sparrow nor Gogs liked to offend Bull by saying anything against her. But for another thing, old Mrs Hind really did know a lot that no one else in the village knew. She had told Bull some of her old stories, but she always said, "Now keep that to yourself, so it doesn't get out," and Bull would do as she said – except that, very occasionally, he would tell Sparrow and Gogs a little of what he had learned.

"There's dragons," said Gogs pleasantly, trying to head off an argument.

"What about dragons?" Bull snapped.

"There's dragons in stories," Gogs said.

"So?" said Bull, with scorn. "Dragons are animals. They may be magic, but they're still animals: they're real things, not stupid flying tubes."

Bull, with his black hair and his piercing blue eyes that stared unblinking from under fierce, knotted eyebrows, never let his friends forget that he knew more than they did, or ever would. It was through him that they had learned that there was such a thing as magic, and he always talked as if he knew many dark secrets. This made him the accepted leader of the three friends.

Sparrow shrugged. "Anyway, I'm only saying what my grandad said," he mumbled.

"Are we going to hunt rabbits?" Gogs said. "That's what my dad said we should do."

Then Sparrow remembered his idea from the night before and forgot about his grandad's aeroplane.

"It's Murie's birthday tomorrow," he said, "and I wanted to try and find another milkstone to go with the first one."

Bull's scowling face brightened. "I'll help you look," he said promptly.

18

"Me too," said Gogs, "though Sparrow's the best stone-finder there is."

That was true, and even Bull had to admit it. Milkstones, with their delicate gold veins and their white, smooth surface, were very rare, and Sparrow had found the only one in recent times. The only place they could be found was the Cliff of Stones, and the three friends immediately set off through the bright thickets of golden birch and red rowan that climbed towards the deep shade of the pine forest on the lower slopes of the mountains.

In the mid-morning they reached the Cliff. You came on it very suddenly, rearing sixty metres above the dense-packed pine forest, grey-brown, full-face towards the sun. Against the lower half of it there was a heap of loose stones and dust which became steadily steeper, till at one end of the Cliff the land plunged away in screes and rock-falls down towards the Forest River.

The three friends started working along beneath the towering precipice. The morning mists had cleared away and the autumn heat shimmered over the rock.

"There's always amethysts," said Bull after a little. Sweat was pouring off his face.

Gogs' fair skin was beetroot-red. "I bet that's full of amethyst," he said, holding out a lump of rock the size of a small turnip.

Sparrow took the lump and tapped it doubtfully. "I don't think so," he said.

Gogs spent the next ten minutes trying to break open the rock by banging it on other rocks, only to find that Sparrow had, as usual, been right. Disheartened, he sat down, pulled round a leather bag attached to his belt, and fished a squashy parcel out of it. "I'm going to have some lunch," he announced.

Bull sat down beside him. He had food with him too. "I never thought of bringing anything to eat," Sparrow said, "and I'm really quite hungry."

"You'd forget your own ears if they weren't tied on with string," said Bull.

"You'd forget your own legs if your mam didn't stick your body on to them in the morning," said Gogs.

Sparrow accepted their rebuke silently, and Bull spared him a sandwich while Gogs gave him an apple. But not long after they had eaten, Bull and Gogs said they had had enough of stone-searching. They tried to persuade Sparrow to go back with them, but Sparrow went vague, as he always did when his mind was set on something.

"I'll just check along this bit," he murmured, stooping, picking up the stones, turning them over, searching left and right. After a little, Gogs and Bull realized he wasn't coming at all, and started off through the trees.

"We'll tell your mam you forgot your balance and fell off the cliff!" they called cheerfully.

Sparrow only half heard. "I'll just check ten more stones," he told himself, "then I'll follow them, and Murie will have to have one of the amethysts."

But ten stones were picked up and then thrown down again, and another ten, and another, and soon Sparrow had forgotten all about Gogs and Bull, and searched on alone through the silent afternoon.

The boys were not supposed to go to the steep edge of the scree at the end of the Cliff, and as Sparrow worked his way along the cliff-foot, the sound of the river far below reached his ears, deep and drumming, and he knew he was very near the forbidden place. He flattened himself on the ground, crawling forwards on his stomach to peer over.

As he peeped out over the broken rocks, he knocked a stone over the edge. He watched as it bounced and bounded down the drop until it disappeared into the forest gloom.

Looking down the slope where the stone had gone, Sparrow noticed something amongst the grey trunks. He squinted harder, but after frowning and squinting for quite some time, all he knew for certain was that there was a *shape* down there – bundled on the ground, difficult to make out because it was almost the same colour as the forest floor under the shadow of the trees.

He peered and peered, creeping out further than he should have – even for someone lying on his stomach – to the very edge of the drop. In a little while he became certain that the shape he was looking at was the shape of a man huddled up on the earth, lying quite still.

21

That was when the whole thing suddenly became very strange. Sparrow was looking down on the man's shape from high above. He was almost too far away even to be sure it was a man and not a tree trunk or a large boulder. And all the time the noise of the waterfall down below filled the air, too loud for any other sound to be heard. Yet as Sparrow watched, the shape below became clearer and clearer. He gazed, lost in total concentration, and gradually made out that it was a man dressed in a long green-brown coat with a hood covering his head.

As soon as he realized this – almost as if it had been waiting for him – the head moved, and the face under the hood became visible. Sparrow caught his breath, and the hairs on the back of his neck prickled. It was a face wild and old and wrinkled, with tangled grey hair all about it; but glinting through the hair were piercing green eyes – eyes green as birch-leaves, as wild as a windy day. For just a moment, Sparrow thought he had seen that face before, but then the mouth moved, and a quiet voice said – as clearly as if it had spoken right beside his ear – "Boy, come down here to me: I need your help."

the gift

SPARROW HAD TO GO A LONG WAY ROUND TO GET down to the place where the old man lay: through the woods in front of the Cliff of Stones until he found the Forest River; then along beside the river until it fell away spuming and foaming over the jagged rocks of the waterfall; then up again through the trees at the foot of the steep scree.

But the old man wasn't difficult to find. Sparrow almost walked straight into him.

As soon as he saw him, Sparrow realized that he was not able to walk: one of his legs was so badly twisted that it was almost behind his back. "I fell," he grumbled. "Silly old goat."

Sparrow said nothing. He knew the old man wanted his help – he had asked for it, anyway – but he wasn't sure what he could do. He certainly could not carry him!

"Well then, well then, don't just stand there," the old

man chided, "that won't do any good."

"Shall I pull you up?" Sparrow said.

The old man spluttered under his hood, and his eyes glinted like sunlight rippling through the trees. "Pull me up? He wants to pull me up!" he gasped to himself. Then, looking Sparrow full in the face – Sparrow again felt a shiver running up his spine at the glint of those wild forest eyes – "Twenty strong men couldn't lift me up, young one," he chuckled, "not even if they were yoked to a strong team of oxen."

"I think just one strong man could pull you up," said Sparrow, who was beginning to wonder if the old man might be a little crazy. "In fact, I think I could pull you up, if it wouldn't hurt you."

"One strong man, eh?" the old man said. "Or one skinny little fellow no taller than a salt-barrel. Come on then, give it a go and you'll see." He held out his hand with a chuckle.

Sparrow took it. It felt strange – cold, and not quite like a hand: more like a piece of polished wood, maybe.

Sparrow dug his feet into a tussock and pulled. Nothing moved. The old man's grip on his own hand didn't seem particularly tight, but Sparrow had the strange feeling of being pulled downwards. He grasped the old man's wrist with his other hand and heaved for all he was worth, digging his feet firmer into the damp grassy ground. There wasn't the slightest hint of a movement: it was as though he were hauling at the branch of an ancient tree with roots that reached deep into the earth. It wasn't that the old man was too heavy to move: more that he was a part of something that simply *didn't* move. Sweat broke out on Sparrow's forehead; his whole body was taut like a bent bow; he felt

24

as if his arms were being tugged out of their sockets. A high-pitched grunt broke from between his clenched teeth, and just then the ground gave way. The grassy tussock broke under his feet, his shoes skidded forwards over mud and he sat down *bump*, on his bottom, with a shock that jarred his whole back.

The old man hooted with laughter. He coughed and wheezed and spluttered till Sparrow forgot all about his sore bottom and began to worry that the other would choke with laughing.

"Not bad! Not bad!" the old man gasped at last. "You almost shifted my left little toe. You're stronger than you think. You might even move a mountain some day. But you can't move me. No one can move me!"

Sparrow got up slowly, rubbing his bottom. He was quite convinced that the old man was mad now, yet it was true enough, he hadn't been able to move him.

25

"How can I help you then?" he asked.

"That's more like it," the old man murmured. "Questions are better than answers." He looked Sparrow slowly up and down. Then he remarked, "You are in a dream."

"Yes, I think I must be," Sparrow agreed, scratching his head.

"Not in the way you think," the old man said. "You couldn't move me because you are a dream-thing and I am not."

Sparrow did not much like the sound of this, but he said nothing.

"Well, listen," the old man said, "I said I was a silly old goat and that's just exactly what I am. I came out without my stick, I did, and now I've gone and fallen down through the trees and broken my leg."

Sparrow didn't understand what the old man meant by saying that he had "fallen down through the trees", so all he said was, "Where is your stick?"

"Well, listen," the old one said again. "What you have to do is follow the little dark stream up to its source. You'll come to it if you go down beside the river for a little bit. When you get to its source, there's a cave, and in the cave there's my stick."

As the old man described it, Sparrow had a clear picture in his mind of the cave, and a strange bent stick of dark, polished wood leaning against its back wall.

The old man nodded, almost as if he could see the picture that Sparrow was seeing. "That's right," he chuckled. "Now, there's just one thing about my stick: it'll try to play tricks on you. But don't you let it. You remember it's just a stick you're fetching me, and you'll manage well enough."

A short way below the place where he had found the old man, Sparrow came upon the little dark stream running down the hillside in a deep channel among the straight, slender grey trunks of a young ash wood. Keeping as close to it as he could, he started the ascent. By the time he had climbed through the ash wood to where the rocky mountain heights towered above him, he saw from the sun that it had become late. He realized sadly that he would probably not manage to get a stone for Murie at all now.

Up and up Sparrow climbed, and always the little dark stream murmured softly beside him. Soon he was higher in the mountains than he had ever been before, climbing over short grass in a flat space between two rocky walls, with the little dark stream flowing quietly through the greenest part of the grass.

26

Here and there ivy grew, covering the rock walls, and it was eventually into a solid mass of ivy that the little dark stream disappeared. Sparrow forced his way through the thick, cool leaves, and found that the ivy was growing over a cleft in the rock wall just wide enough for him to squeeze through.

He emerged into a circular space: a mountain courtyard with frowning rock walls on every side. Through the courtyard the little dark stream rustled, and in the very centre was the place where it bubbled up through the ground from under some flat, silvery stones. Straight across from it, Sparrow saw the triangle-shape of a cave mouth in the rock wall.

The cave had furniture in it, and was very like an ordinary room. There was a low fire in the grate, a chair beside the fire, a bed in one corner, a table in the middle and shelves with something on them that Sparrow didn't recognize, for the simple reason that he had never seen a book before.

He saw the stick straight away, and was glad that he wouldn't have to look for it, for he found the cave just a little bit spooky. He crossed over to where the stick was leaning against the wall, and was about to take it when – *sssss!* He found he had made a horrible mistake: it was not a stick at all, but a snake! Brown with vivid red markings in a zig-zag down its back, it was the thickness of Sparrow's leg, and its wedge-like expressionless face and blank golden eyes were turned full on him. It must have been hanging down from something on the wall, Sparrow thought as, frozen to the spot with fear, he watched the thing slither down into great heavy coils on the floor. Its head swayed slowly, stretching out towards him, the tongue flickering from the slit of its mouth.

Sparrow's hair stood all on end, and he turned and bolted. He didn't stop till he was right outside the cave, in the middle of the courtyard of rocks, with the little dark stream bubbling out from the stones at his feet. There he waited, expecting to see the snake slithering out of the cave at any moment.

But the snake did not come. Above his head, the colour was draining out of the sky: sunset could be no more than half an hour off. Sparrow's thoughts turned again to the old man's instructions. He forced himself, reluctantly, back to the triangle-shaped cave mouth, and peered in fearfully, watching for the snake but at the same time looking round to see if he could make out the stick leaning against some other wall.

28   How strange: there, against the wall right in front of him, was the stick he had first seen. Twisted and bent, and all of smooth dark polished wood – the same stick he had pictured when the old man had told him about it!

Then he remembered what the old man had said about the stick playing tricks on him. Of course, he thought, there never was any snake at all! His fear left him in a rush. He could almost have laughed.

In he went, and over to the stick. He put his hands on his hips and said to it, "Stick, you think you can play tricks on me! Well, you can't, because I know all about you." And then he took hold of it.

For a moment he felt it in his hand – just for a moment, and then suddenly: *splash!* He was holding nothing at all, but a big splat of water had hit the stone floor, making him leap back with wet legs. Out of nowhere the water had come, and now it was beginning to trickle off into the cracks between the stones.

This time, however, Sparrow was more ready for it. "Oh no, you don't!" he cried, falling to his knees and starting to gather all the water together in a puddle before it disappeared. "You may look like water, but I know you're a stick, and I can see you, I can see you, I can see you!" As he spoke he thought as hard as he could about the stick leaning up against the wall.

And suddenly, there it was again, leaning calmly against the wall as if it had never moved – and the floor was quite dry!

Now Sparrow was more careful. He just held out his hand a little way from the stick, and spoke to it, as if he were coaxing a cat out of a hidey-hole. "Are you coming?" he said. "The old man needs you and he told me to fetch you." Sparrow vaguely wondered if he was starting to crack as well, because he had certainly never heard of being polite to a stick before. But it seemed to work. The stick stood up from the wall, all by itself, and toppled gently into his outstretched hand.

The smooth wood felt pleasant to hold, and Sparrow stroked it gently as he walked back out of the cave. But just as he was crossing the courtyard towards its ivy-grown entrance, the stick spoke to him.

Sparrow knew it was the stick speaking, because it jerked in his hand. "Who do you think you are," it said, "carrying me about as if you owned me – and stroking my head?"

"I'm Sparrow," said Sparrow. "I don't *think* I'm Sparrow: that's who I *am*."

"Oh," retorted the stick scornfully, "he knows who he is! Well –" And suddenly it jerked right out of Sparrow's hand and span round once, twice, three times and up into the air, where it hung still about three metres above his head.

29

"Well," it snapped, "what do you say now, bonehead? Turnip-face?"

"I say, please can you come down and stay in my hand," Sparrow said. "It's time for me to go home now and I have to take you—"

But before he could finish what he was saying – *whizz-whizz!* The stick started whirling round and round, as though being twirled by an invisible hand. Twenty times, maybe, it whirled, then did a series of cartwheels that took it over to the far side of the courtyard. And then it span around, and suddenly came flying straight towards Sparrow – fast, purposeful, menacing as a spear aimed at his head. At the very last moment Sparrow ducked, and the stick crashed end-on into the rock wall and clattered on to the ground.

Sparrow really was a bit scared of it now. That was no joke, the way it had flown at him. Where would he be if he hadn't ducked?

But when he carefully picked it up, it just felt like any ordinary stick, and he decided it must have knocked itself senseless when it hit the rock, because it didn't say another word or try any more tricks on him. He reached the foot of the little dark stream, and a short while later was handing the stick carefully to the old man, who kept his wild green eyes fixed on Sparrow as he took it, stroking the polished wood and speaking quietly to it.

A moment later, the woods, the waterfall and the towering cliffs had all disappeared, and the old man, no longer crippled, was standing in front of Sparrow in the rocky mountain courtyard outside the cave.

Sparrow blinked. "Was that magic?" he asked.

"Magic's in the mind of the beholder," the old man said mysteriously. "Do you think it was magic?"

30

"Yes, I think I do," said Sparrow.

"Then magic it was," he answered. "And now, because you helped me, I'm going to give you three wishes."

"Me?" Sparrow echoed stupidly.

"Who else would he be speaking to, bonehead?" snapped the stick. "Himself?" But the old man slapped it sharply on the head and told it to be quiet. In fact, the old man seemed to be a lot calmer and more sensible now he was holding the stick. But this time, although it was only the second time he had heard it speak, the stick's voice seemed to Sparrow oddly familiar: as though it belonged to someone he had known all his life…

"What's your name?" the old man asked.

Sparrow told him.

"You can call me Puckel," he said in return. "And now be quick and tell me what your three wishes are, for it's time you were home."

Sparrow felt embarrassed, not knowing what to ask for. Like most of the young folk of the mountains, he was quite content and didn't wish for anything he didn't have. It required immense thought, wishing for something. Yet, after all the strange things which had happened that afternoon, he felt quite sure that the old man with the wild grey hair and green eyes was perfectly able to give him whatever he asked.

"Well," Sparrow said slowly, "I was trying to find a special white stone with gold in it for Murie…"

"Oh, oh, oh!" exclaimed Puckel excitedly. "But you don't need magic for that! Look for the stone, and you'll find it – don't come asking me! Think! Think! Think! Think back over one day! There's a hundred wishes you have in each hour!"

Sparrow found that hard to believe, but he did think back over everything that had happened that day. Most of the day had been taken up with looking for the stone, and the old man didn't seem to think that was worth wishing for. He thought of Bull and Gogs. Seeing an aeroplane? Was that worth wishing for? Sitting inside an aeroplane? He tried to imagine that... Looking into the bright, brilliant blue of the sky; somewhere far below, little mountains etched with snowy peaks... Almost as if someone else were using it, Sparrow heard his voice saying, "I would like to fly." Immediately afterwards he seemed to get control of it again, and added doubtfully, "But I don't really know if I could do that."

"You don't know? But of course you could!" Puckel laughed.

He planted his stick firmly on the ground and vaulted over to stand in front of Sparrow. Then he held out his arms, and his broad green-brown coat covered Sparrow's face. It smelled of the woods, of new leaves, of dying grasses, of toadstools in a damp hollow.

"Let him fly," he murmured. "Let him fly, let him fly. Be eagle, be swallow, be wild goose – be Sparrow." Stepping back he said, "And what else? That's only one wish."

"I don't really know what else," said Sparrow, now feeling very stupid. "That's all I can think of."

"Well, well and well again," old Puckel said. "There's a lad who'll never go far. Can't think what he wants, eh? Then you'll have to watch out for unkind spirits. Well, I'll tell you what. One wish you've had. Now go home and think, and when you've thought, come back and call for me, why not? Then I'll give you what you ask for."

"Thank you," said Sparrow.

32

"Oh, don't thank me," Puckel said, as if to himself. "You brought me my stick, and now I'm under an obligation to you, a great obligation. Not many could have brought me that stick, yet you passed the test without hesitation. But now –" and he was no longer speaking to himself "– think hard, and think right, and don't let yourself be fooled by unkind spirits that aren't what they seem. Come back soon – and now, fly!"

Sparrow didn't know what the old man meant about the unkind spirits. But he soon knew that he could fly, for with one great spring he leapt up into the air – and simply hung there, weightless, six dizzy metres above the ground.

He found himself peering over the top of the rock wall round the mountain courtyard, and the angle of the steep mountainside seemed all wrong. He moved his head, and rock wall and mountainside tilted alarmingly to one side, uphill and downhill suddenly changing places. He put out a hand to steady himself and found he was clutching at thin air. He panicked, the whole world rolled right round, and a second later he was looking straight down into the courtyard of Puckel's cave. He had rolled over on to his front, and he was floating: the ground didn't come any closer.

The old man had apparently gone back into his cave without another glance. Sparrow took a deep breath. "It's real," he muttered. "It's all right." He stretched out his arms in front of him, straightened his legs, and something like a shock seemed to take his whole body. He felt like one single piece of bone – a hollow bird's bone with no weight – and he soared upwards, forwards, without effort, while a fierce wind rumbled in his ears and tore at his hair without lessening his speed. He was flying, and didn't know how he was doing it. Higher, and higher again, and he was looking over

33

an impossible stretch of mountain and forest, where everything seemed somehow to have been flattened out.

In the distance, hollowed under the luminous air, he could see the clutter of shapes and shades that was the village and the three round green hills (little tufts, they were more like from here) where his and his friends' houses stood; and the sun was just setting over the mountains on the far side of the valley.

"Whee! Whee! Whoopee!" he called, for the impossible, giddy joy of being fifty metres up in the air without a thought of falling. Then he sped down towards the distant valley, and the ground rushed up terrifyingly towards him. He bowed his back inwards, and his flight immediately levelled out. Below him the rocks of the high ground rushed past, then the pine forests like a dull green mist, till a lurch of the ground beneath him told him he had passed the Cliff where he had searched for a stone.

Sparrow threw his head back and came upright, suddenly breaking his headlong flight. The air whooshed up round him and grew still again. He hung there like a hawk, looking back at the Cliff, for he had caught a glimpse of something that shone and sparkled.

There it was. The last light of the setting sun was picking out a stone, high up on the Cliff, too high and too steep to be reached by climbing. It shone creamy-white, rose-white with the sunset. Sparrow flew straight to it, and hovering close, he reached out and pulled it from the loose rock.

It was a milkstone – just the very kind he had spent all day looking for. As big as his hand, milky white, and streaked with delicate flakes of gold. It was more than a companion for Murie's stone that sat on the television: it was the most beautiful milkstone Sparrow had ever seen.

three weeks alone

IT WAS STRANGE APPROACHING HIS HOME FROM THE air. As Sparrow came down to land on top of the green hill, he was aware that old Puckel's gift would change everything. He seemed to be looking with new eyes at the long, thatched house with its faded white walls and small windows where he had lived all his life. It was as if he were noticing it for the first time. And the fields, forests and mountains rising behind looked new and strange, mysterious and full of things he had never even dreamed existed.

Sparrow landed rather clumsily, tripping over his feet and nearly falling. For a second he thought he couldn't move, until he realized that he was simply feeling the weight of his body which had been left behind when he was flying. Then the cold hit him: it occurred to him for the first time that he had felt none of the autumn-evening chill when he was airborne. He shivered, and at the same time his face burned from the wind that had been blowing into it. There was a drumming in his ears still, but after listening to it for a moment Sparrow realized it wasn't the wind: there was a snorting and whickering mixed with it, and he saw Cairo, his father's ancient horse, careering round the paddock behind the house as if a swarm of bees were after him. Cairo was a stiff-jointed, ill-natured old beast who had never let anyone near him since Sparrow's father had disappeared, and he never moved faster than a sulky hobble. Now he was bucking and swerving around the field like a colt, and Sparrow understood that it must have been the sight of him flying which set the horse off. He laughed, and went indoors.

Before going through to the kitchen, Sparrow softly moved the old milkstone from the middle of the television top to the left-hand side. On the right-hand side he placed the new stone.

"I always seem to find them when Ms Minn goes away," he murmured – not quite accurately, since it was only the second milkstone he had found. "Perhaps it's the bits of her brain that keep falling out..." Murie would never notice the new stone in the darkness that evening, and it would be there to surprise her when she came downstairs on her birthday morning.

Murie had given up trying to prepare the evening meal in the long-waned daylight from the window, and was just placing the glass bowl over the second of the two yellow-gleaming wall-lamps as Sparrow came in. The soft beam from the lamps fell across the homely things in the kitchen which had always been the centre of Sparrow's world: yellow on the solid, well-scrubbed pine table by the window; coppery on the great brown-grey clay stove with its black-iron cooking range built into the front; yellow-gleaming on the huge black pot in which Murie was cooking tomorrow's potatoes for the goat, cow and hens; distant, jewel-like yellow in the depths of the milky-white glass onion that hung on a cord from the ceiling and was always referred to as "the light", even though it never gave out more than a vague reflection…

There was a mingled smell of boiling potatoes, pea-and-duck soup, and honey cake. "I'm starving," Sparrow said, making Murie jump.

"Where have you been all day?" she said. "You've not had any lunch."

"I got some from Bull and Gogs," Sparrow said, "but not enough."

"You should have said; I'd have given you sandwiches. You're such a scatter-brain." Crossly she sloshed soup into bowls standing ready at the stove.

"Bull wouldn't believe that Grandad flew in an aero-plane," Sparrow said.

37

"Nor do I," Murie answered, plonking the bowls of soup, along with two hunks of fresh bread, on the table. "It's just a daft story he used to invent. Eat up."

Sparrow lived alone with his mother. His father had been lost around the same time as Bull's father, when the boys were still babies; but everyone knew what had happened to Bull's father, who had been killed by a horse high up on the Old Road, while Sparrow's father had simply disappeared. He had not been a Trader, like Bull's father, but had hunted, though higher into the mountains than most men of the village, who rarely went more than five or six kilometres from home. But he had not been hunting – at least, not with his crossbow – on the day he disappeared. What had happened to him no one knew, but in that land of fearsome cliffs and crashing waterfalls people did sometimes disappear, and it was supposed that he had slipped on the edge of some precipice and fallen to his death.

"Where were you?" Murie asked as they ate.

"Up at the railway line," Sparrow answered vaguely.

"Not too far, I hope," she said sharply. Sparrow shook his head, but kept his face down.

If Sparrow had stopped to think about it, he would have noticed one immediate change which came from his amazing gift: overnight he became secretive. He told no one, neither Murie, nor Bull, nor Gogs. Without altogether realizing it, he was revelling in having a secret from Bull. For three long weeks after Murie's birthday, while autumn changed gradually to winter, he was on his own and flew so much his feet hardly ever touched the ground.

Every morning he would run off to a quiet clearing in the woods. There he would leap into the air and with a single bound find himself hovering beside the tops of the trees, with the seas of sodden, russet-leaved forests stretching away over his shoulders. Further up, through the rain, and a sudden new country would open beneath him, a country furrowed and ridged, pearl-coloured: the cloud-country, pierced by countless humped islands that were the mountain tops.

High he could go, into the huge silences of the sky – or else he would skim low over the forest and send showers of frightened birds scattering, or he would race to the top of the tallest mountain, stand on the edge of the highest cliff and throw himself into the yawning gulf of air beneath him.

By flying, by going up into the high places, Sparrow learned a lot about the country he lived in – things he would never have learned at the village school even if he had gone there for fifty years. He learned about the mountains, which seemed to stretch endlessly on over towards the east, but which towards the west soon came to an end at a flat calm lake bordered by low hills; about the other villages, which he vaguely knew of but which no one talked of or went to (apart from the Traders, but no one talked of them either). Sparrow found out all there was to know about these villages, though to be sure that was not much. There were four of them, apart from his own, but all as near the same as his own as any four places could be. The railway line went through two of them, then it curved and snaked off towards the flat lake. Sparrow followed it on one occasion, but there were no farms or villages in that part of the country. There were no living trees either, though there were plenty of dead ones, and the ground was a nasty grey colour with very little grass. Something about the lake-side felt unpleasant: Sparrow told himself he wasn't scared of it, but he didn't go there again.

39

In the other direction, the railway line disappeared into a tunnel in the mountains, and Sparrow could find no further trace of it: there was no other end to the tunnel. Nor did he ever find what lay beyond the mountains: always, on the edge of the horizon, there was a curious bank of white mist where the mountain peaks faded from sight. It seemed to move slightly, as cloud does, but it never cleared, not even on the windiest of days. Sparrow tried several times to reach it, but it never seemed to come any closer.

Not surprisingly, Bull and Gogs were meanwhile feeling rather neglected by Sparrow. Gogs did wonder at first if Sparrow might have been offended that day under the Cliff when they had gone off and left him. But it was not like

Sparrow to stay offended for quite so long – he had never had a good enough memory for it. Gogs and Bull came over for him several times, but he was never in.

"Where do you go all by yourself?" Murie asked. "And what do you do?"

"Oh, I just go up to the woods and look at things," Sparrow answered vaguely.

"What sort of things?"

"Rocks and things." It was true enough – he just didn't mention that he was looking at rocks and things from way up in the air!

"How on earth did you manage to get that home?" Murie exclaimed, looking in amazement at the huge branch of a tree Sparrow had brought home one evening to cut up for the fire.

40   "I don't know," Sparrow said. "I just dragged it." In a way, that was true too: he didn't know how he had managed it – it was true that he had found that things didn't seem to weigh anything when he was flying. It was as though his own lightness got into whatever he touched.

One morning Murie, out in their top field, noticed which way Sparrow was heading amongst the trees. Later that morning, Bull and Gogs came up the hill. They had decided to try to visit Sparrow once more and ask him if he had stopped being their friend altogether. On this occasion, Murie was able to tell them where she thought he had gone.

"You'll be getting quite fed up with him," she said. "I don't know what's got into him: I hardly ever see him either."

"We'll sort him out," Gogs grinned, as they set off along the side of Cairo's paddock. The old horse watched them sourly from the far end.

The two friends came to the clearing. Sparrow wasn't there, so they sat down on a log and wondered what to do next. Although the sun was bright, it was low over the tops of the mountains and the air already had a wintry chill.

"I'm not going to sit here all day," Bull said crossly.

"Nor me," said Gogs. "I'm freezing."

They were lucky, however. Sparrow had forgotten to collect the hens' eggs before he left, and had then remembered half-way through the morning and was flying back just as Bull and Gogs were deciding not to sit around.

Without noticing anyone in the clearing, he came down from the air, landed lightly on his feet, and stood still for a moment. He always did that now when he landed, to get used to the feelings of weight and cold that hit him.

But almost at once, something told him that he was not alone. He turned round to see the astonished faces of Gogs and Bull staring across at him.

41

For a full minute Gogs and Bull stared, pop-eyed as startled rabbits; and for a full minute there was silence in the clearing.

Sparrow looked at Bull, whose eyebrows were drawn so tightly together that they looked like a single bar of black across his forehead. He had a mixture of feelings. On the one hand, this was the moment he had been waiting for – the moment when he knew he had impressed Bull more than Bull had ever impressed him. On the other hand, he felt uneasy: he had never crossed Bull before. Without knowing what there was to be scared of, he felt a little scared.

Bull broke the silence. "You jumped down from the tree, didn't you?"

Sparrow shook his head. "No, I didn't," he said quietly. There was another silence.

"You were flying?" Gogs said.

Sparrow nodded.

"No, he wasn't, Gogs," Bull said firmly. "He's having us on. He jumped out of the trees."

"If he'd jumped out of the trees he'd have broken his legs," Gogs pointed out. It was not like Gogs to contradict Bull so sharply. "How did you learn to fly, Sparrow?" he asked.

"I was… Someone made me," Sparrow said. He didn't know how much he wanted to tell his friends. He had grown too used to being alone in the past weeks.

"Someone made you?" Bull repeated. "Do you mean you can't help doing it?"

"No," said Sparrow, "I only fly when I want to."

"How high do you go?" Gogs asked excitedly.

"However high I want to," Sparrow told him.

"Have you been far away?" Gogs asked. "Have you seen places we don't know about? Have you been to the end of the mountains?"

"Did someone teach you?" Bull interrupted.

"Not exactly," Sparrow said. The short moment of triumph was fading and the uneasiness was fading too, but he was beginning to realize that Bull was going to get the whole story out of him. He wouldn't have minded so much telling Gogs, because Gogs was just excited at the thought that someone could fly. But he felt cross at himself because he knew he couldn't stand up to Bull.

"Did you find a wizard or a magician or something like that," Bull said, "and he taught you how to fly? – Was that what happened?"

Bull had of course told Sparrow and Gogs only a few of his grandmother's tales. So Sparrow was completely flummoxed by what seemed like an amazing guess. How did Bull know? The two boys stared at each other, but Sparrow's eyes soon faltered and fell before Bull's keen gaze. Maybe Bull already knew all about such things.

"I don't know if he was a magician or a wizard," Sparrow muttered. "He just held his cloak out and said some words over me, and I could fly."

"Did you find him in trouble and help him?" Bull pursued. "Is that what happened?"

Again Sparrow was amazed at Bull's guess. "Have you met him too?" he asked.

"No, I haven't exactly met him," Bull said mysteriously. "What was his name?" he added.

Sparrow opened his mouth to tell him: he had just got as far as the "P" of "Puckel" – when he found he'd forgotten! It was very strange, considering he had thought of the old man and his name almost every day since he had started flying. Now his mind was a complete blank.

"It was – Puzzle or Piddle or something like that," he said vaguely. "I suddenly can't remember."

"How did you help him?" said Bull, still fixing Sparrow with his blue, unswerving eyes.

"Yes, can we go and help him too?" Gogs burst in, seeing what Bull was getting at. "And then he'll teach us to fly as well and we can all fly together!"

Suddenly, after three weeks of being alone, Sparrow realized that he would love to do that. What did it matter about impressing Bull? He had enjoyed flying on his own, but what was the point of having something so secret that you couldn't share it with anyone?

But there seemed to be no way of making Gogs and Bull find the old man in trouble. It had just been a matter of luck when that had happened to Sparrow.

"He'd fallen through the trees," he told them, "and broken his leg. But it was only because he didn't have his stick with him. I don't think he'll leave his stick behind again – he'll be very careful now."

"Tell us everything that happened," Bull said.

As Sparrow talked, he found that he had been missing Gogs and Bull all the time, and had been longing to tell them the whole story. But whenever he came to say the old man's name he couldn't remember it – or only the beginning and the end – so they decided just to call him Piddle.

Sparrow came to the end of the story.

"And what were the other two wishes?" Bull asked.

Incredible as it may seem, Sparrow had actually forgotten about them! His memory was like that: if he had one important thing to think about, he concentrated so much on it that he simply stopped thinking about anything else.

"I didn't know what to wish for," he told Bull.

"So you threw them away? Two wishes?" Bull asked, his eyes wide with disbelief.

"Well, not really," Sparrow remembered. "He said I could go back and see him when I'd thought."

"You mean you still have two wishes to make?" Bull exclaimed.

"Hooray!" Gogs cried. "You can make a wish for me, and a wish for Bull, and then we'll all be able to fly!"

Sparrow had never thought of this. It seemed a wonderful idea.

"Let's go and find him right now," Gogs said, "and we'll all be flying by the evening!"

"No, I've a better idea," said Bull. "Sparrow can fly to him now, and we'll have our wishes by lunchtime."

"All right, I'll do it," said Sparrow, and he would have flown off there and then.

But Bull stopped him. "You haven't heard what we want yet," he said.

"I thought you wanted to fly," said Sparrow in surprise.

"Well, not just," Bull said. "I want you to tell Piddle that I want to be a shape-shifter…"

"What's a shape-shifter?" asked Sparrow.

"Never mind," Bull said. "Just tell him I want to be a shape-shifter and I want to understand the language of beasts and birds."

"Oh, that's good," Gogs put in, "I'd like that too."

"Isn't that two wishes?" Sparrow asked.

"Not really," Bull answered, "and if you say it all very quickly – Bull wants to be a shape-shifter who can understand the language of beasts and birds – I'm sure Piddle will think it's just the one wish."

"All right," said Gogs. "Then will you say that Gogs wants to be a flyer who can understand the language of beasts and birds – very quickly, so that he thinks it's just one wish?"

"I'll try," said Sparrow, "but if I ask for those things, how will you be able to fly with us, Bull?"

Bull just smiled mysteriously. "Oh, I'll manage," he said. "Don't worry, you won't leave me behind."

So, in great excitement, Sparrow left them. He leaped into the air, and hung there a moment above their heads. Gogs gasped.

"Don't forget!" Bull called up.

"I won't!" Sparrow called back, and was off.

* * *

High in the air he went, straight towards the huge rounded peak of the great mountain that stood over the valley. Puckel's cave was somewhere in the shoulders of that mountain.

Puckel's cave! The moment he sprang into the air he had remembered the old man's name. He realized there was something very odd about this, but continued his flight nevertheless.

He looked down. There was the Cliff where he had found Murie's stones, and the Forest River and the waterfall below it. And there was the little dark stream winding down towards the river! Sparrow's eye followed it up through the hillside into the crags and rock walls of the mountain.

But though he peered and peered, he could see no sign of the rocky courtyard outside Puckel's cave, where the little dark stream rose. He flew down, and hunted over the rocks and through the ravines: but somehow, try as he would, he could not make out the two ivy-covered rocks he had squeezed between.

At last Sparrow flew right down to the foot of the little dark stream at the Forest River. He had an idea that if he followed the stream, just as before, he might find what he was looking for. He wouldn't fly, he wouldn't even skim: he would go on his two feet, just as he had done that first time.

It worked. Sparrow followed the little dark stream up into the mountain, over the grassy floor in between the climbing rock walls, and at last found the place where it flowed out between the two huge ivy-covered rocks. Minutes later he stood in the little rocky courtyard where the stream bubbled up from the stones. But all about there were only rocks. He turned round and round; there was no cave.

"What's wrong?" Sparrow said to himself. "I'm sure this is the right place."

Sparrow thought. What had he been told? "Come back soon," Puckel had said: maybe he'd come too late! Maybe he would never see Puckel again and Bull and Gogs would never be able to fly with him.

But what did "soon" mean, anyway? What else had he said?

"Go home and think" – that's what it was – "and when you've thought, come back and call me…"

Call me? Well, it was worth a try. Sparrow rounded his hands at his mouth and shouted, "Puckel!"

As the echoes of his shout faded, something happened. A large ivy-covered rock nearby in the rock wall made a splitting sound. *Crick*, it went, then *crack*, then *crick* again, and suddenly, just as though it had always been there, there was the ivy-grown entrance of the cave.

two things as if they were one

.

48 OUT OF THE ENTRANCE SOMETHING FLOATED – something dark and thin. Puckel's stick wavered gently towards Sparrow and remained suspended in front of him like the bar of a gate. Sparrow reached out and held it with both hands.

With a sound like a short, stony laugh, the stick took off, dragging Sparrow into the air. He was more amused than frightened, thinking the stick was just being mischievous. But when it flew very close to the rock wall and suddenly made a sharp mid-air turn, Sparrow's legs flew out to the side and cracked painfully against the rock. "Ow!" he cried, and decided to let go.

But he couldn't. His hands seemed to be stuck to the wood.

"Good sticking power, that!" the stick cackled, and proceeded to drag him on a most alarming ride, at high speed, close around the wall of the courtyard. Again Sparrow banged his legs on the rock, and yet again. And now he realized that there was more malice than mischief in the thing's performance.

"Puckel!" he called again. But by this time he was so dizzy he couldn't see if the old man had come to answer his call. Suddenly the stick did another turn, and hovered in the air near the rock wall.

"What's the matter with you?" Sparrow gasped. "What have I done wrong?"

The stick made no answer, but jerked again into movement. Backwards this time and gathering speed at an amazing rate, it was hurling Sparrow towards the opposite wall of the courtyard. "Help!" Sparrow screamed. In a moment he would hit the rock wall, and then –

"Put him down." Puckel's voice was quiet, but it cut through the noise of the air whistling in Sparrow's ears. With a sharp jolt, the stick halted, so suddenly that Sparrow flew backwards to his arms' length. He felt his shoulder-sockets wrench, and then the stick let go of him – that was what it felt like anyway – and he fell to the ground. He felt dizzy and battered and sick.

He sat up and tried to look at Puckel. He had forgotten how wild the old man looked. At another word from him, the stick floated obediently down into his hand. He looked steadily at Sparrow. "Well," he said at last, quite ignoring the state Sparrow was in, "flying's been good, I see; it's been good, very good. I thought you would have been back to me a long time ago, asking for more – but flying was so good you forgot all about your other wishes."

"Yes, I did," agreed Sparrow, trying to focus his eyes.

"But now you've remembered about them?"

"Yes, I have," said Sparrow. "That's why I came back

looking for you."

Puckel waited, looking hard at Sparrow. Sparrow began to feel better. He smiled weakly. It looked to him as though the old man were about to break into uncontrollable chuckling as at their first meeting, but he remained grave. He never actually smiled, Sparrow realized, but there was something about him as though all his insides were shaking with barely-suppressed mirth.

"Why were you so difficult to find?" Sparrow asked. He felt he'd been looking for Puckel for days.

"Because your brain's full of bone," the stick snapped, before Puckel could say anything.

Puckel slapped the stick on the head. But he was barely more polite himself. "Do you think I want every fool in the mountains coming and calling my name?" he said, turning towards the cave. "One's quite enough."

He passed out of sight through the cave mouth. Scared it might close again, Sparrow jumped up and followed him in. He felt better and his legs weren't sore any more, but he had no time to be surprised about that.

There was a brown stone bowl in the middle of the table in the cave, and Puckel was holding his stick over it as Sparrow came in. As he watched, the stick seemed to go soft, to melt and go smaller, and in a moment what Puckel was holding in his hands was water, which he allowed to pour gently into the bowl. Puckel looked intently at its black shining surface in the wavering light from the fire.

"I don't like what you're here for," he said suddenly.

"Can't I have my other two wishes?" Sparrow asked.

"Oh, you can have them," Puckel replied, "you can have them and welcome. I promised them, and I must give them. But they're bad wishes, and you'll be sorry you made them."

"But I haven't told you what they are yet!"

"You haven't told me, but now you will tell me," said Puckel, and waited.

"Well," said Sparrow, "Bull wants to be a shape-shifter and understand the language of beasts and birds, and Gogs wants to be able to understand the language of beasts and birds and fly. I thought they were asking for two things, but they said they weren't."

"Your wishes," said Puckel, looking up at Sparrow. "They are *your* wishes, not your friends'."

"I know," said Sparrow, "but…"

Puckel interrupted him. "They are good wishes. Shape-changing, and understanding the wild creatures and the tame creatures, the fish in the water, the bees gathering honey off the flowers. They are good wishes, yes."

51

"What's a shape-shifter anyway?" Sparrow asked.

Puckel disappeared. As Sparrow was looking about him, the chair by the fire suddenly spoke: "Come and sit on me." It was a strange voice, a little like Puckel's, but somehow stiffer, harder, more grating – a wooden voice, as though it were possible for Puckel to be speaking with a chair's voice.

Sparrow went and sat in the chair. It felt just like a chair and creaked as he sat down, but as he settled himself in it, the creaking became a muttering voice: "All right, all right, you needn't wiggle so much. What a great hefty wriggling lump you are! Goodness knows how you ever manage to fly…" A second later Puckel was standing in front of him again.

"Shape-changing," he said, "is the power of going into the shape of any other thing or creature, and becoming that creature for the length of the change. I was the chair. Now I am Puckel."

"Does that mean you can become an animal, too?" said Sparrow.

"As long as there's an animal to become. You can't change into something that isn't there, unless you learn to step out of the dragon's dream and become a master of transformation. But a thing that's there – bird, beast, fish, fly, stone, chair, fire, water, cloud, ring, tree, book, bed, spider or speck of dust – any of these things you can become as a shape-changer, while your own shape disappears."

Sparrow heard Puckel's mention of the dragon's dream, but it was not until much later that he remembered it again. Too many questions were crowding into his head. "What happens to your shape?" he whispered.

Puckel screwed up his eyes. "Let it be enough for you to know that it disappears so that it's there for you to return to," he said. "If everyone could see it when you were out of it, it wouldn't be your own any more."

Sparrow scarcely heard. Another question had already occurred to him. "What about people?" he said. "Can you change into another person?"

Puckel was silent for a moment, before saying one word, so softly that Sparrow could hardly hear above the hiss of a stick in the fire. "Yes." And Sparrow felt a cold fear inside him, for as Puckel said it, all the old man's inner laughter suddenly disappeared.

"I don't want you to change into me," Sparrow said quickly.

"I won't," Puckel replied quietly. "And no shape-shifter who is wise should ever change into another person – and nor should you, when you have the power."

"I won't," said Sparrow. He had forgotten for the moment that it was Bull who had asked for this wish.

"Do you want this wish?" Puckel asked. "They are your wishes and you can have them for yourself."

Then Sparrow remembered. With an effort, sadly, he said, "No, I'd better not. I said I would get the wishes for Bull and Gogs – that's what I told them."

"You could fly back to them," said Puckel, "and tell them you'd changed your mind and taken your wishes for yourself."

"I could fly back to them and tell them you couldn't give my wishes to them, only to me," Sparrow suggested.

"No, you couldn't," said Puckel, "because it wouldn't be true, and that's a fact. And we do not tell lies."

Sparrow felt quite scared he had even thought of telling a lie.

"If you want the wishes for yourself, that is what you must tell your friends," said Puckel.

Sparrow considered. He would have loved to have the power of shape-changing, but he had not forgotten how being able to fly had made him feel so different from the others. What would it be like if he was the only one who could understand beasts and birds, and the only one who could shape-change? It might be good, but it would be terribly lonely, maybe even too lonely to bear… On the other hand, it would be something that Bull didn't have. Bull could keep his secrets and his gran's stories. Perhaps he would let Gogs have his wish and take Bull's for himself…

"No," he said at last with an effort, "I want Gogs and Bull to have magic powers too."

"Then make a wish for each of them to fly like you," said Puckel, "and then you'll all be the same."

53

"Could I tell them those were the only wishes you'd give me?" asked Sparrow doubtfully.

"No, you couldn't," Puckel answered sternly.

Sparrow sighed. "Then I'll just have to ask you for the things they told me to ask you for."

Puckel said, "I can grant you these wishes, though I don't want to do it. I must if you ask me, because I promised you."

"Bull and Gogs are my friends," Sparrow explained, "and I want to be able to do things with them."

"Then you must have what you ask," said Puckel. "Now you are like a glass of clear water, little Sparrow," – his voice sounded quite sad – "and your friend can look straight through you. In the end it will be a good thing."

"And now," he continued, "are you listening?" Puckel's wild old eyebrows were drawn close together – he was frowning, and his green eyes seemed to shoot out dangerous little tongues of fire.

"Yes," said Sparrow.

"Then come on, come on, come here and look."

He sounded impatient, so Sparrow jumped up from the chair by the fire and went over to where Puckel was looking into the bowl of water on the table.

Sparrow did as he was told, and there, clear and small, like a perfect little picture in a book – but moving and alive – he saw the trees round the clearing he had left less than two hours earlier, and Bull and Gogs wandering about, looking bored and a little annoyed. It was so real he felt he could have reached into the bowl and touched them.

"Now," whispered Puckel, "tell them that they have their wishes."

"Bull," began Sparrow – but in the moment he spoke,

the water in the bowl became rippled and ruffled. Sparrow could still see Gogs and Bull, but they were pulled out of shape by the twisting water, so that it looked as if two small black monsters were wandering about in a jungle of nightmare.

"Go on," whispered Puckel. "Tell them."

"Bull, you'll be able to change your shape," said Sparrow, "and understand beasts and birds, and Gogs will be able to understand beasts and birds and fly." And as he spoke, the little figures of Bull and Gogs twisted and jumped and danced in the writhing forest, till it looked as though they were being torn into pieces and thrown up among the branches of the trees. He watched, horrified, but as soon as he had finished speaking, the water calmed down and the picture became clear and still again. There were Gogs and Bull standing in the clearing, but now they were looking about them with strange expressions on their faces.

Puckel said, "When you watched them without speaking, the picture was clear. That was because you were doing only one thing. When you watched and spoke, the picture was pulled out of shape: that was because you were doing two things. Your friends each asked for two things as if they were one. They will have those two things, to be sure they will have them: they will not be half-gifts. But nothing will turn out as clear or as straight for them as if they had only asked for one. Remember this, young Sparrow."

"All right," said Sparrow.

"Then off you go now, and when you need me, call me and you'll find me."

Puckel passed his hand over the bowl, and the water in it shot up into the air like a fountain. Just before it hit the

55

ceiling, it arched over and came twisting down in a spiral, not at all like water. For a moment, Sparrow caught a glimpse of the snake in that curling, coiling water, before suddenly, brown and hard and shiny, there it was again – a twisted stick in the old man's hand.

This time Sparrow didn't fly up into the air, or at least he didn't remember doing it. Puckel, his stick, the cave, the bowl, the table, the chair and the fire, all simply disappeared and Sparrow was left floating in the air, high above the mountain tops.

He felt strange and – even though he was floating – heavy and so tired. He floated more than he flew, rocking down like a leaf from the mountains over the forest, softly and slowly back to the clearing he had left with such high hopes.

He landed, stopped, and looked around. The clearing was empty. Gogs and Bull had gone.

Sparrow walked home. The tiredness would not pass and he went to bed early, and slept and slept, right through till lunchtime the next day. It was such a deep, black sleep that it was like being buried in the earth; and when he woke up again, he could hardly remember who he was or where he was or what day it was.

Slowly things began to come back to him: the events of the day before; Puckel; Bull and Gogs getting their wishes. He had better get up and go and see if he could find his friends.

But on the way down the path, Sparrow met a boy coming up from the village with a message: Ms Minn was back, and school was to open again the next day. Sparrow turned back and went to tell Murie.

It was a windy, sunny day, and Murie decided then and

there to wash all Sparrow's clothes so that he would have something clean to wear to school. Sparrow had to take everything off, and went about for the rest of the day in a warm old shirt which had belonged to his father. It was so long it came down past his knees, and although it was comfortable enough he felt embarrassed about going off to find Bull and Gogs dressed like that.

He spent the day wondering why his friends hadn't waited for him, and whether they really had received their gifts and were going about flying or listening to what the beasts and birds said.

When he thought about this, he began to feel a little miserable – he realized properly for the first time that the gifts of Gogs and Bull were much more than his own.

That night Sparrow dreamed he saw an aeroplane. It was just as he had imagined it would be – a tube with stiff wings sticking out at the sides – and he felt delighted. Then it was right up close to him and he was standing on one of the great flat wings, tipping backwards and forwards on it to keep his balance, and bending down to peer inside the windows that ran all along the tube.

Sure enough, there seemed to be people inside it, but Sparrow was only able to make out one, and that was Ms Minn. She was sitting in the very front, hanging on to a set of horse's reins and apparently steering the aeroplane with them. The wind was blowing her hair about, and with a faraway, foolish expression on her face she was chanting the words, "At the third stone, the time has come! At the third stone, the time has come!" over and over.

At that moment, Sparrow felt himself slipping. He wrapped his arms round the wing of the aeroplane and looked down: down, down, to empty air beneath him –

nothing but empty air, and far, far away, a dark splodge that could have been the earth. And a horror grew in him that he could no longer fly…

When he woke he was trembling and sweating. But it was morning and time to get up for school.

His dream had seemed so real that Sparrow felt certain he had lost the power of flight. On the way down the path from the house, he glanced round to make sure he was alone, then jumped and – oh, the relief! – yes, he could still fly. He dropped down a bit, and skimmed on just above the road. A little further on and then I'll walk, he was thinking, when – *slam!* Something caught him hard between the shoulders and sent him staggering forwards, landing and tripping on the hard road. He came down on to his knees – not too hard, but just hard enough to make him feel annoyed.

He looked behind him. There was Gogs, hovering a little above the ground and grinning all over his freckly face.

Now Sparrow felt really annoyed. "Where were you?" he shouted crossly. "Why didn't you come and see me?"

Gogs stopped grinning. "I was coming up to see you just now. Then I heard a bird saying you were flying down the path, so I thought I'd hide and surprise you. I couldn't come before, because all my clothes were getting washed. So were Bull's. It didn't stop Bull though. He turned into a bird and came across to tell me, though when he turned back into Bull he didn't have any clothes on!" Gogs laughed.

"Why didn't Bull come to see me? Why did he just go to you?" Sparrow said.

Gogs shrugged. "I wished I'd asked to be a shape-shifter

too," he went on, "but Bull says that when you turn into something else you can't see things properly and you can't think properly, so maybe it's better fun just being able to fly."

"What's it like hearing the beasts and birds?" Sparrow asked. He was curious, even though he did still feel cross.

"It's confusing," said Gogs, "because you hear these voices going on all round you, big ones and little ones and high ones and low ones. But Bull told me you can make it go quiet if you think about it, and you can. I don't hear anything talking just now, but if I wanted to listen I could."

"What's that bird saying?" Sparrow asked, pointing to a chaffinch in the bare elm tree across the road. It was chuff-chuffing to itself in a contented fashion.

Gogs listened. "Nothing very interesting," he said. "Just something about some barley spilled down at the mill. I think it's swelling up inside him. He says he feels like a stuffed turkey."

Sparrow giggled, though inside him something was regretting, regretting. Why had he let Gogs and Bull have his wishes? Gogs didn't even seem particularly interested in his. If I'd got the gift of understanding beasts and birds, Sparrow thought to himself, I wouldn't make it go quiet: I'd listen to everything, for days and days…

Bull appeared on the road ahead. He might have been walking down from his house, but Sparrow suspected he had been shape-shifting.

Bull's brooding face looked unusually pleased. "You should see what we can do," he said. "I can do just about anything now."

Sparrow immediately felt that something was not right about Bull. Or had Bull always been like this and Sparrow just hadn't thought about it properly? A new wave of anger swept over him. Bull hadn't so much as thanked him! Yet mixed with the anger there was that fear again. Only now he understood at last what he was scared of: he was plain scared of Bull. Had he always been, or had it only become real fear now that Bull had this awesome power? He swallowed his thoughts, and said, "We'll have to hurry. We'll be late for school."

"Huh! School!" said Bull scornfully. "Why go to school when you can do what we can do? You don't learn anything at school!"

Gogs looked horrified. "Oh, we've got to go to school," he said. "Everyone does that."

"Who could make us?" said Bull. "They couldn't make us stay in the classroom, and they couldn't even catch us if we decided to fly away. Or I could turn into a brick or a tree or something and they'd never even know I was there. Or I could even turn into Ms Minn herself, and then I would know everything that she knows and I could be your teacher – and I could easily just shut the school up and say there'd be a holiday for as long as we wanted."

"You wouldn't really do that, would you?" asked Sparrow. "P— the old man told me you shouldn't shift into other people's shapes, you know."

"Well, he never told me that," said Bull unconcernedly. "Anyway, I tried it with my gran last night when she was knitting. She just thought she'd been knitting in her sleep. She found she'd knitted a whole sock without even knowing! 'I knew I was good,' she said, 'but I didn't know I was that good!' I didn't tell her I'd been doing it for her!"

If Bull changed into his gran, Sparrow thought, does that mean he knows everything that she does? Is that why he's different? Then a worse thought struck him. Was that why Bull had said Sparrow and Gogs wouldn't leave him behind when they were flying – because he would simply change into one of them? The thought horrified him. "Aren't you going to school today then?" he asked tensely.

"I'm going for one day," Bull announced. "I'm going to ask Ms Minn one question – I'm going to ask if she can teach us anything real."

"What do you mean, *real*?" said Sparrow.

"What do we do all day at school?" said Bull with a scornful twist to his mouth. "Sit all day and add up numbers – what for? And why do we have to fiddle about with calculators when we do it? What difference does that make?"

Gogs looked worried, but Sparrow shrugged. "Why do you have to know why you're doing it?" he said. "It's just what you do."

"Well, it's not good enough for me," said Bull. "Not any more. So I'm going to ask her. And if she can't tell me, I'm going to turn into her, and that way I'll find out if she really does know anything or not – and then I'm going to go away, or if I feel like it I might come back and teach you all some of the things I know."

They went on in silence, Sparrow and Gogs walking a little ahead of Bull.

Ms Minn hadn't changed a bit. She was wispy and wild and vague as ever; she was dressed in the same dusty old black clothes, and she talked in just the same way. Everyone was very quiet, and she made them press the buttons on their calculators all through the morning while they did money-counting sums in their heads.

Sparrow glanced over at Bull a few times, but he seemed

to be thinking very hard about something, and not noticing anything that was going on. He was certainly not pressing his calculator buttons.

But after lunch, Ms Minn announced in her dry, scrapy voice, "Now children, this afternoon I'm going to test you to see if you remember how to address a Prospective Employer. Bull, will you come forward, please? You are the interviewee for the job of advertising agent, and I am the interviewer."

Bull stood up, but he didn't come forward. He folded his arms across his chest, looked Ms Minn straight in the eye, and said, "Ms Minn, could you teach us something real, for a change?"

bull and the dragon

THE SILENCE THAT FOLLOWED BULL'S QUESTION was the quietest, most breathless silence imaginable. You could have heard the mice squeaking behind the walls, only they had fallen silent too. You would have thought the little black beetle crawling across the floor would have gone on tiptoe. No one had ever spoken in that way to Ms Minn before.

But for all her strangeness, Ms Minn was not easily surprised. She stood quietly, clasping her hands together as she always did, and looked straight at Bull with her frail old head on one side, like a thrush about to spear a worm.

"Very well, my dear," she said. "What would you like to know?"

Bull was not flustered. "Well, you want us to speak to a Prospective Employer," he began.

"Yes, of course," Ms Minn put in.

"But we don't even know what a Prospective Employer is!"

JET SMOKE AND DRAGON FIRE

"But you know how to talk to him," Ms Minn said quietly.

"What's the use of that," said Bull, "if we never meet one?"

"No use at all," said Ms Minn.

"Well, that's just what I mean," said Bull angrily. "You don't teach us real things. You make us press buttons on calculators – but what do the calculators do?"

"Nothing, I don't think," Ms Minn answered simply.

"That's what I mean," said Bull. "So what is a calculator? What's it made for? Who made it? Why did we sit and press buttons on calculators all morning? You make us sit and count money, but what's money? What's it for?"

"Nothing," said Ms Minn again.

"Well, why's it here?" said Bull. "Where does it come from? Who made it? Why did they make it? Those are the things I want to learn."

Ms Minn straightened up. And something about her seemed to change, almost as though someone inside her had suddenly woken up – someone who had been hiding behind Ms Minn's sometimes foolish exterior, waiting for years for this moment to arrive.

"Then I shall teach you the things you want to learn," she said in her quiet, dry voice. "I shall tell you a story. About a dragon."

"Is this a fairy story?" Bull demanded.

A whisper of confusion ran round the class. Apart from Sparrow and Gogs, no one in the class even knew what a real fairy story was. For that matter, no one knew what a dragon was, any more than they knew what a Prospective Employer was, or an advertising agent.

"This story," Ms Minn said – and her voice became as

quiet and as cold as ice creeping across a pool of water – "this story is everything. It is a fairy story and a true story, a history and a mystery."

"Long, long ago," Ms Minn began, "a dragon came down from the mountains. The dragon was full of marvellous ideas, and was always thinking of wonderful things to make. And it would have made them, but it couldn't because it was only a dragon. I think that may have been why it left its home.

"As soon as it came to live among people, it started giving them the ideas for all the things it had dreamed up. It was the dragon, long ago, who dreamed up all the odd things we see around us but have no use for: the calculators, the televisions, the telephones, the glass light-bulbs that hang in our houses, the railway lines and the roads that disappear in the distance.

"Why we don't use them will be explained in due course, Bull, so you don't need to interrupt. There were other things, too, that most of you won't have heard about. I can't tell you about them all, because there is no time – but I can tell you that the dragon thought particularly about things which would take a lot of people quickly from one place to another. There were boats as big as villages to travel on the water, strings of waggons like giant snakes that rushed along the railway lines, and shining tubes that people could sit inside and fly through the air in –"

Sparrow looked triumphantly over at Bull, but Bull seemed to be sunk deep in thought again.

"The televisions, the telephones, the lights and the calculators," Ms Minn went on, "had the same kind of purpose, because all the things the dragon dreamed up were things which made people think about what was far-off and forget about what was close at hand. There were little windows in which people could see what was far away, horns into which they could speak to people who were far away, little boxes to keep their memory in so they didn't have to keep it in their heads, lights that turned night into day because the people liked to sleep through half the daylight.

"All the things the dragon invented may seem magical to you, but they were not. For though the dragon is a magical beast, when its ideas are made into things, their magic goes: they were just machines, just ordinary things like spades and cups and millwheels. And the dragon did not like this, for a magical beast likes only magical things. So the dragon became unsatisfied and restless, and often angry. It was its own fault, because it should have stayed in the mountains, but knowing that didn't help its temper at all.

"The dragon, you see, is not supposed to live where living creatures live, because its breath is poisonous. When it breathes, smoke comes out of its nose and mouth, and if people or animals or even plants and trees breathe in the smoke, they become very sick. The animals and trees and plants just die when they get sick, but people who breathe the dragon-breath go mad.

"The people built a city round the place where the dragon lived. A city is like a thousand villages all built together, and because there were so many buildings and so many people, there wasn't room for animals and plants: no one noticed that everything died when it came near the dragon. But of course all the people went mad. Only they went mad so slowly that no one noticed.

"As I told you, the dragon became angry when it saw that none of the things the people made were actually magical.

So it began to dream up machines that would destroy all the wonderful things it had invented. And by now the people were so mad that they were quite happy to make these machines and to use them. In this way, whole cities were destroyed, and even whole countries, and the dragon would join in the destruction and fly over the land bellowing and blasting out flames and smoke. Thousands upon thousands of people were killed, but those left simply buried their dead and forgot about them and went on with the work of making and destroying. You must not forget how mad the dragon's breath had made them.

"But the dragon itself was not mad – just very angry – and at last it flew off to find somewhere to cool down before it burst with rage.

"The place it chose was a lonely part of the world where there was a great lake. It plunged into this, and the water bubbled and boiled, and mist and steam rose up and covered the land all around, and where the mist and steam settled everything died. There the dragon stayed for a long time, making itself cool and hiding from the people.

"Not far from the lake, up in the mountains, there lived an old man. He wasn't like other men. For one thing he was much, much older, and for another he didn't go mad with the dragon's breath. He would go down to the side of the lake and speak to the dragon, for days, weeks, months at a time. The dragon wouldn't agree to go back to its own place, but it did stop being so angry – it was a lot cooler with the water by now – and it began to trust the old man.

"At last the old man said to the dragon, 'You can't stay in the lake all the time. Your skin will go wrinkly and soft and before you know it you'll be nothing but a wriggling, slimy worm. Follow me and I'll show you a place where you can hide and no one will find you.'

"The dragon agreed, and one dark night it came out of the lake and followed the old man up into the mountains. The old man walked slowly along a quiet railway line, with the dragon creeping along behind him like a gigantic white lizard. It was white because of the water: normally it was green and golden. At last they came to a place where the line went into a tunnel that cut right through one of the biggest mountains. The line led to a city hundreds of kilometres in the distance, but the old man didn't intend to take the dragon there. He waited until they were in the deepest and darkest part of the tunnel, and then suddenly he ran on ahead, so softly and quickly that the dragon didn't hear him going. But when the old man had got far enough through the tunnel, he let out a shout. It was such a terrible, long, deafening shout that the roof of the tunnel cracked, and the whole mountain slipped. The tunnel was completely blocked at one end, and the dragon was trapped in the ruins. To be quite accurate, it wasn't really trapped. The tunnel was still open behind it. But you must realize that the dragon was very long, and fitted closely into the tunnel, so that it couldn't turn round. And although the dragon is very magical, there isn't a part of it that would ever think of going backwards. So there the dragon stayed.

"The old man ran on, almost to the end of the mountains, but long before the city was in sight he turned and shouted again. And the shout that he gave then echoed from mountain to mountain, till rocks and boulders started breaking off from the tall stony peaks, and came bouncing and spinning down in a deafening, crashing shower that shook the ground and made underground waters spout and hiss up through cracks. By the time the din had stopped and the waters had settled down again, the rocks that had shaken loose from the mountains were half filling the valleys in great ruinous heaps, and the railway line was completely hidden from sight.

"Meanwhile, in the tunnel, the dragon was snorting and bellowing with rage at the trick the old man had played on it, but because of the disturbance in the mountains all the fumes and smoke it snorted found their way through vents and fissures under the ground and rose up in a wall of cloud all around the mountains where the dragon was trapped. This dragon-mist, like the dragon's breath, was poisonous, but now, after seeping under the ground, it didn't exactly make people go mad: it just made it impossible for them to see things properly. So no one from the world outside was able to find where the dragon was: the dragon-mist made the mountains seem invisible, or at most like great white clouds heaped on the horizon. The people from the world outside simply stopped using the railway line that led nowhere, and gradually forgot about it. They were still quite mad, poor things, and forgot very easily. And the people in the five mountain villages forgot about the world outside.

"And now the dragon sleeps beneath the mountain where it was trapped. But as it sleeps it dreams, and everything that happens in the world passes through its mind. And sometimes, very occasionally, someone will stop and think he is living inside the dragon's dream; and when that happens it means that the time has come when— "

Suddenly Ms Minn stopped and frowned. "Bull," she said quietly, "are you listening?"

Ms Minn's words were just beginning to stir something in Sparrow's memory, but what happened next made him forget what it was until a good deal later. Everyone looked over at Bull, but Bull didn't seem to notice. He was sitting at his desk, with his hands hanging over the front of it and his head drooping till it was almost resting on his arms. Sparrow thought his eyes were not quite closed, but he looked very much as though he were asleep.

Bull still did not stir or answer. Ms Minn went over to him. She stood beside him a moment, and then she put her hand on his head. "Bull, you're cold," she said.

She put her hand under Bull's chin and raised his head. Then one of the girls screamed. Sparrow saw that Bull's eyes were open, but they were rolling, and you could see only the whites under his lids. Steadily, the hair of Bull's head lifted until it was all standing up on end. The girl screamed again. One boy whimpered and others were shifting uneasily in their seats. But a second later the whole class became utterly silent.

Ms Minn's hand was still under Bull's chin, but now, as she raised his head up, the whole of Bull's body rose from his seat. As his legs came up, he knocked over his desk with a crash.

"Goodness," said Ms Minn. Bull was in a position as if still sitting at his desk, but he was floating a metre from the ground. Ms Minn let go of his chin. Bull remained up in the air.

Very slowly, Ms Minn stepped back. One step, then another. Bull floated after her. She stepped back again, never taking her eyes off him, until she had retreated as far as she could go, and her back was against the blackboard at the top end of the classroom. Bull floated slowly, steadily towards her, as though he were in an invisible flying chair.

Just in front of Ms Minn's nose, he stopped. He hung there, completely without moving, for as long as it would take you to count to ten quite slowly.

Then he began to float backwards. At the far end of the classroom there was a large, high window, and towards this he travelled with gathering speed. Through the window's polished glass you could see the mountains climbing, one behind the other, to the heights where the first snow had already fallen. Faster and faster Bull went now, backwards, straight towards the window.

"Ms Minn! Please! Stop him!" the girl screamed again. Bull was hurtling backwards now, his dark hair lashing wildly on either side of his face. The classroom seemed to have got longer, to have stretched out like a tunnel, because still Bull went flying giddily, as fast as a stone dropped over the edge of a cliff. A whining, buzzing noise filled the air and one by one the children clapped their hands over their ears to keep the noise out. Soon it was almost unbearable, even with their ears covered. And still Bull hurtled backwards. Dimly they saw Ms Minn standing with her back to the blackboard. The blackboard seemed to have got smaller, or else she had suddenly grown. Quiet and calm and tall, she stood there looking at Bull, while the horrible air buzzed and whined about her...

And then – *smash!* and straight afterwards *crash!* and then an icy tinkling as the broken glass showered down the classroom wall on to the floor. The air cleared immediately, and the whining stopped. The classroom shrank back to its proper size. So did Ms Minn. Bull had disappeared, and only a gaping hole in the window showed where he had gone.

Like a flight of starlings leaving a tree, everyone leaped up and ran to the sill.

Bull was far away up the street that led to the middle of

the village, sitting on his bottom as though he had just landed. He was looking more normal now, gazing about him as if he were wondering how he came to be there in the middle of the road. He didn't seem to have been injured by the glass, and in fact the glass looked more as though it had shattered and fallen out of the pane before Bull hit it: it was all lying in a heap on the classroom floor, and there seemed to be none on the ground outside. One of the doors of the houses out on the street opened, and a fat woman came out and looked at Bull, wiping her hands on a cloth. But the moment he saw the faces appearing at the schoolroom window, Bull did a backward somersault, leaped to his feet, and rushed off up the street through the village and up towards the mountains like a mad rabbit.

"Goodness me," Ms Minn said again. "Oh dear. Oh dear, oh dear, I must see my brother. Oh dear, that's possibly it then, isn't it?" She turned round, went to the classroom door and opened it. As she went through, "That's all, dears," she said absently. "School's over."

And school really was over, after only one day. Such a thing had never happened before, and in fact none of them ever had Ms Minn as a teacher again. But it was quite a long time before the village people realized that she would never come back.

"What do you think happened?" Sparrow muttered to Gogs as soon as he got the chance.

"I don't know," Gogs whispered back. He looked scared.

"Come on," said Sparrow, and they slipped through the commotion of excited children and left the school.

Before long they saw Ms Minn striding across the village square ahead of them. "We'll have to tell her," said Gogs.

"Tell her what?"

"Tell her we know what's happened."

"But we don't!" Sparrow exclaimed.

"Well, he must have shifted shape or something…" Gogs tailed off.

"He didn't shift shape, did he?" said Sparrow. "Something else happened."

"Well, we should tell her it's because of magic, anyway," Gogs insisted.

"What was that she was muttering about her brother?" Sparrow said. "Who's her brother?"

Gogs shrugged. "Come on," he said, "or we'll never catch her up."

They ran, but even so the old lady was going at such a rate that they didn't begin to catch up with her until they were under the bare elms on the street that led up from the village on to the Old Road.

"Ms Minn!" Gogs panted as she flapped on ahead of them. "Ms Minn!" But there seemed to be a wind blowing here – almost as though it were blowing round Ms Minn because she was walking so fast – and she appeared not to hear him.

"Ms Minn!" Gogs called a third time. Suddenly Sparrow gave an exclamation, stopped, and bent down to pick something off the road. With his eyes fixed on the old teacher, he had seen something drop from the ragged edge of her black dress – something that gleamed in a quite unmistakable way…

Gogs stopped and turned back to look at what he had found. Sparrow was gaping in disbelief at the thing he was holding in his hand: a milkstone.

"It fell from her clothes," Sparrow said, as both boys stared down at it. "I saw it falling. It came from her."

It was a perfect stone. Smooth, round, flawless, like a milky gleaming egg, its two layers of gold flake forming two perfect rings round its surface. "We'd better give it back to her," Gogs breathed.

But when they looked again, there was no sign of Ms Minn, either on the cobbled road or up on the Old Road. She had simply disappeared.

"I want to see P—" Sparrow stopped and frowned. "The old man," he finished. "I don't know what's going on." Vaguely, deep inside him, he did know, but his mind was racing too much for him to stop and think.

"I'll come too," Gogs said. "I'd like to practise my flying anyway." And as soon as they had reached the Old Road they flew.

Within moments, Gogs had forgotten all about Bull in the sheer delight of flying. Sparrow was more used to it, so he didn't forget, and Gogs was content to follow him. They flew over the forest, over the Cliff of Stones and down to the waterfall. Here Sparrow landed. He did not intend to waste time again trying to find the old man's cave by flying. He came to the foot of the little dark stream and started labouring up the hillside on foot, following its course.

"Come on," Gogs urged when they had reached the ash wood. "Fly!"

"No use," Sparrow panted, "we won't find it."

"Why?" Gogs demanded.

"I don't know," Sparrow puffed, "we just won't."

"That's stupid," Gogs scoffed. "We'd be quicker if

we flew."

"I'm walking," Sparrow replied, "it's the only way to get there."

"Where is old Piddle's cave?" Gogs asked.

"Up at the top of the stream," Sparrow answered, "but you've got to keep near the water."

"I know what," said Gogs. "I'll fly on ahead, and if I get lost, I'll ask the birds. They're bound to know."

"All right," said Sparrow. But the idea still did not tempt him to fly.

Sparrow watched Gogs skimming away over the stream amongst the trees. But long before he was out of sight between the straight grey trunks, Sparrow saw him land, scratch his head, look about and seem to speak. Sparrow guessed he was asking the birds, having somehow lost sight of the little dark stream. What he didn't know was that when Gogs asked the birds, the air all around filled with chirping and cheeping, but all Gogs could understand was, "Pickle, piddle, prickle, puddle, puckle, poker, kittle, cuddle, fiddle, fuddle, flimsy, mimsy, poodle, strudel, tickle, tuckle," and so on and on. Sparrow saw Gogs rise into the air again – higher this time, and higher again, until he lost sight of him in the lacing branches of the forest trees. He toiled on, keeping close to the little dark stream. A quarter of an hour passed, a stitch crept into his side and his breath was rough in his throat, but still he kept up the steepening slope. The milkstone in his hand felt greasy with sweat.

"Ow!" Sparrow suddenly yelled out loud. Something like a blow to his back jolted him from head to foot and brought him to a standstill. What on earth was wrong? He found he had started trembling all over, and his legs

75

wouldn't hold him. Gradually his knees gave way and he slipped down the bank into the little dark stream.

Cold water round his lower half revived him, but whatever it was that had jolted him had also left a thought in his head. Something he had not even started to consider in all the excitement of the last half hour…

Ms Minn's story was about their own mountains – their own railway line, the dead lake – the tunnel!

And the dragon in the tunnnel? Well, what about the dragon…? Sparrow had no wish to meet any dragon, head-first or tail-first, and yet his curiosity was gnawing him. Suppose he went down to the tunnel now and looked – not far, but just a little way in – just to check if Ms Minn's story really ended in that particular tunnel; just to check if the story was really true. It was strange how urgent that thought became in his mind, because he knew that the sensible thing to do just now was to go on and find Puckel and ask about Bull. And yet the thought of climbing up another kilometre of steep mountainside did not seem very inviting – and how did he know that Puckel would even be there at the end of it?

He pulled himself out of the water and squelched up the bank. He didn't feel like making decisions: he was wet, and he wanted to fly and he wanted to have a quick look at the tunnel. He rose through the trees. High up and higher he went, until he could see all that part of the mountain region spreading out beneath him: the white-capped peaks, the dark, greyish forests, the village far below with its blue haze of smoke, the old railway line climbing and winding up from the village, disappearing behind a rocky mound, appearing again, higher all the time.

There was a small dark figure wandering along the railway track. Sparrow didn't waste a second: he plunged straight down towards it like a falcon, and within seconds was landing in a small shower of water on the track behind the figure. It was Gogs again.

"Gogs," he called, "have you seen Bull?"

Slowly Gogs turned and looked at Sparrow. Sparrow stopped and frowned. There was something wrong with Gogs – Sparrow couldn't quite put his finger on it. It was something about the way Gogs turned and stared at him that wasn't like Gogs. For an instant it actually reminded him of Bull. Gogs waited for Sparrow to catch up with him. "What's wrong?" Sparrow asked anxiously.

"Bull's dead," Gogs said, almost in a whisper. He half glanced at Sparrow, then looked down at his feet.

Again, just for an instant, just before he thought about what Gogs had said, Sparrow thought there was something wrong with Gogs' voice; something wrong with the way he wouldn't look straight at him. Next moment he took in the meaning of Gogs' words and forgot all about his strangeness.

"Dead?" he echoed. "How can he be dead? He was at school this afternoon."

at the third stone

"HE FELL OVER A CLIFF," GOGS ANSWERED IN THE same level, quiet voice. "He was running along the steep path, and he must have slipped. All the birds were talking about it, so I came to see."

Sparrow looked hard at Gogs. "Where is he?" Sparrow said. "And where are you going?"

"I –" Again Gogs looked up in that strange, half-glancing way at Sparrow, and looked away again – "I was just coming to see if I could find you."

"Why didn't you fly then?" Sparrow demanded.

"I forgot," Gogs replied promptly. "I was too upset."

"Where is he?" Sparrow asked again.

"That way," said Gogs, pointing back down the railway line.

"Did you fly down to him?" Sparrow enquired.

Gogs remained looking at his feet. He shook his head. "I was scared to," he muttered.

Sparrow felt his own legs going wobbly. He remembered his dream of the night before. "Come on," he said. "Show me the place."

They walked back down the track in silence, stepping from sleeper to sleeper. Everything around them was quiet. They came to a place where a path led down from the railway line and Gogs took this path until it levelled out near the edge of the cliff. Then he stopped and pointed down.

For a moment Sparrow could see only rocks: huge boulders, smaller stones, all tumbled together in a long grey scree at the cliff's foot. Then he saw the tiny, sprawled-out human figure. He could not make out properly what the figure was wearing, but somehow he knew it was Bull.

He had been going to say to Gogs that they should fly down to him and perhaps carry him back up. But he couldn't bring himself to do it. Looking down there, he simply felt scared. Sparrow, who had flown so high above the mountain tops that he could hardly breathe for the thinness of the air, looked down that hundred metre cliff and was sure that if he jumped he would end up the same way as Bull – smashed over a rock. He felt dizzy and sick.

Then – "Something's moving," he said, peering down.

"I can't see anything," Gogs said.

"Maybe not," Sparrow mumbled. "I thought I could see something moving."

"Bull won't move again," Gogs said with a catch in his voice as though he were fighting back tears.

Sparrow felt his own throat knotting up. "We'll have to tell someone," he said thickly.

"Have you seen the old man?" Gogs asked.

"No," said Sparrow, without explaining why.

"You go and see him," said Gogs, "and I'll fly back to the

79

village and tell someone."

Sparrow agreed to this, and on the railway track they parted, Gogs flying back down the hill while Sparrow left the track and made off again in the direction of Puckel's cave.

Sparrow was still shaking with the shock and he made sure he didn't do any high flying, skimming instead. But he was not used to flying through the mountains this way, and soon he came to a ridge where he landed and looked around, uncertain of his direction.

The land here was a tumble of forest, gullies and ridges, and glancing back the way he had come, Sparrow saw a part of the railway line again between the folds of rocky ground. And at that very moment, he saw a figure on the track – or rather not quite on the track: surely it was flying above the track…

It must be Gogs again, Sparrow thought – and then he frowned. For Gogs was going back the way he had come: not down towards the village but up, in the direction he had been going when Sparrow first found him – into the mountains.

Towards the tunnel. And as the thought struck him, again there came that overwhelming urge – forgotten because of the shock of Bull's death – to go and investigate the tunnel. For the second time, Sparrow was on the point of abandoning his search for Puckel to go back there, to follow the track into the dark, deeper and deeper into the heart of the mountain – where, in the mountain's heart, surrounded by its poisonous smoky breath that made you go mad, the terrible, wise, magical dragon lay stuck, trapped with its tail stretching back towards the open air!

Trapped. And by whom? Of course: by the old man who wasn't like other men. He had to be – Puckel!

Sparrow span round like a top. He had to get to Puckel! But then there was the dragon in the tunnel. Vividly he imagined the fearful beast, and Gogs tiptoeing over the sleepers towards it, closer, closer…

The dragon, Puckel. Puckel, the dragon. They both seemed to pull at him, dragging him this way and that as though he were the bone in a dogs' tug-of-war.

In the end, Puckel proved the stronger thought. But it was hard: hard as getting out of your warm bed early on a cold winter morning. Sparrow managed to decide, but only just: whatever Gogs was doing, the only way of getting help was to get Puckel.

He reached the little dark stream again and ran, ran and ran, till his chest was heaving and painful and his breath tasted of blood. His legs, already chilled from their wetting, seemed too heavy to move, till gradually all the feeling drained out of them – and still he ran, automatically, and barely noticed it when he at last pushed through the close, cooling leaves of the ivy. There in the courtyard of rocks stood Puckel, and Sparrow collapsed at his feet where the little dark stream bubbled up through the stones.

"Puckel," he gasped. "Bull's fallen off the cliff – he's dead – and Ms Minn dropped a milkstone and she's off again; something happened with Bull and she's off to see … and Gogs isn't going down to the village and I think there's something wrong with him too, and I got this bang in the back and my legs got wet and—"

Puckel held up his hand, and Sparrow found his mouth clapping shut. The next thing he knew was that he was half lying in Puckel's chair by the fire, and Puckel was sitting cross-legged on the table staring intently into the brown bowl. Dully Sparrow's eyes moved round the room in the cave. There was no sign of the stick or the snake, so he assumed that Puckel had turned it into the water for the bowl again.

At last the old man looked up, nodding solemnly. "Yes," he remarked, "it's bad: it's very bad, it's very, very bad indeed."

"I know it is," Sparrow said, "that's what I was trying to tell you. Bull's dead." And then his chest heaved, once, twice, and tears overwhelmed him.

"Hush," said Puckel, after Sparrow had quietened a little. "His body – his body is all broken, although it is already quickly mending. That is being attended to, as you'd have noticed if you had sharper eyes. But Bull's not dead."

"You mean we can still help him?" Sparrow gulped.

"Not in the way you think," Puckel replied briskly. "What you saw, below the cliff, is beyond your help. But Bull is not dead. You saw Bull."

"I know," Sparrow answered, rubbing his eyes feverishly, "he had fallen over the cliff."

"You saw Bull," Puckel repeated impatiently. "You saw him, and spoke to him, and you didn't see who he was."

"But I did," Sparrow protested, "I mean – the only person I spoke to was Gogs."

"You spoke to Bull," Puckel insisted.

Sparrow gave one last almighty sniff. "I don't know what you can see in that bowl," he said rudely, "but I think you must be disturbing the water. Gogs is the one with red hair—"

"I know, I know," Puckel interrupted, "the red hair and

82

the idiot's grin. I saw him before. This bowl, boy, doesn't show me pictures – it's not a silly circus trick that you do with a stick and a slop of water." He held the bowl up and turned it towards Sparrow, who saw that it was quite empty – a dry, rough earthenware hollow. "It tells me things in here," Puckel said, tapping his head. "I don't make mistakes from seeing what isn't there. You spoke to Bull, not Gogs."

"You mean Bull turned into Gogs?" Sparrow gasped. Of course: Gogs had been so strange. "But then what – why could we still see Bull's body? It should have disappeared."

"When someone dies suddenly," Puckel said, "it can sometimes take a little time for them to realize they're dead. And of course someone who doesn't realize he's dead isn't properly dead. That has saved Bull. He should have died when he fell, but in the brief time given to him, he saw Gogs looking over the cliff at his body below – and he took Gogs' shape. It was lucky and it was very close. But the thread that held him to his body had already been broken, so when he took Gogs' shape he had to leave his own body behind."

"Can't he get it back?" Sparrow asked.

"We shall see," said Puckel. "There's a good chance of it. But Bull has been very foolish – as I expected him to be. Don't say I didn't warn you."

Sparrow was silent.

"I'll tell you what I read," Puckel said. "The teacher in the classroom –" He paused.

"You mean Ms Minn," Sparrow said.

Puckel grunted, a grunt that was nearly a chuckle. "Ms Minn," he repeated. "Well, she told her story. Bull listened. He was very foolish – very, very foolish. She wasn't going fast enough for him. She wasn't going fast enough, so what does he do? He tries to get inside her – he tries to shift shape with her. Silly puppy. Silly noodle. No one – not the great Kadellin, not Shabab-el-Din, not Solomon himself could have done that – not even tried it. Why? Because it's impossible! There's nothing to shift shape with! You can't get into – what's she called?"

"Ms Minn," Sparrow repeated, bewildered.

"Ms Minn!" Puckel broke out into a great roar of laughter and immediately was shaken by a fit of wheezing. "Ms Minn," he choked, "Ms Mi-hi-hi-hinn. Well, anyway," he went on, recovering himself at last, "he was thrown back, as you saw."

"Yes," Sparrow agreed, "he went right through the window and then dashed off up the road."

"I'll tell you what happened," Puckel interrupted, "you don't have to tell me. Off he went, up the road, off up into the mountains, with no other idea in his silly head than to get up – yes, yes – into the tunnel." He paused, then added solemnly, "And to what is in the tunnel. Yes, young Sparrow, Bull's one thought was to make contact with the dragon – because Bull thinks quicker than you, and knew at once that the dragon of the story must be in these mountains."

"I wanted to get to the tunnel too," said Sparrow, "as soon as I started thinking about Ms Minn's story."

"Of course you did," said Puckel. "The dragon was calling you."

"Calling me?"

"In his sleep," Puckel said impatiently. "Didn't she tell you about that? Or had you decided to doze off just then?"

"Oh yes – she did say something about someone thinking he was in the dragon's dream," Sparrow said, "– and I was just going to ask you—"

Puckel snorted. "That's one way of putting it. But who

does the dreaming, that's what no one can answer: the dragon, or the person who thinks of the dragon's dream? You're lucky, young Sparrow, you had a narrow escape. It could have been you, not Bull. It comes of not knowing what you want."

"I don't understand," said Sparrow.

"The trouble with telling stories about the dragon," said Puckel carefully, "is that he calls out in his sleep – to those who can hear. You heard it, and Bull heard it. He's too greedy, Bull, and he heard it too soon: he has never met me, he has not been given a gift of his own, he had no protection, and now nothing turns out as it should."

"So how did he change into Gogs?" Sparrow asked.

"Gogs was there too," Puckel replied, "led by the birds. Gogs wouldn't hear the call of the dragon: he has too much sweetness in him. But he tried to stop Bull because he was anxious about him after what happened in the classroom. There was a scuffle, the birds twittered and confused things, they slipped to the edge of the cliff…"

"But then where's Gogs?" Sparrow asked anxiously.

"Safe enough, in his own body," Puckel told him. "But asleep. Bull has him. Gogs is Bull, and Bull can't leave his shape."

"Why not?" Sparrow said.

"He has lost the power," Puckel answered. "Bull's shape is no longer hidden: anyone can see it now – so it's no longer his own. We all need a home, to come from and go back to. A shape-changer's home is the body he has kept hidden. Without it, he would simply float away – that's why Bull is imprisoned in Gogs' body now for his own good."

"So what can we do?" Sparrow said in horror.

"Oh, we'll manage something," Puckel replied vaguely,

staring off out of the triangular mouth of the cave. Gradually his expression became grimmer, and his deep-lined old face began to look sad and haggard. "He can't change," he said, "but he can be changed into."

"Who could change into him?" Sparrow gasped.

"Not could, but would," Puckel corrected. "Only one creature would."

"Not – not the dragon?" Sparrow exclaimed. "But how could – I mean – I thought the dragon was huge!"

"Only to look at," Puckel said. "Don't be fooled by appearances. Oh, he wouldn't have much use for Bull's mind or Gogs' shape, not for long. But there's one use he can make of them."

"To get out of the tunnel," Sparrow breathed.

"To get out of the tunnel," Puckel repeated solemnly. "Precisely that."

Sparrow gaped. "What can we do?" he said again.

"We wait," Puckel snapped. "When the business that is being attended to is finished, we can move. Now sit quiet – your tongue's like a bell-clapper."

Sparrow obeyed, but after being quiet for a minute, he remembered the milkstone and, opening his hand, dumbly held the shining thing out for Puckel to see.

Puckel looked at it. "The third stone?" he questioned.

Sparrow nodded.

"Then the time has come," Puckel said. "Now there's not long to wait."

Sparrow couldn't answer. He seemed to have forgotten how to speak. Strange things were going on, beyond even the strange things that were happening to him. Puckel obviously knew something about Ms Minn – and he apparently knew her silly rhyme about the stones. Or maybe it

86

wasn't so silly after all… What did Ms Minn know? Who was she? Where had she gone? Who was her brother? For a moment the ridiculous thought crossed Sparrow's mind that *Puckel* must be her brother – at any rate he didn't know of anyone else who lived up in the mountains – but then he realized that if he were, she ought to be already here.

As these thoughts crossed his mind, Sparrow noticed a subtle, secret movement among the shadows on the floor. A silent thing glistened and slid over the stones of the cave. Presumably Puckel's stick, in its snake disguise, was entering the cave. Quietly, it glided over to the table leg, wrapped itself round it and climbed, coil upon coil. At last the head shot up over the edge of the table, and Puckel, absolutely still until that moment, grabbed it. A moment later he held the strange, twisted, polished stick in his hand.

"The time has come," he said again, "and we must go."

87

Flying with Puckel was unlike any other flying Sparrow had ever done before. It was more like flying in a whirlwind. Puckel held on to Sparrow by the neck, like a bird of prey, and his green cloak swelled and billowed all around them while the air bellowed in their ears. Their speed was incredible.

Within minutes they were rushing down towards the railway line. They landed, and gradually the turmoiled air grew quiet around them. Right in front of them was the dark archway of the tunnel.

Puckel paused, and seemed to be listening. You could see the railway line for a little way after it passed into total blackness.

Puckel shook his head. "This is not good," he remarked. "Come on." And he stepped along the sleepers into the tunnel.

Gradually the light faded, until all that was left of it was a pinhead far behind them – except that it didn't seem far because there was no feeling of distance in the stuffy darkness. Sparrow's skin crawled with the dankness and the closed-in feeling of the tunnel. Minutes before, they had been flying in the light, in the free air. Now he felt as if the whole weight of the mountain were on them, crushing them into the darkness. He clutched on to Puckel's cloak, tripping on the unseen sleepers of the railway track.

For minute after minute they crept forward, almost without a sound, except when Sparrow tripped or kicked a stone. Puckel never tripped.

After an age of darkness, the old man stopped so suddenly that Sparrow ran into him. Puckel ignored his mumbled apology. "Light," Sparrow heard him muttering, "now we need some light."

Sparrow agreed with him, but said nothing. If Puckel was able to make light, he was thinking, why hadn't he done it before?

But the light that Puckel made was no thin candle-flame, nor wavering torchlight, nor even a pale magical glow. It was a burst of flame, a great orange-red fireball that enveloped them in a burst of heat and singed their eyebrows. With a husky roar, the fireball flooded the tunnel around them with reddish light, and slowly began rolling down the line away from them, casting fierce lights and shadows as it went.

On and on it rolled, while Puckel and Sparrow watched silently until it dwindled to the size of a football far along the long straight tunnel. It was so far away that Sparrow could no longer see Puckel when the old man murmured, "No, not a trace, not a sign, not a scale on the wall."

"Has the dragon gone?" Sparrow asked, as relief flooded over him.

"Gone he has," Puckel confirmed.

"What about Bull?" Sparrow asked, as panic rose to take its place.

"Bull, Bull, Bull," Puckel muttered, "there's only one use for Bull, and that's in a field of cows. I don't have time for him. Come on!"

And with that he seized Sparrow by the neck again, and they flew back along the tunnel. If the air had rushed and roared when they were flying outside, inside the narrow tunnel it was deafening, and Sparrow felt his eardrums were going to burst.

They rocketed out of the tunnel mouth back into the dazzling air, and up, up, up they soared – as high as the swiftly-moving clouds where the sunlight still basked golden, although the sun was setting on the earth below.

89

There they paused and hung, and Puckel searched the tumbled ground spread beneath them. Sparrow looked with him for a little, but could see nothing, and as Puckel went on and on searching the ground, patiently, bit by bit, he became restive. If Puckel could see things in the bowl, he thought, why couldn't he have found out from that where the dragon was?

The mountainous clouds billowed up and drifted past, golden and crimson. Sparrow could see far down through the valleys to the dead lake. The sun was low over the low black hills, which he could now see clearly at the lake's end, and the black water glinted with sombre gold. Up in the clouds again, something glinted between the great misty golden shapes, catching Sparrow's eye. Then the clouds shifted and covered it.

Sparrow frowned, searching over and under the massing billowy shapes. Then – there it was again! Something that glinted and flashed in the late sunlight, something that must be very large and very far away. Could it be the dragon?

Sparrow didn't want to disturb Puckel just yet, intent as the old man was on the ground below. So he kept his eyes fixed on the golden glinting thing as it disappeared and appeared again amongst the high clouds. Whatever it was, it was coming nearer.

It was still quite small when Sparrow realized at last that what he was looking at was no living thing. The shape of it was now distinct. Something thin, pointed, like a piece of stick with another piece of wood nailed across it, though shining and glinting as though it were made of metal.

Sparrow had thought about aeroplanes, argued about aeroplanes, dreamed about aeroplanes, but what he first felt, looking at a real aeroplane at last when he had been expecting the dragon, was that there was something slightly sad about it. It looked so fixed and helpless, a thing that couldn't help itself, that had been thrown into the air and left to float or fall as chance allowed.

"An aeroplane," he murmured. "There are aeroplanes, and I can see one. A tube with wings out to the sides that don't flap. It's an aeroplane."

"Eh? What's that?" Puckel broke off his searching and looked sharply at Sparrow.

Sparrow pointed. "Look," he said.

"Quick, come quickly, come quickly!" a voice called behind them. And there was Gogs flying towards them, white-faced, his red hair flying back in the wind of his speed.

the time has come

"HAVE YOU SEEN THE DRAGON?" SPARROW CALLED.

"Yes," Gogs called back frantically – or was it Bull? – "it's this way, come quickly!" He turned and swooped down, with Puckel and Sparrow hammering down the air behind him. Down they plunged, nine hundred, a thousand metres, while the mountain tops rushed up towards them – and into a mist. When they came clear of it again, there was no sign of Gogs, but still Puckel flew on. It was only then that Sparrow remembered that Gogs might not even be Bull, but – worse…

He twisted his head round to see where the aeroplane had got. There it was: larger now, much larger than Sparrow had at first realized – but then he saw something else behind, something hurtling upwards as fast as they were hurtling down, something with a strange twisted lizard-like shape and tattery wings and flames billowing around it…

Sparrow's first glimpse of the dragon was nothing like his first glimpse of the aeroplane. There was nothing sad or hopeless about it. This was a living creature that knew exactly what it was doing; dangerous, fearsomely intent.

A glimpse was all he had before he found himself grabbing at Puckel's arm, pinching and scratching, screaming at him to stop and look.

It seemed an age before Puckel did, and by then they were skimming over the mountain tops. Sparrow pointed behind them, screaming into the roaring wind.

When at last Puckel saw, he let out a roar that fairly shook the mountains. Sparrow clapped his hands over his ears and shut his eyes, for Puckel began spinning round like a tornado. When he dared look again, they were shooting upwards, and the dragon was straight ahead of them. There was still no sign of Gogs.

Fast as the dragon was climbing, Puckel was climbing faster, heading off the great green and golden beast.

Was it possible, Sparrow thought, that *that* had been in Gogs' shape a minute before?

All of a sudden, the dragon became aware of them. Although it did not check its speed or its onward, upward rush, it turned its head, let out a bellow like a mad bull, and shot out tongues of bright red flame. It seemed still too far away to do any harm, but a second later Puckel and Sparrow were enveloped in warmth, then heat – then a scorching furnace blast. Puckel slowed, but a moment later they were clear again, unharmed, and closing on the dragon. Sparrow saw now that it was huge, huger than any lizard could possibly be, knotted, spiked, taloned, green with golden scales and skinny golden wings, horribly ugly and yet, somehow, beautiful too.

Suddenly it disappeared, and immediately afterwards Puckel and Sparrow were lost in the midst of a thick grey mist. They had risen into the clouds, and all was cold, wet and silent.

Just as quickly, they shot out again, still climbing into the darkening blue air. Sparrow heard a whining roar that was not the wind, nor the beast-like roar of the dragon. An evil-smelling smoke hung around them which set him coughing. Then Sparrow saw it full-size: they had come up out of the cloud and crossed behind the path of the aeroplane, which was thundering away from them with what looked like four red eyes glaring back from under its wings. Where was the dragon? Puckel paused and turned in the air, looking wildly about.

With an explosion of flame and smoke, the dragon burst up out of the cloud like a fish leaping out of a pond.

The noise drowned out even the noise of the aeroplane. The dragon roared, and roared again; and mingling with the smoke left by the aeroplane, the dragon's flame went spinning and coiling. For a moment, Sparrow could not understand what was happening, for the dragon had shot its flame away from them, not at them.

But in that moment, Puckel let go of his neck. Sparrow let out a scream and fell like a stone.

"Fly, you bonehead!" Dimly Puckel's voice – or was it the stick's? – came down to him as he plunged into wet grey cloud again. "Help them as you can!"

At first it seemed to him that he had forgotten how to fly. But after a little, Sparrow realized that that was because the cloud was so thick that he couldn't see which way he was going. When at last he emerged into the clear air, he found he was flying after all – though slowly, so slowly, it seemed, after the terrifying rush of Puckel's flight.

Sparrow saw the mountains and the setting sun first. And then he heard the din of roaring ruin above him. He looked up, and all became plain.

First he saw the dragon, but it wasn't flying straight – it seemed to be twisting and turning, as a cat might do if you caught it by the tail and swung it. A second later Sparrow realized why. Puckel was clinging madly to its tail. He looked like a tiny black blob at the end of the colossal stretch of the magical beast, but it was clear that what the old man had hinted about his fantastic strength had been no boast.

But some way off there was a roaring cloud of flame and smoke spinning down towards the mountain tops. It was all so clear now, horribly clear: the dragon had attacked the aeroplane and set fire to it. That was what Puckel had meant when he yelled to Sparrow to go down and help!

Sparrow left the scene of the dragon-fight and followed the flaming aeroplane – though what he could do he had no idea.

Sparrow did not know how aeroplanes behave when out of control. Otherwise he would have realized that someone in this one was still desperately trying to guide it and save the people inside. First one way, then the other, it tilted, slant-ing all the while towards one of the mountains that stood out flat as a table-top and pillowed in a deep covering of snow.

Very slowly, it seemed to Sparrow, the aeroplane hit the mountain top, its wing slicing into the snow and scattering a fine white shower of flakes. Very slowly, the dark body fol-lowed the wing, and then the flaming tail, sending a billowing mixture of black smoke and white mist boiling and coiling up together. Just before the smoke covered it completely, Sparrow saw it sliding to a halt at the very edge of the flat top. It had tipped slightly over when it finally stopped moving. Sparrow raced down towards it, still with no clear idea of what to do, except that he must help.

Now he was directly above the crashed thing, he circled, coming down more slowly as he tried to see what was happening. The tail was still in flames, and more fires seemed to have broken out along the body and on the wing that stuck up in the air like a fish's fin. But a door had opened in the top of the body, and in the dark entrance something was moving.

The door was in fact in the side of the aeroplane, but because it had crashed on to its side the door was facing upwards, a black mouth out of which a tiny figure struggled, crawled along the body a little, then slid over the side, plopped into the snow and disappeared. An instant later a second figure appeared, even tinier.

By this time, Sparrow had realized what he must do. The tube was full of people: perhaps it was full of smoke too. They would have to be helped out as quickly as possible. He dived towards the door in the plane's body, where the second figure seemed to be hesitating, as if afraid to jump over the side to the snow below. A third head was appearing out of the door. Without another thought, he had skimmed in, grabbed the figure teetering on the side of the plane, and flown on past.

He barely had time to register it was neither as big nor as heavy a person as he had expected when, with a deafening crash, a blow hit him in the back, and sent him staggering forwards through the air. Somehow he held on to his burden, though he lost considerable height before he recovered and could fly properly down to land on a rock well below the mountain top.

Sparrow had never seen an explosion before, and did not know what happens in explosions. What had hit him in the back was the blast from the exploding aeroplane, which scattered pieces of it all over the mountainside. A tower of black smoke, orange-lit from underneath, was rising up from the mountain top, while through the darkened air all around them tiny pieces of metal came whizzing and smoking down on to the stones. Sparrow watched, open-mouthed, almost unaware of the body he was half supporting in his arms, as the black smoke raged and gradually grew less dense.

At last he took some notice of his companion. It was a girl, apparently about his own age, with hair that was probably meant to be blonde, but just now was extremely dirty. The girl was in a dead faint.

Sparrow looked down at her, and couldn't quite decide what was wrong. She looked unharmed, so he left her lying in a heap and flew back up to the mountain top.

There he looked around in amazement. Everything had changed. There was hardly a sign of the aeroplane except a fiercely burning thing like a huge twisted skeleton. The heat was tremendous. The snow was grey and sunken and all covered with water. There was a horrible smell in the air that he had never smelled before, and mixed with it a smell like burning feathers. There was no sign of life. The explosion seemed to have destroyed everything. The only person left alive was the girl lying down on the mountain-side.

When he was older, Sparrow thought a lot about that

moment – had nightmares about it too: that moment when he knew that the people who had been in the aeroplane were simply not there any more. But at the time, he felt nothing at all. He left the mountain top and flew back to where the girl was.

When he landed, he saw that her eyes were open, and staring at him, but she didn't move. Sparrow stood and watched.

At last she made a sound. She was clearing her throat. Her lips worked silently. Then the voice came: "What's your name?"

"Sparrow," said Sparrow.

"Sparrow," the girl repeated. "Is that because you can fly?"

"I was always called Sparrow."

"Oh," the girl said, and closed her eyes again.

"What's your name?" Sparrow asked.

The girl opened her eyes again. They were grey-blue eyes, like mist that was about to clear and leave a blue sky.

"It's Kittel," she said.

"Skittle?" said Sparrow, wondering vaguely if she was called Skittle because she'd been knocked down.

The girl made a little grunt, which was actually a short, painful laugh. "No," she said, "my name is Kittel, K-I-T-T-E-L," she spelled out.

But that meant nothing to Sparrow, who had never done spelling. "Kay, Eye… What?" he repeated, bewildered.

"Kittel. I'm called Kittel, that's all," the girl moaned tiredly.

"I'd better take you back," Sparrow said. "You can't stay here: everyone else has gone."

"I know," Kittel murmured, "I was very lucky."

97

"Come on," Sparrow said, and Kittel let him lift her up, away from the wrecked aeroplane, across the mountain tops, and down to the forest on the lower slopes.

Sparrow had been going to take the girl to Puckel's cave, but he quickly saw that she would never be able to climb all the way up beside the little dark stream. She seemed very drowsy, and kept closing her eyes. What had Puckel expected him to do? There was nothing for it, he decided: he would have to take her home.

He really wanted to go back up and find out what had happened between Puckel and the dragon. There was no sign of them in the sky and the air was quiet – no sound of roaring or thunder. But he couldn't leave Kittel lying in the forest: she needed help. Sparrow realized what it would mean if he took her home: he would have to tell Murie exactly how he had found her, and give away the secret of his flight. But he scarcely stopped to think about that. He flew again over the forest in the gathering twilight, past the Cliff of Murie's stone, and down the slopes towards the village. He flew over the clearing where he normally started and ended his flights. He flew on down to the round green hill where his home was, and landed in front of the house, while Cairo – as once before – reared and snorted and went thundering off to the far end of the paddock. He sat Kittel down on the bench outside the house and flung open the door.

Darkness was falling, and the soft yellow lamps on their wall brackets were alight inside. Murie was in the warm kitchen as Sparrow rushed in. She looked flustered and cross, and Sparrow hadn't had a chance to speak before she turned towards him from the stove, putting her hands angrily on her hips.

"Sparrow," she said accusingly, "what have you done with my milkstones? Did you take them to school without asking?"

Sparrow stopped and gaped. "No, I haven't touched them."

"Well, someone has," Murie returned, "and I've been alone in the house all day. It's not fair, you know, giving me things and then—"

"Honestly, Murie," Sparrow protested, "I never touched them, I –" And suddenly Sparrow remembered the third milkstone. But where was it? He had had it in his hand; he had shown it to Puckel. And then what? The snake had come in after that and he didn't remember anything more about it. Had he dropped it in the excitement?

"I found another one," he muttered, peering into the pouch at his belt, "but it's gone too."

"What are you saying?" said Murie irritably. "And why are you so late back from school?"

"School?" Sparrow frowned.

"School," repeated Murie dryly. "Down in the village with a bell in a little tower…"

"Oh, school!" he remembered. "School's over again."

"Over!" Murie exclaimed. "But it's only just begun."

"Murie," said Sparrow, "there was an aeroplane crash."

"A what?" Murie said. "What are you talking about?"

"An aeroplane," Sparrow repeated. "Once Grandad said he went in one, when he was very young."

"That was a daft story he used to tell," Murie retorted. "It was just a joke. He never flew."

"There *are* aeroplanes, Murie," Sparrow said steadily. "I know because I've seen one."

"Fiddlesticks," Murie snorted. And then she seemed to

notice Sparrow properly. "Goodness, look at you! What a mess you're in! You're black from head to toe. Oh, Sparrow, your clean clothes…"

Sparrow interrupted. "I know," he explained. "I'm black because the aeroplane crashed, and there was a huge bang, and fire, and a lot of smoke. But I've rescued someone."

"What?" said Murie blankly. She thought Sparrow had gone quite mad. "You've rescued someone. Who did you rescue?"

"A girl," Sparrow said simply. "She's called Kittel. She's here, outside. I saved her just before the bang came. It was on top of a mountain."

Of course it never even crossed Murie's mind that Sparrow could be telling the truth, but what worried her was that he seemed so serious about his story. Was he really going mad? She didn't know whether to laugh or shout at him.

"How could you possibly save a girl from a mountain top?" was all she could manage to say.

Just then a soft voice spoke behind her. "Because Sparrow can fly," it said. Murie wheeled round to see Kittel standing in the kitchen doorway.

Murie found it all too much: there were simply too many things all at once. The loss of her precious milkstones; Sparrow's flying; Kittel; and, in due course, Kittel's description of the world she had come from.

"What do you mean, the television's *for* something?" Murie exclaimed in wonderment. "What? You see people on that screen? What size of people, for goodness' sake? You speak to a telephone? What a crazy idea. What do you say to it? Are they all mad where you come from, or what?"

And the more Kittel tried to explain, the more confused Murie got. And when Kittel tried to tell her about electricity, it was the last straw. Murie actually fetched a wet towel from the wash-house and wrapped it round her head. "I'm fevered," she muttered.

Sparrow wanted to know if Kittel often went round in an aeroplane. "This was just the second time," she said, "but it was the first time on my own. I'd been away on holiday to my uncle's." This was impossible for Sparrow. The only person he had ever known go away when there was a holiday was mad old Ms Minn. And how could Kittel have been on her own when he himself had seen that there were other people in the aeroplane?

"Our flight was very late," said Kittel, "because there were so many other planes waiting to land." And Sparrow had a picture – half nightmare, half miracle – of a sky dark with the great roaring things with their backward-glaring red eyes circling towers and spires of stone like ravens round a crag.

So much was new that it was a mercy Kittel needed to sleep a lot in the first two days after her arrival. Then Sparrow and Murie would sit together in the kitchen in stunned silence, trying to digest it all. For Murie it was just plain bizarre, but Sparrow had the added complication of Ms Minn's story to deal with. He knew of course that all the wonders of Kittel's world were the inventions of the dragon – the same dragon that he had just seen destroying the aeroplane. But Kittel, it seemed, had not heard of any dragon. It was people who had invented everything, she insisted, just clever people. Then he remembered about the people being mad, and he wondered if Kittel were mad, too, though she didn't appear to be.

When she was asleep, Sparrow would constantly creep into the room just to look at her. It seemed so strange to think that there was only a wall of mist between Kittel's place and the mountains, and yet here she was, so different she was like a creature that had come down from the stars.

By the second day, Sparrow felt he must go and find Puckel again. Of course he had to tell Murie all about what had happened, because she had wanted to know how he could fly. She seemed to believe him quite easily: perhaps because so many impossible things had happened already. But he said nothing about Gogs or Bull or the dragon. Eventually, telling Murie where he was going, he flew off up into the mountain; and she watched him go, shaking her head in disbelief.

He found the old man without difficulty, but there was little comfort to be had from him. It seemed the dragon was secure for the time being. "I've got him here somewhere," he said, and bent down and rummaged about in the drawer behind the chair. When he stood again, he had a bottle in his hand. It was an ordinary clear glass bottle with a cork in the top, and a heavy green seal keeping the cork in. Sparrow could hardly believe his eyes: inside the bottle was the dragon.

It looked extremely cross, and when Puckel lifted the bottle for Sparrow to see it, it spouted smoke and tiny red flames at them. The smoke drifted up and gathered in a black clot in the neck of the bottle. At the bottom was a little rough pyramid of rock.

"I shrank him," Puckel explained, "but a stupid mountain went and got in the way of the shrinking spell and I let it into the bottle too. I shall have to put it back when I let the dragon out, because you shouldn't steal mountains and that's a fact."

"Why are you going to let the dragon out?" Sparrow protested.

"I have to," answered Puckel. "I've only got him here for the time being. You can't really shrink dragons, and I only managed because he hadn't woken up properly from being in the tunnel. I pulled him out of the sky and banged his head against a mountain and that knocked him out for a moment or two, just long enough to shrink him. But that doesn't mean that everything's safe – oh dear me, no. The dragon may be little, but he's slowly boiling up. Feel the bottle."

Sparrow reached out his hand and touched the bottle. It felt hot. Not so hot that you couldn't touch it, but pretty hot all the same.

103

"It's getting hotter all the time," Puckel said, "and when it gets too hot – ping! The bottle will split apart, out will come the dragon and grow to his proper size again in no time at all."

"Why don't you put it back into the tunnel before it can get out of the bottle?" Sparrow asked.

"Bull is there," Puckel replied.

"We'll have to get him out," said Sparrow.

"Easy, isn't it?" the old man replied. "We'll just go into the tunnel, whistle, 'Come along now, Bull, it's time to go home,' and along he comes!"

"Well – not exactly," said Sparrow, "but something like that."

"Can't you get it into that rock-hard skull of yours," said Puckel severely, "that things are *not easy*? Bull is in hiding and he is waiting. He is hiding from the people of the village, because he knows they will think he is Gogs, and he thinks they will think he has killed Bull."

"But they'd know he wouldn't do a thing like that!" said Sparrow.

"They would know, but does he know they would know? There is something you did not understand. Bull can't see anything clearly any more. The dragon has been in his – or rather Gogs' – shape once already, and more than anything Bull wants that to happen again."

"Why on earth?" Sparrow gasped.

Puckel shook his head sadly. "Ah now, that is a great why indeed. Why does Bull want to do everything the wrong way? Why did he send you to get magic gifts for him that he had no right to? Why does he keep things to himself? He's scared of being small, I suppose. But now he's walked into just about the deepest trouble he could have. He'll end up less than small if he's not careful: he'll end up nothing at all. If Bull took your shape, to you it would be like falling asleep. You would remember nothing of what he had done while he was in your shape. It's different with the dragon: if *he* takes on your shape it doesn't feel like being asleep; you remember everything the dragon does – it can even seem as if you did it yourself. You feel very powerful. That's all happened to Bull. It wasn't for long – just enough for him to walk out of the tunnel and then distract our attention from that bit of flying ironmongery – but it was enough. For that little time he felt what it was like to be the most powerful creature on earth. He remembers and he liked the feeling. In the end the dragon will devour his mind."

"But why?" said Sparrow.

"Why what?" Puckel snapped.

"Why does it want to?" Sparrow said.

"I never said it wanted to," Puckel responded. "I said it will. It can't help it. That's what dragons do. Sensible people keep away from dragons. You can no more expect the dragon not to devour Bull's mind than you can expect water to flow uphill."

"Isn't there something you can do?" Sparrow pleaded.

"He must do it," Puckel said sharply. "He must decide, simply, 'No, I will not have anything more to do with the dragon.' Returning him to his own body, and helping him to make this simple decision, are the two things that must be done for Bull."

"And what about the dragon?"

"Eventually I will free him from the bottle. I will go into the tunnel and try to make sure that he is facing inwards and not outwards. But I cannot do this until we have got Bull and Gogs to safety. Nuisances they are – nothing but nuisances. I should never have listened to you. This has all happened because of you and your silly wishes. Now go away and leave me in peace. Come back in three days' time and I'll give you a rope and some other stuff."

And that, very suddenly, was the end of the conversation, for Puckel and the cave vanished and Sparrow was left, once again, floating in the air above the forest.

kittel

SPARROW DRIFTED HOMEWARDS. THERE WAS AN unpleasant feeling, like a dark mist, hanging over everything: a feeling of threat, a feeling that things weren't running in their proper courses. He was also annoyed that he hadn't been given a chance to tell Puckel about Kittel.

When he got home, Sparrow found Murie had a visitor. It was Plato Smithers, the master-builder from the village. Smithers was also a kind of policeman in the village, and he had come to investigate the strange goings-on.

The village folk had no idea about Puckel or the dragon or about the magic powers Sparrow and Bull and Gogs had been given, or even about magic of any kind. But what they did know seemed strange enough.

This is how it looked to them: Ms Minn had opened her school again after one of her long absences. But on the same day that she opened it, she had started babbling some nonsense about a mad inventor of some kind, and in the middle of it had suddenly gone over to poor Bull, picked him up by the throat and thrown him right out of the school-room window. Just how that dry old stick had even managed to pick up a big strapping lad like Bull – let alone throw him through a window – was a complete mystery, but thirty-six children had seen her do it. Then she had stormed off without a word to anybody and had not been seen since. The fire in her little cottage on the edge of the village was out and had not been re-lit, and her cat was sitting on the doorstep looking very hungry and cold.

Everyone thought Ms Minn was a bit dottled anyway, but it was a lot more serious when they found that Gogs and Bull had disappeared as well.

On the day after Kittel had arrived, the men from the village went into the mountains to look for the missing boys. They found no sign of Gogs, but it was not long before they found Bull's body lying on the rocks under the cliff. It took them all day to get down there and attach ropes to pull it up.

When they took it home, Bull's grandmother got such a shock that she had to take to her bed. Gogs' mother was not much better – and of course she didn't even know whether her son was alive or dead.

However, a big argument now broke out over Bull. The old doctor from the village was brought to look at him, and he insisted that Bull was not dead at all. Nobody believed that you could fall off a cliff like that and survive, and as far as anyone else could tell Bull was dead as dead could be. They thought the old doctor had gone mad. But the doctor was very definite. Nor did he stop at insisting that Bull was alive: he also said that although many bones in the boy's body had been broken, they were already healing – in fact healing far more quickly than broken bones usually do. Bull narrowly escaped being buried, and was wrapped up warmly and laid in his own bed instead.

The day after Bull's body was found, Plato Smithers started his investigation. So when Sparrow came back home from seeing Puckel, he found Murie and Smithers sitting together in the kitchen with very serious expressions on their faces.

Had Sparrow known anything about Bull's death? they wanted to know. Sparrow said he hadn't. It was a lie, really, but Sparrow told himself it was pretty nearly true, because he didn't know anything about Bull's *death*: Puckel had said Bull was alive! What about Gogs? Smithers asked. Sparrow said he had last seen him heading towards the old railway tunnel. That was true enough. Had Sparrow been to the tunnel? Smithers wanted to know. Yes, said Sparrow, he'd been there to look for Gogs, but hadn't found him. That was true, too.

Sparrow found to his dismay that Murie had told Smithers about Kittel. And then – to his relief – that she had not told him everything. She had been very sensible and simply told him that Sparrow had found her wandering about the mountains in a daze. Smithers went into the room where she was in bed. Thankfully she was asleep, or she might have told all. Smithers said he would send a message through the mountains to the next village to see if anyone had lost a small girl. Sparrow was quite surprised to hear Smithers saying this, because he had never heard anyone talk openly about the other villages before. Then Smithers left, shaking his head and saying it was all a terrible tragedy.

You don't know how bad it really is, thought Sparrow,

as he watched the big man walking down the steep path from the house.

Kittel recovered so quickly that when Plato Smithers returned two days later, she was up and about. Sparrow and Murie had warned her not to say anything about where she really came from, and Kittel quite understood: in the city where she had lived the people were exactly like the village people and never wanted to speak about magic. She also saw that Plato Smithers would consider that an aeroplane had quite as much to do with magic as any dragon.

Smithers said he had heard no word about a girl gone missing in the mountains and he wanted to speak to Kittel. But however many questions he asked her, Kittel just put her hand on her forehead and said, "I can't remember anything." She said it in such a high waily voice that Smithers was quite convinced that she really had lost her memory, though Sparrow and Murie had a hard job keeping straight faces. Smithers said Kittel might as well stay with them until they found out more about her.

This she was perfectly happy to do. She didn't behave like someone who had narrowly escaped from a plane in which everyone else had been killed. Sparrow found this odd but Murie explained that the shock of the crash had probably really made her forget things. Meanwhile Kittel was delighted with everything in Sparrow's house.

"I like the light of the lamps better than electric lights," she said, "and I'm sick of television and I didn't want to come back from holiday yet anyway." She was fascinated by the old crossbow in the hall, and she loved the cats and wild old Cairo out in the paddock, and the goats and the cow and the ducks with their waggling tails, and the lizard that scuttled across the kitchen floor every morning and every night. She had only a dog, she said, in her home in the great city where her mother and father lived.

"I'm going down to the village," Murie told Sparrow the next morning, "so you must look after Kittel. Don't let her go too far from the house."

But soon after she had gone, Sparrow, clasping Kittel, flew swiftly over the forests. As they flew a strange thing happened. Talking with Kittel, telling her all about the extraordinary happenings of the last three weeks, Sparrow suddenly found he could remember Puckel's name! This had never happened except when he was on his own or actually with the old man.

They landed at the foot of the little dark stream, but as soon as they had reached the high place where it rose in the courtyard of rocks, Sparrow saw that something was wrong. Mist was rising from the bubbling water. "It was never like this before," he muttered.

"Puckel!" he called softly. "Puckel, are you there?"

"Just here," said a quiet, watery sort of voice, out of nowhere in particular.

"Where are you?" Sparrow turned round, puzzled.

Suddenly Kittel laughed. "He's there, Sparrow, look: he's hiding in the water!"

"Where?" said Sparrow, even more bewildered. "I can't see anything."

"There!" Kittel sounded impatient, but she was still laughing, pointing down at the water as it bubbled and chuckled up out of the ground.

"He can't possibly be hiding there," Sparrow said, "he'd never fit in."

"I can see him though," Kittel insisted. "He's hiding there, he's looking up at us, he's – oh! he's disappeared."

"Did you say you could see me?" Puckel's voice suddenly came from behind them. They wheeled round, and there he was, leaning on his stick, as large as life, but with an expression on his face Sparrow had not seen before. For a moment he thought that the old man actually looked offended.

"Did you say you could see me?" he repeated, looking at Kittel.

Kittel wasn't laughing any more: she looked a little scared. She nodded.

"Come here," Puckel ordered.

Kittel went up to him, hesitantly. But when she stood in front of him, Puckel reached down and ran his brown hand through her golden hair, very gently, for a minute or two. "Hmmm," he said at length. "Hmmm, Hmmm. Well, that makes a big difference, now, doesn't it?"

111

"This is Kittel," said Sparrow. "I found her."

Puckel snorted. "She found you," he corrected. "These eyes saw through the dragon-mist, and not many could have done that. Could yours?"

Sparrow understood properly then that the mist that lay all around the mountains was the dragon's breath that made the mountains invisible to people from the world outside. He shook his head.

Puckel turned back to Kittel. "A gift as natural as daylight," he remarked, "and as rare as milkstones."

"I saw her though," Sparrow broke in, "and the other people on the plane."

Puckel screwed up his eyes. "The time and the place," he said mysteriously. "The dream of the dragon and the one who wakes in the dream of the dragon. This breaking through of a thing from outside has long been expected."

Sparrow felt less than satisfied with this, but there was something about Puckel's manner which suggested he wasn't prepared to say more on the matter. Instead Sparrow asked, "Why is there mist over the water?"

"Haven't you ever put your jug of milk in a stream to keep it cool?" Puckel demanded.

"Yes, of course," said Sparrow, "but—"

"Well, that's what I've done with my bottle of dragon – put it in the stream to keep it cool."

"It's like an electric kettle!" Kittel exclaimed. "The dragon in the bottle's bringing the water to the boil!"

"It's no joke, by no means, not at all," Puckel broke in. "And I can assure you the water by itself isn't enough to keep him cool: I have to spend most of the day in the stream myself. It's very tiring, and it doesn't leave me any time for the other things I should be doing – like making it possible to get the dragon back into the tunnel."

"So you *were* hiding – no, you were shape-shifting," Sparrow exclaimed. "You'd turned into the water of the little dark stream! So how did Kittel see you?"

"You want to watch your step with golden-haired Kittel, young Sparrow," Puckel chuckled. "You won't keep many secrets from her, no indeed! You want to keep her as your friend, that's what you want to do."

"She is my friend," Sparrow declared.

"Good, good, good," said Puckel. "Then listen, for we haven't much time left. The dragon is growing hotter by the hour, and I will not be able to hold him for very much longer. Bull is in the tunnel, in the shape of Gogs. If this continues, Gogs will wake up a little inside his own body, and Bull will go to sleep a little, and you will be left with a dopey, half-witted sort of person inside Gogs' shape which is not Bull and not Gogs but a little bit of both of them. That is not good by any manner of means. And if Bull cannot be freed from the dragon's hold on his mind, then Gogs will be lost with him. So this is what must be done."

Puckel explained his plan, and though neither Sparrow nor Kittel liked it much, they agreed it was the only thing they could do and that they must set out right away to do it.

Soon they were ready to leave. Sparrow was carrying some things Puckel had given them which he said they would need. There was the rope he had promised – a silken-smooth thing, light as a feather, which Sparrow slung over his shoulder – a package of bread and cheese and two apples ("Not magic," Puckel said, "just plain, ordinary grub.") and a strange short, fat stick with a white ball on the end of it, rather like an overgrown clove in shape. Puckel described this to Kittel as "not merely a torch, but a multi-purpose implement." He was very precise in explaining exactly how everything was to be used.

"There's just one problem," said Sparrow.

"What's that?" Puckel snapped.

"I can't shape-shift," said Sparrow. For Puckel had suggested shape-shifting as a way of making his plan work.

But the old man looked very hard at Sparrow and said, "Yes, you can."

"Since when?" Sparrow said in confusion.

"Since Bull fell, of course," said Puckel. "You felt the jolt, didn't you? That was the power passing into you."

Sparrow was staggered. He remembered the jolt well enough! And ever since then, if he had wanted to, if he had only known…

"What Bull had was yours by right," said Puckel sternly, "and to give it to you I have taken it back from where it should not have been given. When the rope is used, Bull will have the power to change shape once more, but only once: and he must be made to change back to his own body. If he does not, then the only thing that will save him will be the first light of the sun on the place that is not on the mountain and not in the valley, and finding that place is no easy matter. Now go!"

In a moment, with Kittel holding Sparrow tightly round the waist, they were in the air and high above Puckel's courtyard. They turned and sped down towards the distant tunnel.

They landed on the railway line. "How could you see Puckel when he was shape-changing?" Sparrow demanded.

"I don't know. I just could," Kittel shrugged.

"I'm going to turn into something," Sparrow said, "and I want to see if you can see me."

"Hurry then," said Kittel, looking anxiously towards the tunnel.

The real reason for Sparrow's suggestion was that he wanted to see if he really could shape-shift. Next moment he had slipped out of his own shape and into that of a nearby rock as easily as changing his clothes! It happened so naturally that the only way he knew that he had actually changed was because he suddenly found himself hard and cold, without movement or breath or any need to breathe, and he could see all round him at once, though to be sure everything, including Kittel, looked very dim and shadowy. He saw straight away what Bull had meant when he told Gogs that you couldn't see things properly. His strange rock-vision amused Sparrow immensely, but he could understand that Bull wouldn't have liked it much: you had to let go of yourself, somehow, to enjoy it, and Bull never did that.

"You're hiding in that rock," Kittel said, looking straight at him.

Sparrow was so surprised – at himself and at Kittel – that he changed back into himself again. "Have you always been able to do that?" he said.

"Do what?"

"See people when they've changed into another shape?"

"I never knew people could change into other shapes till you told me about Bull, so how could I?"

Sparrow opened his mouth to say something, forgot what, and closed it again. In fact he even forgot to be amazed at his wonderful new power because he was so amazed at Kittel.

But Kittel didn't seem to be amazed at anything. "Come on," she said, "we don't have much time."

They ran up the railway track and came to the mouth of the tunnel. There was no sign of anyone.

"Don't hide in anything too difficult," said Kittel, "or I might miss you."

"I just hope I don't get mixed up and turn into something I didn't mean to be," said Sparrow.

"Practise a bit when I'm in the tunnel," Kittel advised.

With that, she turned and went under the dark archway. Sparrow still had Puckel's rope, but Kittel took the bread and the cheese and the stick with the globe on it. As she disappeared into the darkness, Sparrow, watching from outside, saw the stick gradually begin to glow softly, casting a golden halo of light round Kittel. The light dwindled into the distance, but soon Sparrow heard Kittel faintly calling, "Gogs! Gogs! Are you there? Look, I've got food for you!"

Quickly, Sparrow looked about him. What was there? There was a thorn bush, a rock, a rowan tree still full of golden-brown leaves, a blackbird in the tree, the sleepers on the railway line, a rabbit peeping out of its burrow thinking Sparrow couldn't see it.

One by one, Sparrow quickly changed into all these things (except the rabbit) as quickly as a bird hopping from branch to branch. He went stiff and many-branched and prickly with the thorn bush, hard and cold and cracked with the rock, waved tall and gentle with the rowan tree, pirouetted and went "trr-tucka-tucka-tucka-tuck" with the blackbird, and lay flat on his back, heaving up at the steel line, with the railway sleeper. No wonder it's called a sleeper, Sparrow thought to himself as he changed back into his own shape: he had started to doze off!

He missed the rabbit because it had scuttled off when the blackbird sang. Sparrow wondered what he had said in the blackbird's voice that had so frightened it.

He wasn't sure what shape to take while he was waiting. The sleeper would have been a good choice if it had not made him feel so drowsy. He tried changing into the railway line itself, but that made his vision so thin and stretched-out that he was afraid he would not notice Kittel when she came out again. Then he saw the spider crawling up a mossy crack between two bricks on the tunnel arch. He changed into it, and began his wait.

He would have had a splendid view, because he was right above the railway line – except that his spider's vision wasn't

116

good enough to make things out at any distance. Then he remembered that he could spin a web, and softly let himself fall from the top of the arch. He felt the spider's cord unravelling itself swiftly from somewhere on his back, a pleasant, slightly tickly feeling. The cord felt amazingly strong and secure. Sparrow hung upside-down over the railway line in his spider's form and peered into the darkness of the tunnel.

Perhaps because a spider's brain is so slow (for some things anyway) he felt he had hardly waited any time before he saw Kittel's light approaching again. He tensed, straining his eyes to make out if she was alone.

No. There was someone with her – Gogs! It was Gogs walking beside her.

He looked so pale and thin! Sparrow hardly recognized him, though admittedly everything did look a little strange upside-down. With a shock that made him drop half a metre on his cord, Sparrow realized what it must have meant for Gogs to have gone without any food at all for nearly a whole week. What had Bull been doing? If he'd let Gogs' body starve to death, how could that have possibly helped him?

Sparrow suddenly felt very sorry for both Bull and Gogs. He had been so happy with his magical power, flying through the mountains, but Gogs and Bull had had nothing but trouble from theirs. It seemed unfair.

Now Kittel and Gogs were almost below him. Dimly, high in the distant air, his spider's eyes could make out a blur of shadow which Sparrow guessed was the rowan tree he had turned into before. He turned into it again. Kittel and Gogs were coming straight towards him – they seemed far below, because he was now four metres tall.

Kittel looked straight at him and grinned. "Come on,"

she said to Gogs, "we'll sit under the tree. I've got some bread and cheese for you now, and you'll feel much better after you've eaten it."

Gogs – or Bull rather, in Gogs' shape – was looking around warily. He was obviously afraid he might be walking into a trap. This was precisely why Puckel had said Kittel should go into the tunnel to fetch him out: because she was a total stranger, Bull wouldn't think that she had been sent by the village people. Now Kittel took his hand and led him over to the tree. If Gogs' body had not been so weak with hunger, Sparrow thought, Bull might have struggled – he might even have tried to take the food from Kittel by force. But he didn't. He let himself be led, sat down on a root of the rowan tree and waited for Kittel to unwrap the package of food.

Before Kittel did this, she put down the torch she had been carrying. Bull-in-Gogs'-shape looked at it lying on the ground beside him.

"Where on earth did you get that?" he mumbled.

"I was given it," Kittel said. "I have some very strange friends."

Bull-in-Gogs'-shape frowned. Sparrow could see he was puzzled by Kittel.

"It looks magical," Bull remarked. "Are you a fairy?"

Kittel gave a very un-fairy-like guffaw. "There's no such thing," she scoffed. "There's no such thing as magic either."

"I wish you were right," said Bull.

bull in bonds

KITTEL UNWRAPPED THE BREAD AND CHEESE, AND handed it to Bull-in-Gogs'-shape. "Eat it slowly, and chew it properly," she ordered. "I've got another apple, if your mouth feels too dry." She put the second apple on the ground.

Then she sat beside him, first moving the torch back, so that when she sat it lay behind them. At the same moment she looked up into the branches of the rowan tree and nodded.

The blackbird was still sitting in the branches, eyeing Bull's bread with interest. Suddenly Sparrow took the bird's shape and fluttered down to the ground behind where Kittel and Bull were sitting. Bull jerked round at the noise, and almost choked; but when he saw it was only a bird, he relaxed again.

"You're all right," Kittel soothed. "No one's going to get you."

"How do you know so much about me?" said Bull-in-Gogs'-shape.

"I know lots of things," Kittel said teasingly.

"Can you understand the language of beasts and birds?" said Bull with his mouth full.

"Don't be silly," Kittel said, "people can't understand what animals and birds say."

"I can," said Bull.

The blackbird that was Sparrow hopped softly towards them. He put his three-toed foot on to the torch where Kittel had laid it in the grass. Then he took the foot off it and stretched a wing over it instead.

"Sometimes," Kittel said, "people who have a pet think they know what it's trying to say. But animals can't speak, not really."

"Well, I know what they're saying," Bull insisted. "I've only got to listen and I can hear them saying all kinds of things."

"What kind of things?" Kittel asked sweetly.

"Well," Bull began – he had finished his bread and cheese now, and was reaching for the apple. But he never got any further, either with the apple or with telling Kittel about the birds and beasts.

Soundlessly, the blackbird behind them had changed into Sparrow. For a split second he stood weighing Puckel's torch in his hand. The next instant he brought it smashing down on to Gogs' head.

There was a shattering sound like breaking glass, and a sweet drowsy perfume that for an instant floated past them. Bull-in-Gogs'-shape slumped forward, tipped off the tree-root and lay stretched on the ground.

Kittel leaped up. "Quick, the rope!" she cried.

120

Sparrow still had Puckel's rope slung round his body. Quickly now he unwound it. Although it was so soft and light it seemed very strong. A minute later, Gogs' body was bound round and round with the rope.

"Can you manage to carry both of us?" Kittel asked him anxiously as they prepared to fly off.

"I think so," Sparrow said. "Things don't seem to weigh very much when I fly."

They arranged that Kittel should hang on to Gogs, and Sparrow should hang on to Kittel. So first they had to heave Gogs' limp body on to its feet, and then Kittel got a good grip of him round the waist and held him upright. Then Sparrow took hold of Kittel's waist from behind, and leaped. "We're airborne!" Kittel shouted.

Bull had to be kept away from the dragon at all costs, so they couldn't go back to Puckel with him. Sparrow flew slowly down the mountain, over the forest, over the clearing, and straight home. They landed in front of the house, and laid Gogs' body down on the damp ground under the tall kale plants.

"Will that be all right?" Sparrow fussed.

Kittel was stretching and rubbing her aching arms. "Of course it will," she said. "Come on, let's get inside."

Murie was not yet back. That was good: it would look better if he was found by someone else.

All went according to plan. Half an hour later Murie came bursting into the house. "Gogs!" she cried breathlessly. "He's lying in the garden!"

"Gogs?" Sparrow and Kittel said together. Although he tried his best, Sparrow couldn't manage to act as surprised as Kittel. Her eyes went so round that for a second even Sparrow believed she knew nothing about Gogs.

"Didn't you see him?" Murie demanded. She was flapping about in the cupboard beside the fire, hauling out blankets and pillows.

Sparrow and Kittel shook their heads. "You told us to stay in the house," Sparrow said.

"I did not tell you to stay in the house," Murie retorted angrily. "I said you weren't to go far from the house. And he's lying out there in the blooming cabbage patch – you could have seen him from your bedroom window. He could have caught his death of cold. Come on, you'll have to give me a hand to get him in."

In a while Sparrow was running helter-skelter into the village. He had called at Gogs' house but there was no answer. So he ran straight down to Plato Smithers' house, where the big man was sitting in his office, still "conducting the investigation" with the aid of a bottle of parsnip wine.

An hour later about twenty people, Plato Smithers and Gogs' mother and father included, were crowded into the living room of Sparrow's house, gazing in disbelief at the still form of Gogs lying on the couch. He was still wound round with the rope from head to toe but no one so much as mentioned that. It did not take Sparrow and Kittel long to realize that, as Puckel had hinted, the rope was quite invisible to anyone else.

There was no argument over Gogs' body. Everyone agreed he was alive. He seemed deeply asleep, but no one was surprised at that, because they could see he was half starved.

He was taken on a stretcher over to his own house, and tucked up in his own bed with a roaring fire in the grate.

* * *

Sparrow and Kittel found him there when they walked over the next day. Gogs' mother looked at Kittel strangely, but she told them that Gogs had been awake for a while in the evening, although he was sleeping again now. They could go in and sit with him if they wanted.

Sparrow and Kittel went softly in. Gogs' head lay half turned on the pillow, his face pale and thin. He had his night-shirt on now, but even so they could still see Puckel's rope.

As soon as Gogs' mother had closed the door, Sparrow and Kittel bent over Gogs' body. Sparrow took him by the shoulder and shook him – though not too hard, in case the bed creaked.

"Come on, Gogs, please come on," he muttered, hopping impatiently from one foot to the other.

Gogs' eyelids flickered, but remained closed. "Come on, come on," Sparrrow said through his clenched teeth.

Kittel did not waste time hopping around. She pushed Sparrow out of the way, and bending over Gogs, gave him a vicious slap across the cheek.

"Kittel!" Sparrow remonstrated, but she ignored him. Gogs groaned, stirred, and a second later his eyes popped wide open.

His lips moved. "You said... You said..." were the only words that came out.

"I'm sorry," Kittel whispered. "I'm sorry I had to trick you."

"Bull," said Sparrow. "Bull, is that you?"

Gogs' eyes moved round and stared at Sparrow, cold and hopeless. Looking at his friend's eyes, Sparrow felt a knot in his throat as though he were going to start crying.

"Bull, please," he said. "P— I mean the old man – says

you've got to change back into your own body right away. You and Gogs are both going to be lost and the dragon's going to burst out and everything'll be terrible. Please, will you change back into yourself and help us all?"

Gogs' face was still. Then it frowned. The eyes were hard.

"Will you do it, Bull?" Kittel said.

"My body's … it's under the cliff," Bull said in Gogs' voice. "I can't go back to it. I'd be dead."

"It isn't," Sparrow told him. "It – you've been brought home. Your body's lying in your own bed. I – we – don't think you'll die if you change back into it. But think about Gogs. If you won't leave his body, it'll be like killing him, won't it?"

"Gogs tried to kill me," Bull said. "If I hadn't shifted into his shape, I'd be dead and he'd have killed me."

"He didn't try to kill you," Sparrow said. "It wasn't his fault; you've forgotten what happened. You just fell."

Tears sprang into Sparrow's eyes. "Please, Bull," he begged, "please do it. I – I just want my friends back, Bull and Gogs, the way they were before…" He had not meant to cry, but he felt he was losing the argument, and it was horrible how Bull seemed not to trust anyone.

"You've got *her*," Gogs' voice said, as his eyes moved round to Kittel. "You don't need your friends. You always thought you were better than us anyway – you went off and got magic powers without even telling us. That's just like you."

"That's not true," Sparrow sobbed. He sat down and buried his face in his hands. Kittel had turned away and was fumbling with something at the bedroom window. Now she came quickly back and slipped her arm round

Sparrow's shoulders.

The bedroom door opened. It was Gogs' mother. She saw Sparrow sitting shaking with sobs. "Come on, Sparrow," she said gently, helping him up. "Gogs will be all right; you'd better come out now."

"No!" Sparrow exclaimed. "You don't understand – he's got to…"

But Kittel cut in, loudly and sternly. "Sparrow," she said, "Gogs' mum is quite right. You're overwrought." And she gripped his arm so tightly he almost yelled, and led him out of the room.

When Sparrow and Kittel got outside they walked silently away from Gogs' house and started for home. Soon they passed the path that led up to Bull's house. There was a tree stump beside the road. Sparrow sat down on it and groaned.

125

"What'll we do now?" he said. "Everything's spoiled. We won't be able to see Gogs until tomorrow, and I'm sure we don't have enough time. We'll just have to get Puckel, that's all."

"No," said Kittel determinedly, "we can't risk that. Puckel's busy keeping the dragon cool, and if he's taken away, anything might happen. We've got to try everything we can."

"But what can we do? We can't make Bull leave Gogs' body and go back into his own. Only Puckel could do that."

"We don't know that even Puckel could," Kittel pointed out. "You mustn't give up so easily. Listen, here we are at Bull's house. That's where Bull's body is, right?"

"Right," said Sparrow.

"Then why don't we try taking Bull's body over to Gogs' house?"

"How?"

"You could change into Bull."

"But Puckel said no one's supposed to change into another person!" Sparrow protested.

"This is different," Kittel argued. "For one thing, it's an emergency. And for another, Bull's not really a person – I mean, his body isn't. It's just a body."

Sparrow had to see the logic of this, and somewhat unwillingly consented to try Kittel's plan. Quickly, they walked up to Bull's house. An old lady from the village was there to look after his sick grandmother and see if there was any change in Bull.

"Sparrow wants to see Bull, please," Kittel asked, very politely. And the old lady let them in.

A minute later, Bull was walking out of his bedroom with Kittel, towards the front door. Of course Kittel knew that it was not Bull, only Sparrow-in-Bull's shape. But the old lady didn't know that. She fell down in a dead faint.

"Oh dear," Kittel said. But she kept going, and she and Sparrow-in-Bull's shape set off down the path again.

"Are you all right?" Kittel asked Sparrow.

"I – think so," Sparrow answered, "but I feel very strange. Bull's body doesn't feel right at all. I feel like I did when I was a tree."

"I think Bull's body must be a bit dead after all," Kittel said cheerfully. "You're a living corpse."

"Shut up," said Sparrow, "it's not funny."

Exactly what was wrong he could not tell. It didn't feel as though any bones were broken in Bull's body, and he felt no pain. But by the time they had reached the bottom of the path and started to walk on level ground, he knew he could not go on. He tried to sit down on the tree trunk again, but missed and crumpled on to the grass. "I'll have to change out for a bit," he mumbled, and did. Bull's body immediately tumbled over, the lids slowly closing on the bleared blue eyes. "Like one of those dolls with eyes that shut," Kittel murmured with interest.

"What'll we do?" Sparrow moaned. "I'll never make it at this rate."

Kittel was at a loss only for a moment. "I know!" she announced suddenly. "Let's get Cairo!" Sparrow was about to object that Cairo would let no one near him, when Kittel added, "You can change into him and carry Bull and me."

Sparrow managed to move Bull's body out of sight behind the tree trunk. It lay looking pale and ghastly in the daylight.

127

They climbed up the white-pebbled path to Sparrow's house, and went straight round to where old Cairo's paddock was.

Cairo was standing in the corner of the paddock, looking very grumpy. He was holding one of his back hooves up off the ground as he always did when the ground was cold.

Sparrow got a severe shock when he shifted into Cairo's shape. Cairo, he suddenly understood from the inside, was old and cold and couldn't be bothered. He spent all his days longing for Sparrow's father to come home, and dreamed of eating sweet apples out of his master's hand. The horse's emotions were almost too much for Sparrow and nearly made him change back into his own shape again. But he held on, remembering the need for haste, and made Cairo's body run over the grass towards Kittel – strange and small and stick-like to his horse-vision. He relished the sound, *ba-da-doom, ba-da-doom*, of the heavy hooves pounding the turf.

Kittel used the gate to climb on to his back, and gripped him desperately with her knees as he picked his way down the steep path. When they reached the tree stump again, she dismounted and, going over to Bull's body, put her hands under his armpits and heaved him up. He was too heavy for her: she tripped over Bull's dragging feet, and both of them, girl and boy's body, jolted against Cairo's leg. Sparrow had to restrain his immediate reaction, which was to give Kittel a hefty kick. "You're so high!" she gasped. "I'll never get him on your back."

"What can I do?" Sparrow mumbled through his horsy teeth.

128 "You could lie down like a camel," Kittel suggested.

"But I'm not a camel," Sparrow mumbled. "I'm a horse." He didn't like the feeling that he was speaking through his nose.

"Don't be so stupid," Kittel snapped. "Look –" and she kicked him, hard, behind the nearer of his front knees. The knee buckled.

"Let your knees go, like that," she said.

Now Sparrow realized what she meant, and he let his knees go. Somehow his back legs followed, and soon he was lying on his stomach beside Kittel.

Kittel heaved and humped, and in a couple of minutes she had Bull's body sitting on Cairo's back, while she sat behind, holding him upright.

"Right, get up now," she ordered.

*　　*　　*

Bull-in-Gogs'-shape was lying awake in Gogs' bed. There was no one in the room with him – which was just as well because Sparrow didn't wait for Kittel to check. Gogs' bedroom window suddenly flew open, and Cairo's nose was shoved in.

Kittel had hatched her plan while they had still been at Gogs' house before, and quietly taken the catch off Gogs' window. Now she pushed Cairo's head out of the way, and peered down from his back into the room. "Hello, Bull," she said. "It's us again – we've brought your body."

Gogs' eyes stared at them, but Bull could not move because of Puckel's invisible rope.

"I don't want it," Gogs' voice muttered hoarsely.

Kittel ignored him. "Are you ready, Sparrow?" she said to the horse's ears. The horse's ears twitched back. "One – two – three – now!" And Kittel let go of Bull's body and swung her leg off Cairo's broad back. At the same moment, Bull's body came to life, because Sparrow had shifted into it. But as soon as Cairo became Cairo again, he reared and bucked and bolted, and Kittel and Sparrow were shaken from his back like turnips off a cart.

Kittel and Sparrow-in-Bull's-shape landed in a heap. "Are you all right?" Kittel said, and Bull's head nodded.

Bull, looking through Gogs' eyes, could only gape in utter amazement as first Kittel, and then his own – Bull's – body clambered in through his – Gogs' – bedroom window and stood beside Gogs' bed.

panic

THE SHADOWS WERE GATHERING IN GOGS' ROOM.
The short winter day was passing, and night was coming
on fast.

Kittel whispered, not wanting Gogs' mother to know
they had come back, "Bull, you mustn't be afraid. We want
to help you." She pointed to Sparrow-in-Bull's-shape.
"This isn't you, it's really Sparrow. And if Sparrow can go
about in your shape, so can you, can't you?"

There was a long silence. At last Gogs' mouth moved,
and Gogs' voice spoke. It was really Bull speaking to
Sparrow, but it was Gogs' voice which spoke the words,
and Bull's ears which heard them. "What does it feel like?"
he asked.

Sparrow answered in Bull's voice, "It feels fine." It was
not really true, because Sparrow felt so very strange in
Bull's body – cold and sluggish and far-away – but he
thought he had better not tell Bull that. "It feels just like

me," he said, "only not quite like me, because it's a bit bigger – I mean, you're a bit bigger than me, if you see what I mean."

After another long silence Bull said, in Gogs' voice, "I don't think I can change. I tried to change before, when I was in the tunnel, and I couldn't. Nothing happened. And Gogs would wake up sometimes, and –" he stammered, and a catch came into his voice, as though he were trying not to cry – "I felt he was trying to eat me up. He would fight with me, and I'd rush about hitting myself, punching myself all over, and twisting my arm up my own back – well, Gogs' back I mean. It's not really my own back at all, I suppose."

"It must have been very nasty," Kittel said sympathetically. "But P— I mean…" She paused. "What's the old man's name, Sparrow? I've forgotten."

"So have I," said Sparrow. "I always do."

"Did you know his name?" Bull asked Kittel.

"Yes," Kittel said, puzzled.

"I never knew it," said Bull. "I don't think he could have liked me."

As Bull spoke, Sparrow realized his friend had changed. To begin with, he had thought it might just have been because it was Gogs' voice he could hear and Gogs' expressions – or nearly Gogs' – that he could see, and of course Gogs was always trying to patch up the quarrels that threatened to break out between Bull and Sparrow. But as Bull spoke, he saw that it wasn't just this. Bull, he understood, must have been through a terrible time. He had very nearly died, he had lost his own body, he had been starved, he was frightened, and inside him there was someone else – his own best friend – who he knew might wake up at any time and try to destroy him. Dimly it came to Sparrow that, whatever happened now, Bull could never be the same again – never again be that secretive know-all who was their leader and who took all the decisions. And, now that he knew this, it made him feel sad – sad that their friendship had changed, and sorry that it had changed because of him.

"Well, anyway," Kittel told Bull, "the old man wants to help you. You see the rope you've got around you?"

"It's a magic rope, isn't it?" said Bull. "No one else could see it."

"Yes, it is," Kittel agreed.

"I thought you said there was no such thing as magic," Bull said.

"I was tricking you," Kittel replied. "I'm sorry. But it was just because we all wanted to help you. P— the old —"

"We call him Piddle," Bull put in.

Kittel looked doubtful. "Anyway," she went on, "he says that if we take the rope off you, you'll be able to shift your shape one more time."

"And never again?" Bull said.

"I don't know about never again," Sparrow said. "I'm sure if you went up to see him and asked him properly, he'd let you do it again." Though he was not sure at all.

"Are you a shape-shifter now?" Bull asked wistfully.

"Yes," said Sparrow, "I became one when you fell. Look."

He sat down against the wall. And then quickly, effortlessly, as if he were pulling off his clothes, he slipped out of Bull's body, and stood there, Sparrow, in his own proper shape. "See?"

"If I can only shift shape once more," said Bull, "do you

mean I have to go back inside that?" – and he nodded towards his body, slumped against the wall like a rag doll someone had thrown away.

"You'll be all right," Sparrow assured him.

"I want to see you shape-shifting," Bull announced suddenly.

"Why?" Sparrow asked.

"Go on, just do it – change into something else."

"All right," said Sparrow. There was a bowl of Christmas roses by Gogs' bed. Sparrow changed into one of them. "Hello, here I am," he said in the flower's voice.

Bull grinned. It looked just like Gogs' normal wide silly grin. It was hard to believe that it was Bull grinning and not Gogs. "I like that," he said. "Now be yourself again."

Sparrow changed back into himself.

"I want you to change into that horse again," Bull demanded.

"Cairo?" Sparrow said. "He ran away. There's no sign of him."

"He's not far," Bull said. "He's eating the raspberry canes in the garden."

"How do you know?" Sparrow said.

"I heard him just now," Bull explained. "He said, 'This is the best thing I've tasted for years. I'm not going back to eating that muck in the paddock again.'"

Sparrow had forgotten Bull could still understand the language of beasts – or was Bull using Gogs' power? "I'll change into Cairo if you really want me to," he said, "though I don't really see why you do."

"Please," said Bull.

Sparrow clambered out of the window and disappeared into the deepening twilight to look for the horse.

133

"Will you take off the rope now?" Bull said to Kittel. "I'll change back into me while Sparrow's out, I don't want him to see me do it."

She pulled back the bedclothes, and untied Puckel's rope from Gogs' ankles, pulling it through from underneath him, unwrapping him bit by bit. She unwound it from his neck, and so came to the last knot. "All right?" she asked encouragingly.

"All right," Gogs' head nodded.

Kittel untied the last knot. Stiffly, Bull-in-Gogs'-shape got up. He crossed the floor to where his own body was sitting propped against the wall, and knelt down beside it.

At that very moment, Cairo's head pushed through the window again. "Hello," he snorted, his mouth full of chewed-up raspberry leaves.

Kittel sighed. "Just go away a minute, Sparrow," she said.

"No, it's all right now," Bull said, looking up at Cairo's head. "I don't mind now. I'm ready. You come in, Sparrow," he said. "I want you here with us."

What followed took less than ten seconds, though it takes longer to describe it.

First Sparrow changed out of Cairo's shape. Kittel saw him climbing in through the window, beside the horse's head. Cairo's eyes looked utterly confused for a moment, and he stopped chewing his raspberry leaves. Then he noticed Sparrow climbing past him, and lunged his mouth round to give Sparrow a vicious nip on the bottom.

Sparrow yelled and fell forwards, tripping over Bull's legs on the floor and knocking over Bull-in-Gogs'-shape as he was kneeling beside his own body.

"Ow!" Gogs' voice exclaimed, as Sparrow fell on top of

him. But immediately afterwards Sparrow felt Gogs' body go quite limp, as if it had suddenly fallen asleep.

Meanwhile Cairo swung his head round, smashing the glass in the window, and then – "Quick, Sparrow!" Kittel yelled at the top of her voice. "Turn back into Cairo! Quick! Be quick!"

Cairo was looking dazed, and beads of blood were breaking out beside his nose where the glass had cut it.

Kittel screamed again, "Sparrow! Sparrow!" But Sparrow was dazed too, kneeling over Gogs' body lying on the floor. What brought him to his senses was Kittel's savage kick in his ribs. "Get off your knees, you idiot, and get inside that horse!"

Sparrow looked round to the window. Cairo was just rearing up, tossing his mane. Without another thought he changed, and even as he took on the horse's shape, panic seized him and he was carried away on the horse's hooves in a frenzied gallop.

At that moment, in the house behind him, the bedroom door flew open and Gogs' mother and father rushed in. They saw the smashed bedroom window hanging open and Gogs lying on the floor with Bull's lifeless body slumped beside him, and the girl Kittel standing in the middle of the floor, screaming wildly.

Gogs' mother started screaming along with Kittel, and Kittel saw that the best thing she herself could do was to carry on.

So it was left to Gogs' father to pick Gogs up off the floor and carry him back to his bed. For a moment, Gogs' eyes opened. "Oh, I'm glad to see you again, Dad," he muttered, and then went back to sleep.

* * *

Meanwhile, Sparrow-in-Cairo's-shape was galloping through the gathering night uphill over a field of rough grass. He had forgotten he was Sparrow, forgotten about Bull: he was almost all horse.

What saved him was the fence. It loomed up right in his path, and the horse swerved from his headlong gallop. Cairo had grown fat from not working, and could not have jumped. He ran along beside the fence, snorting, shaking his mane. Soon the land was sloping downhill again, and he galloped faster.

The fence flicked by, post by post. As this was the field Kittel and Sparrow had come through to get to Gogs' bedroom window, the gate was still open, but the horse was running the wrong way to come to it quickly: before Cairo could find the gate he would have to pass the house again.

And it was the screaming from the house which cut through the rushing of the horse's panic. Cairo's ears heard the screams, and he reared up, fell on to four feet again, then stood stock-still, listening.

It was just what Sparrow needed. He remembered straight away that he was Sparrow and not a horse, and when he heard the screaming he thought he had better become himself again. He would have changed back into his own shape then and there but just in time he remembered about Kittel's having been so anxious for him to change into the horse. And as he thought about this, he realized that being Cairo did not feel at all the same as it had done before. There was a breathless, confused feeling about it, almost as though he were being squashed.

Cautiously, he edged forwards to the open window of Gogs' bedroom, where a light was now shining.

At first it was difficult to make out what was going on

inside the room: he was looking through a horse's eyes, and horses' eyes are made for being outside and looking at the weather and grass and gates, not for peering into bedrooms.

Gradually he made out the bed, and Gogs lying in it, asleep. And Kittel standing beside it, and – Bull still sitting slumped by the wall. What was wrong? Sparrow wondered. Why hadn't Bull got up?

Gogs' mother was nowhere to be seen, but just then Gogs' father came in. Kittel had apparently just finished screaming, and Gogs' father patted her on the head, then bent down and picked up Bull and turned to carry him out of the bedroom. Kittel immediately looked up and saw Cairo standing outside the window. She frowned in a puzzled way. Sparrow-in-Cairo's shape moved closer to the window.

Suddenly Kittel clapped her hands against her cheeks. "Oh good gracious," she exclaimed. Then, "Wait outside the house, Sparrow," she ordered. "I'll be out in a moment. Don't change out of Cairo!" Then she turned and ran out through the door.

137

It was only a minute later that she had rejoined Sparrow in front of the house. "Come on," she said, "straight home. It is you, Sparrow, isn't it?"

"Yes, it is. What's wrong?" Sparrow mumbled. He couldn't get used to talking through a horse's mouth.

"I'll tell you when we get home. Can you come over to the fence so I can get up?"

Sparrow stood by the fence while Kittel scrambled up on to his back. Neither of them spoke until they were home again.

"Into the paddock," Kittel said curtly. "I think that'll be safe enough."

Sparrow-in-Cairo's-shape stood by the paddock gate until Kittel had tied it shut. "Now be Sparrow again," Kittel said.

Sparrow stood beside Kittel. Cairo stood beside the gate, looking sorrowfully over at them. Kittel stared intently at him.

"Bull," she said solemnly, looking at Cairo, "that was a very silly thing to do."

Cairo turned his back on them and flicked his tail.

"What do you mean?" said Sparrow. "Why did you call him Bull?"

"Because it is Bull," Kittel answered. "Bull changed into Cairo instead of himself."

"But he could only change once more!" Sparrow exclaimed.

138 Kittel lowered her voice, so that Bull couldn't hear. "I know," she replied, "but after all, we did trick him before. Maybe he was so scared of going back into his own body that he thought he'd risk being a horse."

"Maybe he wanted to gallop off to the dragon," suggested Sparrow.

"Well, he didn't make it," said Kittel grimly. "And now he's a horse and he'll have to be a horse for the rest of his life."

"That won't be very long now," Sparrow whispered. "Cairo's an old horse – he's much older than me."

"I thought if you turned into Cairo straight away you'd push Bull out and he'd have to go into his own shape," said Kittel. "But it wasn't as simple as that. You were both inside Cairo's shape together."

"I hope that doesn't mean that I became Bull," said Sparrow anxiously, "because Puck—"

"I wish you'd stop rabbiting on about that," Kittel snapped. "Can't you understand everything's different in an emergency? Anyway, you didn't become him. You squashed him."

"Did I? I thought it felt funny, being Cairo," said Sparrow, "but I didn't feel Bull there at all."

"I don't think he's such a strong shape-shifter as you," Kittel said. "I could see you both inside Cairo, but Bull did look sort of squashed-up."

"What'll we do now?"

"Well," said Kittel thoughtfully, "I think you'll have to take Bull's shape again, and then try to get him over here. Of course! Once you've got him out of the house, you could fly and carry him! Why didn't we think of that before?"

"I've never flown round here, that's why," said Sparrow, scratching his head. "But why do you want him over here anyway?"

"We'll have to persuade Bull – Bull the horse, I mean – to carry us up to Puckel's cave so we can get Bull and Cairo sorted out. Remember Puckel said there was only one other way – something about being in the place that wasn't on the mountain or in the valley."

"In the first light of the sun," Sparrow remembered. "But he said it wouldn't be easy."

"We'll have to take Bull to him all the same," Kittel answered. "He's the only one who'll know how to do it."

Sparrow looked doubtful. "All right," he agreed at length, "I'll go."

"Bull will be safe enough here," said Kittel. "He won't get out, and I'll try to talk to him. Bull's body is in a bedroom upstairs in Gogs' house, so you'll have to be careful no one sees you getting in or out."

139

"I'll be careful," Sparrow said. "I'll be straight back."

He flew off. Kittel immediately turned and started speaking softly to Bull. Although he went on flicking Cairo's tail at her at first, slowly he began to listen as she explained that he would have to see Puckel or he would stay a horse forever.

But Sparrow was back even quicker than he had said, and he was alone. Although it was almost completely dark now, there was enough light from the house for Kittel to see that he was looking very worried.

"Over here," said Sparrow, and led her to the side of the house where they couldn't be heard. "Bull's body won't move," he told her.

"What do you mean?" Kittel frowned.

"I changed into his shape," Sparrow said, "but I just lay there. I couldn't move as long as I was in it. I felt like I did when I turned into the rock."

"You'll have to get Puckel down here now," Kittel said.

"I'll have to get Puckel down here now," Sparrow said at exactly the same moment.

When Sparrow had left Kittel and flown over to Gogs' house, it was almost dark. When he set off to find Puckel, the night came on in earnest. The sky was overcast with cloud, and it soon became too dark to see anything.

Sparrow was making his first flight by night, and within a quarter of an hour he was completely lost. But when he landed – quite by accident – on a rocky ledge somewhere close to the tops of the forest trees, he found that something extraordinary had happened. Standing on the ledge in the pitch darkness, he whimpered Puckel's name out loud, and to his surprise was answered by an owl, which whooed and wheezed once or twice before Sparrow understood it was saying it thought everyone knew where Puckel was. The owl turned out to have a very low opinion of Sparrow, but Sparrow was so delighted to discover that he had received the gift of understanding birds and beasts that he scarcely noticed its ill humour. He guessed this new power must, somehow, have come to him when Bull left Gogs' shape – though whether he had received Bull's gift or Gogs', he could not know.

After being rather rude to him, the owl offered to guide him to Puckel's cave. Sparrow gratefully accepted, and the creature was luckily as good as its word: after a mere five minutes' flight it hooted that it was time to come down. Sparrow made a blind landing in the darkness, and as his feet touched the ground he tripped, took a big step, and landed, *splash*, in water. He let out a yell and jumped back. The water was boiling hot. Above him, he heard an owlish mutter concerning the stupidity of humans and sparrows, as the bird whirred off into the night.

141

Sparrow understood straight away that he was in Puckel's courtyard, but didn't stop to wonder that he had reached it by flying. "Puckel?" he called. "Are you there?"

There was no sound, except the bubbling and hissing of the little dark stream, hot against the cold rocks.

"Puckel?" Sparrow inquired again.

Still there was no answer. Sparrow did not wait longer. He took a deep breath, and changed.

Immediately, he felt as if everything were pouring out of him. On and on it went, as if it had never started and would never stop, pouring on, stretching out, pouring until he could not understand how there was anything of him left to pour. But there always was: more and more, oceans and oceans – any amount of water could go on flowing through him for hundreds of years.

He had changed himself into the little dark stream. But he scarcely had time to think what it felt like just then, for in a moment he was aware that Puckel was flowing beside him. Sparrow could see no sign of him, but he sensed that the old man was huffing and puffing there, very hot and bothered.

"Did you get him?" Puckel's voice murmured.

"Yes," Sparrow answered, in the murmuring voice of water. "At least, he made his last change. But everything's gone wrong."

"Wrong?" Puckel bubbled. "How, wrong?"

"He's changed into a horse," Sparrow answered.

"All is not lost," Puckel rippled. "When the first light of the sun falls—"

"I know," Sparrow interrupted in his watery voice, "but Bull's own body feels all wrong, and I couldn't move in it: I think it's dying."

"What?" A great spout of water burst out of the stream and broke into a cloud of steam.

"I'm sorry," Sparrow murmured. "We did the best we could. Isn't there anything you can do?"

Silence followed, a long liquid silence, in which Sparrow could feel eddies of icy, then boiling water, curling and slipping around him as Puckel thought.

At last, sadly but with resolve, Puckel answered. "You stay here," his voice swirled thickly, "and try to keep the dragon cool. But you must promise me one thing. You must promise me that if the dragon escapes, you will not change from the stream until he's gone – you'll let him go."

"But," Sparrow faltered, "he might attack the village!"

"You'll not stop him," Puckel's voice swirled again. "Now promise me, or else I'll not go to help Bull."

"All right, I promise," Sparrow told him.

"Think cool," Puckel's voice came. "Don't let the dragon trick you into feeling too hot." And Sparrow was alone.

The moment Puckel had gone, Sparrow felt himself bubbling like water in a kettle. The dragon was making him boil. What could anyone do against heat like that?

But gradually, despite the bubbling, Sparrow realized that the stream he had turned into was much more than just the water swirling round the bottle with the dragon in it. It stretched. It rose to the surface of the ground out of the depths of the earth, endlessly deep and endlessly cool.

He saw what Puckel had wanted him to do. He thought cool. He brought up more and more coolness from the deep, sunless rocks inside the earth, and wrapped it round and round the bottle where the angry dragon glared through the thick glass with its tiny, terrible, raging orange eyes.

143

Hours went by, slow watery hours with no sense of time.

Sparrow stuck to his task, and as he grew more used to the feel of the stream, his confidence grew and he seemed to manage better and better. In due course he began to feel pretty pleased with himself. But even Puckel had said it was tiring trying to keep the dragon cool, and Puckel was much older and stronger than Sparrow. After a while – it was hard to say how long, but the night continued pitch-black as ever – Sparrow wondered whether he *could* keep thinking cool when all the time he could feel the dragon thinking hot – oven-hot, furnace-hot, volcano-hot. And as he grew tired, he began to feel, quite unreasonably, that Puckel had simply nipped off and left him with the most dangerous and difficult task of all. It wasn't fair!

Puckel should never have left him in charge of a dragon which had once terrorized the whole world!

Just as dawn was making the sky pale Sparrow knew he had lost the fight. Try as he might, he could not think cool at all. And now the dragon had grown so big it filled all the bottle, coiled round and round and in and out of itself, its sides pressed against the sides of smooth glass.

And suddenly – *plick!* A crack was running through the glass of the bottle, all down its length.

Sparrow wasn't going to lie there and let the dragon get away with this! Without a moment's thought he changed himself into the bottle. He had some idea that as long as he could hold himself together, the dragon wouldn't escape.

But he had not reckoned on the heat and the pain. In the shape of the bottle, Sparrow felt as though his very bones were melting from the fire inside him. And the split that ran from his neck to his foot was like a red-hot whiplash. And then another crack ran through him. Another crack of the whip. And then another, and another, until Sparrow felt his bottle-body laced with cracks, up, down, from side to side, and all around him.

He yelled, and as if in answer, the dragon inside him roared. Very softly, but menacing, that roar began; then it grew, like an express train coming out of a tunnel, until Sparrow's whole brain was full of the roaring and he felt his head was going to burst.

Just in the nick of time, he changed back into the shape of the little dark stream, just as the bottle burst and its fragments spun off through the water. The water boiled, turned into steam, and dragon smoke gathered and rose up into the air.

Exhausted, Sparrow sank back into the water that was himself, and the little dark stream flowed on as he slept, unaware of the dragon which sat in Puckel's mountain courtyard, spouting black smoke and growing, growing, by the minute.

a job for kittel

146 "I DON'T MIND BEING A HORSE," BULL SAID. "BEING a horse is better than being dead."

"But you wouldn't be dead," Kittel said – though even she was no longer sure about this. She didn't try too hard to persuade him.

She tried another approach. "I like horses," she told the horse that had been Cairo. "At home I always used to go riding at the weekends. I've never ridden bare-back though."

"I don't like horses," Bull snorted. "My dad was killed by a horse."

"I'm sorry," Kittel said humbly. "All the same you'd better start trying to like them a bit if you're going to be one. And you must admit, you'll be an extremely clever horse – and you'll be able to talk."

Bull-in-Cairo's-shape seemed to think about this.

"Would you let me ride you?" Kittel asked after a moment.

The horse flapped his ears. "Perhaps," he huffled.

At that moment, with a thundering of the air and a small hurricane that sent Bull-in-Cairo's-shape bolting off into the darkness of the other side of the field, Puckel flew down out of the night and landed beside Kittel.

"Where?" he said, in a deep, commanding voice.

"Over at Gogs' house," Kittel replied.

"Show me!" cried Puckel, and seized Kittel by the arm as the hurricane whirled them off the ground again.

Puckel burst into Gogs' house just as the doctor was coming out of Gogs' room. The doctor had been pleased to hear that Bull had walked over to Gogs' house, because that proved he had been right about Bull not being dead. But when he went to the upstairs room where Bull's body had been laid, he took one look at him and said, "Well, he may not have been dead before, but he's dead now, in my opinion." Then he had gone downstairs to see Gogs, found him asleep, but quite healthy, and had come out to see if he would be offered any parsnip wine. That was when Puckel and Kittel entered the hall of the house.

"Where is Bull?" Puckel demanded in a voice that rattled the slates on the roof.

"And who might you be?" enquired the doctor, sticking his thumbs in his braces and peering at the wild-haired, wrinkled, green-eyed old creature in the moss-green cloak.

"I," said Puckel – and his voice, though quiet now, made the doors clatter in their frames and blew the dust from under the carpet – "am the boy's godfather."

"Never seen you before in my life," the doctor answered, "and let me tell you I know everyone in this district. Let me also tell you that young Bull is – regretfully – dead. If you're a relative, you may go up and see him. Otherwise, I think you had better go back to where you came from."

"Bull," said Puckel simply, on a soft high note like a bell. In a twinkling, the hall had transformed itself into the upstairs room, and Puckel and Kittel were standing beside the bed where Bull's body was laid, while downstairs the doctor was looking around in bewilderment.

Puckel got to work. First he sealed the door by drawing all round it with his thumb, muttering meanwhile. "Now no one can get in," he announced. Then he sealed the window in the same way – "And nothing can get out," he said. He put out the lamp beside the bed, but after a moment of darkness, the whole room began to glow with a deep yellow light, like golden moonshine. Then the old man propped up his stick in a corner of the room, went over to the bed and sat on it. He looked at the still body, utterly without movement under the bedcover, for a long time. Then at last, he took Bull's pale head in his lap. And slowly, softly, Puckel began to sing.

No one but Kittel ever heard that song, and what was in it she never told anyone, not even Sparrow. Quite possibly she could not have said, even if she had wanted to, because more than likely it was in no language that she could understand. But that song was something she never forgot, and for the rest of her life, if she stopped still and listened in a silent moment, she would hear it softly streaming from the wrinkled brown lips of the wild old man of the mountains.

It was a song of waking, a song of life, a song which would not leave sleeping things alone to sleep but made them move, breathe deeply, raise their heads, grow, stretch towards the light. And as Puckel sang, softly his stick slid down from the wall of the room where it had been propped and silently, slowly, glided across the floor towards the bed.

It had become a snake.

Kittel did try to speak. She felt she ought to warn Puckel that the stick wasn't behaving as sticks should. But she couldn't speak: her tongue seemed to have stuck to the roof of her mouth, and not a sound would come out. Slowly the snake reached the bed and raised its head. Silently its neck stretched, waved to and fro and stretched again, and silently its body followed, up the leg of the bed, on to the cover, and over the mound of Bull's feet.

Puckel never paused in his singing, and never looked towards the snake. The snake stretched its way up Bull's body, and when at last it lay on top of him, along his length, with its head at Bull's throat, it grew still.

All that long, dark night, as the snake lay stretched on Bull's body, Puckel sang, or was silent, or sang again. Dimly Kittel could hear people outside the room, shouting probably, or even banging at the door. But they seemed very faint and far away, and Puckel took no notice of them.

Through the window, behind the mountains, Kittel saw that the sky was growing paler. She had never stayed awake through a whole night, but this night she had not even felt like yawning, and now the dawn was growing and the day would soon be here.

Puckel's song had become quicker, full of a pulsing rhythm like a drum beat that made Kittel want to get up and dance. The snake was still motionless, but she could see that its lipless mouth was open and its tongue was flickering black over Bull's pale throat.

All of a sudden, Puckel jumped to his feet and abruptly stopped his song with a single clap of his hands. Bull's head was shaken out of his lap as he leaped up, but as it hit the pillow it moved twice, once to one side, once to the

149

other. The snake's head reared up and drew back, as if it were about to strike at Bull's face. And suddenly Bull's still chest gave a great heave, and he started to breathe as if he were deeply asleep, while a soft, slight flush stole over his cheeks.

Kittel felt a thrill through her whole body. She had known all along that Puckel had great power, but until now she had not realized just how powerful he really was. When they had come into that room before, Bull's body had been dead. Now, it was certainly living. Kittel went cold and hot with amazement, but mixed with the amazement there was a little fear.

She had no more than a minute to think about what she had seen. Not then, anyway. For Puckel was still standing with his hands together over his head from clapping when the floor and walls and window all started trembling. It was a very quiet, slight trembling to begin with, but there was something about it which made Kittel think it was caused by something unimaginably strong. Puckel's triumphant expression changed. He froze, his hands still together, and glanced towards the window.

Kittel looked towards the window as well, where the dawn had filled all the air with soft grey light. The great round-topped mountain was humped black against the pale sky. But there was something wrong. Gradually Kittel realized that the whole land – with its forests and mountains – was shaking, as if something too big to even see had got hold of it like a table and was rattling it. And gradually, as she watched, the noise grew – a deep, drumming, thundering sound that became louder and louder until the whole house was vibrating and little puffs of dust plumed up round the edges of the carpet. Kittel clapped her hands over her ears to keep out the din.

And still the noise grew, until suddenly, with one gigantic *boom!* and a shock that hurled Kittel and Puckel back against the wall of the room, it stopped.

But out through the window Kittel could see an immense cloud of thick black smoke gathering and rising on a shoulder of the mountain, blotting out the sky. Fearfully, she grabbed Puckel's arm. "What is it?" she whispered.

Puckel made no answer. He gave a shout. Not a loud shout, though a very sudden one – and the window of the bedroom burst open. In fact, the whole window – glass, frame and all – simply blew out of the wall and smashed on the ground below. It seemed that Gogs' house wasn't having much luck with its windows: near by lay another scattering of glass where Cairo's head had broken the pane of Gogs' bedroom the night before.

Puckel and Kittel followed the window. Kittel couldn't tell how: one moment she was standing with her back to the bedroom wall – the next she was outside on the frosty grass beside the shattered window frame.

"Too late," Puckel was muttering, "just a little too late."

"Is it… Is it…?" Kittel whispered – she found she couldn't speak properly.

Puckel nodded his head. "The dragon," he said. "He's broken out."

Puckel looked at Kittel long and hard. He seemed to be saying something to her, without words, with his eyes. At last he did speak. "A job for you and a job for me," he observed. "Remember the first light of the sun! Now I must go." And with that he threw back his head and let out a shrill, piercing cry towards the sky.

"What about Sparrow? Where is he?" Kittel asked

suddenly. At that moment a black, rushing shape came whizzing down from the air above. Kittel could not see it properly, though she could hear it – but whatever it was was coming straight for her head. She threw herself to the ground, and as she fell, she heard Puckel calling, "He was with the dragon!"

Nothing hit her. Nothing hit the ground beside her. She looked up, and saw no sign of Puckel. All she saw was a huge, wide-winged bird whirling off and upwards, in the direction of the smoke and the mountain.

Upstairs in the house, Kittel heard a sudden bang and then a shouting of excited voices coming through the empty window hole. Without stopping to think, she took to her heels and ran off towards Sparrow's house.

152   When she arrived back there, she felt weak and sick and trembling. She had to force herself to go on. First she ran round to the back of the house to check that Bull-in-Cairo's-shape was still there. He was – careering about the paddock in a frenzy. Whether it was the horse part of him terrified at an earthquake, or whether it was the Bull part of him realizing that the earthquake had been caused by the dragon, she didn't stop to ask. She looked at the sky. It was almost full daylight now, although she knew that it would be two hours still before the sun cleared the mountains and shone into the valley. She ran back round the house, and went in through the front door.

The house was empty. Kittel called for Murie, but there was no answer. It suddenly occurred to her that Murie was probably at her wits' end worrying where she and Sparrow had got to.

But there's no time to look for Murie, she thought, I've

got to help Sparrow. She still didn't understand what had happened back at Gogs' house when Puckel had stared at her and told her she had a job to do. All she had known then was that she had to help Sparrow. Otherwise there seemed to be no clear thought in her head: she was like someone in a dream.

On the wall in front of her hung the crossbow which Sparrow's father had used. Like the telephone and the television and all the other things which lay unused about Sparrow's house, the crossbow was kept well dusted and polished. Well-oiled, too. On the wall beside it, the crossbow bolts looked fresh and deadly in their oiled paper wrapping inside the quiver. Unlike the telephone and the television, the crossbow still worked.

Kittel quietly went into the living room and fetched one of the chairs from the table. She put it against the wall of the hall and climbed on to it. She reached up and lifted the crossbow off its hooks on the wall. It was heavy but she could hold it easily enough in one hand. With the other hand she unhitched the quiver of bolts.

Kittel climbed down to the floor. She put the crossbow on the chair and gently eased out one of the bolts from the quiver. She ran her hand over it, and carefully touched its point. It was sharp as a newly ground knife, a heavy, deadly thing. Slowly, dreamily, as though she were asleep and someone else were moving her hands and arms, Kittel picked up the crossbow again and laid the bolt along it. Then she slowly wound back the string, painfully turning the stiff mechanism until the bolt snapped into place with the string snugly behind it. The crossbow was loaded.

Cautiously, Kittel raised it and pointed it towards the wooden end-wall of the hallway. She looked along its length. Her finger was on the trigger, the bow against her shoulder. Her finger squeezed the trigger.

Zoomph! She staggered back, as the whole house seemed to shake with the force of the bolt. It had stuck fast, half buried in the timber. Without pausing, Kittel pulled out another bolt from the quiver, fitted it, and loaded it. Then she looked down at the quiver, wondering whether to take that too. No, she decided. One bolt was enough. Kittel left the house and went round to the paddock, carrying the loaded crossbow.

Cairo was no longer careering about. He was standing near the gate, almost as if waiting for Kittel. Kittel, numbed from lack of sleep, half in a dream, put her hand on the latch of the gate. "Time to go, Bull," she said.

"What's happening?" Bull asked through the horse's mouth, but he shuddered as he spoke. And Kittel understood then that the dragon did indeed have a firm hold on his mind.

"The dragon's broken loose," she answered.

"Time to go where?" Bull asked.

"Up to where the dragon is," Kittel replied.

"I may want to go there," said Bull, "but why do you?"

"I just do," said Kittel. "Will you take me?"

"Open the gate and you'll see," said Bull.

"Bull," Kittel said solemnly, "I know all about you and the dragon, and I just want to say this: I've been with P— the old man, I mean – all night, and I've just seen him bring your body back to life. It had *died*, you know, but it's all right now. P— the old man – sorted it, but it was all thanks to Sparrow. He's put himself into terrible danger so that you could get help. He may even be dead now. That's what your friend's like, Bull – that's what he'll do for you. Just like he let you have his magic gifts back at the start. He didn't have to let you have them, you know."

"I don't have them anyway," Bull muttered sulkily.

"Well, that's not his fault, is it?" said Kittel.

Bull was silent. It was impossible to know what he was thinking because he just looked horsy, but Kittel had a feeling that what she'd said had sunk in. Finally she asked, "Now are you going to let me ride on you up to where the dragon is?"

"I still don't know why you want to go," said Bull, after a pause.

"Nor do I exactly," said Kittel. "But I know I've got to get up there with you, as soon as possible."

Then Bull noticed the crossbow. "What's that for?" he said.

"I don't know that either," Kittel replied.

155

"You don't think you can shoot the dragon, do you?" he said, the horse's head trembling as he spoke. "Is it loaded?"

"Yes," she answered.

"Even I can't load one of them," – in his surprise, Bull's words came out like a whinny – "how could a girl load one?"

Kittel did not reply.

There was another pause. "All right," Bull said softly. "I'll take you."

Ten minutes later, Cairo was trotting smartly up the narrow forest track where Sparrow and Gogs and Bull had gone all those weeks before – on the day Sparrow had looked for Murie's stone and their lives had been changed.

Half an hour later, there could be no doubt about which way they had to go. The noise in the mountains was deafening. The trees were shaking this way and that, and great gusts of hot wind and ear-splitting roars came tumbling out of the air all around. But nearly another half-hour passed as they made their way through the forest, following the din, and they saw nothing until they came at last to the rise of land that overlooked the railway tunnel.

Nothing was happening at the tunnel mouth, but up in the forest in the other direction, Kittel and Bull soon saw what they were looking for. Indeed they could hardly miss it, for the air was full of smoke and flames, where a deadly fight seemed to be on between Puckel and the raging dragon.

The dragon must have been growing at a tremendous rate if it had still been in Puckel's bottle at dawn. Kittel wondered if it could get even bigger; as it was now, it was the most frightening thing she had ever seen.

156

Everything was in a flurry of confused activity, but after a while they could make out what was happening. Puckel was facing the dragon. Every other moment he was reaching out to either side, and immediately afterwards they would see a massive fir tree shoot up into the air where it would suddenly catch light and hiss and roar like an airborne bonfire, before crashing down beside the dragon, burning furiously.

Puckel was tearing the trees out of the ground! He was throwing them up into the air above the dragon, and every time he threw a tree, the dragon turned its head and set it alight. The burning trees were doing it no harm, but all the while Puckel was stepping slowly backwards and the dragon was advancing on him. Puckel was apparently distracting the dragon with the fir trees, and was slowly leading it towards the tunnel!

Kittel and Bull watched as, moment by moment, Puckel and the dragon came closer towards them. Kittel never moved, and neither did Bull. Quite possibly they would have waited there for ever, not knowing what to do, until the dragon had seen them and burned them up. But something happened which sent them into furious action.

Sparrow appeared. He came skimming over the forest towards Puckel and the dragon, but from behind the dragon, so that only Puckel could see him. He was carrying something.

At that moment, there was a change: a glint caught the corner of Kittel's eye. She glanced round, distracted from the fight. The top of the tall rowan tree down by the tunnel mouth was glowing with golden light. The first light of the sun was pouring through a gap in the mountains and lighting up the tree top. That's all very well, thought Kittel, but what place is not on the mountain and not in the valley? It was impossible – you had to be in one place or the other!

not on the mountain and not in the valley

158 SPARROW AWOKE TO THE DIN OF BATTLE IN THE forest lower down the mountain. He lay for a minute wondering where his body was and how he seemed to be getting a vague picture in his head of Puckel and the dragon chasing each other through the trees, while crashings and roarings and tremblings of the ground went on all around. Then the reason came to him and he changed back into his own shape. The picture in his head, which must have been what could be seen from lower down the little dark stream, vanished, and he was standing in Puckel's courtyard of rocks.

I'd better find out what's going on, he thought wearily, and rose into the air. But he rose too high: he was blinded by the sun rising clear of the mist on the eastern horizon. He swooped towards the forest, which still lay in the shadow of morning, and very soon he spotted the cloud of dark smoke above the trees which must mark the spot where the dragon was.

He was not at all certain what he should do. He had no wish to get close to the dragon or the cloud of its poisonous breath, but on the other hand he felt rather guilty that he had let the creature escape. Should he fly down to the village and find out what had happened to Bull?

In the end he made for the scene of the battle. He selected a tree top that seemed to be reasonably free of smoke and flew down and settled in its topmost branches. He peered towards the forest floor, and began to make out what was happening.

What was happening was a most incredible game of hide-and-seek. Somehow, Sparrow knew that Puckel was there, and that he was shape-shifting, though there was in fact no sign of the old man himself. What there was instead were animals that appeared and disappeared, apparently leading the dragon on a crazy course down the tree-covered slopes of the mountain.

159

From his hiding-place, Sparrow saw a wolf spring out and snap its jaws at the dragon's toes; a mountain lion dropped down out of a tree and attacked the dragon's eyes. He saw another dragon break out of the ground and tear at the first dragon's throat. He saw other shapes and beasts he had never seen before nor could put a name to.

If this was Puckel shape-shifting, it was a kind of shape-shifting that was quite different from Sparrow's. Sparrow could only take the shape of things he saw already there. Puckel seemed to be inventing the shapes and then turning into them. Was this because Puckel was not inside the dragon's dream? Or was the dragon not dreaming at all, now that it was awake?

And soon Sparrow saw that Puckel was doing more than

just turning into one thing at a time. The dragon was suddenly attacked by a fiery black bull on one side and at the very same moment by a giant lizard on the other. When it turned its head and snapped its teeth at the bull, the bull simply disappeared, and beside the giant lizard reared a giant brown bear, its red fangs snarling, while from the trees above swooped an osprey with raking talons.

None of the beasts harmed the dragon, as far as Sparrow could see, but they certainly kept it busy.

And then the whole forest suddenly seemed to be full of beasts of every shape, size, and description, and the noise of them all – snorting, grunting, baying, roaring, bellowing and bleating – rose even above the din of the dragon. Surely these beasts couldn't all be Puckel! It seemed impossible, yet Sparrow guessed that somehow, the old man had indeed transformed himself into all of them at once. And the dragon went quite mad, chasing this way and that on its huge, clumsy, scuttling legs, until it was out of sight amongst the trees. The rest of the animals romped off after it, hooting, howling and yammering.

In the brief quietness after they had gone, Sparrow flew down from his perch. Almost immediately he saw a large white billy goat trotting through the trees towards him. Its beard was so long it was brushing against its knees, and although it had very long, thick horns, it looked quite friendly. This was partly because its nose was so squashed-up and pink, which made it look very silly. The goat stopped and waggled its head from side to side. Sparrow could not help grinning at the creature. But then suddenly he remembered something, something from way back, something – in fact almost the first thing – Puckel had ever said. "Silly old goat." He could almost hear Puckel snapping it, apparently enraged at his own stupidity.

"You're Puckel, aren't you?" he said to the goat.

The goat went on waggling its head. And now there was something else. That silly old goat had...

"Puckel! You've forgotten your stick!" Sparrow cried. The goat waggled its head so hard that its beard whipped its knees. "Where is it? Oh!" – Sparrow ran his fingers through his hair in desperation – "It must be still at Gogs' house? In the room where Bull was lying? Is that it?"

The goat vanished. Sparrow blinked. Had he been dreaming? Did Puckel have his stick? What made him think he'd forgotten it? Why hadn't Puckel appeared to him in his own shape if he wanted to tell him so?

There was no answer to these questions, and Sparrow stopped no longer than a moment to think of one. If Puckel was busy with the dragon and didn't have his stick, Sparrow would have to fetch it.

161

Ten minutes later, Sparrow was at Gogs' house. He flew straight to the front door. He didn't care if anyone saw him.

But no one did. There was too much going on. Standing at the front door, Sparrow could hear that the house was in an uproar. Excited voices were coming from the kitchen, as everyone tried to shout everyone else down in explaining what was going on. He thought he caught Murie's voice amidst the hubbub.

He could also hear a noise outside, from lower down the valley. A large crowd of people were standing at the top of the road from the village. They were shouting as well, gawping and gazing up towards the great humped mountain where the black smoke had been seen after the earthquake at dawn.

Sparrow slipped softly into Gogs' house. He didn't

bother to shape-shift: everyone was in the kitchen. Quickly and silently he ran up the stairs to the room where Bull had been. The door was open and he rushed on in…

And stopped dead. Bull was there all right, lying on the bed – Sparrow even noticed he was breathing. But sitting by the bedside –

Ms Minn! Sparrow could scarcely believe his eyes. There was his frail old teacher, with her trembly hands and her wild, wispy hair. Sitting on a chair beside the bed where Bull lay, she was looking Sparrow full in the face, but she said not a word. As Sparrow stood there, his eyes fixed on her in amazement, she nodded at him, slowly, silently as if she were saying, "Yes, that's how it is, and now you've guessed it, my dear…"

And as she nodded, Ms Minn faded. She became fainter. A second later, Sparrow could see through to the back of the chair she was sitting on. Another second, and she was gone altogether.

Puckel's stick stood propped against the chair. Sparrow was sure it had not been there a moment before. Could it be – Ms Minn – the stick? Was it possible? It flashed through his mind that the last two times he had found Puckel without his stick had been the last two occasions that Ms Minn had closed up the school… And then there was that last thing she had said – about having to go and see her brother… And then – the milkstones that he found each time she disappeared – one had even dropped from her coat… What was that crazy old woman? All that time, all those years when she had been going off alone and disappearing in the mountains, was that where she had been – in Puckel's cave, in Puckel's hand…? And what had been the movement near Bull's body when they had looked down from the cliff? The snake, surely – and was that why Ms Minn had not been at Puckel's cave that time?

Twice before Sparrow had been alone with the stick. On both occasions, it had behaved very dangerously. On both occasions it had seemed as though it were trying to kill him. Just for the very smallest moment the thought came to Sparrow that it might do something dangerous again; but almost in the same moment, he realized that things had now changed for ever between the stick and him. Ms Minn had been there, where the stick was now – dear, gentle, mild old Ms Minn: he *knew* something about the stick now, even though he didn't understand it. And knowing that something, he knew the stick would never harm him.

He wasted no more time on it. He grabbed it, leaped out of the hole where the window had been, and flew like the wind back towards the mountain.

163

When he found Puckel, Puckel had stopped changing into animals and was throwing trees about instead. They were quite near the railway tunnel, and not far off Sparrow saw Kittel sitting on Cairo's back.

"Throw it!" shouted Puckel, and Sparrow threw the stick to him. It whizzed over the dragon's head towards Puckel's outstretched hand. Light it was to throw, as any stick, but as it curved in a low arc over the dragon's head, Sparrow seemed to see in it a whole variety of different things: a stick, certainly, but also a coil of silver rain such as you see drifting through the mountain valleys on a grey autumn day; a brown and red snake with wings held close in to the long, sinewy body; and – yes, there was no doubt about it – an old woman with hair as wispy as mist... Surely that stick was the most mysterious thing he had come across yet!

But even as these stray thoughts flashed through Sparrow's mind, the dragon threw back its great head, rolled its fiery eyes, and – *snap!* – the stick, or Ms Minn, or whatever it was, disappeared into its jaws.

Aghast, Sparrow swerved forwards, though he did not know what he could do. He could see Puckel there, frozen like a statue: even old Puckel had been caught out! How could he ever control the dragon now, without his stick? He couldn't go on playing tricks with it forever.

Snap! The dragon's jaws clashed again. What was it after this time? With a shock, Sparrow realized it was after *him*! And as Puckel stood there, frozen, unmoving, the dragon spun round like a gigantic flicked whip, and Sparrow fled, up, into the air, as a fiery blast swirled around him and singed his hair. Looking back, he saw the dragon stretching out its bat-like wings, starting to row them backwards and forwards. In a moment it would have left the ground, thought Sparrow, and then… He wondered how long he could go on flying, how high, how fast, how far, before the dragon caught up with him and turned him to a flying cinder. Well, at least he might give Puckel time to think of something.

He glanced back again. The dragon's forequarters had left the ground. It was beginning its slow, lumbering flight up into the air, though its tail still dragged on the grass. Soon it would gather speed…

But Sparrow had reckoned without Kittel. So, apparently, had Puckel. Kittel took in everything at once. She saw the stick disappearing, she saw Puckel at a loss, she saw the dragon whirl round and begin to chase Sparrow. Urgently she leaned forwards to whisper in Cairo's ear. "Bull," she said, "I've got one bolt for my crossbow. I'm going to use it on the dragon."

Bull shook Cairo's mane.

"You'll never manage," he snorted scornfully. "I told you before."

"Bull," Kittel whispered fiercely, "if I don't use it on the dragon, I'm going to use it on you."

"Why?" the horse's mouth gasped.

"Because either you're going to help me, right now, and do what I say, or I'm going to think you're the dragon's friend: and if you're the dragon's friend, I'll kill you – I will! It's now or never, Bull. Either you're on the dragon's side, or you're on ours. If you're on our side you'll help me now."

The horse's ears twitched and were still. "One simple decision, Bull," Kittel said. "Remember all Sparrow's done for you. I know you think the dragon's wonderful, but are you going to watch it kill your friend? Do you think so much of yourself?"

165

Bull was still. It was impossible to be quite sure what he was thinking about the dragon. Horses' eyes always look a bit wistful, so it would be wrong to say that Bull was gazing wistfully at the great, terrible creature. It was impossible to know why he had agreed to come up into the mountains with Kittel: to help her, or to get nearer to the dragon. Kittel didn't want to think about it; she just waited. But Bull thought – for hours, it seemed (although it was really only a couple of seconds) – agonizing hours while the wind whipped round them in the winnowing of the dragon's awful wings. Slowly, inexorably, its legs, body, and massive tail were rising clear of the ground. Then –

"All right, let's get on with it –" Bull spoke through Cairo's mouth, and immediately trotted forwards.

Kittel sighed with relief. "One simple decision..." She

knew now that, whatever was about to happen, Bull's mind would be safe from the devouring mind of the dragon. Cairo trotted on. He's much braver as a horse than he would be as a boy, she thought, and then she raised the crossbow.

"Faster!" she called to Bull.

Cairo cantered. Kittel squinted along the crossbow, but the horse's canter was making it too bumpy to aim.

"Faster!" she called. And Bull galloped. That was better! Kittel could hold the heavy crossbow steadier now.

Kittel never knew how she did what she did that day. She had never galloped bare-back on a horse before. She had never aimed and fired a crossbow before. But that day she did both at the same moment. She thought she must have borrowed some kind of magical power, that morning of the fight with the dragon.

166

The dragon had left the earth. Its flapping wings were creating a whirlwind on the ground below, and the trees were tossing wildly. It rose slowly, beating up after Sparrow, who was now distant in the air. It took a long time to get off the ground, but once it had got going Kittel knew only too well how fast it could fly. Sparrow didn't stand a chance.

Kittel, galloping towards the dragon, saw its grey belly lifted behind its massive chest. There was a cleft running down the middle of its belly. That's the place, she thought – and fired. Her finger seemed to choose its own moment for pulling the trigger.

Straight for the dragon Kittel's one-and-only bolt flew. Straight for the cleft in its belly. And soundlessly into the dragon's belly it disappeared.

Kittel had believed Bull. She had never thought she

could kill a dragon. And she was quite right. But what she did not know was that her crossbow bolt went straight through the thin hide on the creature's belly and clove into its liver, and that was like a long sharp icicle thrust into its tenderest part. The dragon let out an almighty roar, so loud that the trees split and an avalanche of rocks broke loose on the hillside. The arch of the railway tunnel collapsed and stones and earth filled up the tunnel mouth in seconds.

The dragon glanced down, searching out its unexpected attacker, and then swooped, coughing, gasping out great gouts of black smoke. Round and round like a helter-skelter it came down on Kittel, and suddenly Cairo's legs were knocked from under him as the end of the dragon's tail caught him like a lasso and sent horse and rider spinning off over the ground, past the glowing rowan tree, past the tunnel mouth, over the railway line, over a stretch of open grass to –

167

"Watch out!" screamed the horse. "We're –"

And Kittel did watch out – but there was nothing she could do about it. They were teetering on the edge of the cliff, with nothing below them but the empty air and little fir trees dotted about on the distant floor of rocks.

A split second they teetered, and then with a scream from Cairo and a scream from Kittel, they were over the edge, falling, falling, falling.

Kittel closed her eyes tight, hung on to Cairo's neck, hung on to the crossbow, and wondered if she would feel the crunch when they hit the ground. A bit of her felt annoyed that she was going to die when there were still so many things she wanted to do – telling her mum and dad that she was safe was the first of them. But another bit of her was not thinking that sort of thing at all. It was just falling, falling.

In fact the falling didn't feel too bad: it was like going very fast down a roller-coaster. In fact, falling off a cliff really felt quite pleasant, once you had time to get used to it...

Kittel opened her eyes. The ground wasn't rushing up to meet her. She was looking into the sky.

"I'm flying," she said aloud. "I must be dreaming. I must be dead."

"No, you're not," said Cairo's mouth. "You're alive."

"Sparrow?" said Kittel. "Is that Sparrow?"

"Yes, it's me," the horse's voice came. "I changed into Cairo when I saw you going over the edge."

"I didn't know you could fly when you were in Cairo's shape," said Kittel.

"Nor did I," said Sparrow. "I just knew that if you were going to be smashed to pieces, I wanted to be too."

"I feel funny, I'm going to faint," said Kittel.

"Please don't," said the horse's voice. "You'll fall off."

"All right," Kittel whispered. But she let the crossbow slip from her hand.

The horse flew higher. Kittel saw the dragon sprawled near the ruined tunnel mouth not far below. All in an instant, she noticed that its jaws were standing apart and Puckel had rushed forwards to grasp something in its mouth.

She felt more dreamlike than she had felt all that dream-like morning. She understood exactly what was going on. Her arrow had not damaged the dragon, but it had made it cough and retch. And now it had coughed up Puckel's stick and the stick had got wedged between its jaws, and Puckel was going to pull the dragon by the wedged stick...

Higher they flew, and all of a sudden Kittel saw Cairo's dull brown back turn to glossy chestnut, while his mane turned to gold.

Of course, Kittel thought faintly: the first light of the sun – and in mid-air. Neither on the mountain nor in the valley, it was so obvious! And as she thought it, the horse under her gave a shudder, then a great sigh, and flew on. To Kittel, the change was obvious. A minute before, Sparrow and a squashed-up Bull had inhabited Cairo's body; now there was just Sparrow.

And at that moment, in the upstairs room in Gogs' house, Bull's blue eyes opened and he looked about him. The sun reflecting off the high mountains cast a rosy light on the walls and the bedcover, although down in the valley it had not yet risen. Bull stirred and sighed and looked about: everything felt right. He tried out his arms and his legs: they moved. Everything moved. But if Sparrow or Gogs had seen him in that moment they would hardly have recognized him: the closed doors of his eyes had been broken open, and he looked as contented as a baby. The nightmare was fast fading – the nightmare of animals that gibbered human words, of having a body that couldn't keep its proper shape…

Kittel knew none of this. Gradually her arms loosened round Cairo's neck and her knees loosened where they had been gripping Cairo's sides. "Here I go," she murmured, and tumbled off the horse's back in a dead faint.

Sparrow became aware of her a second later, falling down below him. There was only one thing he could do. He could never fly under her and catch her in Cairo's shape. There in mid-air he left the horse's shape and became himself again, swooping down to Kittel before she fell too far away into the abyss below.

He caught her long before she had reached the tree tops

and, holding her in his arms, he flew up again. At the same time he heard the scream of Cairo's voice, the one word "Master!" as the old beast went plummeting down and smashed through the trees. The crossbow and old Cairo had been the only things left which had belonged to Sparrow's father, and both were suddenly lost together; now the paddock behind the house would always be empty. Sparrow's eyes felt hot and pricking and he found he was muttering, "I'm sorry, I'm sorry," in answer to the horse's dying scream that echoed over and over in his ears. "Master! Master! Master!" Had he been given the gift of understanding animals just to hear that? "I'm sorry, sorry," he howled, as tears poured from his eyes and splashed on to Kittel's head.

Sparrow hardly thought about where he was going. The place where they landed at last was none other than the courtyard outside Puckel's cave, near where the little dark stream came bubbling up out of the rocks. And Sparrow never even wondered that he had reached it for the second time by flying. "I'm sorry," he groaned, "I'm sorry."

Kittel, who had recovered from her faint, seemed to understand that Cairo was gone, and why. She stood silently with Sparrow beside the little dark stream and held his hand till his tears turned to sobs, his sobs to rough heaving breaths, and at last he was quiet.

It was from here that they saw the last of the fight with the dragon.

It appeared high in the air above them, locked in combat with old Puckel. Puckel was holding the dragon by the stick wedged in its teeth, as if the dragon were a fish on a hook. The dragon thrashed and roared, but though clouds of smoke kept belching from its nostrils, it seemed to have lost

170

its fire. Below it, its long tail whirled round and round, coiling and coiling in a demented spiral. Higher and higher Puckel and the dragon whirled, and higher and higher again, until they were no more than a tiny coiling black spring up in the clear blue air. And still they went up, coiling and – very faintly now – roaring, until at last they could be seen and heard no more.

Bloop! came from Sparrow's and Kittel's feet. Then, *bloop!* again. Great bubbles of air were coming up from below the ground in the water of the little dark stream.

Bloop! The stream faltered. The water was becoming less. Minute by minute there was less, until only a trickle was pushing up through the flat stones.

Then, *bloop-schschschschsch ...* the water stopped. The little dark stream had dried up.

Sparrow looked round the rocky courtyard. There was no sign of Puckel's cave, not a crack, not even a hollow. It was as if there had never been magic there.

"I think Puckel's gone away," he said in a slightly wavering voice.

"I know he has," Kittel answered.

"I don't think he or the dragon will be back," he said.

"I know they won't," said Kittel. "Let's go home now."

"You know what that means," Sparrow said – and now his voice was wavering in earnest – "it means that the dragon-mist will disappear, and your people will be able to come and look for you, and then you'll be taken away, and—"

"Hush," said Kittel, "we don't know what's going to happen." And Sparrow hushed, but he kept biting his lip.

After a while he said, "Maybe Cairo thought he was going back to his master. Maybe he's happy now."

"I'm sure he is," said Kittel.

Just before they turned to go, his eye caught something gleaming amongst the flat stones where the stream had once emerged into the light. He went down on his hands and knees and peered.

Suddenly he laughed. He put his hand between two stones and drew out a small piece of rock. Two fragments of glass tumbled off it and fell with a tiny tinkling sound in the dead quiet of the courtyard. "It's heavy!" he gasped.

Kittel looked at the piece of rock. It was like a little rough pyramid, and when you first looked at it, it seemed to be made of just ordinary stone. But as Kittel stared on, she realized there was something a little strange about it – almost as if, somewhere deep in its core, there were a glowing light. "What is it?" she said.

172   "It was a mountain," Sparrow grinned. "Puckel's been forgetful again: when he shrank the dragon, he shrank a bit of mountain too by mistake, and it went into the bottle. He said you shouldn't ever do that to bits of mountains, and he meant to put it back after he'd got rid of the dragon."

"He won't do that if he never comes back," said Kittel.

Sparrow chuckled. "Then I'd better keep it for him, hadn't I?"

As Sparrow flew with Kittel towards the village, they saw two small figures making their way through the open birch woods near the railway line – one dark haired, the other red. Sparrow turned towards them and came to land not far away. He rubbed his face which was itching from dried tears, and wondered anxiously how he should speak to his friends.

For the first time Sparrow could ever remember, Bull

hung back and appeared to be shy. It was Gogs who came forward and said, "Is this her?" looking at Kittel in some amazement.

"I suppose so," Sparrow answered, remembering that Gogs himself wouldn't have seen Kittel but had probably heard about her from Bull. "She's Kittel," he added.

"Skittle?" said Gogs in even greater amazement.

"I told you," Bull interrupted from behind him.

"Bull says it's six days since – since –" Gogs faltered.

"I know," said Sparrow, looking at his feet.

"I can't believe I've been asleep so long," said Gogs. "I've missed all the excitement."

"Can you still understand beasts and birds?" Sparrow asked uncertainly.

Gogs shook his head and grinned – the same old silly Gogs-grin they had always known. Nothing could change Gogs, Sparrow thought to himself. "Neither of us can," Gogs said. "Can you?"

173

Sparrow nodded. His third gift seemed to have slipped into his life almost without his noticing. Apart from the owl and Cairo's dying scream, he had not heard any birds or beasts talking – he hadn't had time. Now he became aware that there was a murmur all about him, like a hint of distant voices, that he only had to stop still and listen to: a whole unknown world waiting for him...

"I can't even remember what it was like," said Gogs.

Sparrow shook himself. "What?" he asked.

"Hearing the animals talk," Gogs said. "I can't remember it. It's like a dream."

"Oh," said Sparrow. "It's a bit odd, really..." He tailed off, listening again.

"I'm glad," said Gogs decisively. "I mean, we don't mind

if you – I mean—"

"I want to say it," Bull broke in.

"Go on then," said Gogs, and turned red.

Sparrow found he had turned red as well.

"I want us to be friends again," said Bull.

"All right," said Sparrow, a little doubtfully.

"I know we can't be just as we were before," Bull went on. "But nearly – as nearly as we can manage…" Bull's expression was almost pleading.

Sparrow relaxed and smiled. "All right," he said again.

"It wasn't really Gogs," Bull said. "It was just me. You should stay friends with Gogs anyway. I should never have tried to get your gifts. They were yours. I'm sorry – I've been wrong all the time. I almost died. Twice, I think." He gulped. "Just being alive's better than having magic gifts – for me, I mean." He had been looking somewhere around Sparrow's stomach as he said this, but now he looked him full in the face, and Sparrow saw that his bright, piercing eyes no longer had their old command. They were a little bleak, perhaps wiser, certainly sadder, and – Sparrow realized with a shock – Bull looked up to him now. Sparrow had something that Bull knew he could never have. "I'm sorry and I'm glad too," Bull said firmly. "I mean – I think you deserve to have magic gifts. I don't."

And fixed with Bull's keen stare, Sparrow, as so often before, didn't know where to look – but now it was for a new reason.

"Perhaps if we ever see Puckel again –" he began, and then realized what he had said.

"There," said Bull. "That means we won't. Or at least, not to get magic gifts from him." Then he added, in a strangely solemn voice, "That part's finished."

"What do you mean?" said Sparrow. Did Bull still know something he didn't?

"I'm not sure," said Bull quietly. "Really, I don't know anything about it. But I feel – down inside – that something's just starting. I don't know what: something that's to do with all of us."

"That's what I think too," said Gogs. "And Skittle's arrived as well. That must mean something."

"It's Kittel," said Kittel tiredly. "Kay—"

"Well, I think it means something anyway," said Gogs.

"For one thing," said Sparrow, "I don't think Ms Minn will be coming back. We won't have a teacher any more. So I think instead we ought to get Kittel to teach us all the things she knows. And Bull as well – if you want to, that is."

Bull nodded slowly. "Yes, I'll do that. There're a lot of things I could tell you. But why do you think Ms Minn won't be coming back?"

And then Sparrow told them all he suspected about Ms Minn and the stick. And as the four of them returned to the railway line and set off homewards, stepping slowly, sleeper by sleeper, they talked over the whole adventure, gradually piecing things together. At the end of it, though, they found they still had no answer to the business of the milkstones.

"Maybe they were really snake's eggs," said Kittel, "and they hatched out."

"What into?" said Gogs.

"Baby Ms Minns?" Kittel giggled.

"They felt like stones to me," said Sparrow.

"Now Sparrow's the best stone-*loser* there is," said Gogs brightly.

"Sparrow's lost three stones," said Kittel, "and got three

175

magic gifts. That doesn't sound like a bad swop to me."

"I wish Murie saw it that way," said Sparrow ruefully. "And I'm going to have to explain about poor old Cairo and the crossbow too."

They went on down, until in an old orchard the railway line stopped and a wide track of grey-frosted grass continued in its place. Sparrow halted on the last sleeper and looked down to where the first houses of the village could be seen between the bare boughs of the apple trees. "There's one other thing," he said.

"What?" said Kittel.

"Well," said Sparrow, "When I first met Puckel he said I was in a dream. I know what he meant now. Because we were all in a dream, like Ms Minn said – the dream of the dragon. But what about now? The dragon woke, and I suppose it must be up there, up among the stars…" He stared into the wintry blue sky.

"And…" Kittel prompted.

"And that means," Sparrow went on, "that we can't be in its dream any more."

"That's right, because it woke up," said Gogs.

"So – I don't know what that means," Sparrow tailed off. "I don't really feel any different – not because of that, anyway."

"In magic," said Bull, "there are a lot of things you can't explain."

Sparrow shrugged. "I suppose so," he said. He stepped off the sleeper and continued on to the grassy track into the village.

into the spiral

frustration

THE CHILL DUSK OF A SPRING EVENING FILLED THE VILLAGE square with a dreamy, violet light. Everything looked wet, dark and distinct – the bare linden trees, the carved rams' heads on the gable ends of the village hall, the low grey houses on the other side of the square with their purple slates or chocolate-brown thatch. The air was almost misty, and there was a scent of wet earth mixed with the scent of wood-smoke from the chimneys.

In the bare garden of one of the houses two women were talking. A large lady in a hat decorated with artificial fruit was towering over a small thin one standing on the doorstep. The small thin one nodded towards something across the square, and the large one turned to watch a girl and a boy who had just come out from under the lindens and were making their way up the side of the hall away from the square. The girl, who was a little taller than the boy, had curly hair the colour that the roof-thatch would turn in the summer, and the boy had a large black crow perched on his shoulder.

The two women watched the boy and the girl until they were out of sight. Then the large woman turned to the thin one and looked down her nose and said, "Talking to crows that come and perch on his shoulder! There's something not at all right about that boy."

The smaller woman sniffed, like a weasel coming up out of its burrow. "His father was a queer one too," she remarked.

"And look what happened to him," said the large one, who was called Ms Redwall and who had the whitest lace curtains in Copperhill. "Not a Trader, but just as bad as a Trader." Her head, and the imitation fruit, nodded twice. "Not a trace of him left, all those years ago, and poor Ms Overton left with a baby to bring up all by herself."

182

"Little wonder he talks to crows now," said the smaller woman, and sniffed again.

"That's where it starts," said Ms Redwall, "but what will it be next?"

"What sort of ideas is he putting into that young girl's head, that's another thing," said the small woman.

"That is another matter altogether," said Ms Redwall, and pursed her lips. "I gather *she* has enough queer ideas of her own – and I should know, because she's friends with poor Ms Clodish's daughter next door."

"What sort of ideas?"

Ms Redwall's mouth pursed even more, and the imitation fruit nodded several more times. "Ideas," she murmured, "about – other places, if you know what I mean."

The small woman obviously did know what she meant, and looked suitably shocked. "Whoever heard of a young thing like that in charge of the school, anyway?" she said.

"Something ought to be done about it," said Ms Redwall, and looked thoughtful.

After a few more minutes of talk Ms Redwall and her fruit parted from the small woman, who disappeared into her house and shut the door. Presently there was no one to be seen in the square and the grey dusk deepened, helped along by a mist that rolled down from the great cloudy mountain towering above the roof-tops.

The boy and the girl meanwhile were making their way up a steep cobbled road that led out of the village under a line of tall ragged elms. Into one of these trees the crow had just flapped up in a rather clumsy fashion and the boy was rubbing his shoulder where the bird's claws had been digging into him.

183

"Good night, Herold!" he called in answer to the squawk that came down from among a tangle of bare branches. Then he said to the girl, "He's – really, he's just not like a bird. I can't explain it."

"You're imagining things," the girl, Kittel, said firmly. "It's getting to you at last. You're getting confused – probably going mad. Poor Sparrow."

Sparrow ignored her. "He's not sort of – flighty, like other birds," he said. "He's not like other crows either. Crows are always sort of ashamed of themselves. Herold's not. Maybe he doesn't have to be, because he doesn't eat the sort of things other crows eat."

"With the amount of food you give him to eat," Kittel retorted, "he ought to be the sleekest and glossiest crow ever. Instead he's the most awful flying mess anyone's ever seen. So maybe you're right after all. Maybe he became a bird by mistake."

"Do you think so?" Sparrow said with a frown.

"I was joking, stupid," said Kittel.

The mist became thicker as they climbed, and the chill of the air was a reminder that the mountain above them was still half covered with snow. The last part of their journey was up a steep, winding path, whose white pebbles shone in the gathering gloom. Quite suddenly they were at the top of the hill and looking down to a long, whitewashed cottage, whose lights made a golden halo in the mist. The door was open, letting the light stream out from the hallway.

Sparrow stopped just before they went in. "I'm going to tell Murie tonight," he said.

In the year and a bit since Kittel had so unexpectedly come to live with them, Murie, Sparrow's mother, had become extremely fond of her. Murie had always wanted a daughter of her own. She knew that, one day, Kittel would probably have to try to find a way back to her own home, which was a mysterious and dangerous-sounding place somewhere away beyond the mountains. But as nobody even knew how far the mountains stretched, it seemed like the sort of thing you could always put off till next year, or even the year after. They had thought to begin with that people from Kittel's place would come to look for her, but there had been no sign of them.

"It's because of the wall of mist," Sparrow said. But, as the months went by, it seemed that the wall of mist was fading away, and still no one came, and Kittel became more and more settled in her new home with Murie and Sparrow.

*   *   *

"My roof worked," Sparrow announced, as the three of them sat dipping bread into their broth at the large table in the lamp-lit kitchen.

Murie, bread dripping in her hand, looked up and looked blank, as she often did with Sparrow. "What roof?"

"On the cottage. In Kittel's valley," Sparrow said with his mouth full.

Murie continued to look blank.

"I told you about the cottage, back last year. Remember? I was asking if my father could have built it and you said I was talking nonsense."

"Oh, that cottage," Murie said, with deliberate calmness. She was noticing an excited expression in Sparrow's eyes. "Don't run your fingers through your hair, it'll get all full of soup and bread."

"I went back to it yesterday and it's as dry as anything inside."

185

Murie picked her spoon up and took two mouthfuls of soup before saying, "Are you telling me you want to be a thatcher, or what?"

Sparrow glanced at Kittel, but Kittel was examining her bread carefully, pulling out the small black seeds in it and eating them separately.

"Kittel and me are going—"

"Kittel and *I*," Kittel murmured.

– "to try and find the way back to her home. We're going to start from the cottage…"

Murie put down her spoon again. "You're going to start from the cottage," she repeated. She knew quite well what Sparrow was saying, but she was determined not to understand.

"We can spend the night in the cottage, and start off from

it in the morning."

A deep silence fell, a silence made somehow deeper by the gentle bubbling of the large iron pot on the fire. Even Kittel, who came from a different place, knew Sparrow had said something awful.

"I've been out at night before," Sparrow said at last, when the silence seemed to have gone on long enough.

"That was different," Murie snapped. "You were with what's-his-name."

There was another silence.

"People don't stay out at night," said Murie finally.

"We wouldn't *be* out!" Sparrow exclaimed. "There's a door, and now there's a roof! It's a real house!"

"It's out in the middle of nowhere," Murie said firmly. "Miles and miles out into the mountains."

186

"Someone must have lived there once," Sparrow argued.

"Well, they're not there now – so what happened to them?"

"Traders are out at night," Sparrow said, though he knew by now he had lost the argument.

"Traders are different," his mother said. "Traders take their life in their hands. Look what happened to Bull's father."

Sparrow sighed.

Murie got up from the table and turned to the black cooking range that crouched by the wall under the huge clay oven. She started slamming the embers about with a poker and throwing fresh logs in. "What does Kittel think about this?" she demanded. "Do you want to find your way home?"

"Well – there's the school," Kittel murmured, "and Lissie, and – other things… No… Yes… I don't know."

She was not often at such a loss. Her misty blue eyes looked mistier than usual. "I like it here, you know," she finished lamely.

Sparrow looked offended.

"But I do think we should try to find a way home," she added hastily.

"I see what it is," Murie said, jamming a last log in under the black pot. "Sparrow wants to go exploring, so's persuaded Kittel out on this wild-goose chase too."

"I don't! It's not that!" Sparrow protested.

Murie started ladling out more broth. "Right," she said, "I'll tell you what. We'll leave it for just now. The nights are too dark, and the weather's not good enough at the moment. When the spring gets going, there'll be a lot of work to do. After that, say at the beginning of summer, the nights will be brighter; and then perhaps – *perhaps* – I'll let you go for a couple of days: as long as you don't get into any scrapes in the meantime."

187

The spring came on. Mist came and went on the mountain above the village and the dark patches grew bigger on its snowy upper slopes. The tender crocus spears pushed up in the flowerbed in front of the house; snow came, flattened them, and melted the next day. Daffodils began to make yellow masses amongst the tired yellow grass, and birds began to sing amongst the budding trees. Kittel watched it all rather wistfully, Sparrow impatiently.

Gogs Westward and his father came over with their team of horses to break the ploughed ground in Murie's steep little fields, and Sparrow and Kittel went up and down behind them, scattering corn, then up and down behind them again, poking in the grains of corn the rake hadn't covered. There was digging, sowing, planting and weeding to do in the vegetable garden, and everyone had to lend a hand. Whenever they finished a job on their own land, they went over to Bull Hind's house on the next hillock and helped Bull and his grandmother on theirs, and sometimes on to the next to help with Gogs', though Gogs' family was big enough not to need much help.

The days grew longer, the sun climbed higher above the mountains day by day. The handsome black cockerel would make sure no one stayed in their beds after four o'clock in the morning.

"Any day now…" Sparrow was muttering to himself one May morning as he climbed up through the heavy-scented gorse towards where the forest began at the top edge of their fields. "She's got to – she's got to – if we don't go now we'll never go…" He wasn't saying it to anyone in particular and he got no answer back, except that there was a lark high above his head, trilling something that sounded like "easy easy easy does it, easy does it, easy does it," which Sparrow found faintly irritating.

188

As he climbed, he kept glancing round, stumbling and hurrying on. Just learn to be patient, Murie had said the night before, but already he was beginning to feel that the summer was ticking away. Kittel seemed to be losing all the interest she had had in his plan and spent most of her free time out of school with her friend Lissie. Perhaps it wasn't surprising, since the last time she had seen the cottage it was just four damp walls and no roof and certainly didn't look inviting as a place to live in. It wasn't his fault that she hadn't seen it with its amazing roof on, its shutters of woven twigs, log chairs and pile of sticks stored ready for burning in the huge fireplace.

*   *   *

An elder tree leaned over the wall that bounded the top edge of the field, its bony trunk pushing the stones out of place so that it was easy to climb over. Sparrow hauled himself up by the yielding branches and stood on top of the wall, scanning first the fields below him and then the sky above him. Then all at once he sprang up off the wall, looking to begin with as though he were going to jump back into the field…

Except that he didn't come down, but rose higher into the air: flying, not jumping. He hung for a moment above the field, and then with an effortless twist of his body rose over the elder and disappeared into the glistening green canopy of the beech tree that overhung it.

High among the lattice of the tree's silver branches he paused and landed, straddling a slim bough and peering down, around, and up towards the blue sky mottled among the topmost leaves. Then he smiled, straightened, and seemed about to launch himself upwards again – when suddenly his expression changed, he slumped limply back on his branch and heaved a deep sigh.

Directly above him, perched half hidden in a thicket of leaves, was the crow, Herold. Herold was the most marvellously untidy bird Sparrow had ever met, with hardly a feather that wasn't askew or moth-eaten looking, but for all that, he had an uncanny knack of knowing exactly where Sparrow was going to be at any time of the day or night. Faint churring noises were coming from his beak now, which was what had caught Sparrow's attention, and one black eye was glaring stonily down at him. Sparrow sighed again.

The churring noise changed to a series of soft squeaks and rasps, then the beak snapped shut.

189

"To the cottage," Sparrow said tiredly, in answer. "I wanted to try and go a bit further today." He glanced down at a squirrel, which had suddenly gone scampering like a russet whiplash down the trunk of the tree. He smiled slightly as he watched it dive into a drift of dead leaves on the ground far below and gaze back up at them, bewildered.

But the crow was squeaking and rasping again, and this time there was an edge to the sound which was just a little threatening. Sparrow stopped smiling. "Of course I haven't had enough of you, Herold," he said pleadingly. "You're fine. You're wonderful. Honestly. It's just you can't – I mean, I can fly faster by myself. You get tired, flying there, and back; you won't manage to go further."

At that the crow seemed to explode, hopping off its perch and sending a flurry of leaves and feathers round Sparrow as it flapped furiously and let out a torrent of squawks and screeches. Sparrow covered his head and closed his eyes, and didn't open them again until the noise had died down and the crow had resettled itself on two twigs, with its legs straight out and rather far apart, looking very much the way people do when they stand with their hands on their hips.

Sparrow was quite used to the crow's rages, and had an excellent reason for covering his head, but he also knew they never lasted long. After a few moments he said, "So what about Kittel? She can't come with us if we do it your way, you know that."

The crow made several more, rather quieter noises, at which Sparrow snorted, "Of course she can't walk. There's forests and rough ground and boulders and bogs. She'd take days getting there."

Herold clicked and clacked his beak and squeaked several times. Sparrow sighed a third time.

"Oh, all right," he said at last. "But she'd be a lot more interested if she could come and see for herself. Come on then."

A moment later the crow had flapped itself clear of the treetop and was wheeling in its odd, lopsided fashion over the green masses of forest on the lower slopes of the large mountain. Of Sparrow there was no sign, either amongst the trees or in the air.

the linden lady

IF MS REDWALL HAD KNOWN THE FULL TRUTH ABOUT Sparrow, her concern would have become deep shock. For her, the idea of his having a pet crow was bad enough. If she had known that it was not a pet at all but a wild bird, and that it sat on Sparrow's shoulder because Sparrow could understand the speech of beasts and birds, her disapproval would have changed to horrified amazement. If she had known that the crow had first started speaking to Sparrow because it had seen Sparrow flying, she would probably have had a seizure – which certainly would have saved everyone a lot of trouble.

However, Sparrow kept his remarkable gifts a close secret from all but a small circle of people – his best friends Gogs and Bull, Bull's grandmother, Murie, Kittel and Kittel's friend Lissie (who lived next door to Ms Redwall). Apart from that, there were only rumours – hints dropped by Kittel in the classroom; strange things Sparrow said or did which couldn't be accounted for; and memories of the startling events of eighteen months before, when Kittel had suddenly appeared in Copperhill village after being rescued by Sparrow from a crashed aeroplane on a mountain top. It was these things which made some of the ordinary village people whisper and wonder and shake their heads; but none of them knew enough to make any reasonable guesses, and the truth wouldn't have occurred to them even in their wildest dreams.

Apart from being able to fly and understanding the language of beasts and birds, Sparrow had one other gift, possibly the greatest and strangest of the three. As the crow flapped steadily onwards through valley and over ridge and among the tall mountains, it was this third gift that Sparrow was using: he was in the crow's shape.

This was why he was not seeing the world quite as he usually saw it: in crow-shape he could view all at once the ground speeding below him, the great arch of sky above him, and the sunlight and shadow of the hillsides on either side. The only direction – apart from behind – in which he found it difficult to see was straight ahead. He had to make his crow-eyes roll together if he wanted to do that – as you have to do if you want to focus on the end of your nose –or else turn his head first to one side and then to the other. A crow isn't normally thinking about getting anywhere in particular, and its eyes are more made for searching for food and keeping out of trouble.

In fact, after the interest of it had worn off, it was a bit of a nuisance flying in the crow's shape – part of the nuisance that life had become since Herold had befriended Sparrow the previous autumn. Sparrow hadn't been able to use his gift of flight properly for months now, because Herold refused absolutely to let him; every time he tried to, the crow was there to stop it. Herold did this mainly by reminding him of all the help the birds had given in building the roof on the cottage, and saying that if friendship meant anything at all, Sparrow should let himself be saved from the obscenity of being a flying boy. He should leave the flying to the birds.

It was afternoon by the time Sparrow wheeled over the last ridge and glided down into Kittel's valley, and his crow-shape felt tired. In a way this didn't matter, because after perching in a pine tree and dropping down to the ground in his own boy-shape, Sparrow didn't feel tired at all. Herold felt as though he'd just woken up from a long sleep – that was what it was like for him when Sparrow was in his shape.

194

Kittel's valley or, as she called it, "the Valley of Murmuring Water, like in a Chinese fairy-tale", was a secret, remote place far beyond the furthest limits that the people of Copperhill ever travelled to. How the cottage had got there Sparrow couldn't begin to guess, which was why he had vaguely wondered if it could have been built by his lost father.

If you stood outside and looked around, you felt you were in the bottom of a deep bowl, on whose edges rough heathery ground gathered into sheer, rocky cliffs as the mountains towered up all round. Down a long cleft in one of the cliffs a thin white waterfall poured, filling the bowl with a constant soft noise as though the mountains were gently breathing. But where the water ran across the floor of the valley it was in a deep, dark channel, and there it made hardly any sound except for the occasional swirl and *ploop* when a trout hit the surface. Kittel had given the valley its name when Sparrow first flew there with her in the autumn.

The cottage certainly looked different now from the way it had looked then. Not everyone would have said it looked better. Herold and his army of birds – Herold had grown up amongst them, though he looked down on them now that he lived in Copperhill – had been most interested in Sparrow's idea of getting a roof on. They had put a huge amount of time and energy into building the "great, upside-down nest" which the boy wanted.

For that was how it came out. A real thatcher wouldn't have recognized that it was a roof; he would just have seen an untidy mound of twigs and leaves and dead grass heaped like a haystack on the roof-timbers of the ruined cottage. Yet it proved thick and dense enough to keep out the roughest winter weather.

195

Ignoring Herold's complaining croon from the pine tree, Sparrow walked down to the cottage. He wandered round it, as he always did when he arrived in the little valley, and sighed. It wasn't much use without Kittel.

The queerest thing about it – apart from its new roof – was its doorway. It was an extraordinary doorway to find on such a tiny building. Its two massive stone doorposts were not upright but, when looked at from the front, leant out to the sides. Over them, the two lintel-stones were set together to form a point over the centre. Into this five-sided space there fitted a massive five-sided door.

After a while, there seemed nothing more to check about the cottage, and Sparrow stood by the door and gazed off eastward where the stream took its way out of the valley. The afternoon sun was shining full on a rocky ridge cut by a sharp, dark, gully. If he went in crow's shape, that was the way he would have to take. If he flew himself, a single bound would take him high above the ridge and into sight of the lands beyond. He had seen these from a distance but had never followed the stream. Following the stream was the course he and Kittel had agreed would be best, as long as it went eastwards – eastwards was the direction of the old railway line before it got lost in the mountains not far out of Copperhill. They knew the railway line had once, long ago, linked the village with Kittel's place.

Murie was right, of course. Sparrow wanted Kittel there as his reason for going on, but it was really for himself that he wanted to find the way to her place. He was hungry to see the incredible world she had described to him so often – televisions full of colours and people talking, lights that made a whole room bright just by touching a thing on a wall, traffic roaring, crowds of people rushing through the bright-lit streets, people who didn't know you, people you'd never seen before. He wasn't sure if he would feel safe to go there without Kittel to guide him: on the other hand, just a glimpse might be safe enough … if he could get there quick enough … if he flew by himself…

A loud squawk behind him put a stop to his thoughts. Herold always knew: always. It was like having a nanny looking after you, never letting you alone, never letting you grow up. Sparrow bit his lip, and his eyes prickled with frustration.

He took a deep breath and nodded towards the ridge.

"That's the way we'll have to go," he said.

Herold complained that the sun was hot enough to frazzle his feathers.

"You don't have to come," Sparrow said.

That set the crow off into a rage again and it started half flapping, half running, round and round the roof, screaming the sort of abuse that crows scream at each other in their more excited moments. To save it from exhausting itself, Sparrow took its shape again, picked himself up from the somersault down the roof which the sudden shape-change caused, and set off at a glide for the gully, skimming over the bright grass of the valley and the fragrant birch forest at the eastern end.

When Sparrow insisted to Kittel that Herold was different from other birds, it was because of a faint feeling of difference he had every time he took the crow's shape. It was hard to say exactly what it was. Normally, with birds he changed into, he felt that his bones were full of air: birds were so light they hardly seemed to belong to the ground at all. It was as if the crow somehow felt its own weight a little bit – a tiny bit – more than other birds. It was like the ghost of an old sadness. Sparrow wondered if it was simply connected with Herold's being so fond of sleeping. He didn't believe Herold was a very old crow, though he did think he was probably very lazy. Whatever the feeling was, he never got entirely used to it – either that, or it was getting stronger.

The effect of the gully on his crow-vision was dramatic. The rocky walls drew suddenly, blackly, in, like a lid slamming on either side of his head. The sunlight was cut off. The echo of the water battled to and fro and grew to a monotonous drumming, a dizzying noise that swirled round the small black thing he was, wrapping him in cocoons of sound. Sparrow could almost see the sound, spinning away like a tunnel ahead of him – a black tunnel, stretching on and on, flecked with flashes of silver that were

197

the continuous boom-boom-boom of the drum…

He was not flying any more. He was walking, in his own shape, down that black and silver tunnel, dreamily, vaguely, stumbling as though he were walking in his sleep. He couldn't think what had happened to Herold, though that didn't seem to matter. He almost let his eyes close as he stumbled on down, down, down…

A cool, laughing voice cut across Sparrow's dulled senses: "You were going a dangerous way – you're lucky I was here to find you!" He stopped, wrenching his eyes wide open, blinking stupidly.

He was no longer in the black and silver tunnel, but in what seemed to be a wide, low-roofed chamber with walls of bluish stuff like ice or frosted glass. The walls let light through but no glimpse of anything outside. Sparrow hardly noticed this, for he was staring, goggle-eyed, at the lady who had so unexpectedly interrupted his strange journey.

Sparrow had seen plenty of girls and women before, but never anyone he could exactly have called a lady. This person was. You could see she had never done a stroke of work in her life, had never been out in burning sun or cutting wind or chapping frost. She was very beautiful, with long reddish hair that looked as though each strand had been polished a thousand times. Her skin was smooth and pale as ivory. Her dress was green, covered with a jungle of designs in gold thread.

"Come," she said, smiling, "you must be hungry after coming so far."

Sparrow frowned. He had not remembered being hungry; but now, as the lady spoke, he realized that he felt ravenous. He felt as if he hadn't eaten for a week. His stomach seemed like a gaping hole that would need a barrow-load of food to fill it.

"Yes, I am," he said, puzzled.

He let the lady take his hand. The touch of her fine, long-nailed fingers was soft and cool as water in a sun-warmed pool. Round her there hung a faint scent like the smell of linden blossom, and he fell again into a strange dreaminess. They crossed under a low archway in the bluish wall, and there in front of them, in a second chamber like the first, was a great table of glass, laden from end to end with the most tremendous feast Sparrow had ever seen.

The dishes, bowls, trenchers, pitchers and platters seemed too many to count, and each was filled with something that looked delicious. There were pastries and pâtés, roast fowl and fondues, fruit and fish and a great fat-oozing pig's head with an apple stuck in its mouth. Sparrow's stomach seemed to be howling with agony, and his mouth watered so much he couldn't speak. He had never felt such hunger.

199

"Eat – whatever you like," the lady said, delicately picking up a piece of succulent skewered meat and sinking her crystal-white teeth into it.

It was too much for Sparrow. He felt his sides were caving in for want of food. He rounded on the glass table, ready to seize whatever was nearest…

But he stopped, his hand poised above the plate from which the lady had eaten. A pickled eel in a yellow sauce on a nearby dish had moved. In fact, it was crawling. It slithered off the plate and across the table, winding between the dishes; and as it passed under Sparrow's hand it raised its yellow-streaked, pickled head and spoke.

"First, the stone in your pocket," it said.

Sparrow, although stunned, became quite clear-headed. It was true that he had his stone in his pocket – or in the pouch that hung from his belt, to be exact. He always kept it with him, in case he got the chance to hand it back to old Puckel. Puckel was the only person who would be able to turn the stone back into the mountain it really was. It was Puckel who, a year and a half before, had given Sparrow his magical powers.

He glanced at the lady. It seemed she had not noticed the talking eel. He picked up a piece of skewered meat like the lady's, but at the same time he drew the stone out of his pouch.

He was immediately seized by a giddy feeling of being hurled backwards very fast; yet nothing moved. The bluish, translucent walls became like clouds which seemed to shift slightly, so that he could see through them glimpses of the way he had come, the stony gully. The lady was changing in front of his eyes, withering, drooping, her hair falling away from the front of her head, leaving her a big bald dome of forehead, and something strange was happening to her arms. Sparrow went on clutching the stone, gritting his teeth against the awful feeling of falling backwards. He still seemed to be clutching the skewer of meat, too, but when he glanced down, he saw it was Herold he was holding.

And now the lady had become a shadowy figure in a straggly grey cloak, an ungainly humped thing that shuffled along over stony ground. The feeling of violent movement lessened, and Sparrow saw a second, then a third, figure exactly like her: deep-shaded humps of grey cloak, no faces visible. They were shuffling slowly, and now Sparrow could see that they were on the shore of a still water, where swirls of deep mist made it difficult to make out anything clearly. They were moving away from him and paid him no attention. If it were really the lady he was seeing, she seemed to have lost all interest in him.

"I don't understand," Sparrow said aloud. He looked down at the crow in his hand. Herold was as motionless as a stuffed bird.

With a ripple and a swish, the waters of the lakeside parted, and Sparrow found the black, beady eyes of an otter fixed on him. The animal's glistening wet fur was black as jet, but for a strange streak of vivid yellow-gold across one side of its face. It was a very unusual-looking otter, but seemed real and solid compared with the deep-cloaked figures receding into the mist. The otter brushed a paw across its whiskers. Sparrow heard it say, "What you don't understand is pretty much."

201

There was something about the creature which made Sparrow think immediately of the eel. The same sinuous, winding way of moving, the same sound to the voice. "What on earth's going on?" he demanded, and heard the otter reply, as it brushed its other paw forward across its face –

"Not on earth, but under earth, through water, and by the Secret Way of the Mountains."

Sparrow saw that the animal's eyes had a queer, slightly glazed look – more than a little like the eyes of the pickled eel. It turned its blunt muzzle side-on to him and arched its back. Then he heard its voice – which somehow didn't sound as though it quite belonged to it: "There they go – see? This is the moving of a stone from where it should be to where it shouldn't be. And that puts everything out."

The otter gazed after the three figures, almost out of sight now in the swirling mist. Then it turned away towards the water. "Puckel must know this quickly," it added. "That stone will take you. Under the Pole Star, only then." With a soft ripple it disappeared.

The mist seemed to be drawing back from the water and from the stony shore. Silently, uncannily, it grew clear.

The light was dim. Sparrow found himself in the twilight of evening beside the shore of a long, pale-shining lake with tangled trees growing all along its edges. Through their trunks soft clouds of mist went creeping. Seized by sudden panic, he gathered himself and leaped into the air.

High above the shimmering silver of the water's face, he paused, hovered, and looked down. The lake spread eastwards for what looked like several miles. But westwards, there was a rocky defile where a stream that fed the lake flowed through. He flew a little higher – and there, over the far end of the defile, he saw the little valley he had left that afternoon: his own valley, with the cottage and its heaped-up roof.

Holding the still body of the crow against his chest, Sparrow sped homewards.

return to copperhill

IN THE DUSK OF THAT SAME EVENING KITTEL SAT BY THE Cold Stone, waiting. The lights were twinkling in the valley below and the Old Road was a pale band, glimmering between rock walls and low bushes off up into the mountains.

The only sounds were the occasional calling of a lamb from down in the fields round the village or the call of a curlew somewhere above; and all the time there was the soft, restless tinkle of water falling into the stone trough at the Cold Stone's foot.

Kittel was waiting for her friend, Lissie Clodish, who was coming back with her father from the next village. Lissie had been staying in Villas for the last three days. A visit by one of the young people of Copperhill to one of the other villages was something which had not happened before. This one had come about after a terrible row between Lissie's mother and father about his work as a

Trader, and it was all being kept very secret.

"There are four other villages in the Mountains," Kittel announced one day to her class in school, to gasps of disbelief. "Sparrow has been to them all."

"What are they like? What are they like?" came from all sides of the schoolroom.

"They're just like ours. They're not very interesting," Sparrow assured them. But it made no difference – now everyone wanted to see them. It was a far bigger sensation than when Kittel had spoken about astronomy and people having been on the moon.

The only problem was the parents. No one's parents would talk about the other villages, or even admit they existed. A couple of boys were beaten for mentioning them. One girl was stopped from coming to school altogether.

204

As a Trader, Lissie's father, Don Clodish, regularly made journeys to Villas, Drakewater, and even Springing Wood and Uplands, bringing back glass and scythes and salt in exchange for the copper pans and distilling vats which were made in Copperhill. But no one would talk about the Traders either. Lissie's mother simply pretended she didn't know what her husband did for a living.

"It's so silly!" Kittel laughed. "I just can't believe it. It's like long ago, when they wouldn't believe the earth was round."

"I know," Lissie said, hanging her head. "But you can't do anything about it."

"They're all mad," said Kittel scornfully.

"You'll have to be careful, Kittel," said Lissie. "People are starting to talk about you. I can't talk about school with my mum any more. I'm sure there's going to be trouble."

"Stupid," Kittel snorted.

*   *   *

The dim cloppity-clop-clop of hoofs echoed down towards her from a distant bend. In a while the dark shapes of two horses appeared and came slowly down the road.

"Whoa! I almost missed you there, Kittel," came Don Clodish's voice. "Had you fallen asleep?"

Kittel got up and smiled. Lissie scrambled down from in front of him on the leading horse. "The poem first!" she said, holding up her finger.

Cut in the stone of the little water trough were the words:

> Take of my water
> Enough for your need;
> Then onward, true-hearted,
> I bid you good-speed.

205

Before Kittel had arrived in Copperhill, no one had been able to read the words at the base of the Cold Stone; now Lissie made a point of reading them aloud whenever she passed. Lissie was fond of rhymes.

"Hello, Kittel," she said when she had finished. Her eyes were shining in the dark.

"What was it like?" Kittel said.

Lissie sighed. "It was wonderful – oh, I just can't tell you what it was like… There was this boy… and there was the dog, Boffin, and a house all covered with yellow roses, and a ruin in the garden – I want us to move and live there – and great oak forests, and the garden's really big and there's a pool with these enormous holly trees – it's called the Hollywell – and Ormand's mum doesn't bother about anything and – did I tell you there was this boy called Ormand…?" She broke off and sighed again.

They walked along behind the two tall horses, all mis-shapen in the twilight with their bags and bundles. The road came down to the apple orchards on the edge of the village, then climbed again past the foot of the three round hillocks of Overton.

They parted there, and Kittel climbed on up the path to the house on the top of the nearest hill. In the kitchen, Murie was bad-temperedly washing dishes. She was bad tempered because she was worrying about Sparrow not being home and she had broken a plate as a result.

But Kittel had barely begun to help her when Sparrow ran into the house with his hair wild and his eyes wide.

Murie rounded on him. "Where have you been?" she demanded. "I've been worried to death!"

"He – He – Herold –" Sparrow panted in return, ignoring her question. "Something's happened to him!"

Murie looked with distaste at the ragged bundle of feathers in Sparrow's hands. She didn't care much for crows, however interesting and intelligent Sparrow might claim they were. "He looks all right to me," she said. "As cheeky as ever, anyway."

"What?" said Sparrow in surprise, and held his dark handful up to the light. Herold's eye winked at him maliciously. "Herold!" he exclaimed. "I thought you were dead!"

The great beak snapped a few times and the eye rolled anxiously in Murie's direction. Herold was convinced that Murie had murder in her eyes.

Sparrow hurried out – not that he really thought Murie would try to murder Herold – and Kittel followed him, anxious to hear what had happened. Murie, grumbling to herself, returned to the sink. She didn't really want to know where Sparrow had been; she found his doings too dizzying anyway, and the main thing was that he was back.

Kittel was just in time to see Sparrow release the crow, who flew up to the nearest treetop, squawking with indignation. Sparrow told Kittel of his strange adventure in the gully, and the message he had been given by the otter; but long before they had got anywhere near understanding what it was all about, Murie called to Sparrow that he might at least come and eat the supper she'd made, even if he didn't intend telling her where he'd been.

The next day there was school. Lissie wasn't there; and Sparrow fidgeted and couldn't settle to anything. A couple of times Kittel told him to get out if he wasn't going to take part. He didn't go.

School was definitely not what it used to be. It couldn't be, when the teacher was no older than the older pupils. To start with, when she had first become the teacher over a year before, Kittel had tried Ms Minn's old method of standing up in front of the class and telling them things. It was Lissie who had changed all that. Lissie was a great mimic, as well as liking rhymes. (She could do Ms Redwall's turned-up nose, pushed-out bottom and snooty voice quite beautifully.) One day she had got up in the class and done such a perfect imitation of Kittel's teacher-ish, rather bossy, manner that everyone was soon rolling about in helpless laughter. Kittel had been a little offended, but things had become a good deal more relaxed after that, and Kittel and Lissie became close friends.

When Lissie had done her famous Kittel-imitation, she had spoken a little nonsense rhyme, which went:

Honey is sour and vinegar's sweet
If I were a cow I'd never eat meat;
A wheel is square and a brick is round
If I were a fish I'd never get drowned.

Everyone loved it. "Go on, do some more," they urged her,
and Lissie added another rhyme that came into her head:

So when you're sorry and want some fun
Fling a bucket of water up to the sun,
Then all join hands, with winks and grins
And shout like mad when the rain begins!

There was an uproar of delight. The two rhymes were put
together, a tune was found for them, and "Lissie's Song"
became the basis for a wet and rowdy playground game.

So far, no one had interfered with the youngsters at
school. Most of the parents were grateful to Kittel for taking
their little ones off their hands now that old Ms Minn had
gone. But Lissie was right – there were murmurings. Ms
Redwall seemed to be constantly hanging round the school
these days, though she always made it look as though she
had just stopped for a chat with someone or other. Not long
after she had first decided that "something ought to be
done" about Kittel, she had persuaded her sister to remove
her son – Gogs – from the school. It was "not nice", she
said, for the lad to be taught by a girl of his own age, especially when dear Ms Minn had been taken from them so
tragically. Next on her list was her neighbour, Lissie's
mother, who, thanks to Ms Redwall, now firmly believed
that Kittel was trying to turn the children against their
parents.

"Why does she always have to be around?" said Bull as he left the school with Sparrow and Kittel at the end of the day. He stared rudely at Ms Redwall as they passed her, turning his head to go on staring behind him as they went on up the road. As Bull had piercing blue eyes and frowning black brows, a stare from him was quite impressive, and Ms Redwall was left flushing and muttering about the manners of the school children now that they didn't have a real teacher. Bull laughed. "My gran says that if there was a prize for stupidity she'd even come ahead of the donkeys," he said.

Bull's house was on the middle one of the three rounded hillocks which the village people called Overton: there was Overton itself, where Sparrow and Kittel lived, then Hind – Bull's home – then Westward, which was where Ms Redwall's sister lived. Bull always went home with Sparrow and Kittel. When they were out of the village and under the row of elms where Herold spent most of his time, Sparrow began to tell Bull about his strange experience of the day before. Bull was a good person to turn to when you had a problem: he listened carefully and thought deeply, and even if he couldn't come up with a new way of looking at the problem himself, he could go and get his grandmother's advice. And that was normally the best advice you could get anywhere in the village.

As if to back up Sparrow's story, Herold came fluttering down from his tree like an old leaf in a storm. In fact his flying was so bad today he did a complete somersault before landing half on, half off Sparrow's shoulder.

Sparrow waited patiently as the crow scrabbled back into position beside his ear. "What's wrong?" he said. "Why are you flying so queerly?"

The crow rasped and rattled in reply.

"Where's it gone?" Sparrow asked.

"What's he saying? Where's what gone?" Kittel broke in impatiently.

"His trailing edge," said Sparrow. "He says it's missing."

"His wha— ?" Kittel was beginning, when Herold burst into a fresh series of excited squeaks and clicks, and stretched one of his wings out in front of Sparrow's eyes. Sparrow had to grab hold of it to stop the crow toppling off again. Then he stared. "Look at that," he said.

There was a half-moon of feathers missing from the edge of the wing. From the look of them, they could only have been chewed off. In his mind's eye, Sparrow saw the pearly teeth of the linden lady sinking into the piece of meat. He shivered. "I'm sorry, Herold," he said. "I don't know what happened. We're trying to think what to do."

The crow subsided, though the wiffling noise that came from his closed beak was almost a hiss.

They were interrupted just then by Gogs, who quite often found an excuse to come down the road about the time school was coming out. Although he had never been terribly good at things like reading and arithmetic, he missed being with his friends since he had been stopped from going to the school. He was carrying a twisted bit of rusty iron on his shoulder and holding another in his hand. His curly red hair was a shade darker than usual, as though he had been under a shower of rust. Which was pretty well where he had been. "It's off the ridge-plough," he explained with one of his broad grins. "It broke. We were putting in turnips. I've to take it to the smiddy."

His eyes grew round with amazement when he heard Sparrow's story. "What will you do?" he asked. It was

210

never any use asking Gogs for advice.

The others were silent.

"Why should an otter know anything about it anyway?" Kittel said.

"Otters eat fish," Bull said. "My gran says that anything that eats fish gets wise."

"Even so," said Kittel, who didn't take the sayings of Bull's grandmother all that seriously.

"You should do what it said," said Bull. "You should take the shape of your stone."

Sparrow fingered the rough pyramid-shape of the shrunken mountain in his pouch. "I have," he said. "It doesn't make any difference; it's just like being changed into any other shape."

"Wait till you can see the Pole Star," said Bull. "Then try it."

"That's a good idea," said Gogs. "You should try that." He made his piece of iron more comfortable on his shoulder and prepared to go on down into the village. "There's something going on," he said. "My aunt's got Plato Smithers to hold a big meeting in the hall. She's been round everyone telling them they have to go to it. They won't say what it's about – but she found out about Lissie's dad taking her off to what's-its-name and she just about took a purple fit. I'll let you know if I hear any more."

As the others were thinking more about Herold's wing and linden ladies just then, they didn't find this piece of news as alarming as they should have done.

Kittel arranged to be back with Sparrow when the stars came out, and then went over to hear all about Lissie's adventure in Villas. However, apart from sighing rapturously every time she mentioned the boy, Ormand, Lissie was more concerned about what had been happening since her return to Copperhill. It seemed that something had snapped in her mother after the row about her father's work and then his taking Lissie with him on his travels. Worse still, Ms Redwall had lost no time in discovering the shameful secret of their trip to Villas.

"She was there," Lissie told Kittel. "I mean, waiting in the living room with my mum. They were like a couple of china cats. We were caught red-handed. Dad looked like a little boy that's been nabbed stealing apples. It was much worse for him – I didn't really care."

"What did they say?"

"They? Mum didn't say anything. It was old Redbottom that did the talking. Honestly, Kittel, she's completely taken over the house. And Mum's gone really queer. The way she looks at you … I think she's going mad, I'm not joking."

"What did they say?" Kittel said again.

"Oh, I don't know. All this stuff about being corrupted and 'seeing things that no young person should see', and how they weren't true-blooded human beings in the other villages – you wouldn't believe it, honestly. So I said I'd kissed Ormand and he felt quite human to me. I didn't really, I just said it to shock them. Old Redbottle just about expired, I really thought she'd had it!"

"Pity she hadn't," Kittel said thoughtfully, remembering Gog's news.

"Anyway, Dad's off again tomorrow," Lissie went on. "He said I shouldn't miss school again. But I'm worried Mum'll do something drastic when he's not there to keep an eye on me."

"Like what?"

Lissie shrugged.

*   *   *

When Kittel got back home, Sparrow was already waiting in the bedroom, straining his eyes into the pale northern sky, which could be seen from the window. Peering out through the whiskery thatch, gradually their eyes could make out the elusive pinpricks that were the stars. Five here, seven there, and one lonely light in a great space of sky – Cassiopeia and the Great Bear, following each other ceaselessly around the Pole Star.

"All right?" said Sparrow.

"Let me light the candle first," said Kittel quickly.

"Why? You won't see the stars so easily."

"We don't need to now," said Kittel; "we know they're there. I don't want to be left alone in the dark."

"I'll be right here!" Sparrow exclaimed – Kittel seemed to be behaving very queerly. "I'm only changing into the stone."

"You're supposed to be looking for Puckel – and I don't know what'll happen to you when you turn into the stone."

Sparrow realized she might have a point. The fact was that, with Puckel, it was difficult to know exactly where you were. The weird, wild old man, whom Sparrow had met in the mountains, was an uncertain and magical person. Sparrow and Kittel had helped him in an attempt to recapture the dragon – indeed, the last they had seen of him was locked in desperate combat with the terrible creature, spinning off up into the higher reaches of the sky. Towards the Pole Star? It was possible.

"I'll be right here," Sparrow said again, all the same. "Nothing's going to happen – it never has before."

Nevertheless he went downstairs and lit a candle at the kitchen fire. He brought it back and put it on the little table at his bedside. For a moment, a monstrous shadow of his head flickered on the sloping ceiling of the room as a draught caught the candle flame. Then the room brightened – the shadow, and Sparrow, were gone.

Kittel waited, and watched. Kittel, too, had a remarkable gift, though as far as she knew no one had given it to her – at least not in the way Sparrow had been given his gifts by Puckel. Kittel could see through shape-changes. Sparrow had never been able to hide from her by taking another thing's shape. Just now she could see him within the stone's shape, still gazing out northwards. What else *could* have happened? A puff and a bang, and Puckel appearing? It was no different from times before, it was just like changing into any other thing's shape.

214

"It's no use, Sparrow," she said. "Nothing's going to happen. You'd better change back."

The candle flickered a little from her breath. There was no answer from Sparrow.

"Sparrow?" said Kittel. "Can you hear me?"

Something had happened after all. Kittel waited. An hour, maybe, until her eyelids grew heavy and she found she had nodded off to sleep.

The candle guttered. She opened the drawer to take out another, but there was none there. Sparrow was always running out. It was at times like this that she longed for an electric light with a switch near to hand. By the time she had carried the candle through to her own room, it had gone out. She hesitated, then groped her way to her bed and settled herself to sleep.

The morning sun woke her. She leaped up and ran back through to Sparrow's room. The stone was still on the table where it had been before. Sparrow was still in its shape, gazing northwards.

Kittel turned it round. Sparrow went on staring. She didn't like to leave it there. Murie didn't know about it and might throw it out – anyway, she felt uneasily that she ought to keep an eye on it. She told Murie Sparrow had left early in the morning but that she was expecting him at school in time. That was true, in a way. She did Sparrow's jobs as well as her own, and set off for school herself.

Lissie was not at school again, although she had said she would be. Sparrow stayed in the stone's shape all day. Kittel's anxiousness grew. After school she screwed up her courage, and went and knocked at the door of Lissie's house.

Lissie's mother appeared. She looked wild and dishevelled and grey, which shocked Kittel considerably; Ms Clodish was the neatest and most house-proud person in the village. She didn't seem to look at Kittel but somewhere over her shoulder. She seized a broom that was beside the door and brandished it at Kittel's feet. "Out," she said. "All dirt goes out – out – out!" Then she slammed the door again. Kittel could only hope Lissie had gone with her father after all.

In the evening of the next day – the day after the meeting – Kittel slunk down to the village square and stood listening amongst the linden trees outside the hall. There were murmurings of a crowd of people inside, but she could make nothing out. The stone rams' heads glared down balefully at her from the gables.

Kittel went miserably home. She had had to tell Murie what had happened with Sparrow so that Murie wouldn't send out search parties. Now Murie was as worried and jumpy as she was. They quarrelled, and went to bed early. Kittel kept the stone by her bedside, and Sparrow went on staring.

The next morning, only about half of the school turned up. There were none of the little ones, and of the older ones only those who lived on the edge of the village – like Bull, who had come down the road with her.

"Well," Kittel said when they realized that as many children as would be coming had come, "I said I would tell you what I know about evolution, so that's what I'll do. Where I come from, everyone says that people came down from monkeys. But Sparrow says a very, very old rat once told him that people had come from rats. Anyway—"

"Where is Sparrow?" asked one of the children.

"He's – he's away just now," Kittle stammered. "For a – a little. He'll be back soon. Anyway, I was saying—"

She never got any further, because at that moment the classroom door opened and Ms Redwall swept in, followed by the huge form of Plato Smithers. Everyone stared in silence.

Ms Redwall sailed to the front of the class, but Plato Smithers hung back, looming in the doorway and looking a little embarrassed. Kittel suspected that the big man had never been in front of a class before and was feeling he ought to try and squeeze in at one of the desks.

Ms Redwall placed herself almost on top of Kittel, who stepped back. "All right, Mr Smithers," she said. "Do your duty."

Smithers shuffled forwards towards Kittel. He was holding his felt hat in his hands and wringing it repeatedly as though it were soaking wet. "Well, miss, it's like this," he said, looking at Kittel's feet. "We need you to make a promise, you see…"

The sight of the huge man being so bashful about speaking to a young girl was making the class whisper and giggle. Ms Redwall drew herself up, quelled them with a terrible stare, then turned towards Kittel. "Continue, Mr Smithers," she said coldly.

"Well," Plato Smithers went on, "if you can make this promise and keep it, well, everything will be all right. But if you can't make it, then I'm afraid that this village just isn't the place for you. We know you've said you can't remember where you came from, but—"

"But we think that a couple of nights out alone in the mountains will soon bring your memory back," Ms Redwall put in. And she shuddered till her pink double chins were shaking too.

Kittel swallowed. "What is the promise?" she asked.

"Well," Plato Smithers said, "you must promise not to speak to any of the young ones in the village again."

"How old do they have to be before I can speak to them?" Kittel asked innocently.

Her simple question threw Plato Smithers into such confusion that he was left quite speechless. He was not a man who thought very quickly – nor was he a harsh man.

But Ms Redwall was there for that very reason. "Doesn't that just prove everything I said about her?" she hissed. "Cool as a cucumber, isn't she? Have you ever seen such ice-cold impertinence? And don't think it doesn't spread, my word, no…" She looked as though she thought Kittel the most hateful, dangerous thing she had ever seen.

However, here Kittel saved Plato Smithers from further awkwardness. She wanted out of the whole horrible situation. Smithers she could stand, but this Redwall woman

217

gave her the creeps. "All right," she said hurriedly, "I promise. But I'd like to say goodbye to some of my friends if I'm not to speak to them again."

Plato Smithers didn't look at Ms Redwall – probably, Kittel thought, in case she made him say no. "That seems quite reasonable to me, miss," he said. "Just you go ahead and do that." He seemed relieved.

But now Kittel sprang her surprise. "Thank you," she said politely. "And, just so that you know I'll be keeping my promise, I'll do the other thing you want, too. I'll leave the village."

In the stunned silence that followed this announcement, Kittel, holding herself very straight, walked out of the school.

the pole tower

To begin with, turning into the stone was like all the other times he had tried it before. Sparrow felt his pyramid-shape, his coldness, his hardness, the slight confusion from not needing to breathe any more, the inner silence that came because there was no blood rushing round his body. There was nothing new in all that.

But he couldn't see Kittel, and he should have been able to; in fact, he couldn't see any of his bedroom. In the form of a stone he could normally see all round him at once. Now, he could see nothing – no bedroom, no Kittel, no candlelight. It panicked him, and he tried to change back to his own shape, but couldn't. Nothing happened. He was alone, in darkness. Could Kittel see him? Even if she could, how would she know he was in trouble?

Sparrow's panic didn't last. Stones aren't made to panic. After a moment or two, he began to do what stones always do, which is wait.

At last – whether it was sooner or later he couldn't tell, because stones don't feel quick or slow either – there was light again, the tiny, distant light of a star: the Pole Star, in the midst of an empty space of sky. Rapidly it grew brighter. Soon it was as bright as a clear, freezing night of winter, and it grew brighter yet. It was twice – five times – as bright as the Pole Star ought to be. Ten times. There were no other stars to be seen, but gradually a pale mist seemed to form round this one, to become brighter, to glow like starlight. The mist took on edges. It was a spiral, a glowing, silver spiral that slowly turned about the Pole Star...

Sparrow was approaching the edge of the spiral – whether walking or floating, and whether from below or above, he could not tell. Whichever it was, he had reached the outer arm of it. It was turning in his direction; that is, he found himself moving along the spiral arm. It was like travelling along a road of glimmering mist.

On and on he went, until he realized from his circling motion that he must be near the centre of the spiral. Did that mean he was approaching the Pole? There seemed to be something ahead of him, though there was no longer any sign of the star. There was a faint blue light, but most of the thing – whatever it was – was black as midnight.

Then Sparrow realized – or had come close enough to see – that what he was approaching was a tower – a peculiarly-shaped tower, thin at top and bottom, fatter in the middle, like an elongated egg. There was a single lighted window. He must have been floating, he thought, for next moment he was at the window, peering in, with his nose pressed against a cold pane of thick, bumpy glass.

Because the glass was so bumpy, it was hard to make anything out at first. There seemed to be a small, bare room with a bed, some shelves, and a small, round table. But next moment – coming towards him with a strange, waving motion because of the uneven glass – he saw Puckel.

It was so strange, seeing the old man so unexpectedly after so long! And so frustrating, too, because although he was quite close, the glass of the window made him seem almost as distant as if Sparrow were looking at him through the wrong end of a bad telescope. Yet there was nothing strange, or distant, about the croaky old voice that snapped right in his ear. "That took you long enough," Puckel said.

The old man was unchanged. His wild white hair still looked as though several bird's nests might be concealed in it; his brown skin still looked like an old leather purse that had lain in water and then dried in the sun; and even through that glass, there was no mistaking those piercing, wild green eyes that were like living pools among the rocks. In his hand he held the curious, gnarled stick he always had – even more twisted than usual, because of the glass – and on his face Sparrow could make out the familiar scowl that he had long ago decided Puckel must put on to stop himself bursting out into uncontrollable laughter.

The only thing that was different about him was his cloak. The shabby old green and brown thing he had always worn, that smelled of must and mushrooms and sometimes looked more tatters than cloak, was gone. In its place Puckel wore a splendid, sweeping coat of dark blue with silver embroidery around the collar and cuffs, and a coiling silver brooch. He would have looked very magnificent if he had not seemed so out of place in it: its splendour just made him look more like an old tramp than ever.

Sparrow tried to ignore the old man's complaint. "I like your new coat," he said.

221

"Stuff and nonsense," Puckel snorted. Although Sparrow could barely see his mouth moving because of the distorting glass, the voice was as clear as if the pair of them had been sitting next to each other.

"It's very grand," Sparrow persisted.

"Absolutely unnecessary. It was part of the agreement, and if you ask me, calculated to make a donkey out of me."

"What agreement?" Sparrow enquired.

"I came to an agreement with the dragon."

"You mean you didn't beat the dragon?"

"You don't really beat dragons," Puckel said carelessly; "at best, you try to knock 'em about a bit so that you can make an arrangement with them. That's what I've done. It's a nuisance, and it keeps me tied up here, but at least it keeps him out of mischief. Someone would need to call his name out before he could get back to earth – but no one knows his name, so it doesn't matter."

As Puckel said this, Sparrow thought he turned a strangely searching glance on him – though it was difficult to tell through that thick glass. "Where is the dragon?" he asked, glancing anxiously over his shoulder.

"You came in along his tail," Puckel said.

"I came here along a sort of road of mist," Sparrow said.

"You came along his tail," Puckel repeated firmly. "Young man, it's time you learned a bit more about what's what. What took you so long, anyway?"

"Well, I didn't know how to find you!" Sparrow exclaimed indignantly. "I didn't even know if you wanted me to find you."

"What do you think I left that lump of rock behind for, then?" Puckel demanded.

"I found it by accident!" Sparrow protested. "I thought

you'd forgotten it."

"Hmph!" Puckel snorted.

"What's happening?" Sparrow exclaimed, for the glass seemed to have begun to move, like thick water, and Puckel and the room began to waver and pull out of shape.

"It's because we were talking about you-know-who," came Puckel's voice, as the room seemed to make an effort to straighten itself out again. "It's difficult enough to get him to sleep up here in the ordinary course of things – so as soon as we start talking about him he moves in his sleep. Better tell me what you have to tell me before we get dragged out of shape altogether – or he wakes up."

Sparrow told Puckel about his meeting with the linden lady and the otter. As he spoke, Puckel and the room in the tower became reasonably clear again, though every so often a corner of what he could see would start drifting off into a swirl of colour.

223

"Hm," Puckel grunted when he had finished. "You brought all that on yourself, so don't ask me for sympathy."

"How?" Sparrow gasped.

"By trying to get to Kittel's place out of time, of course. There's a time for you to get to Kittel's place and a time to stay put. It was a false move. You've a lot of things to learn before you can make that journey."

"But I thought—" Sparrow began.

"What you thought," Puckel interrupted, "was based on some nonsense that crazy old schoolteacher told you about a wall of dragon's breath that no one could get past. Well, I've news for you: it's a lot more complicated than that, and as I say, you've a lot of things to learn first – like the Secret Way of the Mountains, and the secret of the Hollywell…"

"The Secret Way of the Mountains," Sparrow murmured after him, remembering that these were the very words the otter had used.

"…these things are needed," Puckel was saying, "because the Polymorphs have to be controlled. All that about a stone being moved from where it should be to where it shouldn't be just means the Polymorphs have upset the balance between the Star Wheel and the Vault of the Bear. That throws the whole balance out and it'll lead to disaster if it's not checked soon."

"And what—" Sparrow began again.

"The Polymorphs, boy," Puckel interrupted in a low, solemn voice, "are masters of the dragon's dreaming."

Sparrow felt his own voice sinking to a whisper. "And what's that?" he asked. He had always found talk of the dragon's dreams unsettling.

"Mind-stuff, that's what – all that comes into your mind; the rock that feels hard to your hand and the hand that feels the rock. The wind that blows from the way you're facing to the emptiness that's behind you. It's all there because that's how you think it. All things are made of thought. These masters of the dreaming are quicker than thought; they break up the way you expect the world to be and puff! the world vanishes like smoke, and you're left with chaos – madness."

Sparrow had an inspiration. "Like the skewered meat and Herold's wing!" he said.

"Exactly like that," Puckel nodded sagely. "Things would all swim together if the balance moved too much in the Polymorphs' favour. The dish would run away with the spoon. It's no laughing matter. Up to now we have kept the Polymorphs in check – I, and those who work with me. Now we can't any more, because I'm stuck up here with my pet lizard."

"So how can you set the balance right, now?" Sparrow asked.

"I need you to control them," Puckel said.

Sparrow thought back to his encounter with the linden lady. Yes, he thought – perhaps, with the shrunken mountain, he could learn to control them…

"You needn't start thinking along those lines," Puckel said sharply, as though he guessed Sparrow's thoughts. "They're a lot trickier than you think. They take many forms; they can be in many places at once; they are not easy to master. You had a very close shave with the creature you met. The food it offered you was the shape you were in – the crow's shape. If you had eaten it, you would have been eating your own chosen shape. You would have vanished. You would have been in limbo. It could have happened."

Sparrow listened in horror. "Is that what she was trying to do to me?" he asked.

"I suppose you thought you were living in some sort of mountain wonderland where nothing bad ever happened," said Puckel. He sighed, and then spoke more gently. "Well, it might have been – once. It should have been. But things haven't been as they were meant to be in these mountains, not for many a long year now.

"It all comes back to the dragon being out of his proper place, of course. There hasn't been much we could do about that, but we've got by, in most respects. Nothing's been what you'd call satisfactory – one result which you would notice is the way the people of the different villages have fallen out of touch with each other. The Polymorphs have cast their shadow over all the lands between them. Now each village is like an island in a sea of shadow."

"But I've been going miles from the village for ages," Sparrow objected, "and nothing's ever happened to me before."

"That stone's played its part in protecting you up to now," said Puckel. "But they've just been biding their time, ever since I left the mountains. They had no reason to hurry. Now they've moved at last, and as soon as you made a false move, they were in there – like mould into a broken fruit.

"They have certain ways of trapping you. Eni and Tho get in there, under the skin, if you fall into a quarrel; Ur offers you food to eat, or hides common things in a cloak of deceit and seeming; Eych plays on your fears, and can strike you dumb or blind; Yo lies in wait if you get a swollen idea of yourself. They don't always work the same way, but these are the most common. I expect it was Ur you met. Bur it certainly wasn't: that's their leader. If you'd met Bur you'd have known about it! The six Polymorphs, with Bur their leader." He fell silent.

"What am I supposed to do then?" said Sparrow. He had started to feel very small, lost amid a world of unguessed dangers.

"Now you're talking sense," Puckel answered. "'Supposed to do' is the kind of talk I like to hear. There are two things which can be done. One – the better – would be to loose the dragon on the creatures; that would bring them to heel immediately. But of course, that's not possible…"

As he said this, Sparrow thought the old man glanced at him again, with a strange gleam in his green eyes. But he scarcely paused in what he was saying. "The other," he went on, "is to learn the Secret Way of the Mountains and

226

continue to do what I was doing until I was forced to come up here—"

"What? Me alone?" Sparrow burst out.

"Why not?" Puckel replied. "You're good enough material. Some bits missing, of course – one big one in particular. That'll need patching up to begin with."

"What part of me's missing?"

"The part you've never known, and so never missed."

Sparrow looked anxiously down at himself.

"I don't mean a bit's fallen off you, numbskull – now look what we've done…" Puckel's voice suddenly grew dimmer, and the swimming and swirling of the glass got rapidly worse.

Sparrow thought he heard Puckel saying something about his mother, but he couldn't make out what, because the old man's voice had become fuzzy and indistinct. Sparrow felt he was slipping altogether out of reach. "What bit?" he cried, as a feeling like panic began to grow in the pit of his stomach. "What bit's missing?" But there was no answer, and the swimming and swirling of shapes was going on all round him. He guessed it was the dragon moving again, and waited for things to clear. But minutes passed and there was no sign of anything he could recognize: even the swirling colours were fading, as though he were plunging gradually into deep water.

"Return as soon as maybe!" Puckel's voice seemed to call, out of a great distance, and then everything became very confused. He had a glimpse of the village hall in Copperhill, but all from the wrong angle, and Ms Redwall striding across the picture from top corner to bottom corner waving her arms about. He saw one of the stone rams' heads on the hall gable looking round and winking at him. Then there was blue sky and clouds, and the waving of Ms Redwall's arms became the flapping of a dark wing which blotted out the light.

"Look at that! Just look at that!" Herold's voice came screeching. "There's a part of me missing – there's a big part of me missing! "And Sparrow saw once again the half-moon of chewed-off feathers, only where there should have been empty space there was something like an egg stuck to the edge of the wing. "My feather!" Herold's voice screeched again. "See it? It's missing! My father, that's what that is. My father – faa – faa!"

Then complete darkness, complete silence, fell, and Sparrow found himself sobbing, and whispering through the sobs: "My father, that's what's missing. Myfather – myfather…" until all at once the breath left him and he was utterly still, waiting.

the shadow

IT WAS TWO DAYS FROM THE CLOSING OF THE SCHOOL
before Kittel saw Lissie again – two awful, anxious days in
which she stopped even peering at the stone to see if there
was any change in Sparrow. Lissie suddenly appeared at
the door. Her normally rosy cheeks were pale and she
looked gaunt and hollow-eyed.

"Where have you been?" Kittel gasped. "What's
wrong? Where's your dad?"

"He's up at Bull's gran's," Lissie said. "Oh, Kittel, it's
been awful!"

"Where were you? What happened? I thought you must
be away!"

"I was in the wash-house."

"What? Why? You mean – locked in?"

Lissie nodded. "As soon as my dad went away. She took
a hold of me and told me my clothes were filthy and I was
to get in to the wash-house and take them off. I said, they're

fine Mum, or something like that, and she went on repeating 'fine Mum, fine Mum', to everything I said. It was horrible. Then she pushed me into the wash-house and locked the door before I realized what she was doing. Then she said I was a cat and cats belong in cages."

"Did you get food?"

"She pushed it under the door."

"What about –"

"I used the boiler as a toilet, if that's what you mean. She can boil her clothes in it if she likes. I never want to go back there again – never." Lissie's voice shook, but her face remained hard. "Dad came back and let me out just now. I thought he was going to kill her. I've heard about the meeting – and the school."

"This wouldn't have happened to you if it hadn't been for the Redwall," Kittel said in a low voice.

"I don't know," Lissie said. "Mum didn't have to be like that. She didn't have to do everything Redwall said, did she?"

"Yes," Murie said when they went indoors, "a visit to Mrs Hind sounds like an excellent idea. Let's go over there right now and have a conference."

A voice spoke again at Sparrow's ear, but it was not Puckel's. This was a voice Sparrow seemed to know quite well, though he couldn't think who it belonged to. A woman's voice, perhaps…

"Once the Traders' work was honoured as it should be," the voice said. "People in Copperhill knew there wouldn't be much hay or harvest taken in if it wasn't for the fine scythe blades from Drakewater. In Springing Wood people knew they wouldn't be able to brew their fine apple spirit without the copper coils from our village. And so it went round.

"I don't know what happened. Something must have gone bad. The Traders call it the Shadow. They say the villages are like little islands in a great sea of shadow. The forests and the rivers and the mountainsides look good – but there's an unseen danger in them always there, always waiting.

"Few people know of the risks the Traders run. Once they did. When my son was killed – when his horse went wild and threw him, then turned on him and trampled him – people just said, 'Well, what do you expect with a Trader?' You can't blame them, really. Those dangers are always there. It's been known for men to go crazy and throw themselves shrieking over a cliff. I don't say that's what happened to Mistress Overton's father or her husband, for they weren't Traders, and no one knows…"

231

Because it was all so quiet inside him, Sparrow could hear everything very clearly. He had a feeling that the voice was not speaking to him; there were other people there somewhere listening to it. But where was he? And why couldn't he see anything?

"But the Traders believe they're protected," the voice was saying. "The tale's still told among them of how once – a bad time it must have been, for there were eight of them all together, for safety, up on the Old Road – all of a sudden they heard music and singing in the trees. Before they knew what was happening, they were dancing to the music and, believe it or not, their horses started dancing too. But this was no ordinary dancing. No, they were dancing up and down like dolls on a string, and they couldn't stop. They danced from noon of one day right through the night and into the afternoon of the next day.

"It seemed they must dance themselves to death – but just in time they were rescued. A man appeared, dressed all over in bright, shining copper, with a bear's head for a hood. He slashed his long, bright knife at the trees where the music was coming from, and the sound died away to a whimpering and the men and horses were able to stop their dancing. The man with the bear hood said he was the Guardian and that he was there to protect the Traders from the Danger of the Road.

"He has been seen again since then, not once but many times. We say that as long as the Traders use the road, the Guardian will be there to protect them; and as long as the Guardian's there to protect the Traders, the villages will be safe. But down in the villages no one speaks of these things any more – they pretend the other villages don't exist, they pretend they don't know what the Traders do.

"But what if, sometimes, the Guardian goes away? He wasn't there to protect my son. I remember it was in that same year – the very same year that Mistress Overton's husband went missing – the apple blossom fell early from the trees and there were no apples that autumn. I say the Shadow came into the village that year, even though it went away again. Perhaps that's what's happening now with that donkey-of-a-neighbour of yours, Don."

Then a man's voice said, "Yet there's been no sign of anything wrong up on the Road – else I'd never have taken Lissie."

Then Sparrow realized who the speaker was. The man who was killed by the horse was Bull's father, which meant that it was Bull's grandmother speaking – and obviously she

232

was speaking to Don Clodish. But how was he hearing her?

With an effort, he realized that he was again in the shape of the stone – if he had ever been out of it. "Polymorphs!" he exclaimed, and changed back into himself.

"Sparrow! Where did you come from? Where have you been?" seemed to burst from half a dozen people all round him. He seemed to be sitting, gazing into a small, bright fire. Then –

"Ow! Get off!" a voice bellowed in his ear, and a hefty shove landed him crack on a wooden floor. He looked up, bewildered, and realized straight away that he must have been sitting on Kittel's knee when he took his own shape again. They weren't alone, and they weren't in Sparrow's bedroom. They were in the kitchen of Bull's house, and apart from Kittel, there was Mrs Hind herself, Bull, Don Clodish, Murie and Lissie.

233

"How did I get here?" Sparrow said, rubbing the leg he had fallen on.

"I brought you," Kittel said, "in my pocket." She seemed unaccountably angry. "And don't you ever do a thing like that to me again!"

"Or me," Murie put in, from the other side of the room.

"What do you mean?" Sparrow said. "What have I done?"

"What have you done?" Kittel railed. "Oh, only been away for five days and nights. Only left us thinking you'd be nothing but a lump of rock for the rest of your life."

"I was just away for a few minutes," Sparrow protested, uncomfortably aware that Mrs Hind and Don Clodish, who knew nothing about Sparrow's shape-changing, were looking rather confused.

"I can assure you Kittel is quite right," Murie said; "and I'm beginning to think your tricks are getting just a bit dangerous and out of hand."

Kittel realized that Sparrow was anxious not to discuss his magical doings in front of everyone; and despite her anger, she changed the subject, though with a look that plainly warned: "you've not heard the last from me!" What she said out loud was, "Anyway, you couldn't have chosen a better time to be away."

"Why?" said Sparrow. "What's happened?"

"Oh, nothing much," said Kittel, "except that the school's been closed, and I've been told to get out of the village."

"*What*!?" exclaimed Sparrow, unable to believe his ears. "But – how – how – what – they can't…"

"We'll have to go to the cottage," said Sparrow after everything had been explained to him. "We'll get Kittel home to her place, then I'll come back here. If they don't want a teacher, they don't have to have one." Sparrow had already forgotten Puckel's warning about the time having to be right.

"And how long will it take you to find how to get to Kittel's place?" said Murie.

Sparrow shrugged.

"What about the winter?" Bull said, taking up Murie's question. "It's all right going for a picnic in the mountains, but what if you have to spend a long time searching for a way? Supposing you're still searching in October? How will you manage then, when the bad weather starts and Kittel's not allowed to come back to the village? You'd die out there in the mountains."

"I could come with you," Don Clodish said unexpectedly. "Lissie would come too. We'd been going to leave here and go to Villas, but it's all one really. If we did that, we could help prepare the house for the winter, and Kittel could come back to it if she couldn't find her way home."

"I'll come as well," said Bull; "I want to help too."

"You need to stay and look after your gran," Don Clodish said.

After much argument, both on that day and the next, it was agreed that Murie and Gogs should be the ones who would go with Sparrow and Kittel to the Valley of Murmuring Water. Murie, who was feeling a little impatient with the talk of invisible shadows and guardians who couldn't be relied on to do much guarding, simply felt so angry with the people of Copperhill that she wanted to leave the village and would have been quite happy never to come back. Gogs particularly wanted to come because his family was divided over the whole business of Kittel. His mother was standing by her sister, and had never cared much for Kittel anyway. His father, like many others, was deeply shocked at the decision to put Kittel out of the village. He secretly encouraged Gogs to go with Sparrow's party because he believed it would do a lot of damage to Ms Redwall's cause if her own nephew left the village in support of Kittel.

Murie was leaving the house for Bull to look after. Bull was none too happy at being left behind, but he saw that he couldn't leave his grandmother without help. Murie's hens were to be left behind, but the cow and the goats were to go with them, and they were also to take two large bags of meal, gardening tools and vegetables to plant. It was all a bit hare-brained, but Murie thought that if they worked hard to begin with, they might just manage. "If we run out, Sparrow will just have to fly back and steal some more," she said.

235

Don Clodish decided that things would not remain safe for himself or Lissie with Ms Redwall right next door, so he decided to go on with his plan to leave Copperhill with Lissie and settle in Villas.

There was a painful parting between Kittel and Lissie. The two friends realized they might never see each other again, however things turned out. Both girls felt, in their different ways, that they were being forced to leave the village. Lissie didn't think her father would ever come back to live at Copperhill.

"He's going to rebuild the ruined house in Ormand's garden," she said. "He says he'll have to come back for Mum when it's ready, because he doesn't think she'll be able to look after herself, the way she's going. Perhaps he's right, I don't know. I hate her – I really do – but I suppose we can't just abandon her."

236

Kittel said nothing, and Lissie fell silent too. Now that the thing had actually happened, neither of them wanted to say the word "mad".

As Lissie watched her friend walking off under the elms by the street out of the village, she felt that the whole world she had known was coming to an end. "Well, that just leaves Ormand," she told herself; and the thought of his surprised-looking eyes, under his cap of fuzzy brown hair, comforted her.

On the morning of the fourth day after Ms Redwall's meeting, Sparrow, Kittel, Murie and Gogs, along with the cow and the goat and its kid, set off on their journey into the mountains. They each had a heavy pack to carry, while the cow was laden as well, and the goat, much to its disgust, was harnessed to the small goat sledge.

It was a grey, drizzly morning, and none of them felt in the least adventurous – apart from the kid, which did mountaineering exploits on its mother's back. They looked back at the low, white house with its rain-darkened thatch and dripping eaves, and the cloak of grey cloud behind it, and seemed to feel the same grey coldness inside them. The house meant everything that was safe and warm and secure, that they were leaving behind.

From his flights in crow-form, Sparrow now knew the way well, and their journey through the forest, if slow and soaking, was uneventful – apart from troubles with the goat. Occasionally Sparrow had to unhitch it from the sledge so that he could fly, with the various sacks and bundles, over some particularly rough part of the ground. He could do this quite easily, as he never felt the weight of anything he carried when he was flying, but after he had finished there would be a mad chase as they tried to recapture the sulky creature. A couple of times Sparrow had to take its shape in order to bring it back to the harness, and then had to endure the goat hissing reproaches at him under its breath for the next half-hour.

Not long after lunchtime on the second day, the grey clouds broke up, and pale blue sky, then sparkling sunlight, followed. It was at that stage that Herold caught up with them. Sparrow had been feeling very pleased with himself for having given the crow the slip, because Herold was bound to object to him and Kittel flying off to search out her way home. He realized he should have known better. "Now I'm for it," he muttered as the crow descended on them with a triumphant squawk.

Herold perched on the branch of a tree and gave Sparrow a long harangue on the virtues of loyalty and steadfastness. Although the others couldn't understand his speech, it was obvious that Sparrow was getting a good scolding. When they laughed, Herold got so infuriated that he lost his balance and finished up on the next branch down. There, he took a deep breath, stuck his beak in the air and, taking on an expression of great dignity, told Sparrow he had decided to return to the home of his fathers and that it was a mere accident that they were going the same way.

Sparrow took a biscuit from his pouch and crumbled it. "Would you like something to eat?" he said.

Herold accepted this offer promptly, but refused to eat from Sparrow's hand like – he said – a pet parrot. He stood by his word, too, and didn't journey with them. Sparrow wondered if this new mood would last long enough for him to be able to get away with Kittel, when the time came.

238

Near the end of the fourth day from leaving Copperhill they arrived at Sparrow's cottage.

No one found the valley very welcoming, even after three nights in the open. The cottage looked like a gigantic bee-skep in the twilight, rearing up in the gloom of an alien place. Even the fragrance of lush grass and meadowsweet and sun-warmed pine that filled the air seemed unfamiliar and threatening.

Sparrow creaked open the massive, five-cornered door. It was pitch dark inside, but he easily found his way to the corner where the bedding material was piled. It had to be spread out rather, as there were four of them and not two as he had originally expected; but they had brought blankets, and no one could deny that it was the cosiest night they had spent since leaving Copperhill.

* * *

Plato Smithers was now finding little time for his work as a stonemason. He seemed to spend all his days cramped in the little room at the back of the village hall where he had his office. The room was barely big enough for him to sit at the broad oak desk with his legs stretched out, and the only times he really liked it were when he had a bottle of parsnip wine to keep him company. But there wasn't much chance of that these days, as the reason why he was being kept busy in his office was that Ms Redwall kept pestering him. Ms Redwall didn't approve of his drinking parsnip wine.

On this particular morning, just over a week after her famous meeting, she had been in to tell him that as the children of the village were now desperately in need of proper schooling, she was prepared, "for the good of the community", to take over the school where Ms Minn had left off a year and a half ago. Smithers said he would "think about it".

Plato Smithers had found Kittel a puzzle ever since she had arrived in the village. He was inclined to think that she really came from one of the other villages, whatever she might say, and that her stories of a world of incredible machines and huge cities were mere make-believe. On the other hand, there was the question of her amazing knowledge. There was no doubt she had taught the youngsters how to read. He had even learned a word himself. Up on a dusty shelf in a corner of the office there was a television. Beside one of the buttons were some of the white squiggles which Kittel said were letters. They made the word "POWER".

Plato Smithers sighed several times and shook his head several times. This meant he was thinking.

The door opened and Bull Hind came in.

"Well, lad?" Smithers said. Ms Redwall had particularly

complained about Bull on several occasions.

"There's something you should know," said Bull. "Kittel's gone, but she hasn't gone alone."

Plato Smithers shifted uncomfortably. He had, of course, heard that Sparrow's house at Overton was empty. "Well?" he said, trying to look as though it had nothing to do with him.

"There's four of them went," Bull said; and smiled grimly as he saw Smithers' fingers moving slightly on the table: the big man was trying to count out if he had the names of four missing people.

Eventually he sat up, scratched his head, and looked hard at Bull. "Who else?"

"Gogs Westward."

You could almost hear the sound of Smithers' brain working. Then he blurted out, "But that's – her nephew!"

"That's right," said Bull, and left the room.

Smithers leaped to his feet and roared after Bull as he made his way up the side of the hall, "Where have they gone?"

Bull turned, fixed Plato Smithers with his coldest stare, and shrugged. "How should I know?" he said.

As Plato Smithers settled himself in bed that night, his none-too-quick brain was in a spin. That afternoon he had learned – through yet another of Ms Redwall's visits – that Don Clodish had left Copperhill and had taken Lissie with him again. "The whole fabric of society is collapsing!" Ms Redwall had wailed.

Smithers did not sleep that night. Never had such things happened before in his life. People didn't leave the village – especially young girls. The deep fear which the people of the village had, but never spoke about, never thought about

– the fear whose cause was only remembered by the Traders – came over him. "It wasn't right," he muttered to himself. "It wasn't right. It should never have been done…"

In the forests somewhere between the village and the Valley of Murmuring Water, a strange music was playing softly in the branches of the trees, drifting slowly westwards. Only the night creatures heard it, a meandering, unreal sort of music, sometimes like the thin, reedy music of pipes, sometimes mixed with a deeper thrumming and twanging like drawn strings. Owls shifted restlessly, the snouts of hedgehog and badger worked this way and that, as if trying to pick up an elusive scent. But there was no scent – only a pale shadow that crept about the foot of the trees or high in the topmost branches, following wherever the music led. A shadow that wavered and broke like mist, but was not mist.

Softly westwards the music and the pale shadow crept, and down through the woods of birch and rowan above the village of Copperhill, while another arm of it ran like a gentle tide along the Old Road – where Lissie and Don Clodish had gone only the day before – flowing gently at last into the great oak forests of Villas.

As the dawn came, the pale shadow faded, leaving something that the wild creatures could only sense, as animals can sense a thunderstorm or an earthquake – a feeling that something had changed, something had grown less certain, less reliable, more dangerous. Only Puckel, wandering as he once did in the forests, would have known it was a sign that the Polymorphs' power was now growing fast – though if Puckel had been there in the forests, and not trapped up among the stars, the Polymorphs would never have dared to move beyond their limits.

a test run

"COME ON, WE'VE GOT MONTHS OF WORK TO DO ALL IN A few days!"

That was the brisk message Murie woke them up with on their first morning at the cottage. She seemed to have left her normal, easy-going self at Copperhill, as they found out when she started giving them a seemingly endless list of jobs to do.

She soon had Sparrow and Gogs sweating and groaning, digging over the ground at top speed to get the vegetable seedlings planted. "We won't get much of a crop," she said, "but every little helps."

They took it in turns to stop the goats and the cow from trampling the area of grass which Murie decided would be for cutting hay – they had to have hay at all costs to keep the animals through the winter. That was the only rest any of them got, and the goats made sure it was never too restful.

In all, the four of them were working flat out for a fortnight, day after day in the growing heat of the summer. Herold came and went, but was never there long enough for Sparrow to know if he was still in disgrace or not. The crow certainly never came for food. It was a fortnight in which there was no time for anything but work, eating (never enough of that) and sleep (even less of that). There was no time for thinking. Sparrow almost forgot about Puckel and the Polymorphs and finding Kittel's home: they seemed like vague, uneasy dreams out on the edge of a world of sweat and hot sunshine and his aching back.

At the end of the fortnight, Murie said the work could now go on at a more relaxed pace. But she added that Sparrow and Kittel should set out the very next day on the next stage of their journey. Straight away, all the uncertainties and worries about the way ahead came back to Sparrow in a rush. They might be safe enough here in the Valley of Murmuring Water, but just beyond was the gully where he and Herold had been ensnared.

Sparrow had never gone against Puckel's instructions before, and the truth was he didn't really mean to now. It was just such a long time since he had spoken with Puckel. And at that time Puckel hadn't known that Kittel was going to be put out of the village – at least, Sparrow told himself that he hadn't.

He didn't tell Kittel about his worries. He did mumble that he ought to go and see Puckel, but she refused to let him. "You're not going off to see him just now, and that's all there is to it," she said. "Last time you changed into that stone we didn't see you for nearly a week. I'm not hanging about here that long every time you can't make up your own mind about something."

Kittel had had to screw herself up to go; now she was

afraid that any delay might make her change her mind. Besides, as Gogs pointed out, the quicker Kittel went, the sooner their problems would be over.

"I wish I could come too," Gogs said, "but I think I'll be needed here." Murie nodded grimly.

The following morning Murie and Gogs were out to see Sparrow and Kittel off. Murie wrapped up enough food – mostly hard little bread-biscuits and cheese to last them a good few days – and Kittel slung the package on to her front.

"Make sure you turn back when you've eaten *half* your food," Murie warned, "not the whole lot." They expected to be back again in a few days to let Murie and Gogs know how things looked. The only other thing they took with them was Sparrow's stone.

244

"Good luck," Gogs said; and "Be as quick as you can," said Murie. Herold was, thankfully, nowhere to be seen. Sparrow lifted Kittel off the ground and rose up with her into the clear, midsummer sky. Murie and Gogs watched them speed off eastwards towards the sun, rising high over the rocky ridge at the end of the valley.

"Time to start cutting hay, I think," Murie remarked to Gogs.

Sparrow was anxious to get as high as possible above the stony gully, but he need not have worried. No evil spell wrapped them round, and soon the long lake was glinting like a fat blue serpent below them.

"Whee-ee!" Sparrow called out, as a cool wind tugged at their hair and beat against their eyes. It was ages since he had last made a proper flight, and the joy and excitement of the high spaces was all coming back to him.

"Don't get too excited!" Kittel shouted over the rumbling of the air in her ears. "I don't want to join in any aerobatics!"

Beneath them the long lake came to an end in a wide waterfall that gathered itself into a stony, fast-flowing river, stretching off eastwards.

"I suppose we just keep following it!" Sparrow yelled.

"It's bound to get us out of the mountains eventually," Kittel yelled back.

But it came as a great surprise to them both how quickly the mountains ended. It was well before lunchtime when they saw one last, massive rock wall rearing up ahead of them. It was right in the path of the eastward-flowing river; but the river, which was by now broad, deep and powerful, had carved itself a deep, steep channel through it. And where it poured out at the far end (with a thundering that shook the air even where Sparrow and Kittel flew), suddenly, abruptly, the mountains stopped. Below them stretched a green land such as Sparrow had never seen before.

He circled and came down to stand on the rocky top of the ridge through which the river roared. The thunder of it made them feel the ground was dancing. The most tremendous waterfall they had ever seen crashed in gigantic steps down a cliff towards the green country far below, but they could not see the bottom because of the clouds of mist and spume thrown up by the water.

What made the green land so unutterably strange to Sparrow was that there were no mountains: it was quite flat, and stretched in paler or darker greens, until it became swallowed up in a blue haze at the edge of sight. It was all too far below to make out anything properly, apart from a line of tall grey shapes that disappeared off into the misty distances.

"What are those giant things?" Sparrow whispered.

"Electricity pylons, stupid," Kittel giggled.

Their eyes returned to the tumbled drop of rock and scree below their feet.

"Look down there!" Sparrow suddenly exclaimed. He pointed. "There's something moving."

Kittel followed his finger, and in a moment picked out something bright coloured about half-way down the long grey screes beneath them. "It's people," she said at length. "They're climbing up. I knew they'd come eventually!"

For a while they watched as two bright blobs, one red, one yellow, crawled upwards across the cliff face.

"It'd be easier if we flew down," Kittel said at last.

"All right," said Sparrow. Yet he was feeling strangely shy as he took hold of her and flew from their high perch to circle down. They found then that the climbers were actually following a narrow path which threaded its way across the cliff face, and they landed on this some distance from the strangers.

The cliff towered above them on one side and dropped away giddily on the other. They were out of sight of the great waterfall here, and though the air still throbbed with its steady boom, the noise was no longer so violent.

They waited. "Some reception committee, two climbers," Kittel muttered.

"What did you expect?" said Sparrow absently.

She grunted. "Twenty at least, and carrying a banner with WELCOME HOME, KITTEL on it. I don't know," she finished crossly, "it's as if no one's cared, and we were so near all the time…"

There were actually three climbers: one was a dog, a tall, reddish, lanky animal that was now racing up towards them.

"It's a red setter!" Kittel exclaimed as it bounded closer. "Just like the one we had – Max. In fact…"

At that moment the dog reached them and stopped suddenly. It held its long nose out as far as it possibly could without actually moving forward, while the velvety-chocolaty end of it twitched suspiciously.

"It *is* Max," said Kittel in a soft, unbelieving, husky voice.

"How do you know?" Sparrow said. "Because he's my dog, idiot," Kittel answered, dropping down on her knees and holding out her hand. "Max?" she said softly. "Maxy? It's me. Don't you know me?"

And then she drew back her hand rapidly, because the dog let out a long, low growl. "Max," Kittel said in a hurt voice, and then suddenly looked up towards the two advancing figures. They were in single file, and she looked at the leader without recognition. "Perhaps I was wrong," she muttered, standing up again.

But Sparrow, watching it all, knew she was not wrong. The dog did recognize her. He knew that because when it growled, Sparrow had heard it say, "Of course I know you, silly bitch; I want to know what you're doing here."

He had no time to wonder if this was just ordinary doggish behaviour, or if there was more to it, because the moment Kittel stood up again she was hailed. The figure walking behind – the one in yellow – who they now saw was smaller than the leading figure, suddenly pointed and waved and called out, "It is! It's her!" in a high, excited voice.

247

It was a woman and a girl who were approaching. Sparrow thought their jackets must be bright enough to glow in the dark. He felt very shabby in his old, worn clothes. When he got a proper look at the girl he got a shock: she was so like Kittel he could almost have mistaken the two of them. Then he saw that the stranger was quite a lot younger, her hair a lot darker and her skin a lot paler, and –

"It's Trina!" Kittel's voice broke in on him. "It's Trina! Trina, what are you – ? Have you – ?

"Looking for you, of course!" the other girl burst out, running forwards past the woman. Unceremoniously she shoved the dog out of the way, grabbed Kittel by the wrist, and beamed with unbelieving happiness. "And I've found you!" she exclaimed.

At this, Max seemed to become a different dog. He started bounding about, letting out small, squeaking barks, flapping his long ears and weaving in and out between the feet of the humans, while Sparrow even heard him singing a clownish song in his tuneless dog-voice.

Above the doggish din, Sparrow heard Trina introducing the woman as her schoolteacher, Miss Meggan; while Kittel said who Sparrow was and rattled off everything that had happened to her since the plane-crash when – from Trina's point of view – she had gone missing. She did that too quickly even for Sparrow to follow, but Trina seemed to be quite satisfied with her account, while old Miss Meggan beamed and nodded and tried to pat Max's head whenever he brushed past her. After three minutes of hard talking, the two sisters were agreeing to sit down and have lunch, and a large flat rock in a wide part of the path just there seemed the ideal place.

But as they were making their way towards it, Max pushed past Sparrow and paused for a second. And Sparrow heard him growl, "Not a bite – do you hear? Not a bite of her food!"

Sparrow frowned in puzzlement. Was the dog being unfriendly? Or…? No, he thought, surely not … Kittel would know her own sister.

The sun, moving round from noon, had almost disappeared behind the towering wall of rock, and their picnic spot was one of the few places where it still shone. The ground went on shaking, and it almost felt as if the warm slab they sat down on were trying to tremble its way to the edge of the drop. Kittel opened their satchel of provisions. "We don't have to be so careful now," she said. "We've no more searching to do."

"We're on holiday – well, sort of," Trina explained. "Dad's got some special work here, just for nine months, and so we all came, and I'm doing a year at the school and, anyway, when I saw the mountains I knew I had to come and look for you but they thought I should go with someone who knew the paths properly, so Miss Meggan said she'd come. We've left the car down at the bottom there. Mum thinks I'm just being stupid, expecting to find you in these mountains, but I knew I was right, I just knew it – and I was."

"And we came to meet you just on the very same day that you came to look for us!" Kittel put in excitedly.

"This was just a sort of test expedition, to see how we got on," said Trina.

"So was ours," said Kittel, "just a test run."

"We thought we might all come with the tent when the real holidays started," said Trina.

Kittel and Trina beamed at each other. Miss Meggan beamed benignly. Sparrow looked out over the huge expanse of flat green land, misty blue in the distance, broken here and there by the darker green of woods and the dark firm lines of roads and hedges. He could make out very little. In fact, it all seemed very vague, very misty. Was that just the haze of summer heat? Surely that misty blue reminded him of something?

"Taste this," said Kittel, handing Trina a piece of the cheese Murie had given them. "It's the best you've ever had."

"Mmm," Trina agreed, nibbling at a white crumb. "Is that what you've been living on all this time?"

"You look very well on it," said Miss Meggan kindly.

Max, lying over in the shadow of the rock, growled softly.

"I've only got peanut butter sandwiches," said Trina.

"Mmm, peanut butter sandwiches!" Kittel exclaimed in delight. "Oh, can I have one – please?"

"All right," said Trina, with a strange smile.

"You must try a peanut butter sandwich," Kittel said to Sparrow. "I used to stuff myself with them."

Sparrow was not sure he liked the sound of this, and when Max growled again he liked it even less.

Trina took a flat white thing (which Sparrow didn't recognize as bread) out of the blue bag she had been carrying, and handed it to Kittel. The sun was just catching the side of the dog's head, which was resting on the edge of the rock, and it gave him a most peculiar look.

Sparrow felt more and more strongly that there was something he ought to do. The dog was staring straight at him. Trina handed him another of the white things.

Sparrow felt its soft sponginess between his fingers, and then Max growled again. "Not a bite, not a bite," Sparrow heard. Kittel sank her teeth into her own sandwich. "Go on, Sparrow," she urged, "it's really good."

Max sat up. A last ray of the sun made a slash of yellow from the top of his ear to the bottom of his jaw. Sparrow stared.

"Lie down, Max," Trina's voice came dimly, "you're putting him off. He always begs, he's awful."

Sparrow's left hand slipped into his pouch and drew out the little rough stone.

The effect was immediate, devastating, unbelievable. It started with Max, who threw back his head and let out a long, rising, wolf-like howl that seemed to echo off into some immeasurable distance. The next thing was that Trina suddenly leaped to her feet, as a tremor of the ground made their rock jump in its bed as if it had been no more than a pebble. It sounded as though half a mountain had just crashed down the waterfall.

251

"Trina!" Kittel yelled, sending a spray of half-chewed peanut butter sandwich spluttering out of her mouth, as she clapped her hands over her ears – and then again, in a quite different tone, "*Trina!*" for Trina had begun to change.

By now Sparrow recognized what was happening. Just as once before, there was the feeling of being flung violently backwards, falling through sickening space, yet nothing moved; and something was happening to Kittel's sister – Sparrow didn't notice the teacher – a change in her hair, in her face, something changing about her arms. The hair had disappeared from the front part of her head, her arms growing longer, the hands disappearing from the wrist...

He couldn't make it out. "Trina!" Kittel screamed again. "Oh, Trina! No!"

Sparrow leaped up and grabbed hold of Kittel's arm. All about them was screaming, crashing, roaring, wailing and howling, and a distant sound that might have been the waterfall or a mighty wind getting up. It became hard to see, because the very mountainside seemed to be collapsing round them. Rocks fell, waterspouts spouted; fire seemed to be spreading over the distant green land. Dust and smoke and mist gathered. Vaguely Sparrow made out the humped shape of the Polymorph where Kittel's sister had been. He sprang into the air.

The mist grew dark, the crashing of the mountains grew distant, but the noise of the wind continued. Sparrow flew, dragging Kittel beside him, without knowing whether they were flying upwards or down, forwards or sideways. He flew to the very limit of his speed, but without being able to see anything to know how fast they were going. Kittel was whimpering Trina's name. Gradually they seemed to outstrip the dark wind, and light appeared somewhere ahead.

Slowly the light grew – the plain blue light of sky. And something else – dark, swirling shapes, that drew together into dark, hard shapes... And at last, a long mountain ridge with dark forests on its lower slopes, and below the forest, the shining surface of a lake.

A moment later they were standing on the shore. The trees pressed down almost to the edge of the lake, and mist moved amongst their silent trunks. The whole journey had been nothing but a tangled web of sorcery: they had scarcely travelled a mile from the Valley of Murmuring Water, and the sun of morning was still shining.

"It didn't happen," Sparrow said to Kittel, who stood blankly, pale and shivering. "We haven't been anywhere. It wasn't your sister."

Kittel was trembling too much to nod. "I thought she was too young," she managed between clenched teeth. "Trina's bound to have changed since I saw her, but she looked exactly the same as I remember her."

at the lake

"KITTEL," SPARROW SAID URGENTLY, "YOU DIDN'T EAT ANY of that white stuff, did you?"

"The sandwich? I spat it out – you saw me."

"You're quite sure?"

"Yes."

"I suppose you wouldn't be here if you had," Sparrow said. "We'd better get back."

"Back where?" Kittel asked, her voice firmer now.

"To the cottage," said Sparrow in surprise.

"Why?" Kittel frowned.

"Because – well – I don't know," Sparrow stumbled. "I suppose it can't be done – I suppose…"

"Do you think I'm going to let something like that stop me?" said Kittel. Her fright had left her angry.

"But how can we stop it happening?" Sparrow said. "We think we're doing fine and getting somewhere – and all the time we're just stuck in one place."

"It's obvious," said Kittel stubbornly. "We fly holding the stone. Everything disappears when you take it out; so if you have it out all the time nothing can go wrong."

Sparrow couldn't argue with this, but inwardly he was worrying more and more about Puckel.

"Come on," said Kittel. "I'm all right now. Let's not hang about any longer, or I'll never want to go."

And Sparrow let himself be persuaded. Because he had to hold Kittel, they agreed that she should carry the stone, holding it out before them as they flew.

As they took to the air again, Kittel glanced back towards the ridge where the stream emerged from their own valley. "Isn't that Herold?" she exclaimed, pointing.

Sparrow hovered. There was a small dark shape visible against the rocky hillside, a black bird flapping along in an ungainly, haphazard fashion. No other bird flew quite as untidily as Herold.

255

"He'll have to be sent home," said Sparrow. "Perhaps the sight of us flying will send him into a huff."

"I don't know about that," said Kittel. "He's coming straight towards us; he must have spotted us already."

Kittel was noticing a funny taste in her mouth. It seemed like the taste of blood, and she thought it must be from the little cut she had near her lip – perhaps from some spinning stone as the mountains crashed round them. Yet at the same time it seemed very sweet – sweeter than blood ought to be. "It's only the taste," she muttered to herself; "I definitely, definitely spat it out…"

By now Herold had come close enough for them to hear him. He was making the strangest noise – a sort of soft, crooning croak that sounded to Sparrow like, "Blind as a bat, blind as a bat".

Even with things happening so fast and so unexpectedly, Sparrow had a dim memory of Puckel telling him that one of the Polymorphs could strike people blind. Had Herold been attacked by the Polymorphs? Why should he be? All the same, it worried Sparrow.

"What's happened, Herold?" he called.

The crow switched direction slightly and headed straight for them, gibbering loudly about being abandoned in his hour of need.

"Hey! Look out!" Sparrow yelled, rising out of Herold's path. "You're going to knock into us!"

Sparrow turned, preparing to fly alongside Herold to find out what was wrong. But as he did so, Herold again altered course, apparently to follow the sound of Sparrow's voice. When Sparrow glanced back to see where his friend was, Herold was so close up behind them that Sparrow once again lost sight of him.

"Where's he gone now?" he exclaimed, lessening his speed; "where's—"

"Watch out, Herold, you –" Kittel burst out, suddenly aware that there would be a collision. "Don't – oh no!"

There was a bump and a fluttering, another yell from Kittel, a harsh caw and a soft plop from the lake below them. Herold was plummeting like a dropped bit of rag, before picking himself up just above the water, letting out a joyous squawk from which Sparrow understood that he could see again. Then Sparrow realized what Kittel had yelled.

"The stone?" he echoed. "Where? How?"

"There!" Kittel cried, almost in tears, pointing down to the rings spreading out on the calm surface of the water.

Sparrow didn't pause for a moment. Down he swooped,

and would have plunged straight into the lake if Kittel hadn't stopped him with another shriek. Sparrow realized just in time, and straightened out, skimming over the surface.

He had to think quickly. "I'll leave you on the shore," he shouted. "But – I know. Herold, you fly round and round over those ripples, till I get back!" Without another word, he streaked off towards the shore, where he left Kittel standing forlornly in the shadow of the twisted trees.

When, a minute later, he had reached Herold again, he told the crow to go back and wait with Kittel. Then he dived down into the centre of what was now only the vaguest of vague, wide circles on the water face.

Sparrow was not the most expert of swimmers. But just as his dive had come to a slow stop and he was beginning to rise inexorably back to the surface, he noticed a fine, fat carp slithering off towards the weedy shadows.

257

Without a thought he took the fish's shape, and in his new fish-form swam nimbly back to where he thought he had been. It was lucky, for he was able to use the carp's unerring sense of direction under the water. In addition, Sparrow's shrunken mountain was a very special stone – he had looked after it night and day, treasured it, for eighteen months now; it had almost become a part of himself. He did not take long to find it sitting on a ledge of rock, and swam joyfully towards it.

And stopped, at a loss. Even before he had quite reached the stone he had realized the problem. For although the carp-shape had been ideal for finding it, the lippy, gaping fish mouth was nothing like big enough to lift it from its ledge. Sparrow swam round and round it, nudging it, kissing it with his fishy lips, sucking at it, clicking at it with his bony tongue.

Of course, the obvious thing would have been to change back into himself, grab the stone and float up to the surface. What stopped Sparrow was simple fear. In the heat of the moment he had been prepared to dive into the lake. Now he had calmed down. The fish-shape felt comfortable under the water, but the thought of being a boy so far below the surface horrified him. What if he found his lungs empty of air when he changed back into himself? He might simply drown, and no one ever know.

Sparrow was not a coward, but he needed a little time to think. He swam towards the surface. He had an idea that he would change into himself, take a reassuring gulp of air, then change back into the carp. Above his head, the light grew...

258   "Ow! Aagh!" Sparrow didn't exactly yell out loud, because fishes don't yell – but he yelled inside his head. A fearful pressure enveloped his neck and was crushing him, crushing out the cool feeling of breath in his shoulders, filling them with something else they had no right to be full of. A terrible, blinding warmth was around him, while something had pierced him through and through, something like great nails driven from one side of his body to the other.

He changed shape. It was automatic; he didn't even know what shape he was changing into; he was simply saving his own life. Light was bubbling round his eyes, bubbling and breaking round his head. Instead of the languid, swift pushes of the carp's fins, he was propelling himself through the water at a great rate with powerful legs and arms, while a great, sideways-swinging tail kept him on course. In his mouth was something sweet, something savoury, something that made his chops water and his stomach rumble in anticipation of a delicious feast!

The otter pulled itself on to the shore and dropped the fish, which twitched once and lay still. Sparrow changed into his own shape and looked down at the animal, which stared back up at him with black, unwinking eyes. No two otters could have that curious flash of yellow across their face…

"A partnership, the boy and Hnak," the otter said, glancing down at the fish. "The boy rides in the fish; Hnak clenches the fish; the boy rides in Hnak, safe back to the shore. The boy swims like an otter; Hnak feeds like a lion. What joy!" It looked down at the fish again, slavering.

Sparrow was confused at the otter. He realized, of course, that it was making him a sort of offer, but he was more taken up with wondering if it could really be the same one as he had met before. He knew by now that what most animals talked about, thought about, most of the time, was food – which was why the otter had seemed so unusual when it spoke to him after his encounter with the linden lady. Now it was talking – and behaving – like an ordinary otter. What did it know?

"Where's Kittel and Herold?" he burst out. He had got his bearings now. He was standing at the head of the lake, under the shadow of the cliff. And, gazing over to the point where he had left Kittel half an hour before, he saw the shore was empty. There was no doubt of it: the sun was shining brightly on the trees at the lakeside, and there was no one there.

"Your friends, the girl and the rag-bag crow?" The otter was unconcernedly grinding and slurping over its first mouthful of carp. "No hope for them, not ever now. Taken.

259

Coils of mist, round and round, whispering and chuckling. Unprotected, they were. That stone…"

"I was trying to get the stone when you went and caught me!" Sparrow whispered weakly. For a moment, everything went black in front of his eyes. Crunch, crunch, slurp, crunch, went the otter at his feet. "Do you mean – the Polymorphs have captured them? Tell me!" he pleaded. "Will you please stop eating and tell me!"

The otter looked up in surprise. "Hnak can eat and talk together, all at once," it told Sparrow a little huffily. "Hnak can take you back to the stone, too. But no hurry: no hope. Drinking her own blood, the girl: no hope. On the way to the Labyrinth, and no getting out of there. Round and round, all the way in, and then round and round back out again, for ever."

spellbound

THE OLD ROAD SHIMMERED IN THE HOT SUN; THE MOUN- tains baked; the forests hummed and buzzed; the people of
Copperhill and Villas were already complaining of the suf-
focating heat. "Too hot for June," were the words most
often heard in either village.

Plato Smithers wasn't sure if it was anything to do with
the heat, but things had become very sour in Copperhill.
Ms Redwall didn't pester him any more, but he didn't have
much chance to be glad of that. The reason she didn't
pester him was because she simply did things without
asking him now. Ms Redwall seemed to have grown over
the past fortnight – even Plato Smithers felt small beside
her now. There was something about her which he found
a little alarming.

Not that everything was working out for her. When she
marched into the house next door and announced to
Mariett Clodish – Lissie's mother – that she could now

consider herself a free woman, her neighbour had simply cowered in a corner and trembled with fear. Her idea about the school didn't go too well either. When the children heard that Ms Redwall was to be the new teacher, they simply refused to go. She ordered their parents to make them go, but even that didn't work. "Let them have a summer holiday," people said. "It's too hot for school."

In the coolest place in the village, the wheel-room of the mill, Plato Smithers, still wearing his felt hat, stood with a small group of other men and sweated. Two of them, small wiry men with faces like wrinkled apples, were carrying crossbows and had quivers of bolts at their backs, along with heavy packs. Noddy Borrow and Cross Lurgan, two orchard keepers from the outskirts of the village, were preparing for a journey.

"Well, it's goodbye and good luck," Smithers said as he took each of them by the hand. "We know which way they've gone, though for sure we don't know how far they may be by now."

"We'll find them," said Noddy Borrow, who looked like a yellow apple. "Just you make sure and do your bit back here." Cross Lurgan, who looked like a red apple, nodded in agreement. "Put her in chains in the cellar, if need be," he said. "If she can do that to her own sister's boy, she can do it to anyone."

Gogs' father's idea had worked. When people heard that Ms Redwall's own nephew was among the ones who had left the village, it became the start of a secret attempt to get the woman under control. This was not easy, because although a number of people – including all the young people – were against her, she was continually holding meetings now and getting them whipped up about one thing or another, and in this way she still managed to get a lot of the people to think the same way as her.

None of the men meeting in the mill that day knew who had the worse job – the two who were to track Sparrow and his companions in the mountains, or the ones who had to stay behind and do something about Ms Redwall.

As the two men journeyed eastwards, a day's journey to the south of Copperhill the oak forests of Villas lay in stifling heat. Amongst the long lines of pillared trunks, Ormand's dog and the ball he had been chasing had both got lost, and Lissie was getting very short-tempered as they searched for them.

"What's wrong with you?" Ormand said.

"Nothing! Obviously!" Lissie stormed, giving him a filthy look and flouncing off through the chest-high ferns.

263

"He didn't go that way!" Ormand called after her. He was trying to remain good-tempered, but somehow he felt angry at her being so angry – after all, it wasn't anybody's fault. Lissie ignored him and continued out of sight between the still trunks of the oak forest. He made a face and went after her.

He thought she might have cooled down a bit by the time he came up with her, but the moment she saw him she burst out again: "I hate the flies here! I can't stand them! They're everywhere!"

A cloud of flies was certainly buzzing determinedly round her; but to Ormand it didn't seem worse than flies at any other time in bracken-filled woods. "They're round me too," he pointed out.

"Oh, you – yes, I can see they're round you," she spat back. "But you wouldn't even notice! You're used to them!"

"Don't you have flies in your woods, then?" he asked, with just a hint of mockery in his voice.

"No, we don't!"

"Not a single one?"

"No!"

"Huh," Ormand said. "You were probably never allowed to go out of your garden, that's why – in case you got your clothes dirty!"

Lissie flew at him. She attacked him like a wildcat and a donkey rolled into one – scratched him with her hands and kicked him with her feet. It was the most vicious attack Ormand had ever experienced. He was bigger and stronger than she, but even so it was only by luck that he managed to topple her over a tussock of grass and hold her down.

At that moment the dog, Boffin, suddenly returned with a rush and a crash. He stood at the edge of the bracken, looking at them, legs slightly splayed, panting. Lissie relaxed. Ormand released his hold on her.

"It was all your fault," Ormand told him. "Why did you run off? What got into you?" Whatever had got into him was still there. Boffin suddenly began to bark at them; excitedly, sharply, persistently.

"Be quiet!" Ormand yelled. But the barking went on.

"I think he must have found something," Lissie said quietly.

Ormand scrambled to his feet. "Not the ball, anyway. Come on, boy. Show us!"

Boffin swung round and went bounding off through the bracken again. Lissie got up, and quickly they followed his trail through the listening aisles of the forest. A couple of times they lost track of him, but each time he came back, bounding and barking, then whisking round and careering off again.

"These flies are getting worse," Lissie said disbelievingly. Even Ormand had to admit they were troublesome now. They buzzed and buzzed, so close to their heads that they could feel their faces flicked occasionally by the insects' wings.

At last they heard Boffin ahead, squeaking, whining, letting out little jabbing barks. There were more and more flies: the whole air seemed dark with them, and the buzzing of their thousands of wings seemed to fill the whole forest and throb in their ears like drums.

Boffin was leaping and scratching round something in the grass. The flies seemed to be thickest round it. It almost looked as though they were pouring upwards from it.

"Ugh!" Lissie exclaimed, turning away. "It's something dead!" But something made Ormand go on further, to shoo the flies out of the way and get a closer look.

"Lissie, come quickly," he said.

Reluctantly she came to his side. It was a dead animal; a smallish dog. Lissie saw at once why Ormand looked so dumbfounded; apart from a red gash in its side, the dog matched Boffin in every detail. It had Boffin's unusual white patch between the eyes, the same black pad on its left forepaw. There was something about it, dull and lifeless though it was, which simply *was* Boffin. If Boffin hadn't been leaping around in front of their very eyes, they would most certainly have believed that Ormand's dog was dead. And all the while the flies buzzed and thrummed, thrummed and throbbed, in the still air of the oak forest. Both children stared helplessly at the dead creature at their feet, but neither bent to touch it or turned away to leave it. They seemed mesmerized by it, rooted to the spot – spellbound.

265

*   *   *

Several hours later a search party, consisting of Lissie's father, Ormand's uncle and a couple of neighbours, followed Boffin up into the oak forest. They could find no trace of the two missing children. Some broken bracken stems led to a spot where rabbit fur and a rabbit paw were lying in a small, flattened patch of grass – but otherwise, there was nothing.

It was Boffin who roused Ormand and Lissie again – or perhaps "roused" is the wrong word. Something had happened to them; something had changed inside them. They were still aware of what was happening, but somehow it had all become very distant, as if it were a story from long ago.

Boffin was barking again, excitedly and urgently, as if to get them to follow him. The flies buzzed and buzzed. Suddenly he turned and again went rocketing off into the woods. They stirred, looked round, but before they had even had time to think of moving, the dog appeared again, trotting smartly off *away* from them as if he had only that second left the side of the dead dog. So of course he couldn't have appeared again – this must be another Boffin. But which was the real one? The one which had crashed off through the trees, the dead one, or the one trotting off ahead of them now? They followed this last.

Some way further on, the Boffin they were following stopped and sniffed in the long grass. There was another dead Boffin, lying in the shadow of a thicket of young trees. Again the same thing happened: as they looked, Boffin ran off with a yelp into the woods; Boffin lay dead at their feet; Boffin trotted quietly off ahead of them, leading them further into the forest. And they followed. They had stopped wondering, or even thinking, by now. Five times this same scene was re-enacted.

"Where are we, Ormand?" Lissie asked an hour later.

"I don't know," Ormand replied dully.

And suddenly they were out of the forest – on a broad, dreary stretch of moorland that lay between two parts of it. The summer day seemed to have gone; the land lay under a light like a dull evening of autumn. Large rocks were scattered here and there in the heather and rough grass, and Boffin made his way purposefully amongst them.

With a yelp and a howl, the five missing Boffins reappeared. They popped out from behind various rocks, all at once, and began a mad chase, in and out, backwards and forwards, over tussocks, over stones, crossing and recrossing the moor – until suddenly all five of them converged on the one Boffin Lissie and Ormand were following: converged all at once, with breathtaking speed, six dogs becoming one dog.

"Boffin!" Ormand called out, his voice itself sounding sharp as a dog's yelp. As if in answer, the dog did a head over heels, and by the time Lissie and Ormand came up to him, a sixth dead dog lay in the wiry moorland grass. For a moment they stood and stared down. Then softly Ormand bent to touch the still head.

Wowf! The very second he did so, with a leap and a bound that sent him tumbling backwards, one, two, three … five … ten Boffins leaped out of the dead Boffin. Like a hunting pack they went jostling and streaming off towards the forest on the far side of the moor. And Ormand and Lissie followed, running, running, running till their breath came in gasps and their legs ached and their lungs felt like bursting.

267

Closer the forest loomed, and closer again, but it seemed to take an age to reach it. At last they understood why: it was more distant than it had seemed, and the trees of it were oaks three times – six times – as large as any oak trees they had ever seen. Nightmarishly huge they loomed up in the dull sky, and in the roots of the hugest, at the edge of the forest, an immense rabbit hole gaped like an open mouth. They did not hesitate. By now the yelping of the hounds had faded away ahead of them, but they were scarcely up to the forest eaves when it broke out suddenly behind them. Behind them and drawing nearer. They were being hunted…

They dived into the rabbit hole and ran, as all sound faded behind them. They slowed to a walk, then stopped, gasping to get their breath back. There was a velvety silence behind the noise they were making – but behind the silence the ghost of another noise: perhaps a faint whirring, like a flock of pigeons just taking flight. They were completely enclosed in the tunnel, with no trace of an entrance either before or behind them. Yet they were able to see, in a dim, brownish light like a faint echo of the dreary light they had come in from.

"There's no reason why we should be able to see in here," Ormand remarked presently. "If we really were in a tunnel under the ground, it'd be pitch black; we wouldn't see a thing."

"I'm scared," said Lissie. It was the first thing she had said since they found the second dead dog. "I feel dizzy," she added.

"And yet we are underground," Ormand went on after a little, "because this is earth, and these are tree roots sticking out of it. Look." He pulled at a fibrous end and drew an unmistakable tree root from the crumbling tunnel wall. Right up the wall and round the roof he pulled it, as a gentle rain of earth fell on their hair.

"Be careful," Lissie warned. "You'll bring the whole tunnel down."

But Ormand went on pulling, and the root kept on coming. Over the roof, slanting down the opposite wall, and across the floor –

"Ormand!" Lissie cried out – a split second before, with a gentle patter-patter, then a soft, choking *sumph!*, the tunnel collapsed, crushing them to their knees with the soft weight of earth.

They went down without a sound, too surprised to cry out. A moment later they were able to struggle to their feet again, barely up to their knees in earth. Then Lissie smeared the soil out of her eyes – and let out a loud scream: framed in the loose earth of the collapsed wall was a frightful, wrinkled, leering face.

269

"No need to be scared." The thin-lipped mouth moved in an unnatural, automatic fashion as the grinding stony voice came from it. Pieces of earth could be seen falling from it in the gloom as it spoke. "No need to be scared. I'm here to welcome you in."

Then the head detached itself from the wall, and Lissie and Ormand saw a skinny, brown-clad body with long, bony arms, and in one hand a lantern in which flickered a tiny, chocolate-coloured flame. The flame cast no light, but somehow the look of it was the same as the brown gloom that filled the earthy tunnel. "I've come to let you in through the door," the creature croaked.

"What door?" Ormand demanded in a shaky voice.

"Why, this door," the voice grated. And they saw the

plain wooden boards of a door where the tunnel wall had been.

"Where does it go?" Lissie whispered.

"Why, it says here on the door, child. Can't you read it?"

"There's nothing there," said Lissie, staring at the door.

"Look," the lantern bearer rasped, with a black, hollow grin. "It's written on the door. A – M – A – " the bony finger moved across the plain wood of the door as the dry mouth spelled out letters – "Z – E – M – E – N – T. What does that say?"

"I don't know," Lissie replied.

"It says Amazement!" the ancient mouth roared, as the door burst open in another shower of earth. "IT SAYS AMAZEMENT!" The empty doorway seemed to do a cartwheel towards them. "*It says Amazement!*" came a third time, muffled now and echoing and mixed with the slamming sound of wood on wood on the "maze" sound. Lissie and Ormand stood alone in a squared corridor of rock, beside a flickering torch fixed into a bracket on the wall.

And then there was silence, apart from the frenzied thumping of their hearts. Gradually they grew calmer, and noticed there was something oddly peaceful about the place they were in. They looked about them. The corridor was wide, with walls of rough sandstone, clean and dry. At about twice their height there was an arched ceiling of bare earth. In contrast, the floor was of smooth, polished stone flags that gleamed a little with a deep reddish tinge like garnet rock. There was a slight curve to the walls of the corridor, and the torchlight reached just far enough for them to see where it curved out of sight. The torch flame sputtered now and then, giving off a bluish, honey-scented smoke.

"I wonder what keeps them lighted?" said Ormand, who had noticed that the brackets, and the torches themselves, were of stone and bore no trace of the usual material – pitch or tallow – that torches burn on.

Lissie didn't like the thought of torches with no fuel to keep them alight. What was to stop them going out at any moment? "What do we do?" she said. There was no sign of any door now. Where they stood the corridor ended – or started – in a blank stone wall.

"Go on, I suppose. We can't stay here."

They started down the corridor.

"It seems a bit boring, this place," Lissie said when after a while they came to a second, and then a third torch on the wall.

It was true. The passage seemed to go on forever, with nothing happening – no doors, no rooms – just more passageway, all exactly the same, gently, monotonously, continuously curving out of sight ahead. The torches sputtered on the wall, quite far apart, but never far enough apart for anywhere to be in complete darkness. They had already gone a good way, and Lissie had just counted two hundred and forty steps between one torch and the next, when –

"Did you hear a voice?" she whispered.

"No," Ormand replied, stopping. "But I thought I saw something moving, on ahead – away from us."

"What shall we do?" Lissie whispered.

"Keep behind me, close to the wall," Ormand whispered back. "We'll run and catch up. Tiptoe."

They didn't have far to run, and when they suddenly came in view of the next torch they stopped, quite baffled. Kittel was sitting beneath it, with a large crow on her shoulder.

into the spiral

KITTEL'S SMILE WAS FRIENDLY AS THEY CAME UP TO HER. But Lissie immediately had the feeling there was something amiss.

"Hello," Kittel said, without any surprise in her voice. "Hello."

The crow on Kittel's shoulder stuck its head out and hissed, so Lissie didn't go right up to her friend. "Do you know where we are?" she asked, after a pause.

"Ye–es," said Kittel slowly. But instead of telling Lissie, she asked, "How did you get here?"

Lissie told her. She had a feeling that Kittel was only half listening, and when she had finished, Kittel just remarked, in a reassuring sort of voice, "Yes, dogs are like that, really. But there's nothing you can do about it; you just have to take them as they are."

"Kittel, are you all right?" Lissie asked anxiously.

Kittel gave a short laugh. "It's that stuff I took," she said vaguely. "It's just like ordinary bread to taste, really, but you get hooked on it. It's all this junk food, it's stuffed full of chemicals and you don't know what half of them are doing to you. Trina, could you turn that radio down a bit, please?" Suddenly she seemed to notice Ormand. She got up immediately and held out her hand to him. "Oh, hello, you must be Sparrow." She said it in the same unnatural, over-polite way that Lissie's mother had when she spoke to Ms Redwall.

"Its Ormand, Kittel," Lissie pleaded, now thoroughly worried. "I told you about him. Ormand," she said, turning to him, "there's something wrong with her – she's not like this."

"Kittel's told me so much about you," Kittel said confidingly to Ormand. "Can you really fly? It must be *so* exciting!"

"She's gone mad," Lissie whispered; "she's completely lost her head. Oh no, not another one – what'll we do?"

"She is a bit odd," Ormand agreed.

"Now," Kittel said, and her voice had changed again; she spoke in clear, slow tones, like a teacher addressing a rather dull class, "it's really much easier than it looks. Now, pay attention to the map." She turned to the wall and ran her finger over a part of it. "The red arrow helps you. It says YOU ARE HERE – so you can't really go wrong. Trina, take those headphones off – you have to pay attention." (She glanced severely at Lissie as she said this.) "You know the name of the street you want to go to, but you don't know where it is. Now down here there's a list of street names, in alphabetical order, and after each street name there's a letter and a number. Now, look along the side of the map…"

273

"What are we going to do?" Lissie whispered again.

"I don't know," Ormand whispered back. "Humour her, I suppose."

"And it's … this way!" Kittel announced. "Come on!" And she turned and started smartly down the passageway, the crow on her shoulder teetering backwards and forwards with each step she took.

Lissie and Ormand exchanged glances, and then set off after her.

It would not have been too bad if it hadn't been for Kittel. Lissie had long since decided that, wherever they were, it wasn't a horrific place to be in, considering the horror of the doorway into it. The floor was smooth and pleasant to walk on and the passage was never too dark, because of the sweet-smelling torches – even though they did cast rather eerie shadows on the silent, honey-coloured walls. But the constant stream of nonsense coming from Kittel was distressing; especially since she kept changing her voice, and never appeared to be any one particular person for more than half a minute at a time. Through that endless-seeming, torchlit journey, Lissie heard her talking like her mother, like Ms Minn, like herself, like Sparrow, like Sparrow's mother, like some other teacher, like Plato Smithers – and Lissie even recognized herself when Kittel suddenly put out her hand and sang:

Hedgehog, hedgehog, down by the well,
Find me a snail with a curly shell.

In the middle of giving a long lecture to Sparrow about not having cut enough firewood, she suddenly said, "Oh, Dad, you're always hiding behind that newspaper"; in the middle of throwing a stick for her dog, and then pelting off after it as though she were a dog herself (the crow fell off and had to fly along behind her), she suddenly burst into tears and announced, "I have to go away now, dears, and I'm afraid I might never see you again."

All this time a gradual change was taking place in the passageway. For a while they didn't notice it, then Lissie first and Ormand not long afterwards commented on it. The curve of the walls had become much sharper. And the reason they hadn't noticed sooner was that the torches were set closer together. Ormand measured the distance with his feet: there were only sixty steps between them.

Lissie was softly repeating her rhyme about the hedge-hog and the snail. "I know," she said suddenly, "it's a spiral. Like a snail shell."

"What is?" said Ormand.

"What we're in," she answered. "When we get to the centre, it'll stop."

"Oh, Trina, *please* turn that radio down," Kittel broke in.

And in the small silence after she had spoken, they heard a voice.

It was a soft, murmuring, distinct voice, floating easily along the passage towards them, though without words that they could make out. But they only had a second in which to listen to it, because the crow suddenly burst into such a cacophony of caws and screeches and flappings of its wings that Lissie automatically flung herself against the wall, covering her head with her arms.

The silence returned after a moment or two – a silence without any sound of the voice. Lissie uncovered her head. Kittel was wagging her finger at some small, invisible

275

person in front of her. "Tut, tut, tut," she was saying. "That's what happens when you don't do up your shoelaces." There was no sign of the crow.

"What happened?" said Lissie.

"The crow flew off," Ormand said. "Don't ask me why."

"Where?" asked Lissie.

"On ahead," Ormand answered.

After some tense listening, they went on again. There didn't seem anything else to do, and besides, they felt they should keep Kittel in sight. Lissie seemed to be right: the curve of the passageway was very definitely tightening. "Only thirty steps between the torches now," said Ormand.

They paced out the distances together: twenty-five – twenty-three – eighteen – seventeen – and stopped. For about twenty steps the corridor ran on ahead of them and then came to an end in a blank wall. There was one last torch just before it. And the moment they came in sight of the end of the corridor, they heard the voice again.

It was a man's voice, it seemed, though murmuring in a rather high, chant-like fashion, like someone trying to remember a poem by repeating it over and over. But it was no poem the voice was repeating; in fact, it seemed to be plain nonsense.

"Ngamawa cumarana baranaia wumawanga," it murmured, quietly, continuously as a stream bubbling to itself in a shady hollow under the trees. It was right ahead of them, but they could see nothing.

Almost nothing, that is. For on to the floor against the wall opposite the torch, a small black something suddenly flopped – almost as though it had jerked itself out of the wall. It became still. It looked very like the wing of a bird.

Kittel didn't hesitate. "Just coming!" she called gaily and trotted off towards the torch and the thing on the floor. Lissie and Ormand followed.

They caught up with her just as they came to the black thing. It was the crow, which lay, either dead or senseless, in a stone doorway in the wall of the passage. Kittel gave the creature no more than a glance. "Trina," she remarked, "I've told you a dozen times not to leave your underwear lying about," and she advanced through the doorway. Lissie and Ormand were right behind her, and this, and the huge dancing shadows thrown on the wall by the torch-light, meant that they didn't at first see what was in the small, circular chamber they were entering.

When they did, they froze in shock, and Lissie clapped her hand over her mouth.

It was a chamber of rough stone, just like the corridor. In the centre of it stood a round stone table. Just beside the table there was a tripod of some black metal, its three legs meeting at the top and then curling back into a sort of collar of wrought ironwork. Sticking out of the centre of the collar was a spike, and fixed to the spike there was the head of a man.

The dark face was towards them, and the dark eyes were closed or lowered. The face looked utterly peaceful; and the murmuring stream of meaningless sounds was coming from its scarcely moving lips. "Ngathaiathaia rumalinea bumarinoyo haikanaragaia brandulimotho moronigora," it intoned.

Kittel was already advancing towards it. "Oh, you must be Sparrow's father," she exclaimed, holding out her hand. "I'm so glad to have met you at last – I've heard so much about you."

doors in the earth

THE OTTER WAS DIFFICULT TO PERSUADE. EVEN AFTER IT had finished its fish it didn't seem to feel much urgency about Sparrow's problem. Kittel and Herold, as far as it was concerned, were gone; nothing anyone could do would bring them back. It was sad, but life had to go on and fish had to be caught.

It *was* the same otter Sparrow had met before, and it remembered Sparrow quite well, but it remembered nothing about the mysterious message it had given him. It knew of Puckel (Who doesn't? it said), but it couldn't see how Puckel could help; Puckel had left the mountains hundreds of years ago. Nothing Sparrow said could persuade it otherwise.

Eventually it accepted that its scheme for catching fish was too dangerous for Sparrow, and by this time anyway its hunger was well satisfied. It belched a few times, said that had been the best carp it had ever tasted, and agreed to take

Sparrow back to the place where it had caught the fish.

Its sense of direction was unfailing, and with its guidance and then a change into a second carp, which Sparrow made sure didn't swim up towards the surface, he found his way back to his stone a second time. Not knowing what else to do, he changed into it, and waited and thought, though not one idea came to him about rescuing Kittel and Herold from the Labyrinth of the Polymorphs – wherever, whatever, that was. Apart from this, his conscience was badly nagging him: he should have gone back to see Puckel. If he had, he wouldn't be in this mess now.

Time moves differently for stones. He had scarcely decided that the best way of helping Kittel would be to go to Puckel, when he realized by the turning spiral of silver that he was already on the way. That meant it must be night-time and he must have been on the lake bed for hours.

Things were different this time. There was no road of mist. And after a little, he realized that the silver spiral was actually becoming clearer, sharper, smaller. It stopped circling. It was a small, silver brooch, just in front of Sparrow's eyes, and –

It was the brooch on Puckel's magnificent midnight-blue cloak! Sparrow was inside the tower!

"Puckel," he said, "we're in trouble now."

"No doubt you are!" Puckel retorted. "And no wonder. Do you think I've nothing better to do than walk up and down this room, while you picnic and skylark in the mountains?" The old man's hair flew wildly as he stomped this way and that across the bare stone floor.

Sparrow felt a little indignant at having two of the hardest-working weeks of his life referred to as skylarking and picnicking, but it seemed the wrong time to argue about it. "Puckel, Kittel—" he began.

"Don't Puckel-Kittel me!" Puckel snapped. "Attend. The Vault of the Bear no longer offers any protection. The noose draws in. Already the Polymorphs are striking towards the Centre."

Sparrow did not dare to interrupt.

"The strategy is this," Puckel continued. "Bur of the Lamps, their head, has set Eych the Enslaver to guard the source of their power, which is in the Star Wheel itself; Ur is set to guard the perimeters; Eni, Tho and Yo to dim the light of Cold Stone as siege is laid about Hollywell – there is duplication of forms, shapes and shadows in the forest, danger to all who stray from the villages, danger reaching into the heart of the villages, evil from the outside meeting with evil in the hearts of fools. Drakewater, Uplands and the Springing Wood are safe for the present, though not for long if the Centre is endangered. Bur goes among them, unseen, holding them to his will. Bur is the key. Bur must be provoked, brought out into the open. Is that clear?"

Sparrow shook his head. He had not even begun to understand.

Puckel stopped, frowned, sighed, folded his hands over the top of his stick and tapped his foot. "Well, what's so difficult?" he demanded.

"Everything," Sparrow said. "All these names. The names of the Polymorphs, and the names of the villages, and the names of these other things, and the Star Wheel and the Vault of the Bear – I just don't know what you're talking about, that's all."

"You've seen the Door, haven't you?" Puckel said, now tapping his stick on the floor as well as his foot.

"What door?" said Sparrow.

"Why, the door you came through, of course!" the old man exploded.

Sparrow glanced round. Had he come in by a door? Apparently he had. There seemed to be no window in Puckel's room now, but where the window had been there was an empty doorway. Through it nothing was visible but black space and brilliant stars. But Sparrow scarcely noticed that; the door itself was what took his attention. It was identical to the strange-shaped doorway of the cottage.

He turned round again and found that Puckel had somehow got up on the little wooden table, where he was precariously perched with his legs tucked under him. There was no sign of his stick.

"I shall explain," said Puckel. "I might as well, or we'll just be plagued by your stupid interruptions. Listen carefully.

281

"Along time ago – so many years I wouldn't care to count them, years before memory – this world was still in the making. In those days, giants were here. Not the sorry creatures of the nursery tales you're all so fond of down there. These were real giants, out-topping the highest mountains, their shoulders above the clouds. They were the craftsmen, and the mountains and valleys and seas were their handicraft. Well, that's all long gone; their time passed before memory began.

"But they didn't leave the earth – no, they built themselves doors in it and went down below, down to the centre. Mountains slipped and seas washed over the lands, new hills were carved by rivers of ice; the giants' doors were buried. But they are all still there, and where they are discovered, a great power of making and unmaking, of hiding and revealing, can be set loose. This whole mountain-country is such a place."

"Where – you mean…" Sparrow faltered.

"I mean the country you call your country, this lost country of mountains, with its five ridiculous little villages. They're all inside the frame of one of the giants' doors. A five-sided frame, exactly like this one and the one you've seen before."

"But huge," Sparrow murmured. "It must be huge."

"Huge enough," said Puckel, "though you could cross it in a single day – indeed you used to, before you started using that tomfool of a crow as your permanent conveyance. However, the size doesn't matter. What has happened with the Giants' Door is that it has been used to make the Secret Way of the Mountains.

282

"The Giants' Door is like a broken mirror: when a mirror is broken, each fragment is a little mirror of its own. There are nine hundred and ninety-nine doors; each of these is the Giants' Door in miniature. They are all one door. So anyone who has mastered the Secret Way can move faster than thought between door and door. To learn the Secret Way he must first see through the illusions of the Polymorphs and then chain them to his service. Thus he becomes a master of transformation."

Sparrow didn't feel much wiser for this explanation, but Puckel didn't ask him this time if he had understood. "Now," the old man went on, "you've gone and dumped your friend Kittel and that black scraggle of feathers in the maze of the Polymorphs, and they're no use to me there. Those two young well-keepers are in there too, though that's no fault of yours.

"However, as I want you to learn the Secret Way, these

matters will sort themselves out in due course."

"Can I not help them?" said Sparrow.

"No. What you must do for me will help them."

"And what's that?"

"You must go to the Vault of the Bear," said Puckel, "and discover what stone thing the Polymorphs have taken from it. Then you must go to the Star Wheel and find it."

"How do I get to the Vault of the Bear?"

"By the Secret Way."

"But I don't know it."

"Exactly. Because you have been wasting time."

Sparrow at last began to see things from Puckel's point of view. "Do you mean I can't help Kittel and Herold till I learn the Secret Way?" he said.

"Exactly," said Puckel again.

"What about my stone? I can beat the Polymorphs with that."

"Oh, can you?" said Puckel drily. "Then why are you sitting at the bottom of a lake?"

Sparrow was silent.

"Well, well," said Puckel, "it's not the end of the world. Now, listen. There is a place of power in each angle of the great Door. The Vault of the Bear and the Star Wheel are such places. They are hidden, and they can only be reached by someone who has learned the Secret Way. Such a person can, on occasion, open the door between them and the world of everyday. On occasion, though it can be risky—"

He broke off, and stared down at Sparrow's arm.

Sparrow followed his gaze. Wrapped round the arm from wrist to elbow – like a snake, but quite definitely no snake – was Puckel's stick! Polished and gnarled, Sparrow recognized it at once, though how it had been possible for that hard, dry piece of wood to coil itself round his arm like ivy round a tree, Sparrow could not begin to think. He stared for a moment, then looked up and stared at Puckel.

"Well, you couldn't have made it much clearer than that," the old man grumbled. He was speaking to the stick, not to Sparrow. "Not much for me to say, then. She'll teach you what you need to know. None too gently, I'm afraid, but all the quicker for that – and quick is what we need to be now."

"You said I had to find a missing bit of me first," said Sparrow.

"You already have," said Puckel carelessly, "or pretty nearly. Now, go and get on. And when your work has all been done, then throw the water into the sun. Then all join hands, with a wink and a grin, and shout like mad when the drums begin."

Sparrow gazed at the old man. "That was like Lissie's rhyme," he said wonderingly. "How did you know it?"

"Same way as she knew it," Puckel answered, sticking his finger into his ear. "By listening." He stuck a finger into his other ear, screwed his eyes shut, and pursed his mouth. He was like a figure carved out of stone.

"Time to go," said a harsh voice from Sparrow's wrist. "Haven't you wasted enough time already?"

It was the stick speaking, and without waiting for a reply it gently tugged at Sparrow's arm, and he drifted out through the doorway and into the night of stars, along the road of mist.

"I thought it was something to do with my father, when Puckel said there was a part of me missing," Sparrow said as they went.

"Your thoughts are like mud in a sump," the stick replied. "You stir them up and your mind becomes clouded. Let them go."

Sparrow took a deep breath. "What do we do, then?"

"Rise," the stick grated.

"Rise where?" Sparrow asked.

"Up to the air," the stick crackled. "Do you want to drown?"

"I can't drown here," Sparrow said, "there's no wa – oh! Blub!"

He kicked, struggled, panicked, breathless…

Writhing, rising…

And with a crash of breaking water, they were in the air again. Sparrow took great thankful gulps of it as, still, they shot upwards, slowed down and hovered.

He was in full, warm sunlight, with the little pyramid of rock clutched painfully in his hand. Below lay the long, narrow, tree-girt lake. Over the stony ridge he could see down to the little cottage in the Valley of Murmuring Water.

285

"I always seem to end up here," Sparrow remarked.

"This is where you started," the stick said. "Come."

Sparrow swooped downwards, but when they had entered the valley, the stick pulled him away from the cottage, and they landed in the new-mown hay beside the stream. He struggled to put the stone back in his pouch, which was difficult because of the stick round his arm. Then he looked about. There was no sign of life anywhere. "Where are Gogs and Murie?" he asked.

"Prisoners," the stick replied curtly.

"Not – in the Labyrinth too?"

"In themselves," said the stick. "Like most human creatures. It is little different from being in the maze of the

Polymorphs. All you need know is that the boy is beating rocks together and singing love songs to the goat—"

"What? Gogs?" Sparrow exclaimed, but the stick paid no heed.

"That is the work of the Polymorph Ur, though it is possible you would prefer to think of the creature as the lady of linden blossom." There was something about the way the stick said this which made Sparrow go pink with embarrassment.

"Where's Murie?" he asked quickly.

"The woman is riding on the back of the cow down in the wood," the stick replied.

Sparrow gasped.

"She has twined flowers in its horns and carries a leafy sceptre," it went on drily. "Now attend. In all that concerns the Secret Way of the Mountains, the speaking of names is of importance. Names are what hold a thing together. When the time comes, you will find that the cottage is an island of safety. Touch the left-hand doorpost and speak the names of the woman and the boy, then they will come back and be as much themselves as they have ever been. Now cross the stream."

The stream was a little too wide to jump at this point, but considering the imperious mood of the stick – it had given his arm a sharp tug as it spoke – Sparrow didn't dare to waste time looking for a spot where it was narrower. The water, cold even on the warm summer day, swirled strongly round his shins.

"Stop," the stick ordered, before he had quite reached the far bank. He stopped, and waited. The swirling water began to give him a queer, trembly feeling in his legs – almost as if they were turning to water themselves. He glanced over towards the wood, to see if there were any sign of Murie and the cow. There was none. Higher the feeling mounted in his legs…

"Stick me into the ground," said the stick suddenly.

"How?" he asked. "I can't even get you off my arm."

"Straighten yourself out, then you'll manage," it replied.

"What?" said Sparrow, frowning.

Next instant, the whole world seemed to turn inside out. Not only Sparrow's arm, but his whole body – not only his body, but everything round him, the stream, the grass, the wood, the mountains, the sky, seemed to twist itself into one vast corkscrew-shape. It was ridiculous, sickening, dizzying. The only straight thing in the whole world seemed to be the stick. A moment later everything had returned to normal, and there was the stick, straightened out – as much as it ever could be – in Sparrow's hand. Hurriedly he leaned over and stuck it into the soft ground of the bank.

287

"The Secret Way is like the stick on your arm," said the stick. "You thought your arm was straight and the stick was twisted round it. In fact the stick was straight, and you were twisted. The Secret Way is the straight way, but it touches on every part of the mountains. The mountains are crooked, the Way is straight. It is the quickest and truest way."

"Yes," said Sparrow.

"Yesss," the stick hissed back at him, seeming to bend towards him from the bank. "And now you will learn to see."

Sparrow had seen it happen before, but it never failed to surprise him. The stick was bending, was becoming pliable; brown and red coils were lying on the ground, writhing, until with a soft *thluck*! a tail jerked itself out of the ground. The stick had become a snake.

Sparrow stood in the water, gazing at what had been dry wood and was now living creature. Stick handle was now snake's head, and the raised head came closer, closer. A sensation like fear crept through Sparrow, trembling and weak as he already was from the water. Yet it was not like the fear that makes you shrink away, cower in a corner, or even run. Indeed as the snake bent towards him, it seemed that he was also bending towards it. Its eyes seemed to be shining, so that they made a circle of gold light all round its head. Its head, black in the midst of the circle, came closer still, grew larger, swayed from side to side, as though searching for something in each of his eyes in turn.

Sparrow watched, fascinated, as the thin black tongue flickered in and out. Then all at once the snake drew back its lips, bared its fangs, and struck. With a cry, Sparrow clutched at his left eye and fell backwards, gurgling into the stream as the water closed over his head.

out of the coils

SEEING HER FRIEND ABOUT TO TRY AND SHAKE HANDS WITH a head that had no body was enough for Lissie. With a scream of "Kittel!" she launched herself across the circular chamber and grabbed Kittel by the shoulders before she had reached the stone table.

"Trina! Not here!" Kittel hissed at her through her teeth, trying to free herself. But Lissie hung on for dear life. The more Kittel struggled, the more Lissie held on, until, tripping on a leg of the table, they lost their balance and both landed sprawled on the floor, Kittel on top.

They would have gone on struggling, if it hadn't been for the crow.

The crow was lying just in front of their noses. Lissie had barely hit the floor when the bird's still body gave a jerk and then a heave.

One wing flapped, and then the beak opened. But what came out of the crow's beak was not a crow's voice; it was the deep, quiet voice of a man.

"Be still," the crow's beak said. "There's nothing to fear."

Lissie and Kittel grew quite still, and gaped. Ormand, standing in the doorway, gaped.

"The crow is unharmed," the voice went on. "It has only knocked itself senseless. Through it, I can speak to you. Listen: I am what you have come to find."

Kittel's eyes ranged round the chamber in a vague sort of way. It was Lissie who answered the crow. "You can't be," she blurted, "because we're not looking for anything. We – we got lost in here, and we're trying to get out."

"No, stupid," Kittel interrupted, heaving herself up from on top of Lissie and looking not at the crow but straight at the head. "It was Dad we were trying to find – that was the whole point in going."

Lissie was still staring at the crow, but Ormand looked towards the head as Kittel spoke to it. He distinctly saw the lips smile on the peaceful face.

"I think you've got a beautiful face," Kittel told the head. "Now that we've found you, what should we do?"

The head smiled again. "You must go back out," the crow's beak stated in the man's voice.

"We don't know if we can," Ormand put in. "You see, we were shut into this maze thing – we think it's a spiral – by someone. They wanted—"

"They wanted you to be lost in amazement," the man's voice interrupted gently. "But it is not what they shall have. You will keep your feet on the ground – to that extent I can help you. Go now."

And suddenly Herold gave a great jerk, then a great sigh. His eye opened and for a moment glared up at Lissie, who scrambled to her feet and backed away. But Herold flapped his wing free of the wall and flew up to the roof of the small room with a loud squawk of bird invective. Then he flew down and perched on Lissie's head; she clung to Ormand and rolled her eyes distrustfully upwards, but didn't try to remove the uninvited guest.

"But Dad!" Kittel exclaimed. "We've come all this way to find you! You're not going to make us go away again?"

"Ngaio ngomo ignomo naiarabaranara," the head intoned senselessly, out of its own mouth now.

They listened to the stream of wordless sounds for a few seconds more, and then –

"I want you to come with us," Kittel declared.

"What – that?" Lissie squeaked, swinging round towards her friend and flapping her hand towards the head. "You can't touch *that*!" Then – "Ow!" for her sudden movement had made the crow grip tightly on to her head to keep his balance.

"Yes," Kittel replied determinedly. "We've come all this way, and honestly I don't like going on the Underground at the best of times with all those strange people about, so I don't see why we should have a wasted journey."

"It's not your dad, Kittel!" Lissie cried, almost in tears. "It's just a head on a spike – it's horrible."

Kittel stared stupidly through her. It was impossible to tell if she'd even heard what Lissie had said.

Fright was making Lissie angry. "Well, I'm not staying with you if you've got it," she said fiercely. "I'm going."

"We really should stay together you know, Lissie," Ormand said, though his voice was trembling. "It's not very nice in here."

"I know that," Lissie flashed back at him, "so I don't see

why we should try to make it nastier!" And she turned round to leave the chamber.

But Kittel seemed as determined as Lissie. By the time Lissie had stepped out into the passageway (Herold still gripping doggedly to her head), she had crossed the room again, skirted the stone table, and was within reach of the head on its tripod. Ormand remained where he had been, unable to decide whether to follow Lissie or stay with Kittel. Lissie continued on her way, and by the time Kittel reached out to the head, murmuring, "Come on, Dad, don't mind Trina," Lissie was out of Ormand's sight.

But even Lissie, out in the passageway, stopped dead when Kittel touched the head. And Ormand, who was neither coming nor going, clapped his hands over his ears and let himself sink into a huddle on the floor.

292   What happened when Kittel touched the head seemed to happen somewhere deep inside their own heads, but it seemed like other things happening round them. It was as if the light altered, as if it became dimmer, as if a dark mist were starting to blow in front of their eyes; it was as if a low moaning wind got up somewhere far away in some hidden corner of some hidden passageway, and were rising and rumbling down the great spiral corridor towards them; as if the rocky walls were suddenly coming alive. And it was as if a hideous, buzzing voice were speaking right next to their ears, "Beware – beware – beware – beware – beware."

It was that voice above all which made Ormand cower down and cover his ears. There was something about its menace so powerful, so crushing, it almost made his heart stop beating.

Kittel, too, seemed paralysed, her fingers still resting on the smooth, cold hair of the head. Everything else in the room had faded almost to nothing; Ormand was nothing more than a twisted hump of rock on the floor. The dark mist seemed to be growing round her eyes, and she thought with horror that she must be going blind. But if anyone there had been capable of watching her, what they would have seen was her vacant, faraway look fading. The horror was somehow settling out all the confused crowd of faces and chattering voices in her mind – bringing her swiftly back to herself. Without looking at the head, she was tugging, tugging, trying to free her fingers from the cold thing they seemed to be stuck against.

Out in the passageway, Lissie saw the walls and ceiling and floor begin to heave and writhe as if they were all made of glistening skin, while Herold was clinging to her head so tightly it felt as though his claws would dig right into her skull.

Ten seconds – ten minutes, ten hours it seemed like – they remained; all the while Kittel more and more desperately tried to force her fingers away from the head. The nonsense about her dad had faded – of course she wasn't back at home! All she wanted now – all she had ever wanted in her life, it seemed – was to get her hand away from the cold, dead thing under her fingers, and go free, to scream, to panic, anything as long as it would stop the buzzing voice and the moaning wind and the dark mist...

And suddenly her hand was her own again. They were free! Kittel heard the boy across the chamber give a groan, and saw him start to crawl towards the doorway. The dark mist was clearing a little. The voice was still there, the wind, the writhing of the walls, but it wasn't as bad as it had been; it didn't make you unable to move, it left you free at least to –

293

To run! One by one, Lissie, Ormand and Kittel began to stumble blindly, faster and faster, half in terror of some following evil, half in relief at getting away from the awful whatever-it-was that had seized on them in the central chamber. On and on, down the writhing, mist-darkened, moaning corridors, on and on, faster and faster along the way they had so uncertainly come, through the widening coils, on and on, on and on...

Until, surely, they were in the outer circle, stumbling past the now red-sputtering torches, Lissie still in the lead, Herold flapping along grimly beside her, Ormand following, Kittel, her breath coming in painful gasps, bringing up the rear.

They were near the outside, but how were they going to get out? Lissie remembered the door, but she also remembered the blank wall where the door had been; Kittel could remember nothing – nothing but standing on the lake shore with Herold while the soft mist writhed towards them out of the trees... Must they stumble on, round and round this awful outer corridor, until one by one they ran into the blank end wall and had to turn?

With a downward explosion of earth and stones, then a downward explosion of light – the common, blinding light of everyday – the ceiling of the passage a short distance ahead of them was torn open. They came to an abrupt halt, Ormand running slam into Lissie, Kittel tripping crack over Ormand's heel and finishing up on her hands and knees. Herold flew on and seemed to have disappeared in the cloud of settling dust. They had come to the end of their running; but were they free? Was it as easy as that?

Something was moving in the hole that had appeared in the ceiling. Something small, black, wedge-shaped, waving to and fro. The thing disappeared from the bright hole, but a second later reappeared hanging from the ceiling of the tunnel, still keeping up its sinister waving to and fro, extending steadily downwards. Lissie gave a little gasp and shrank back against Ormand, who stepped back on to Kittel's leg and nearly lost his balance. Sliding down into the tunnel from above was coil after coil of black and red snake.

From the ceiling down to the pile of stones and earth on the floor the snake stretched, and when its throat had reached the ground, the remainder of its length slithered down after it. But none of the three children in the tunnel could move, not even Kittel who, still on her hands and knees, was looking more or less straight into the snake's pale, expressionless eyes. Something about those eyes held them absolutely still. They had run to the end of their running; all they could do now was wait for whatever would happen to them.

the vault of the bear

"WHAT ABOUT THAT ROPE?" A CLEAR, PIPING VOICE SAID.

Bull jumped, clean off the ground, for he had thought he was alone. He looked round, but it was several moments before he saw the speaker, sitting in a tree just above his head. It was a white-haired, wrinkle-faced, green-eyed, green-coated old man, and he was so small he could almost have sat in the palm of Bull's hand.

"Who on earth are you?" Bull exclaimed. "Are you – you're not Puckel, are you?"

"Sparrow sent me," the tiny man piped. "I am his messenger."

"He never said he'd be sending a messenger," said Bull cautiously.

"He never said he wouldn't," the reply came. "But if you don't want a messenger, then I'm not his messenger, and be blowed to his message. I'm off." And he leaped to his feet and walked down to the end of his gently swaying branch.

"Wait," said Bull. "I didn't want – I didn't mean to make you angry. It's just – there's a lot of queer things going on. I don't know who I can trust."

The little man put his hands behind his back and pirouetted a couple of times on a twig, looking down at his feet.

"I'm sorry," said Bull. Bull didn't often say sorry to anyone, and the word only came out with a great effort. It was hard to say if the stranger appreciated the effort; he just went on looking down at his feet.

But presently he said, "Anyway, I gave it you."

"Did you?" said Bull. "What did you say?"

"I never repeat myself."

"Then what's the point – " Bull began, and checked himself, at the same time remembering the little man had said something about –

"What rope do you mean?" Bull enquired.

"Aha, so you heard me!" the piping voice said.

"I remember now."

"What else do you remember?"

"Well – there was a rope Sparrow used, way back when… I don't think anyone saw it often. It was Puckel's rope, I know that. It can't still be in Gogs' house, can it? That's when I last saw it…"

The little man jumped from the branch-end to the ground, trailing an arc of green light behind him. He stood in front of Bull, his head no higher than Bull's knee. "A rope to bind the fallen people," he said. "The dead not dead. Those you trust to go armed, day and night – crossed wood, shaft wood. Those you trust to pin down the tricksters with wood and iron. Then trussed in the rope where they fall."

"Did Sparrow tell you to say all that as well?" Bull asked

in some surprise.

"Every word," the little man piped, and melted away into the grass.

Bull blinked, scratched his head. He felt a little shaken, and didn't much like the idea of being watched without his knowing. Where was Sparrow anyway? Had Cross Lurgan and Noddy Borrow found him? And was that Puckel he had just seen? Apart from the size, he looked just like Sparrow's description of the old man of the mountains.

Sparrow said, "Can I see Bull because of the Secret Way?"

"No, clod-head," the stick replied. "You can see him because of me. Your messenger reached him by the Secret Way. I am letting you see this so that you will see how the Way can be used."

298   Sparrow chuckled, despite his aching head and his throbbing, blinded eye. He had found the little Puckel-messenger very droll. "He shouldn't have said I told him to say all that, though," he said. "That wasn't true."

"When you don't even know who you are, how can you say what messages you may or may not have given?" said the stick.

Sparrow was silent, gazing painfully into the pool of water the snake had led him to in the dark, before it had turned back into the stick again. He could see nothing of where the pool was or what kind of place they were in. All that was to be seen was the still surface of the water and in its depths the small figure of Bull, who was now toiling up the hill towards Gogs' house. Sparrow saw him slipping in through the front door without knocking. The house seemed to be deserted, though he saw Gogs' father working with a hoe in the field at the back.

The picture in the pool was changing constantly, showing Sparrow now a wide stretch of field and wood and hillside, now things very close up. He could see Bull in the little downstairs bedroom, scrabbling under the bed, pulling out old boots, an old pan lid, dust and cobwebs and, finally, something that looked like the biggest cobweb of all, but which Bull shook, then wound up and slung over his shoulder: a thin grey rope, the very one Sparrow and Kittel had brought down from Puckel's cave eighteen months before. It wasn't surprising it had been overlooked for so long; when Sparrow and Kittel had used it before, it had been invisible to most people.

The surface of the pool rippled and the scene changed completely. There was a crowd of people in a large hall – the village hall, Sparrow realized, and Ms Redwall was up on a platform making an impassioned speech. Everything seemed confused.

"To sweep out the dirt from under our beds," he heard Ms Redwall declaiming, "to bring back a sense of independence to this village, a pride in ourselves and what we can achieve without the help of any outsiders…" There was a lot more which Sparrow found hard to understand. A tremendous number of people seemed to be there, outside in the square as well as in the hall itself. Gradually, from things he could understand, he realized that Ms Redwall was talking about the Traders, and urging the village people to ban them all from the village for ever. She kept reminding them of Lissie's mother, "her mind quite destroyed", and saying that she had gone mad because of the strain of being married to a Trader, and that that was what would happen to the whole village if the Traders didn't go.

Sparrow felt a cold lump of fear growing in his stomach. What had been going on since he left? Had everything gone quite crazy? He remembered Gogs' deserted house – but then, there was Gogs' father out in the field. No, not everyone would be at this meeting. Some people, surely, wouldn't listen to this awful woman.

Almost immediately the scene changed again. He could still hear Ms Redwall's voice ranting away somewhere in the distance, but what he saw now was a small room full of people, men and women standing silently, listening to the distant voice with despairing faces. Plato Smithers was among them.

The picture in the pool faded. As it disappeared, Sparrow saw Bull come into the room and start to tell the people that he had had a message from Sparrow and that they were to have their crossbows with them at all times.

The water in the pool didn't go completely dark, and presently Sparrow realized that this was because he now had some idea of their surroundings. He seemed to be standing on the ground under a dark, starless sky. The eye where the snake struck him throbbed and seemed to be completely blind – but it was real darkness which was stopping him seeing properly. Dimly his good eye made out the dark massed shape of five huge trees surrounding a pool. They were holly trees, the biggest he had ever seen. "This must be Lissie's pool," he murmured. "Where she went. At Villas."

"It is called the Hollywell," the stick said. "It is most often the centre of the Enclosure. Does your eye pain you?"

"Yes," Sparrow said.

"It will heal. When the time comes, it will be your eyes

which tell you the truth. One eye to see the dreaming, one to see through it. We are at the Centre. From here all the angles of the Giants' Door can be seen. Look into the water."

Sparrow looked. At first he thought there was going to be another picture, but gradually it seemed rather that there was something like a disc of pure, shining blue lying at the bottom of the pool. Then he realized that the sand and gravel at the bottom had actually become transparent and the blue disc was beneath.

"Because you will see through all illusion, you will have no more need of your stone. Throw it into the pool."

"Why?" Sparrow exclaimed.

"Do as you're told." The stick was wrapped round his arm again, and now he thought he felt its grip tightening.

Reluctantly he drew the little rough pyramid out of his pouch and weighed it in his hand.

"It was supposed to go back and become a mountain again," he said. "I'm supposed to give it back to Puckel."

"What you are supposed to do with it, young slug, is what I tell you to do with it," the stick returned. "Now will you throw it, or will I have to twist your arm off first?"

There was no doubt of it – the stick was squeezing Sparrow's arm tighter and tighter. After what it had done to his eye, he thought it would have little difficulty in ridding him of an arm as well. "What'll happen to the stone?" he asked.

"Obviously, it will become a mountain," the stick replied drily. And Sparrow felt the pressure on his arm slackening. He took a deep breath and gently threw the stone towards the pool. It was like throwing a part of himself away.

There was barely a ripple. Sparrow watched, fascinated, as the stone seemed to float gently downwards – as if through thick oil – and then on, down, through the bottom, as if the gravel and sand were nothing but shadows across the blue disc. Suddenly the stone grew rapidly smaller. Sparrow bent forwards to see. It took him a moment to realize that it was not getting smaller but was falling, falling away through a great sky of pure, cloudless blue, falling into some measureless abyss of air. That was what the disc was! Not a disc at all, but a doorway through into some other place. Sparrow gazed and gazed, although by now the stone had fallen far out of sight. Try as he might, he could see no ground, no far-distant hazy earth for the stone to fall to...

Gradually the bright blue of that otherworldly sky changed to dark blue, and from dark blue to black: and the blackness rose up out of the hole in the bottom of the pool and gathered itself round Sparrow. All sight faded, all sense, all sound. Feeling vaguely for his arm, Sparrow noticed that the stick was gone; he was alone. His heart beat fast, then slowed. Time might have passed, there in the sightless dark, but even his heartbeat had grown so quiet and slow that there was nothing by which to measure it.

"We must wait for the moon to rise," said a dry, scrapy voice beside his ear.

Sparrow started, and his heart was beating again. It was the stick's voice, but not quite the stick's voice... It seemed to have grown gentler; in fact, it reminded Sparrow strongly of his old teacher, Ms Minn.

"Be calm," the voice said. "This is a strange place, because it is not really any place but the end of all places.

In the daylight world it can't be found; but here, in the darkness, all things come together. This is the Enclosure. Listen now, and I shall tell you the names of the five angles, and when I finish, the moon will rise.

"The Star Wheel you know of from my brother. The Vault of the Bear you will come to shortly. These make up one side of the Door. Remember the names; one day you will need to know them. Facing these two are the Scroll Cupboard and Mother Egg; and at the top King Puck, which holds the whole doorway together."

And the moon was there. There had been no rising, no slow gathering of light on a dark horizon; simply, one moment complete blackness, the next, the calm, milky moon. Sparrow was standing in a circle of high, steep rocks, and before him there was a cave.

It was not the only cave in that dark, rocky enclosure. He turned a little to the left, and saw another. He turned again; his eyes picked out a third in the deep shadow cast by the moon.

303

There were five caves altogether, spaced regularly round the rocky walls. Five black, secret mouths in a circle round him; and he was alone in the circle in the moonlight; the stick was gone from his arm; the snake was not there.

He gazed up at the blue-creamy orb in the black sky. A wisp of cloud moved across it, like a tangle of hair over a wild old, mild old face. Sparrow asked the moon, "Why did I need to hear the names?"

The moon replied, in the voice that was like the stick's voice but not quite the stick's voice. "Understand," it said, "that you do both the things you want to do and the things which must be done. So, there is a way home for the girl, and you will find it. You have been told this already. Why do you imagine you were given magical gifts?"

"To help her get back home?" Sparrow suggested.

"You say to help her get back home," the moon said. "But this is only what you *want* to do. There is also the thing which *must be done*. The way which you and the girl will find is this thing. You will not find it only for her or for yourself, but for many others. The girl was brought here so that she and you should find the way back. Now, I ask again – why do you imagine you were given magical gifts?"

"Well," Sparrow answered uncertainly, "I helped Puckel when he had fallen down through—"

"You are wrong again," the moon interrupted. "Your gifts were to prepare you for learning the Secret Way of the Mountains. Games to play, but games with a purpose. The learning of the Secret Way also has a purpose, but mastering the masters of the dreaming is no game. It is part of a battle with deadly danger. You were needed for this and chosen for this, and soon you will face the hardest test of all, which will decide whether the choice was a right one."

"What's that?" Sparrow breathed, now thoroughly alarmed.

"If I told you anything about it, it might ruin your chance of coming through," the moon replied. "Puckel believes you will pass the test; he believes you are your father's son."

"What's my father got to do with it?"

"Everything," the moon replied.

There was a silence. For a while Sparrow felt too confused to speak. Then all his doubts and confusion came together in a single question, the question he had been longing for years to ask of someone who might know the answer. And here was someone – or something – who seemed to know. "What happened to my father?" he asked.

"He was eaten by a bear." The moon floated in the black sky, expressionless.

"Oh," said Sparrow. He felt cold.

"Now you must do what you're here to do," said the moon. "The cave you are looking at leads to the Vault of the Bear. You remember your task?"

"I've to try and find out what the Polymorphs have stolen from it."

"Do it then."

Sparrow walked over the uneven ground and entered the cave. Although the rocky mouth was in deep shadow, it was less dark inside than he had expected – or at least he could see more clearly than he had expected to. Ahead of him was a heavy wooden door with a large something carved on it where you would expect the knocker to be. Sparrow stared in the deep darkness at the carved shape. It showed a snarling bear's head – not life-sized, but very realistic. There was a wooden bar across the door. He lifted it and pushed.

305

He was in a small, round chamber – if he had known, very like the chamber which Kittel, Lissie and Ormand had come to in the centre of the Labyrinth. There was a shaft of moonlight slanting across from somewhere high up in the vaulted roof. It fell across a great shape on a stone couch in the centre of the chamber. With his skin crawling, Sparrow went hesitantly over to it.

It seemed to be the statue of a man lying on his back. A stone sword lay at one side of him; at his other side, cupped in his stone hand, was a stone bear's head with snarling jaws. What looked like a huge round plate lay against his feet. "A shield," Sparrow breathed. The man's clothing seemed curiously smooth in some parts – over the chest, for example – and curiously sharp in others. "He's wearing armour," Sparrow whispered. "It's the statue of a knight, like in the stories. And the bear's head is his hood – he's the one who came to help the Traders.

Down one side of the couch Sparrow crept, round the foot, and along the other side. The shaft of moonlight fell full on the great round shield, leaving the shoulders of the statue in deep shadow. Sparrow inched softly towards the shadowed head.

The head was missing. Sparrow had to feel with his hands to be quite sure, because it was so dark at this end. But there was no doubt about it. There was a stone pillow where the head should have rested; but moving his fingers gently along the armour-plated shoulders, Sparrow could feel the stump of the neck ending in a rim of jagged stone. Some enormously powerful hands must have seized the head and broken it off.

So that was it! Sparrow wanted to make sure, and crawled about the dark floor of the chamber, searching to see if the head could simply have fallen off. But he was already certain. *This is the moving of a stone from where it should be to where it shouldn't be* – the otter's message drifted into his memory. A stone head!

At last he got up, went back through the door and let the bar fall into place behind him.

Out in the courtyard of rocks the milky moon gazed down.

"Was anything missing?" the moon asked.

"The head," replied Sparrow. "They've stolen the knight's head."

"Then we must find it. The cave next to it on your left leads to the Star Wheel; I shall go first."

Sparrow went to the next cave mouth and waited. Nothing happened.

"Come on, we haven't all night," the moon's voice came, but with just a trace of snappishness that reminded Sparrow strongly of the stick.

Still he could see no one, but he did notice that a thin moonbeam had cleared the edge of the cave mouth and was shining into the depths. Sparrow went in. And the strange thing was that, although he should have blocked off the light, the moonbeam shone as steadily as ever.

The cave was nothing like the Vault of the Bear: it was little more than a rough hollow scooped out of the rock. Sparrow turned round, bewildered. Then he noticed the floor. The floor was not rough, but polished like marble. And on it was graven a pattern of five sides. "It's the shape of the door," Sparrow said – "at the cottage and in the tower."

307

"You will see doors where there are doors to see," the moon – or the stick – said. "This is your door."

"Will you come with me?" asked Sparrow.

"That will depend on you. If your door is big enough, you will be able to take others with you."

Sparrow considered. "The only thing," he said, "is that it isn't really a door, is it? How am I to open it?"

"Stamp on the floor," the voice whispered.

And Sparrow stamped. Once he stamped, and the floor gave back a dull, solid sound. Twice he stamped, and the floor sounded with a distant echo. Three times he stamped, and there was a noise like thunder in the walls of the cave – and suddenly everything collapsed; walls, roof, rock floor, black sky and moon disappeared and he was standing in the glaring daylight, with a summer sunrise just appearing over the edge of a hill behind him – exactly where the moon had been.

But in the grass at his feet was a great, gaping hole, through which the light fell on a pile of earth and rocks in a reddish-hued passageway. Carefully he let himself down through the hole.

broken stone

IT TOOK SPARROW SOME MINUTES TO REALIZE THAT THE
place Puckel and the stick called the Star Wheel must be
the same as the Labyrinth of the Polymorphs. He had not
been expecting to find Kittel. Even if he had been, he
would certainly not have expected to so soon; he had imagined a labyrinth to be a place like the copper mine outside
the village, full of complicated underground passages
where you could get lost for ever. He gaped rather stupidly
at the three of them before he understood, though even
then he could not think how Lissie and the stranger –
Ormand – had got there.

As for Kittel, Lissie and Ormand, they were so intent on
the approaching snake that for a while they did not even
notice the darkening of the light through the hole in the
tunnel ceiling. Nor did they notice the pair of legs dangling
through the hole, then the body suspended on its elbows
from the top of the hole. Closer the snake slid; and it was

not until it had cast its long, patterned body on the floor all about the group of children and gripped on its tail with its hard black lips that they were able to look up suddenly and see Sparrow coming towards them with – quite how, they couldn't imagine – Herold perched companionably on his shoulder.

He looked a bit breathless and a bit tousled – just like the Sparrow Lissie and Kittel knew – but even in that first moment of seeing him, the two girls immediately sensed there was something different. For a moment, it did cross Kittel's mind that this was not the real Sparrow at all, but another trick of the Polymorphs; she had after all been mistaken about her own sister. On the other hand, if this was a trick, surely they would have taken the trouble to make the trick Sparrow exactly as she remembered the real one – and this Sparrow had the most splendid black eye she had ever seen. No, it was certainly Sparrow; but something had happened to him – apart from the black eye. He was changed.

"That's the way out, I think," he said at length, pointing to the hole in the ceiling. "I don't know exactly where it goes to. But I think there may be something here I've got to collect before we can get away."

"Collect?" echoed Kittel, although she had already guessed. "What?"

"A head," Sparrow replied. "Have you seen one?"

"No!" Lissie brought out in a half scream before anyone could answer.

"Yes, we have," said Ormand, as bravely as he could, though his teeth were chattering; "but I don't think you can just collect it."

"Where is it?" Sparrow asked.

"Oh, it's easy enough to find," Lissie put in again, in a high, wavery voice. "You just follow the passage, and you're bound to come to it."

"Isn't this a labyrinth, then?" Sparrow asked.

"It's a spiral," Lissie said.

Sparrow hesitated. He could see from their faces that Kittel, Lissie and Ormand had had a severe fright. Would he be able to seize the stone head? Certainly he would have a good chance of it if he took the stick; but the stick, in its snake form, had circled itself round the three of them. It was quite obvious it intended to protect them, and not to go anywhere with Sparrow. He would have to do without.

"Is the head guarded?" he asked.

"Well, not exactly," Kittel replied uncertainly. "Not exactly guarded."

"Then what's so bad about it?" Sparrow asked. "It's just a stone head."

"Stone?" Lissie let out in a squeak of disbelief. "You call that stone?" She was shuddering.

"What was wrong with it?" said Sparrow.

"It was alive," said Kittel after a short silence.

"Alive?" Sparrow repeated. "How?"

"I don't know," Kittel said in a low voice. "It was just a head, on a spike sort of thing, and it was speaking. It spoke to us. I can't remember much about it; I came over a bit strange. I think it must have been the head of the Polymorphs."

"No," said Sparrow in a puzzled voice. "No, it can't have been. It doesn't belong here. It's just something they've stolen. But it's only stone."

"Well, this one certainly wasn't," Kittel insisted.

Sparrow was puzzled. He had not been expecting this.

Then at last it occurred to him. Of course! Why hadn't he thought of the most obvious thing first! "You were being tricked," he explained. "It wasn't really alive at all. The Polymorphs were just making it seem alive!"

Kittel looked doubtful. Lissie and Ormand looked blank.

"I'll be back soon," Sparrow said. "You'd better not try to step over the snake. She's protecting you."

"Some protection," muttered Lissie, looking down distastefully at the lithe, glistening creature.

Sparrow had already disappeared. Herold, overjoyed at having his old friend back, had demanded that Sparrow change into his shape there and then, and crow-shape seemed as good a way of getting along as any. So Sparrow ventured into the very heart of the Polymorphs' power without stick, stone, or even the security of being in his own body.

Before long he had drawn into the tight centre of the Star Wheel, and the murmuring voice came to his ears.

He took on his own shape again. Surprisingly, Herold didn't protest; nor did he choose to perch on Sparrow's shoulder, but fluttered down to the floor and walked like a dog at his heel as he crept towards the low voice from the central chamber. It never occurred to Sparrow that the bird was behaving in this odd fashion because it had begun to feel faint. He reached the doorway, and paused.

Slowly the hair on the back of his head began to rise. Was this an illusion? He had come looking for a stone head; without his own stone how could he tell if this talking head were real or a trick? Had he come, here in the heart of the Polymorphs' power, upon the first and strongest of the Polymorphs, Bur of the Lamps? Could he be hopelessly trapped in illusion?

Sparrow stepped backwards out of the chamber and out of sight of the head. Nothing changed, nothing stirred the smooth stream of sound, nothing stopped him from going as he had come.

Finally he went into the chamber again and spoke to the head. There seemed to be nothing else he could do; it was not a stone head, but it was the only head he had come across. "Are you the head of the statue in the Vault of the Bear?" he asked.

The torch in the chamber sent up a spout of flame, blue-edged with sparks, and then died down again; but the head didn't react. "Nongonothara rambara faiallafala," it chanted peacefully.

Suddenly, at Sparrow's feet, Herold flapped, left the ground, and with four or five feeble wing-beats flew up to the little stone table in the centre of the room, where he promptly collapsed.

313

"Herold, what is it?" said Sparrow, going anxiously over to the table.

Herold made no reply. The lids slowly closed over his eyes. His wings were flopped out to either side of him.

"Herold!" Sparrow said again. He did not notice that his voice was the only sound in the chamber. The head had fallen silent.

Then Herold's beak moved. "Sparrow," said a deep voice.

Sparrow looked all round – at the head, at the door, under the table. But he knew the voice had come out of Herold's beak, and it was not Herold speaking. Was it the power of the Polymorphs? In that moment, and against all common sense, Sparrow made a bold guess that it was not.

There was something here, something less strong than magic, but older, deeper rooted, more homely – something he could not quite put his finger on... "How do you know my name?" he mumbled, looking now not at the crow but straight at the head.

The head only smiled, a slow, dreamy, mysterious smile. A smile, somehow, of great fondness. It was almost as though the head had known – and loved – Sparrow for years and years.

But even now, despite all the little hints and glimpses he had been given, Sparrow did not guess. A dozen questions were whirling through his mind that weren't the real question, a dozen confusions that made him unable to see what was obvious.

"Why do you have to talk through the crow?" he asked. "Why do you just talk nonsense when you're by yourself?"

Again came the head's mysterious smile. "It's not nonsense," the voice answered. "When I speak without a living mouth to speak through, what I say is not words, but the thing that words come from, little islands in the ocean of sound. Before the Polymorphs parted head and body, I could speak. Now, without a living mouth to speak through, I can only sing the beginnings of words."

"Is your mouth not a living mouth?" Sparrow said. "You can smile, and you can make sounds, so you must be alive. You can't be – dead, can you?"

"I am neither one thing nor the other," the voice replied. "Don't be frightened."

"I – I don't think I am, really," said Sparrow.

"Good," the voice replied. "Then listen. There is a place where the living and the dead come together. That's all I can tell you. That place is called the Vault of the Bear.

I am not dead; but I am also not alive in the way you are. I have been eaten."

"By a bear?" Sparrow said, in so soft a whisper he could hardly hear it himself.

"That's what we say," the voice of the man replied. "There is a power we call the Great Bear, whose image you see circling in the stars about the Pole Tower. This power is enclosed in the Vault of the Bear. So we say I have been eaten by the Great Bear, and my place is in its belly."

"Do you mean," Sparrow said at last in a small, rough-throated whisper, "you are – the stone man is…"

"Your father, Sparrow. I'm sorry we must meet like this. The Polymorphs have prevented our meeting where we should have met, in the Vault of the Bear itself, where you could have sat by my side, and we could have talked, and from where we could have gone out together to clean the Star Wheel of the murk which was gathering in its coils. That can't happen now."

"But – but, I don't understand," Sparrow faltered. "When I was there, there was a statue, just a statue made of stone…"

The head smiled again. "At times, yes. Though we could still have spoken. That statue was far older than I, and was only inhabited by me after I was eaten, and before me by the father of your mother. But at times the sleep of stone would fall off me, and then my flesh would become as warm and living as when I was alive; the breastplate of my copper armour would shine in the sun. Not now. Not now that the Polymorphs have stolen the sleeping head from the sleeping body. That will never happen again."

"I've been sent here to bring you back," Sparrow said. "Puckel sent me."

"Puckel sent you," Sparrow's father agreed, "but he

didn't send you to bring me back. That can never happen now. He sent you to find me."

"Well, it's the same thing, isn't it?" said Sparrow, while a cold dread crept into him.

"No," his father's voice answered. "Listen. This head contains my power, the power Puckel gave me when I became the Guardian of the Vault of the Bear. Now the power is stolen; but the head is only the vessel the power is held in; it's no more than a bottle, a jug, a bucket. They have the power. You could pick up the head and carry it out of the Star Wheel now, and the Polymorphs wouldn't try to stop you. They wouldn't need to. It would all be illusion. As soon as your back was turned, the head would again be here in the inner chamber. Only dragon fire can now return the power to the place where it should be."

"Then what can I do?" said Sparrow despairingly.

"There is only one thing you can do," the voice replied softly. "You must destroy the vessel."

"What do you mean?" Sparrow gasped.

"The head," the deep voice replied. "You must break the head in pieces."

"No!" Sparrow wailed. He had known, deep inside himself, that this was what was coming, that this was what he feared.

"Two things the Polymorphs did not reckon on," the voice said. "One was this peculiar crow's hunger for sleep. The other was that through the sleeping crow I would be able to speak and so tell you what must be done with the head. Don't waste our chance."

"No," Sparrow said. "I can't destroy it. I can't do that! Never! You're my father! I've always wanted to find you! I can't, I can't!"

"I'm not your father, Sparrow," the voice said when he had become silent. "Think – your father isn't a head on a steel spike! When I was your father I was a man, a whole, living man. When I took my place in the belly of the Great Bear I remained your father, and I remain your father still. We can speak to each other, but we can't do the things that fathers and sons do together. That is something you will never have. But I haven't told you to destroy *me* – only the head which the Polymorphs are using for twisted purposes."

Sparrow was shaking all over. He heard what the voice was telling him, but he couldn't understand it. "No," he said. "No, I'm not going to do it; you can't make me do that – Puckel can't make me – no one can make me. I won't – I just won't!"

And without waiting for his father to reply, Sparrow reached over, seized the head – cold as it was, and heavy, but not quite stone-like – and wrenched it off the tripod. An instant later, he was skimming along the corridor with it held firmly between his hands.

Sparrow had silenced his father – and he had never felt more miserable. He knew he had done something terribly wrong. Because he had not wanted to hear what his father was telling him, he had deliberately left the crow behind, possibly unconscious, entirely at the mercy of the Polymorphs. He knew that was an unforgivable thing to do but it had not stopped him doing it. The one thought that was filling his head was that he had found his father, and he wasn't going to give him up. He didn't concern himself about the fact that a mere head – particularly one that can't even speak – is little use to anyone; somehow, some time, he would get that sorted out. Perhaps Puckel would help, or if not Puckel, perhaps the stick – or even one of the Polymorphs. What did it matter?

It seemed like no time at all before he was rounding the steady curve of the outer circle of the Star Wheel and seeing the light ahead from the hole in the ceiling. Kittel, Lissie and Ormand were running towards him. "Quick, Sparrow, be quick!" Kittel was calling. "Something's started to happen!"

Wondering vaguely what had happened to the snake, Sparrow landed at a run and stopped in front of his friends, staring at them with a wild, confused expression but saying nothing. All three of them were talking very fast and excitedly to him, but all Sparrow could make out was something about a wind rising. It seemed they had not noticed he was holding the head. Then they did, and one by one they fell silent.

318

Kittel looked awed, and Ormand looked scared. But Lissie screwed her eyes tight shut, clapped her hands over her ears, and started screaming.

"I won't go with you! I won't look at that thing!" they made out among the screams. "I'll stay here in the dark and never see anyone again! Get it out of my sight! Get it out, get it out!"

"Come on," said Sparrow after a moment, "we've got to get going. Help her, you two, and follow me."

"Listen to that wind!" Ormand groaned between chattering teeth.

But Sparrow could hear no wind; he could hear nothing but the blood beating in his ears. Without looking round to check whether Ormand and Kittel had managed to get Lissie to her feet, he took a tighter grip of the head and went towards the square of light in the ceiling of the passage.

He had just set his foot on the pile of earth and stones

underneath the hole when a distant squawk of rage cut through the rushing in his ears. He paused, guilt and misery forcing him to stop and think what he was doing.

"Treacherous! Traitor! Disloyal! Unworthy!" the voice screamed at him, echoing down the passageway. Kittel, Ormand and Lissie paused too and turned to see where the din was coming from. They couldn't hear the words as Sparrow could, but they could be in no doubt about what the noise meant. And for Sparrow, though used to the crow's abuse, every word cut like a knife. Herold flew straight towards him where he stood just below the bright daylight.

Straight towards his face. And Sparrow realized now that the strange, swimming motion of the bird's flight was caused by his good eye being full of tears. He blinked, and wondered when he had started crying. He wished he could stop. But he couldn't, and through his blurred vision he saw Herold, magnified to twice his usual size, flapping slowly – amazingly slowly – towards him.

319

Herold was actually heading for Sparrow at great speed. And it was really due to bad luck that he was heading for his face – although he had been beside himself with crow-ish fury, it would never have entered the bird's head actually to attack his friend. It was simply that he had suddenly become unconscious again, in mid-flight. And just at the last moment – the moment when he was filling the whole of Sparrow's blurred vision – his beak opened wide, and the deep, urgent voice of a man filled the corridor.

"Destroy the head!" it boomed. "Quick! Now! Here! Now! Destroy the head!" And Herold came to the abrupt end of his flight.

Sparrow had seen it coming, but he seemed powerless to do anything about it. Herold was heading straight for his eyes. At the last moment, instinctively, he cried out and threw up his hands to shield his face. The head flew out of his grip, fell with a dull thud on to the pile of earth and rolled – with a crooked, swaggering roll – along the floor of the corridor towards Kittel, Lissie and Ormand. Kittel leaped over it. She thought Herold was attacking Sparrow and her main idea was to help him. Ormand hesitated as the head bowled along towards them, but swerved to avoid it at the last minute. Lissie did not notice it at all – until it came to a stop at her toes.

Lissie had been terrified, horrified, had screamed and had sobbed. Now, staring down at the thing on her foot, she found she was angry. There was no screaming from her now; only a whisper, but it was a whisper like the hiss of a snake. "No, I won't have it – I won't have it. Destroy the head? Yes, I'll destroy the head – I'll smash you, I will!" And as she said it, she glanced round for a weapon…

The first thing her eye fell on was not a stone or a piece of rubble fallen from the corridor roof. It was a stick lying unnoticed against the wall. A stick of smooth, polished wood, rather twisted, and not all that solid. But it was enough, and Lissie bounded over to it, kicking the head against the opposite wall as she did so.

A groan – the groan of a man – came from Herold's beak as the head hit the wall. Sparrow, who had sat down with the force of the crow's dive, heard it – but not Lissie. She was too intent on her work. *Thwack*! The stick made contact. The man's voice groaned again from the crow's beak. "Yes," she said, "that's one from me." *Thwack*! Another groan. "And that's –" *thwack*! – "for my mad –" *thwack*! – "mother; and that's for my mad –" *thwack*! – "friend." And now silence from the crow. Sparrow was up on his feet, running towards Lissie, yelling something as he ran. Lissie wasn't even aware of him; she heard nothing but the crack of her club on its target – saw nothing, because her eyes were tight shut. That stick may not have been heavy or solid, but it had cracked the head like an eggshell.

Sparrow launched himself – not at Lissie, but along the floor, right under her stick. When her next blow fell, it was across his back. But for all the notice he took of it, it might have been a feather duster. He lay on the floor, cradling the head in his arms and groaning, "Oh no – no!" For it was already too late – the head lay in two pieces – stone pieces: cold, lifeless, and rock hard; no head of a living man, but a piece of a statue. Lissie stopped flailing, opened her eyes and gaped.

The only one who remained calm in all the confusion was Kittel, who was always good in a crisis. She had heard the voice of the man, and by the time she had reached Sparrow on the pile of earth she had realized that Herold hadn't been attacking him at all, and that the head had taken over the crow again. She didn't know if this was a trick of the Polymorphs, but it didn't seem to make any difference. She knelt down and carefully lifted the limp body of the bird from where it lay half buried in a pile of small stones. Then she turned round to see what was going on. But though she saw Lissie laying into the head with her stick, and Ormand coming up behind her as if to restrain her, and Sparrow diving to shield the head – why was he trying to protect it? – there was something else that was taking up her attention.

There was something menacing, ominous, distantly disastrous about the wind which had again begun to rise and moan in the far-off corridors. Now and then it would gather itself and rise, for a moment, to a thunder that shook the walls (though not a breath could she feel), only to die away again. But all the time, in some way, Kittel felt it was coming closer.

Carefully, she replaced Herold on the ground and ran back to Lissie, Ormand and Sparrow. She recognized the stick. "Go on, Lissie," she said urgently, grabbing her friend by the shoulders and turning her to face the pile of earth and the daylight. "Get out of that hole, as quick as you can – and keep hold of that stick!" She gave Lissie a shove and turned to Ormand. "You've got to help me with him," she said, pointing to Sparrow. "We might have to use force." The broken head was unimportant to Kittel; she was more concerned with getting Sparrow to safety.

But Sparrow didn't need any persuasion. He seemed quite sensible, and when Kittel said they had to get out and not waste any more time, he scrambled to his feet, said, "Come on, then," and skimmed off after Lissie without a glance behind. Once at the hole, he gave her a helping heave up through the broken roof, then turned and helped Ormand and Kittel through as well. Kittel, who had taken charge of Herold again, thought Sparrow must suddenly be feeling better – whatever had been wrong with him – but she noticed he was as pale as putty.

Kittel scrambled up a steep bank of soft, yielding soil, and then she was lying between Ormand and Lissie on short, sweet-smelling grass. A second later Sparrow flew up through the hole in the earth and crouched beside them, looking round him. "I see," he said at last. "I see."

By now Lissie had looked up too. "Where on earth are we?" she exclaimed.

"In the Valley of Murmuring Water," Sparrow answered in a dull voice. "But we don't have a moment to lose."

the rain begins

SPARROW HAD HAD ALMOST AS MUCH AS HE COULD TAKE. Looking round now in the bright sunlight of the Valley of Murmuring Water, he was scarcely able to wonder that, all the while they had been living and working there, the Labyrinth of the Polymorphs had been under their very feet.

Listlessly he looked out over the bright little meadow. What was that strange movement in the grass – as if the land were bubbling? He rubbed his eyes and peered. What was he supposed to be doing?

It was Kittel who raised the alarm and got him moving. "Listen, Sparrow," she said, her voice hard with anxiety, "that's that wind we heard getting up; it's making the whole ground move. We have to get away from here."

Sparrow listened, and looked. The ground wasn't actually bubbling; what he could see as he stared across the valley up towards the cottage and to the foot of the mountain, was the spiral shape of the Star Wheel heaving in the ground, as though an enormous coiled worm were burrowing just below the surface. It was true; something was happening, something dangerous. It was risky, Puckel had said, to open a door between a place of power and the world of everyday. Where were Gogs and Murie? Were they somewhere out here, playing the fool with the cow and the goat?

"Come on," he said, scrambling to his feet, but almost immediately collapsing again to a crouch. "We've got to get there…"

"Where?" asked Kittel wildly. "Where can we go?"

"The cottage," Sparrow muttered, trying to summon up the energy to get up and run. "That's crazy," Kittel exclaimed. "That's right in the middle of it all! Just look!"

"I know," Sparrow answered, a little snappishly now because he was trying so hard to stay sensible and practical. "It's – it's an island. It's the only safe place. We've got to get everyone there."

Somehow they managed it, though the ground was difficult to walk on, and every now and again a great heave of the grass sent them staggering to their knees. All of them could hear the rising of the subterranean wind, growing now and then into gusts which bellowed out of the hole in the ground like the winding of a gigantic horn.

"Here," gasped Sparrow, as they were again tumbled off their feet in front of the little house; "we're safe here. Stay where you are."

The others looked doubtful. Sparrow staggered to the door of the house and seemed half to collapse there, leaning against one of the great stone doorposts. A moment later Kittel heard him repeating Gogs' and Murie's names.

"What's wrong? Aren't they in there?" Kittel said, getting up and coming over.

"Here they are!" Lissie called to him. "They must have been round the back of the house. They're here – so's the cow and the goat!"

Sparrow was sitting in the doorway. "Give me Herold, Kittel," he said, without so much as a glance to see if Gogs and Murie were unenchanted or not.

"I've got Herold – he's quite safe," Kittel replied, gently stroking the still body of the bird.

"Give him to me," Sparrow repeated. "Just give me him, and go and make sure the others stay here – right here, close to the door."

"All right," Kittel said quietly, looking at him anxiously. She handed him the crow and turned away. Sparrow, carefully cradling Herold against his chest, crawled into the dark shadows of the cottage.

325

Kittel, turning back to the others, saw that Ormand and Lissie had got up and were wandering away, looking disbelievingly at the small, hidden valley in the mountains and the wild heaving of its grassy floor. "Sparrow says you mustn't go away from the house!" Kittel called to them.

Ormand immediately came back, but although Lissie didn't go any further, she didn't follow him. Kittel turned to greet Gogs and Murie, who were standing by the corner of the house, looking bewildered. Murie had been having a dream, as she thought, of being the May Queen at a most unusual village festival. But since the "dream" had lasted three days and nights, during which she had had no food, she felt very shaky. Gogs was little better off, but at least he wasn't suffering from a badly-bruised rump.

Lissie was still holding the stick as she watched the

turmoil of the valley floor, and the moment Kittel called, she felt it jerk in her hand, and heard a quiet, but sharp and not very friendly voice say, "Throw me into the air."

Lissie looked round. She couldn't see where the voice had come from. The stick jerked again, very sharply. "Me – me – me, noddle-head; throw me into the air."

It was unmistakable. The voice was coming from the stick. As it spoke, it jerked. Lissie gazed down at it in astonishment. Her hand relaxed, and she let go.

The stick didn't fall. It remained suspended above the ground, just where she had been holding it. Then it jerked again, and seemed to move menacingly towards Lissie.

"Will you throw me into the air – or will I have to knock some sense into you first?" it grated.

"No – I mean, yes," Lissie said hurriedly.

"Then do it – now."

Lissie gulped and took hold of the stick again. "Where will I throw you?"

"Into the sun, of course," the stick retorted. "Then shout like mad when the rain begins. *Remind* Sparrow, since he seems to have lost his wits. Now, whirl me round, and throw, as hard as you can. It's a long way up to the sun."

"Yes, it is," agreed Lissie, and started to whirl the stick, too frightened to disobey.

Whizz – whizz – whizz! Lissie whirled the stick round above her head. A wind – a wind in the air, not at all like the bellowing gale under the ground – seemed to gather around it.

"Lissie – what are you doing?" She dimly heard Kittel's warning yell.

"Now!" cracked the stick's voice; and Lissie let go.

"Lissie!" came Kittel's scream.

But Lissie couldn't have disobeyed the stick, even if she had wanted to. It left her hand and shot up into the air straight for the sun, which by now was standing high above the wood beyond the stream. Quickly, Lissie turned and scampered back to give her message to Sparrow in the cottage.

She sped to the door, then stopped. Sparrow was there, but he was far away, unaware of anything that was going on. And despite the din of the seething earth and the bellowing horn of the underground wind, in the cottage there was absolute silence, and in the silence there was the distinct sound of a man's voice, softly – painfully – speaking. Lissie looked round doubtfully – and that was the moment when the earth burst open, and with a hissing roar like steam escaping from a steam-boiler the keepers of the Labyrinth came into the open. Lissie forgot everything else.

327

Sparrow heard none of it. In the darkness of the cottage he seemed to be enclosed in a shell, like a chicken waiting to be hatched. The man's voice had spoken from the crow's beak almost as soon as he had stumbled through the door, and though it was quiet, scarcely above a whisper, Sparrow had no difficulty in hearing it in the absolute stillness of the four walls.

"Sparrow," the voice said.

"Father?" said Sparrow in a small, wondering voice. "Are you still here?"

"I'm still here," the voice returned. "But not for long. Your friend is dying, and in a moment I must leave you alone with him. You shouldn't part with him while he feels you betrayed him."

"I'm going to lose Herold too," Sparrow blurted out in

a sob. "I'm going to lose everything. Kittel's going to go as well – I don't know when but I know she will, and I'm going to be left alone and Puckel and – and…"

"Hush," his father's voice whispered. "It won't be as bad as that, you'll see. Things are a lot better than you think. The head was destroyed, in the Star Wheel too – just as it should have been. The Polymorphs are in great trouble."

"Yes," Sparrow answered drearily, "but if your head's been destroyed, you won't be here any longer, will you? And if Herold's dying… Father, where will you be? You'll be gone, you'll have disappeared – it'll all be like it was before I found you, before—"

"Well, it was all right then, wasn't it?" his father interrupted him. "You managed, didn't you?"

"Yes, but that was before…" there seemed to be a knot in Sparrow's chest, and he was finding it difficult to speak. "It would have been better if everything had just stayed like that – if I'd never found you at all." He was clutching the body of Herold close against his stomach, cradling it passionately, full of the terrible fear of loss.

"Come," the man's voice whispered back at him out of the crow's beak. "You'd be quite surprised where I can get to. That otter, for example…"

"What about it?" Sparrow's interest kindled, in spite of himself.

The voice chuckled. "Otters are clever beasts, but they're not *that* clever. That was your old dad, letting you know he was in trouble."

"What? How?" Sparrow stammered.

"There's not much time," Sparrow's father answered, "but that was when my head had been removed from the

Vault of the Bear and was being taken to the Star Wheel. I could put my thought into the otter's brain, though at that stage I couldn't talk human words through its mouth. Luckily, you had been well taught, and knew what the otter was saying."

"I would never have thought of my stone – and the Pole Star – if it hadn't been for that!" Sparrow exclaimed. "And then I might never have found my way to Puckel and – what about the other time? Was that you too? But why did…?"

"That's as much time as we can have now. But we'll speak again. No – don't interrupt. You'll have work to do in a moment. The song, remember. All join hands… Goodbye for now, Sparrow. Be sure of yourself!"

"But I'm not… No, wait… Father! Don't go yet! Not yet! I want to…"

But he knew it was too late. The beak had closed. The black, hard eye had opened and was regarding him fixedly. Herold's chest gave a heave. Then the beak opened again, and one or two unintelligible squeaks and whiffles came out of it, as though the bird were clearing its throat. At last the voice spoke – not the man's voice any more, talking in human language, but the bird's voice, speaking the language that only Sparrow knew. "Friend…" it croaked. "Friend."

Sparrow couldn't bear it. "Oh, Herold," he groaned; "I left you behind – you could have been…"

"Nothing," the crow croaked – so softly now it was almost inaudible. "It was nothing."

"I'm sorry, Herold," Sparrow's voice sang the words softly over the top of a sob.

"Bounteous boy," the crow answered, while for a brief second his eye sparkled with its old life. He seemed to be summoning up one last great effort. "Everything I had was from you. Now the vessel is shattered, and your servant can depart in peace."

At any other time, Sparrow would have laughed over the crow's pompous words. As he looked down at the limp bundle of feathers in his hands, the crow's chest gave another great heave – a long, long breath out. Then Sparrow realized that the black beady eye was no longer seeing anything. Herold was gone. Gently, he laid the body on the floor and straightened up.

Without knowing why, he suddenly felt a lot better.

Outside the cottage, Kittel, Lissie, Ormand, Murie and Gogs gaped in horrified amazement. Where the small hole in the grass had marked the outermost circle of the Star Wheel there was now a massive, brown rent. Smoke billowed round its edges, staining the grass a dirty grey. And from the hole itself there coiled and climbed a shape that was not a shape, something that was not something, that baffled the eyes and confused the senses. There seemed to be faces in it, human faces or animal faces or faces half human, half animal; big faces, little faces, ugly faces, sad or furious faces, pudgy faces, noble faces, terrifying faces, faces peeping shyly or mischievously, faces blankly staring into great distances like the faces of statues… But human or animal, bird, fish or insect, the faces all the while seemed to be trying to drag themselves away out of the Thing, but as soon as they came out of it and became almost clear they were dragged back in. And the thing went on and on, pouring out of the hole, filling the air, darkening the sun, pouring upwards endlessly, more and more and more shapes and forms and faces.

330

When it filled half the sky, it changed. The shapes and faces kept pouring on and upwards out of the hole, but now there were whole scenes. There was nothing pleasant – only things decaying, collapsing, crumbling. A castle of stone rose up, and almost immediately slipped and slid into the wide moat of green water surrounding it. A horse was pulling a cart – the axle cracked and the wheels fell off, and the horse collapsed into slime and bones. Dead animals and the branches of trees floated by in the flood of a great, grey swollen river.

Lissie standing next to Murie, felt for her hand and gripped it tightly. "What is it?" she whispered.

Murie shook her head. "I don't know," she whispered back.

"It's horrible," Ormand muttered.

Though spreading over the whole sky, no part of the shadow came near them as they stood at the door of the cottage. But their eyes kept returning to a sort of mass or knot of darkness which seemed to be forming low down in its skirts. "What are we supposed to do?" Kittel said.

331

"Shout!" Sparrow's voice answered her.

Tearing their eyes away from the pouring Thing, all five of them turned round to see Sparrow, standing in the cottage doorway. He looked pale, his eyes were red-rimmed, his cheeks were extremely grubby, but though he gazed upwards at the tainted sky, there was a confident look on his face – almost a smile. And even as he came out from the doorway, gazing upwards, a great drop of water splashed on his nose and rolled down his cheek. Then another hit him smack in the eye and his face screwed up.

Splash! Splash! Massive drops of rain were coming down all round. Two of them were enough to make your head feel wet all over; on the roof they crashed into the warm thatch and hissed and steamed. The young plants in the garden were doing a slow-motion tango as the great gouts of water battered on their leaves. Faster the rain began to fall, but no less heavily, and all over the valley a sound like distant drumming began.

"Of course!" Lissie exclaimed. "That's what I had to tell you, Sparrow. We shout like mad when the drums – I mean the rain – begins!"

The force of the rain grew. Over the valley it no longer looked like rain, but like straight rods of grey steel, and the sound of the stream was already growing to a roar. The noise was becoming unbearable; if they looked upwards it was difficult to breathe for the crashing downpour. With an effort Lissie stared towards the sky. Still the endless procession of shapes and faces was up there, but all was coiling and writhing, and with tremendous relief she realized that the rain was not coming from the Thing spread through the sky, but from something above and beyond it. She looked down, gasping for breath.

"We've got to shout – as loud as we can!" Sparrow yelled above the tumult.

"Why?" Murie yelled back at him.

"I don't know!"

"What?"

"I don't know!"

"Oh – look!" Kittel screamed. "Look at it! Look! Look!"

The knot of darkness had formed into something like a tunnel – a dark, rocky track winding down out of a tunnel of murk; and there were two figures on the track, coming towards them, one bright, one dark, but both surrounded by an air of cruel menace.

"Oh, no," Sparrow heard Ormand whimpering, "it's him, with the lantern."

And it was about then that Sparrow discovered a difference in his eyes. The figures of the two Polymorphs became like shadows round something which he couldn't see properly – as though his eyes were tired and he were seeing double. And there was a third figure, like a shadow, huge, in front of them. What was happening? What had the stick said? One eye to see the dream… Like the way Herold looked at you, perhaps, out of one eye and then .the other. Sparrow covered his left eye – the damaged one – and the two figures became clear again, while the great shadow vanished. There, hastening on with huge jumping strides of its spidery legs, was the lantern-carrying horror which had shut Lissie and Ormand into the maze of the Polymorphs. And there beside it, flaming in gold and green light, strode the beautiful lady who had first ensnared Sparrow in the gully.

Sparrow covered his right eye, and let out a startled cry.

The blind eye could see, but not in the ordinary way; it was showing him what was behind the illusion of the Polymorphs' appearance. He had not had time to look at them clearly on the two occasions he had met them before, and there had been some things about their shape he had not understood. Now he saw the high, domed foreheads properly, the stooped shoulders that did not end in arms but in huge wings that bore the creatures clear of the ground; he saw the unearthly ugliness of them. And there were not two, but three.

The lady and the lantern carrier were advancing behind another huge form that could not be seen at all by normal vision. It was like them; had the same great shaggy wings

333

with the same slow, sickening beat – but it had two heads, and in the centre of each head was a glaring eye. The two heads swung imperiously this way and that, like a hunting beast searching for sight of its prey. The two glaring eyes were like lamps, one of them red-gold, one so pale it was almost white…

"Bur of the Lamps – if you'd seen him, you'd have known about it…" Sparrow remembered Puckel's words. This, he had no doubt, was the head of the Polymorphs; and the three were coming straight for them, stooping out of some unguessed depth of grey sky. Illusion or no illusion, Sparrow didn't like the look of either vision of the Polymorphs, but it was the awful eyes in the wild-swinging heads of the leader that most filled him with dismay.

"Bur of the Lamps; Ur, the linden lady; Eych, the Enslaver," he said aloud.

"What?" Murie said, staring at the advancing figures.

"Their names. They're called Ur, Eych and Bur."

"Ureych?" said Murie. "What sort of name's that?"

"They've stopped," Kittel exclaimed.

They had, but it was only a pause; a moment later they were advancing again. It was hard for Sparrow to tell exactly how far away they were, but on the rocky illusion-road they seemed to be about the distance of the stream.

"That's it!" Sparrow yelled. "Their names! We shout out their names! All their names! After me. There's more than two; just say them after me. Ur!"

The six of them clustered round. "Ur!" they shouted.

"All join hands, like in the song!" Sparrow said. "Now – Eych!"

"Eych!" they shouted, fumbling for each other's hands, but not daring to take their eyes off the approaching danger.

Feverishly, Sparrow cast back in his mind over the names he had heard from Puckel. He felt them all there in his memory, but still he worried he might forget them. Maybe the other three who weren't here didn't matter… Who were they, anyway? There was –

"Yo!" He shouted it as he remembered it.

"Yo!" the others shouted. The figures of Ur and Eych stopped and looked behind them. Did they expect their companions to be there? But twin-headed Bur advanced.

"Bur!" Sparrow screamed, and the others repeated it. The monster halted.

"Eni! and Tho!"

"Eni! Tho!" But now the three were coming forward again. From his right eye Sparrow saw they had crossed the stream and were stepping up through the mown hay.

"Ur! Eych! Yo! Bur! Eni! Tho!" Sparrow yelled, speeding the names together.

"Ur! Eych! Yo! Bur! Eni! Tho!" Their voices seemed to get caught in the rhythm of the teeming rain, the names of the Polymorphs ran together as if the rain had washed their edges away. They repeated them over and over, faster and faster – Ureychyoburenitho! Ureychyoburenitho! The three Polymorphs had halted, uncertain it seemed – or perhaps waiting…

What was Sparrow to do? They couldn't go on shouting the names forever. The Polymorphs had halted, but they didn't look as though they were going to go away…

And then the truth hit Sparrow. How he suddenly understood it he didn't know, but he was in no doubt: Ureychyoburenitho was the name of the dragon. They were standing there in a ring, calling out the dragon's

335

name. And Puckel had said that calling out the dragon's name was the one thing that would bring it back to the earth.

ureychyoburenitho

IN THE SQUARE AT COPPERHILL, SCREAMS AND SHOUTS
filled the air. The glaring eyes of the stone rams' heads on the
village hall did not glare as horribly as the eyes of the two men
who stood under the linden trees, with crossbows raised.
Crossbow bolts were already lodged deep in the wood of a
windowsill and a door, on houses across the square. Another
lay where it had sheared off the top of a stone gatepost, and
one stood through Plato Smithers' felt hat. People were flee-
ing in all directions up the small streets that led from the
square. The two men under the linden trees shouted in
harsh, barking voices, but their words were gibberish. Cross
Lurgan and Noddy Borrow had returned from the mountains empty-handed and stark mad.

The scattering people found shelter, and a watching silence
fell, broken only by the occasional shouts of the two men.

"Eych! Tho!" Cross Lurgan shouted.

"Ur Yo Eni Bur!" Noddy Borrow barked back.

Briefly, Plato Smithers appeared up on the balcony of the village hall, a crossbow in one hand, waving with the other over the square to where a second bowman crept stealthily behind a hedge. A third slipped gingerly from trunk to trunk of the lindens towards the tree by which Lurgan and Borrow stood.

At that moment there was a small commotion in one of the streets, and into full view of those in the square stepped the stately figure of Ms Redwall. Gasps of admiration broke from the hiding people as, without a trace of fear, she swept across the square towards the lindens.

"Boro Bur Oro Ur!" Cross Lurgan screamed.

"Ya Yo Eni Eni!" Noddy Borrow howled.

Ms Redwall's most imperious voice interrupted them. "Just put those things down, you two, and don't be so silly. We've had quite enough of this nonsense."

With more senseless yells, both madmen fired. The cruel whizz of the two bolts could be heard all over the square. Time seemed to stand still. *Thack-whoo! Thack-whoo!* echoed from the walls as Plato Smithers and his comrades fired the bolts from their own weapons. Ms Redwall crumpled and fell, a single bolt through her neck. Lurgan and Borrow, both hit, ran jerking forwards before somersaulting into a heap beside their victim.

The silence went on for a minute or more, before people started drifting slowly back into the square. Plato Smithers leaned over the balcony of the hall, white-faced and shaking in every one of his huge limbs. A wide ring collected about the three fallen villagers, as the people stared down in silent horror. Never before had such a thing happened in Copperhill.

"Mr Smithers!" a clear voice called up from below the

338

balcony, and Smithers turned his head to find himself in the steady stare of Bull Hind's blue eyes. The big man rubbed his own eyes, and his felt hat slipped off, unbalanced by the weight of the bolt through its crown. Was that a tiny white-haired man standing by the boy's knee? Plato Smithers rubbed his eyes again and tried to concentrate. Bull was holding up a rope. "Do you see this?" he asked.

There was something flimsy, almost misty, about the rope, but it was quite visible. Smithers nodded.

"We have to tie them up in it. They aren't dead. We have to tie them up in the rope, all together. Do you understand?"

Smithers pushed himself upright and turned and staggered back through the balcony door. A few moments later he was down in the square at Bull's side, looking a bit steadier. "I don't know what all this is about, lad," he said, "but I'm going to do what you say."

Together they walked over to the silent crowd.

339

Sparrow couldn't help it. He had to shout, he had to call the dragon's name. And strangely, although he knew what he was doing, he found he had no fear. The very sound of the name seemed to fill him with a fierce, wild excitement, and in his mind's eye he saw the great, fiery demon-beast rushing and whirling down from a darkness behind the sun. Nearer it would be coming, nearer still…

Over and again they called out the strange name, none of them except Sparrow knowing what they were doing. And now the three visible Polymorphs were turning round. Round and round, slowly at first and then quickening as though in some weird bird-dance, with their wings flapping and churning about them. Ureychyoburenitho! At first Sparrow suspected a new trick – perhaps they were

dancing up a storm of their own. But presently he became
sure that they were whirling because they couldn't help it,
just as the Traders had danced because they couldn't help
it, all those years before. He laughed.

Ureychyoburenitho!

And with a roaring of the air, and a crackling and a hissing, the dark Thing which had burst out of the ground split
into a thousand pieces. Faces, figures and forms went
whirling and twirling off into the sky, or were beaten down
to the earth by the rain. The three Polymorphs, in their
own shapes – even Bur was just visible to the others now –
went on turning and turning, but they were unmistakably
on the ordinary ground now, down in the hay meadow,
ordinary-sized, unimpressive, ragged figures.

And the dragon came, splitting the clouds apart, while the
sun burst through in dazzling rainbows and the rain turned
to great corkscrew columns that seemed to dance on the
ground. Downwards the massive beast whirled, bellowing
like thunder, landing with an almighty crash on the ground
between them and the whirling Polymorphs. The shock of its
fall knocked the feet from under them and sent them sprawling in the mud. All but one of the dancing columns of water
disappeared, and that one corkscrewed for a while beside the
dragon as it gave a few more roars and blasts and then grew
still. A small figure perched high on its back reached over and
the column of water danced up into the outstretched hand,
and shrank and grew dark; and there was Puckel, holding his
stick again, then digging it into the dragon's side and vaulting
off towards the hidden Polymorphs.

The old man hit the ground just as Sparrow and his
companions were struggling to their feet, and the shock of
his landing was, if anything, greater than the dragon's; they

were flung down again as if there had been an earthquake. They got back to their feet a second time, by now plastered with mud. They huddled together silently, shifting uneasily in the glare of the dragon's eye, just beyond the far corner of the cottage. Everything had gone very quiet, apart from the rushing of the stream.

Then the three Polymorphs appeared again. They came one by one, half flapping, half hopping over the lower end of the dragon's tail, and up towards the cottage. There was little menace in them now; there was something about their flapping and hopping that was a little like the capering of crows on a wheatfield. Puckel, waving the stick, appeared close behind them.

For all that, when the Polymorphs came to a stop not far away, there was nothing pleasant or amusing about them. Everyone could see them now in their proper shapes, winged and hunched at the shoulder, with their heads sticking forwards on long necks. They were not quite solid, though you couldn't actually see through them, except for a little at the edges. Their wings and the rags that hung on their bodies were grey. Their faces – which were almost human, except that they had a glistening, sagging look like newly-cooled candlewax – were grey and expressionless under the huge, domed foreheads. The small, black eyes of Ur and Eych were fixed on the ground. Only one of Bur's eyes – the silver-white one – was open. The head with the closed eye was wobbling and knocking against the other as though it were asleep. The Polymorphs were a drab, dreary sight, particularly with the green and gold magnificence of the dragon in the background, stretched like a battle-mented wall across the garden, with streaks of smoke blowing along its flanks as it breathed.

"Well, a bath wouldn't do you lot any harm," said Puckel, coming up behind and looking askance at Sparrow and his friends. "That's hardly the way to look when you're meeting your neighbours for the first time – particularly you, young fellow."

Sparrow smiled weakly. Now that all the excitement seemed to be over, he was feeling distinctly trembly. What did Puckel mean by "neighbours"?

"Don't think it's all over," the old man said. "Not by any means. I'm not going to do all your work for you. I'm simply going to introduce you to your friends here and show you what we can do to help them."

"Help them?" Sparrow repeated, amazed.

"All in a manner of speaking," Puckel said, giving him a sidelong glance, almost like a bird. "Well done, by the way," he went on. "You came through. I knew you would of course, though it had to be done."

"What had to be done? What have I come through?" Sparrow asked. The worst thing about Puckel was that the more things got themselves sorted out, the more complicated they seemed to become.

"You were told a severe test was coming to you," Puckel said. "That was it. You came through."

"I never did anything," Sparrow said.

"You guessed the dragon's name, didn't you?"

"Not really," Sparrow said. "It was just an accident. The Polymorphs' names just – got knocked together… It was just…" And then Sparrow went quiet, because he suddenly thought about the strangeness of the little Puckel-messenger. Was this another thing about himself he didn't know?

"That's right," said Puckel, who seemed to know what Sparrow was thinking. "You know more than you think you know. You're stronger than you think you are, as I said to you once before. Six names to make one name – not easy to get the order right first time, but you did, without even trying. You're the one we've been waiting for. Now put the dragon to bed."

"What?" said Sparrow.

Puckel had already turned away from him, and was starting to drive the Polymorphs closer to the door of the cottage. "I'd advise you to start at the tail," he said over his shoulder, "it's the cooler end."

Sparrow gaped after the old man, who was ushering the three Polymorphs into the cottage. He turned to the others. "What am I supposed to do now?" he said.

Gogs looked at Murie. Murie looked at Gogs. "You'd better do what he says," Kittel said.

"Thanks," said Sparrow. And because there seemed to be nothing else for it, he turned from them and walked, slithering in the mud, down through the vegetable patch, into the mown hay, towards the dragon's tail.

He reached it and stood, at a loss. Puckel's order had seemed impossible before; now it seemed just silly. The dragon stretched before him like a small hill. You couldn't move a dragon! Here, where the vast stretch of the beast tapered to its thinnest, the very end of its tail was still thicker than Sparrow's body. "Ureychyoburenitho," he murmured, fearful, yet marvelling to be so near the terrible creature. "Ureychyoburenitho." He noticed that the green and golden scales that covered the huge body were strangely delicate, each beautifully shaped, like the petal of a flower. At the very end of the tail the scales disappeared under plastered mud.

In fact the very end of the tail was buried under the mud.

343

And just as he realized that he might actually be standing on it, the ground moved under Sparrow's feet, and the mud steamed and slipped away off the blade-like tip. Sparrow tried to step back, but the rising tail threw him forward so that he fell on the scales he had just been looking at. They felt cold – so how was it that the mud was steaming? Steam, or mist rather, seemed to be everywhere, pouring upwards, enveloping the dragon, which rapidly became a humped island of mist in a broader sea of mist all around…

Everything was becoming very confused. Sparrow seemed to be turning. He saw the sun appearing up on his left, a ball of dull orange fading into the deepening gloom of mist. The dragon no longer seemed to be stretched out across the ground. Its shape was now marked by a great grey coil, a vast misty spiral that boiled and billowed yet was never lost in the rolling mist that covered everything. Sparrow was moving rapidly along a road of mist, towards its centre, which he now knew was the dragon's head. Somewhere within the circle of the coils, a little below him, he saw Kittel, Murie, Gogs, Lissie and Ormand; somewhere on the edge he could see Puckel and the three Polymorphs, all of them standing in the formless mist with nothing else round them; and on the other side of Puckel, on the outside of the circle, there was Bull, and three more Polymorphs lying at his feet. Sparrow was floating, circling round and round them all.

And now Puckel seemed to have picked up a thin end of the road of mist and passed it over to Bull, who was winding it round the three Polymorphs lying on the ground. Or was it the rope?

Then the coils of mist grew suddenly tight, and the edges of the circle were pulled in towards the centre, and the centre was where Sparrow stood. Puckel was right next to him. The mist was thicker than ever, but now it smelled like smoke. There was a vague whirring noise going on all this time. Puckel wheeled round towards the nearest of the Polymorphs – Ur or Eych, Sparrow couldn't tell which – seized its head, and with one almighty twist pulled it right off. "Now," the old man said in his most matter-of-fact voice, "that's one." And he threw the head down in the mist between Sparrow's feet, where it disappeared. A second later there came a dull thud from somewhere below. The Polymorph's body had meanwhile disintegrated into a small white heap, like fragments of burned bones.

Sparrow watched, rooted with shock, as Puckel proceeded to dispose of Bur's two heads, and the single head of the remaining Polymorph.

"Now you," he said, pointing a finger at Sparrow.

It was then that Sparrow saw the other three Polymorphs which had been lying at Bull's feet. They were still lying there, but things seemed to have got twisted round in a peculiar way so that they were now lying with their heads at Sparrow's feet. And it was no longer exactly three Polymorphs, because Sparrow's ordinary eye told him that he was looking at two men from the village, whom he recognized – and Ms Redwall.

"Come on, you know what to do," Puckel said.

"Do I?" said Sparrow.

"Of course you do. All that's needed is for you to get on with it."

"But—"

"Butts are for holding water. Don't waste time."

Turning then, Sparrow saw Kittel and Lissie and Murie beside him, looking down in horror at the three faces at his

345

feet. Gogs was there too, his face sickly green. "That's Cross Lurgan and Noddy Borrow," Murie said.

They saw the crossbow bolt through Ms Redwall's neck. "Are they all dead?" Kittel and Lissie exclaimed together.

"They are bound by iron and wood to the forms they took for themselves," Puckel said softly. "Let them go, Sparrow."

Sparrow gulped several times, for now he understood. "Lissie will like this more than me," he said at last. Then he bent down over Ms Redwall, crooked his elbow under her chin, seized the top of her head with his other hand, and pulled for all he was worth. And with no more effort than pulling up a cabbage, the head came off in his arms.

There was a strangled gurgle from Gogs, but Sparrow knew his friend must now be able to see the real form of what he was holding. He dropped the Polymorph's head down between his feet, and as it fell it made a dark trail through the mist. Gently it floated out of sight into darkness; but just before it disappeared, Sparrow saw it rolling an eye at him and then winking. Again there came the dull thud from below. He turned back to Cross Lurgan and Noddy Borrow, and in a moment two more Polymorph heads followed the first one.

As this was happening, Sparrow became aware that there were shadowy figures over beyond Bull. Bull had turned away towards them, and there was a voice speaking – a man's voice – almost certainly Plato Smithers.

"A young girl, a woman and two young boys are still out there," the voice was saying. "We don't know what might have happened to them by now, and they should never have been made to go, whatever any of them may have done wrong. I'm not even sure that that young lass ever did a wrong thing anyway."

"It was a fine thing, what she was doing at the school," another voice, a little fainter, called, and there was a murmur of agreement.

"We've a lot to thank this young lad for," Smithers' voice came again, and Sparrow saw a large hand being clapped on Bull's shoulder. "He's made us think about a lot of things that we'd forgotten – things that we preferred not to think about. A Trader's son, that's what he is – and a living reminder of what Traders do for our sakes. Remember Tack Hind, the lad's father."

There was another murmur of approval, but it was almost immediately interrupted by shouts of surprise and fright, and the shadowy figures started moving, surging forwards towards Bull – though breaking into mist when they reached Puckel – backwards and forwards, stooping and straightening. "She's moving! She's getting up!" Sparrow heard, then – "Look, Noddy's all right too. Come on lad, take my hand. Come on, Cross…"

The forms faded, Bull became faint and shadowy, and Sparrow thought he heard a woman's voice asking in high, complaining tones why were the children not at school and what was happening and why was everyone looking like a flock of frightened sheep. Then the ground – or whatever it was he was standing on – gave way under him, and he found himself hanging by the elbows to a stone thing, scrabbling and pulling himself upwards as hands reached down to grab his hands and the mist swirled and seethed in front of his eyes.

A moment later it cleared, and he found himself standing on a solid floor, the white ash of the Polymorphs at his feet and black ash of something else still hot and smoking all round amongst fire-blackened stones. The hot sun was beating down, and his friends and Puckel were on the grass just beyond the circle of scorched ground. "Where's the dragon?" he said. "What's happened?"

"Gone to ground, gone to earth," Puckel replied. "Gone to bed, where I told you to put him. Don't be surprised. You did it. You shouldn't doubt yourself so much."

Sparrow saw the large stone he had pulled himself up by, lying half buried in a heap of ash and charred wood. Or – no – there was something else there… He covered his right eye and stared from the darkness of his left… He was at the edge of a well or a pit – a five-sided pit rimmed with five huge stones. Staring in, he found himself gazing down into the baleful, uplifted eyes of Bur of the Lamps.

Bur was standing deep down below him, and the other Polymorphs, winged and in their whole shapes, stood round in what Sparrow now saw was the little torchlit chamber with the stone table and the empty tripod and, poking through the doorway from the passage outside, the blade-shaped tip of the dragon's tail.

Sparrow found out later that after he had gone down and stood on the dragon's tail in the meadow, the others had seen the great creature crawling up over the garden to the cottage, while Sparrow climbed steadily up on to its back. When the dragon reached the cottage it pushed its head through the door and the whole cottage went up in flames and smoke and collapsed. They lost sight of Sparrow in the smoke, and there was no sign of Puckel either. But the dragon continued to crawl and gradually disappeared into the burning heap. As the smoke cleared they saw Puckel calmly ripping off the Polymorphs' heads, and when they ran over to the cottage – all except Ormand, who had fainted – they discovered Sparrow about to pull off the

348

heads of the three villagers, after which he seemed to stumble, slipping under the great stone doorframe, which the dragon had flattened as it pushed its way in.

"The spiral of the right hand and the spiral of the left hand," Puckel remarked quietly, as he gently stroked the head of his stick. "Now this is truly the Star Wheel again, and the haunt of dragons."

"The spiral," Sparrow echoed; and those of them who had been in the maze of the Polymorphs thought of the great body coiled round and round in its silent corridors, snug as a hand in a glove. "Is this where the dragon came from, long ago, before it got away?"

"How do you think the torches stayed alight?" Puckel snapped. "Electricity?" He was fumbling with the brooch of his midnight cloak. With an irritable grunt he tore the fastening and let the garment fall to the ground, leaving the Puckel whom Sparrow and Kittel had always known, clad in an old moss-green thing that was more tatters and patches than coat. "Phew!" he grouched. "That's better. Thought I was going to turn to butterfat in that stupid clobber.

349

"There is a change," he went on, "but we're none the worse for that. The dragon faces outwards now. Before, his head was to the centre. What comes of that we shall see in due course.

"Things are not finished yet, not by any means; and you haven't seen the last of that lot – " he nodded towards the hidden pit – "so you'd better get used to the idea of them."

"Haven't you got them under control yet?" Sparrow asked.

Puckel looked at him sharply. "I have, but you haven't. And you're going to have to, though to be sure you're well on the way already. But that trick with your eyes is just the beginning, to help you to see through their nonsense.

You'll have to master the Secret Way and I'd better tell you right now that that means ruling the Polymorphs stricter than a carter rules his team of horses. A lot stricter in fact; it doesn't pay to be good to them, and you should never thank them. They need a firm hand and no respect. Use them – that's all they're good for. That way they'll take you both far and fast – faster than thought."

"Where will they take me?" Sparrow asked.

"Oh, here and there. Where that idiot crow stands on your father's chest in the Vault of the Bear and says his words for him, for example."

There was a small gasp of surprise from Murie at these words, but Puckel went on – "And through all the angles of the Enclosure, and through all the nine hundred and ninety-nine doorways in the great door. You'll find out – you'll have to, if you want to find what this one's looking for." He nodded at Kittel.

"Her way home?" Sparrow said.

"Well," Puckel chuckled, "maybe her way home's not quite the way you all think it is. However, that's all one. It's time you made your way to where you think your home is for the moment. And it's not here, and that's for sure."

And without another word, Puckel vanished from their sight. Only Sparrow, just for the briefest glimpse of his left eye, saw the old man leap into the pit of the Star Wheel and disappear in a whirring and whirling of great wings. All that was left of him was a mist of dark blue forget-me-nots in the grass, where his cloak had fallen. And all that was left of the little cottage that had been their home for a fortnight was a pile of fire-blackened stones.

"Well," said Sparrow, "it is time we started back home. I've an idea they'll be glad to see us again."

the shining bridge

the quiet street

IN A WAY, BEING FRIENDS WITH PATS MADE UP TO TRINA FOR not having Max any more. Not that Pats was a dog, but he could be very dog-like. Sometimes the three of them – Pats, Pats' father and Trina – would go for walks together, and Pats would run after sticks and fetch them back – except that he would throw them first as well.

"I wish we could get another dog," Trina told Pats' father.

"Can't you?" he said.

"Not now that Mum's working," Trina replied glumly.

"Don't you like her having a job?"

Trina shook her head, sighed. "I don't know. It's all since Kitty – went. The job takes her mind off things. But nothing's the same any more. I like Newborough though. I'm glad we came here."

She hadn't been to begin with. It was all another crackpot idea of her father's, as far as she was concerned. He had wanted them to move away from the city after the riots. "There's going to be more – this is just the start of it," he had said, in his darkest prophet-of-doom voice. And then Max had been run over. Max would have liked it at Newborough; all the places to go, round the edge of the little town.

Now they had got a cat, called Cat; they had moved to Newborough, and things had got better. But then new troubles seemed to begin. Trina wasn't sure how it had happened. Her mother said it was just a stage she was going through; to Trina it seemed her mother was just always finding fault. "Why is it you can't spell properly? Don't they teach you to spell here?" Or, "Don't you ever read the instructions on things?" Or, "Why are you so disorganized?"

And though it was never said, Trina soon began to realize that, somehow, Kitty was always at the back of it: Kitty had been an excellent speller; Kitty had always read instructions and thought everything out before she did something; Kitty was always making lists and never forgot anything and was never late... "Pooh," Trina would mutter to the silence of her room, "Kitty must have been some kind of angel; no wonder she got killed. This world probably wasn't good enough for her."

She no longer had a very clear memory of this perfect older sister; but she did have a memory of the day Kitty went missing. She remembered the feeling of waiting at the airport; waiting and waiting; telephone calls to the uncle and aunt Kitty had been staying with; her father going off to make enquiries; no one seeming to know what was going on, but making up hopeful-sounding stories; and then at last the awful truth dawning, when the world seemed to stop and a huge silence seemed to fall. The aeroplane had simply disappeared. Somewhere in the empty miles of ocean it must have gone down. People tried for months to find it, but there was not a trace: nothing.

There was another memory Trina had, of the time just before they had come to Newborough. Her father had a job for nine months at a university in a town about an hour's drive from the mountains, and one day Trina and her mother had gone for a long walk into these mountains. In a lonely place near a great waterfall they had met Kitty. They didn't see where she had come from, and she was dressed in old-fashioned, rough clothes, and there was a boy with her dressed the same way. The boy had saved her, Kitty explained, and they felt wonderfully grateful to him, but Max growled every time the boy looked at him, as they sat on a rock and ate sandwiches together. They were *357* living, Kitty said, in a place where everything was very old-fashioned and quiet; there were no cars or shops or cities; there were telephones and televisions and an old railway, but none of them worked; there was no electricity. Kitty loved it, but she still wanted to come back home and see everyone – that was why she and the boy had set off to try and find the way back.

It was all too wonderful, but by the next day Trina's mother had forgotten all about it. When Trina tried to remind her, she told her it must have been a dream. At first Trina was certain it hadn't been, but when she found she had no idea where Kitty and the boy had got to, she had to agree that her mother was right. Kitty had told them the boy's name, but Trina couldn't remember that properly either: it was something to do with a bird, which was why she thought it was probably Robin. But she couldn't be sure.

She talked with Pats' father about dreaming. He wrote books, and he liked dreams. "It can be difficult to tell dreams apart from real life," he said. "I keep on having a dream that Pats comes and stands in my bedroom when I'm in bed, and we hold long conversations. I suppose it's a dream, because I know he's never spoken and probably never will – but how can I be sure?"

Their new home was on the edge of Newborough. There was a park opposite, which Trina liked to look out over when she got up in the mornings, though she didn't care for it later in the day when it was full of boys playing football. Another favourite place was the bridge between the two halves of Newborough. It was called the Union Bridge, and she liked to hang over its parapet and watch the brown water swirling round its stone piers.

358

A little way up the broad, straight street into the old half of the town (Trina lived in the new half), was the house where Pats lived with his father; and not far beyond that was the small Square of the old town, with its fine houses and its spacious feel. At the Square, the main road was met by the road from Market Glass, which was the way she and Pats and his father took whenever they went for a walk.

One of the buildings in the Square was a tall, narrow house with quaint arched windows, and next to this was the start of a small road.

From the very first moment she saw it, Trina knew there was something special about that road. Something inviting; something odd. It was narrow, and it was cobbled – its cobbles shining dully as if polished by centuries of long-vanished horses' hoofs. There were no windows in the walls of the buildings on either side of it, and it had no pavements. It ambled off at an angle, then turned a corner as if it were starting to try to get back to the Market Glass road.

The first time Trina noticed it was on a still day in April. It was one of those April days that seem as warm and as close as summer, with hazy clouds stretched across a dreamy blue sky. Half a dozen dogs and cats lay stretched on the pavements of the Square, and old ladies in cardigans sweated by, complaining of the heat. But in the entrance to the cobbled road a slight, chill breeze shifted, and Trina was caught by the sigh of it, and the faintest of faint sounds that was like music far away. Something in the pit of her stomach turned over; it was as though she had been wandering in a desert and suddenly got caught in a shower of silver rain.

Strangely, she felt reluctant to go down the little road. "Some time," she murmured to herself, knowing only that "some time" meant "not yet". The feeling grew in her that if once she ventured down there, she would set in motion a chain of events she could never undo.

"Where does that road go?" she asked Pats' father, as the three of them were setting off, as usual, on the road to Market Glass.

"Oh, it's a road to a farm," Pats' father said. "An old place. No one lives there now. The old branch of the railway used to go down that way – the one that the mystery was all about."

"What mystery?"

"What! You haven't heard about the Newborough mystery? It's quite famous. It was when they were sending children away from the cities during the War because of the air raids. A train of evacuee children came out this way, took

359

the branch line at Newborough Junction – and disappeared. It was never heard of again."

Trina shivered.

There was a fall of snow in the middle of April, but it didn't last long. When it had melted from the ditches, the spring began in earnest; grass and trees sprouted, dandelions opened like miniature suns along the edges of walls, and the fields around the town were full of the sound of bleating lambs.

Then came a Saturday morning at the end of April. Trina's father had promised her a trip to the city; it was actually to see some ancient Burial Ship he had dug up and was very excited about. This didn't interest Trina much, though she thought there would be a chance to get to the shops as well. But something came up at the last moment which meant they couldn't go.

"Next weekend, I promise," her father said.

Trina hung over the parapet of the Union Bridge, staring at the brown water below. She felt near to tears, and when she thought about it she realized that this wasn't because of missing the shops, but simply because there were so few times when she was able to do things together with her father. And since they had come to Newborough, fewer and fewer…

She went on up the street, but didn't stop at Pats' house. She came to the Square. There was a brisk wind, with white clouds racing overhead. She paused beside the tall house, but the wind caught her and blew her against its wall. The sun came out from behind a cloud and blinded her. Quickly she turned into the shadow round the side of the house, and stood on the cobbles of the quiet street.

There was no wind here. There was only the slight, shifting breeze – chill on a warm day, gentle and soothing in this rougher weather. And in the sigh of the breeze, faint and far away, the ghost of a tune on a pipe. Almost despite herself, Trina's feet moved off over the cobbles. Ten … twenty … thirty steps. She was round the corner and out of sight of the Square.

The cobbles stopped at the last building on the street; but the road continued as a stony track. Trina walked on. She could see the line of the road to Market Glass, studded with hawthorns and green elders. She could see the line of the old railway coming out of the Cottage Wood, and the ruined farmhouse. The track wasn't leading anywhere near it. Then she stopped, for she saw something she had never seen before.

It was a hill. A small, green-grown hill, almost a perfect pyramid, which had not been there before. It couldn't be mistaken – in the rolling, soft countryside its shape stood out distinctly. Trina stared; then turned, and began to walk quickly homewards, back over the cobbles. She found she was stepping with deliberate calmness, almost as though she were trying not to panic.

dream friends

THE BUILDING SITE WAS A STRANGELY QUIET ISLAND IN THE
midst of the city hubbub. A wall of wooden boards sepa-
rated it from the street. It was a great square pit of clay full
of leaking grey puddles and mounds of rubble; in a far
corner a large mechanical digger crouching like a sorrowful
yellow spider; and a crane towering overhead, its huge jib
pointing like an arm across the site. There was no movement, no activity; work had been stopped.

The dark timbers of the ancient Burial Ship lay in a pattern like a fish's bones near one edge of the pit, with the soil
carefully dug away round them and piled to one side –
darker, crumbly soil, not the stiff beige clay of the rest of the
site.

"It's only a couple of miles from here to the docks,"
Trina's father said. "It was probably dragged here from the
sea on rollers and then buried." He gazed proudly at his
find. "The prow's missing, that's all. Probably would have

been carved like a dragon or something. There's a prow in the museum, though not from this ship. They found it somewhere else, but this one's could have been similar. Come on, we'll go along and see it, and then think about getting some lunch."

Trina brightened at the thought of lunch, and hoped her father wouldn't get too carried away in the museum, or they wouldn't be out till suppertime.

"What's the little pointy hill called, out on the Market Glass road?" Trina asked her father. She was sitting beside him as they drove home, following a dizzying series of small twisting roads which he insisted was a quicker way than going by the main road.

"There isn't one, that I can think of," he replied after a moment's thought. "We can get over to Market Glass from here and come home by that road, then you can point it out to me." Trina's heart sank at the thought of more twists and turns.

But though he slowed down when they came within sight of Old Newborough, and though Trina craned and peered from the car's open window, there was no sign of the little green hill.

"You can see it from that road," she told her father, pointing to the cobbled road as they drove through the Square.

"Not very likely," her father said. "That road must be pretty well parallel to the Market Glass road. If you can't see it from one, you won't see it from the other. Have a look at the map when we get home."

But when they got home there were other things to think about. Then in the evening her father was out again. Trina spread the map on the dining-table and sighed – half because of the map, which she couldn't make head or tail of, and half because her father never seemed to be there when she needed his help.

"Can we have the telly off?" she said crossly.

"I wanted to watch the news," her mother said. "Don't you?"

"No," Trina said flatly. She slapped down the map and stalked out of the room. The sound of the television followed her through to her bedroom; it seemed able to get through any wall, not so much loud as just penetrating. It drummed at her, even with the door shut. It was always talking about how many people were dead: five, twenty, fifty, two thousand. Trina decided she hated it. She lay down on the bed and covered her head with her pillow. A picture immediately came in front of her eyes – something she had seen in the museum, near the dragon-prow: it was a dark-brown thing, a mummified body sitting on a rough wooden block with its knees drawn up to its chin. The face was sunk out of sight as if it were gazing down at its hollowed-out body and wondering where its stomach had gone.

The next day she went to see Pats, but then decided she would go up to the Square first, just to look…

This time, she didn't hesitate at the entrance to the narrow street. She stepped out decidedly. She would get her bearings right, and then she would pinpoint where the place should be on the map. She would ask Pats' father what it was called. She would…

She stopped and stared. The hill was twice – three times – the size it had been the week before.

There was no doubt about it. It was the same hill; there were no others in the area with that definite, pyramid

364

shape. It was green and grassy, with here and there the darker green of clumps of trees, and on the top a new, darker patch, as if the top was heathery ground. There was the road, there was the Cottage Wood; and there was the hill, exactly where it had been before, exactly the same hill. Except that it had grown…

"Pats," she said, a little later, "I've found a hill that's growing."

Pats stared hard at something just beyond her left shoulder, rocking on his heels. "B–b–b–b–" he said against the back of his hand.

Trina wanted to share her discovery with someone, but she didn't get the chance just then to tell Pats' father.

She told her parents instead, and even managed to persuade them to walk over to the old Square with her, then up the little quiet street. The street became the stony track, and Trina stopped and pointed in triumph.

365

"That's Station Hill," her mother said.

"It's a good way of getting us out for a walk," her father smiled. "Growing hills indeed – I almost believed you! I certainly feel better for it, though."

"But you said there wasn't a hill on this side of the town," Trina protested.

"When did I say that?"

"Yesterday, in the car," said Trina. "We came back this way specially, and we slowed down so we could look properly, and—"

"Not me, darling," her father smiled. "I've always known about Station Hill."

"But it – the size…" Trina tailed off.

"Station Hill's always been that size, silly," her mother

said. "Come on, let's turn back now, it's chilly."

"We'll walk to it in the summer, I promise," her father said.

Trina suddenly felt very tired; there was something wrong. She went straight to her room when they got home and lay down on the bed. Cat followed her in and sat crouched on the chest-of-drawers, regarding her silently from unwinking golden eyes.

It was at this time that she started having dreams. They were not ordinary dreams – they were linked together too sensibly for ordinary dreams. On the first night, there was just a kind of brown gloom that was full of voices. It was almost like being buried under the earth, except that she could breathe normally. A tunnel, perhaps. The voices were most unpleasant – they seemed to be gibbering non-sense, or making a noise like jeering laughter, or occasion-ally breaking into a high-pitched wail. There was also a constant whirring sound, as though someone had startled a flock of pigeons...

The next night, she dreamed of a quiet, sunny place of grass and trees with white blossom. She knew that this place was quite high up in the mountains, though she couldn't actually see any mountains. There were some small, rough ponies eating the short grass among the trees and, always just beyond, behind the ponies, some young people about her own age. She could never see their faces clearly. There were two boys and two girls, she thought.

In the other dreams, she kept seeing these same four friends. She knew they were the same four, though she could never get a proper look at them. Sometimes they would be riding the ponies, sometimes sitting around talking, on one occasion in a dark golden circle of candlelight. Once they seemed to be digging and weeding in a garden, laughing and carrying on as they did so. She began to long to be with them – there was something about their friendship that seemed so close, so easy and comfortable, so right, that she wanted to be part of it all. She would wake up from these dreams feeling lonely, feeling that all the other people she knew were somehow not the real friends she had always wanted.

On another occasion she had the dark dream again, but for a brief instant the tunnel, or whatever it was, split open, and she was looking up at mountains under a clear blue sky. So the two different parts of the dreams were tied together.

The dreams stopped coming so regularly after the first week, but every now and then she would find herself back in them. And almost before she noticed, she was withdrawing, finding it more and more difficult to keep interested in her friends at school because she kept on thinking about the four friends with their ponies and their mountains.

In the middle of that first week of dreams, something else happened. They were not good days: school during the daytime, evenings bickering with her mother, her father away, the hateful television pounding on and on. She was setting the table on Wednesday evening, when she heard her mother give a small gasp and stare at the television. Trina hadn't been listening, but she looked round all the same. The man on the television was talking about how difficult it was to get to some particular place because there were mountains and snow and no roads. Then there was a film taken from the air of some mountains, grey and white and mud-coloured, with dark patches of forest.

"These things always happen in threes," her mother said in a low, tense voice.

"What is it? What's wrong?" Trina asked. Panic was gathering inside her.

"A plane, didn't you hear? It's crashed there some-where. About two hundred people dead, they think—"

Crash. The cutlery fell on the floor. Trina had clapped her hands over her ears. For a moment she gazed down at the scattered steel at her feet, then she ran from the room, her hands still covering her ears, kicked open the door to her own room, kicked it to again behind her and flung her-self on the bed, burrowing her head under her pillow.

And exactly as it had happened before, the picture sprang to her mind of the old hollowed-out mummy in the museum, and a voice in her ears said, *Tell-evasion*.

She threw off the pillow. She could hear no words, just the rhythm of the newsman's voice: *Ba–ba bam bam bom, ba–bom bom–ba–ba...* She raised herself on her arm and looked up.

Cat was on the chest-of-drawers again, regarding her fixedly with his lampish eyes. Trina shook her head. Who had said that – *television* – with a strange accent? Why should she hear that?

She began to wonder what her mother had meant by saying these things came in threes. Had there been another crash recently, or was she thinking about the crash when Kitty had gone?

Cat got up, stretched himself, knocked over Trina's small mirror, and stood listening, as if to the continuing *ba–ba–bam bom* of the television voice. Then he poured himself off the chest-of-drawers, the golden-brown ridge on his back rippling, landed with a soft thump on the floor, and squeezed himself through the crack of the door.

"I wonder where Cat's got to," said Trina at breakfast-time, a week later.

"Who?" said her father.

"Cat," said Trina.

"Who's Cat?" her mother asked.

"Cat!" Trina said impatiently. "What do you mean, who's Cat? Cat – our cat – Cat!"

"What is the matter with you, Trina?" her mother said. "First it was hills that weren't there before, then it was hills that were growing, and now it's cats. You're dreaming too much. I think you're having too much to do with that poor boy."

Her mother's pity for Pats always annoyed Trina. "Look," she said rudely, "whose dish do you think that is on the floor?" She stopped abruptly and shut her mouth with a soft gulp. The place where Cat's dish always sat was empty. There wasn't even a trace of the faint, discoloured ring it left on the floor. "What have you done with it?" she demanded accusingly.

Her father was looking at her intently, his eyes screwed up. "What's wrong, Trin?" he asked gently.

Trina got up from her chair. She scraped it back over the floor and backed away towards the door. She was appalled by the look of worry on both her parents' faces. "Nothing," she mumbled eventually, halfway to the door. "Nothing, I'm sorry."

Half an hour later, she was on the way to Station Hill. It was a grey, drab day but the air was soft – ideal for walking, neither too hot nor too cold.

She was not surprised to see that the hill had grown again. In fact it was no longer a hill, but a miniature mountain. The top reach of it had a grey, moorland look, and there was even a rocky cliff at the very top, but the lower slopes were covered with greenery.

The hard track became a rutted track, and then the rutted track became a narrow path. The path led her straight towards the little mountain before taking her over a stile and then losing itself in a grassy field. Trina continued in the same direction, though she felt a little cheated at no longer having a path to follow. Then she came to the river, and had to turn to go along its bank.

Now things became really difficult. The ground became a tangle of brambles, thorns, and thickets of young trees. Again and again Trina was forced out of the way she wanted to go, and completely lost sight of her goal.

She glimpsed a bank ahead, which looked vaguely familiar. She struggled on, scrambled up it, pushed her way through an old, baggy fence at the top –

And stood on the hard-packed gravel of the old railway course. She grunted, pushing the hair away from her damp forehead; if she had simply gone to the Cottage Wood and followed the old railway she could have had a straightforward journey. But then, she thought frowning, she had never seen her hill from the railway…

But what had happened to her hill? It wasn't that she couldn't see it now; indeed the whole trouble was that she couldn't see anything else! She was looking across the river to a full-sized mountain, with steep heathery slopes and long, dreary screes. She felt closed in, menaced by its great bulk.

Trina had thought she would climb Station Hill that day. Now she had second thoughts, and looked about her, trying to decide what to do.

There was a building ahead, indistinct against the thick-packed stems of the young trees. She went towards it hesitantly.

It was the remains of an old country railway station. The platform was a blue mist of speedwell flowers dotted with yellow dandelions. The station building was little more than a hut with brown planks along the front and boarded-up windows. It was very quiet, very desolate. The only sounds were the murmur of the river and the occasional peep of a bird amongst the trees.

There was a door to the station hut. Trina tried the handle, but it was locked. She sat down on the stones at the edge of the flower-grown platform, gazing for a while at the huge flank of the mountain.

A sound that seemed to start as a soft booming of wind, coming from nowhere in particular, grew gradually louder. Trina only half listened, realizing fairly quickly that it was the sound of a jet somewhere above. After a moment or two she thought, with a slight twinge of unease, that it wasn't fading away again as fast as she would have liked it to. It became an irritating rumbling grumble that seemed to be echoing backwards and forwards among the grey clouds, now louder, now quieter. Trina found that her heart had begun to beat quicker, and there was an unpleasant prickly feeling in her armpits. She frowned, and the thought of the plane-crash on the television came back to her.

She stirred to get to her feet, but then suddenly became quite still, frozen with shock. There was another sound.

It came from up in the sky too – part of the aeroplane sound perhaps, but different, not the same as the to-and-fro rumbling. It was almost like a deep-throated shout, a huge sound though far away, up there in the clouds. A moment later a gust of wind set the leaves shivering on all the small trees round about. When it became still again, Trina could hear that the sound of the jet had changed; it was coming closer, very rapidly closer.

She looked up, but could see nothing but the grey sky. Louder, and there was another noise – a strange whine – mixed in with the jet-rumble. Trina's hands suddenly clutched at her throat, she collapsed on her side, rolled over onto the flowers and then leaped to her feet. The plane was diving towards her – she knew it even though she couldn't see it. The air was banging and roaring.

She must get under cover. Where could she go? She turned frantically, first towards the station hut, then to the thick-growing trees along the railway line. Where would be safe?

The din was incredible. She staggered towards the hut, but tripped over her own feet and came down on hands and knees before she could reach the door. The roaring was behind her now – low, no higher than the top of the mountain. There was a continuous high-pitched scream mixed with it, then a shrieking and grinding, then the sound became strangely muffled. Suddenly it faded, then died away, but smaller, confused sounds followed it – sudden dull bumps and strange creaks. There was something about the quietness that was even worse than the roaring and screaming. Trina crawled, endlessly, towards the door of the shed – she didn't know why, because she knew it was locked; there was no safety there. She had

372

almost reached the doorstep when a tremendous *bang!* followed by a blast of air, sent her sprawling forwards against the wooden boards. Then everything went black.

tell-evasion

374 A DIM *WA–WA–WA* SOUND WAS IN HER EARS, AND WHEN HER eyes flickered open there were grey-green spikes of grass in front of them. Blades of grass, Trina thought, a little tiredly and a little sadly – blades of grass, you can't do anything with blades of grass. She realized she must have fainted. She lifted her cheek from the stones it had been lying against, but the *wa–wa–wa*ing kept her from raising her head too much. She felt sick.

She was looking at two rounded brown things which she thought at first must be large toadstools. But there was something wrong with the shape. They didn't have stalks. There was something behind them – rows of little dark crescents. Where had she seen something like that before?

Bootlaces. She was looking at a pair of boots. There was a stockinged leg in each of them. She scrambled suddenly back, swayed into a crouching position, and gaped up at the person who was standing in the doorway of the shed…

It was not a very alarming person. It was an old woman, not very tall, extremely thin, dressed in a simple shift of mud-coloured wool. On her feet was a pair of heavy, laced boots which looked much too big for her; her white hair hung out all over the place in wisps and wodges.

Trina glanced back over her shoulder. The mountain was still there, but there was no sign of anything wrong. Everything was quiet, quiet enough to hear the distant murmur of the river. No sign of the jet, no burning wreckage – nothing.

"Where did it go? What happened?" she exclaimed, as much to herself as to the stranger.

"Everything is correct," the old woman said. She had a dry, cracked, sweet sort of voice. The sound of it immediately made Trina feel calmer. "That was another's haunting," she went on. "But it is the opening of a door."

"Were you here all the time?" Trina said.

375

"Not when I was not here," the old woman answered. "But everything is in its place. You're not frightened, are you?"

Trina nodded. "I was, a bit. I feel better now. I did think I was alone, though."

"That is a difficult thing to think," the old woman said, nodding her own head thoughtfully. "But it is possible sometimes, it's true."

"I just meant—" Trina began, but the old woman went on, as if to herself:

"There are so many things, you see, that go into making a single person. Yes." And she nodded several times, as though she had just told herself something very important.

Trina began to think she must be a little dotty. "Do you live here?" she asked.

"Do I look as though I'm not alive?" the old woman asked in return.

Trina frowned. She got to her feet, a little unsteadily. "I mean, is this your home?" she said, gesturing towards the hut.

"Actually," the old woman confided, in a trembling, hesitant fashion, "I am a little out of place here – but not in an unbalancing way, if you see what I mean; I mean, it's necessary. I suppose you might say I am here in a temporary capacity."

"Oh," said Trina.

"I'm more of a home myself, you see," the old woman said, nodding again. "That's why it's a little difficult for me. I am Mother Egg."

"Are you?" said Trina. She felt much better now, and she had a vague idea that the stranger was talking so oddly to her on purpose, as a way of making her forget the horror of the plane-crash – or whatever it had been. "I've never heard of Mother Egg, though I have heard of Mother Goose," she added.

Mother Egg bent towards Trina, until her dry old lips were very close to Trina's ear. "Without the Egg," she whispered, "there could be no Goose."

"That's true," Trina replied, drawing back a little.

"Now," Mother Egg said in a business-like way, briskly clasping her hands together. "You must listen." She put her head on one side in a bird-like fashion and said, "There are two things." Trina became very still; something made her feel she must attend. "Firstly, can you find your way back easily?"

"Home?" said Trina. "Yes, I think so."

"That I doubt," Mother Egg said drily; "but that's not

what I meant. I meant, can you find your way back here?"

Trina found the old woman suddenly rather stern, and not at all dotty-seeming. She even began to feel a little scared of her. "I'm sorry," she said guiltily. "Yes, I think there's a quicker way if I just come along the old railway track."

"That is perfectly possible now," Mother Egg said agreeably. "The arrangements are all in place. The second thing is that you are suffering from tell-evasion."

"Television?" Trina said, remembering uneasily that she had recently heard that word pronounced the same strange way.

"Tell-evasion," Mother Egg said slowly, "is a condition in which you are not listening to something you should be listening to."

"What?" said Trina.

Mother Egg turned and walked stiffly back to the door of the hut. For a moment Trina wondered if this would be the time to make her escape. Something stopped her. She had to follow the old woman. She caught up with her just as she went through the door.

377

"Look in there," Mother Egg said, pointing through into the darkness of the hut. "What do you see?"

"Cobwebs," Trina answered truthfully.

"That'll do," said Mother Egg. She sounded quite pleased, as though Trina had given the correct answer to a difficult question. "I too am a spinner, but nothing I make stays together for long. There are too many empty spaces. Another time," she went on, "I may show you the Scroll Cupboard. What's your name at the moment?"

"Trina – well, Katrina really – everyone just calls me Trina. But it's always been my name, you know – and I suppose it always will be."

"Really?" said Mother Egg, looking genuinely surprised. "I shall have to look that up. It's not impossible."
She looked down at the palms of her hands – bony, paper-
white hands – and murmured, "Nothing is impossible."

"I don't understand what's going on," Trina said.

Mother Egg looked sharply up at her. "Perhaps the end
of the world," she said. "Perhaps something a little better."
With that, she went inside and closed the door.

Although she was still quite mystified about the noise of the
crashing aeroplane, and even more mystified by the strange
old woman, Trina found she was feeling a lot better about
things at home as she hurried back towards Newborough.
Her shock over Cat and her parents apparently not remembering him had disappeared in the bigger shock of what
had happened at the old station. She determined now to
deal better with things. She mustn't cause arguments, or
worries. She decided to tell Pats about her meeting with
Mother Egg, but no one else. She would live two separate
lives, one for herself and Pats, one for ordinary people. She
would say nothing about the jet and the bang either, unless
they had heard it too. She couldn't remember much about
it now anyway – the thought of Mother Egg was far more
real.

As she drew nearer to the outskirts of the town, she
turned and looked back. The hill was there. It wasn't the
towering mountain she had seen from the station, but it was
decidedly bigger than when she had showed it to her
parents.

"How high's Station Hill?" she asked her parents next
day, as casually as she could.

"What's that?" her father said. Trina noticed that he seemed to be paying her more attention than usual.

"The hill out on the Market Glass road," Trina said, carefully covering up any impatience in her voice.

"What, the Stack?" her mother said.

"I suppose so," Trina murmured. "I must have got the name wrong again…"

"I don't know," her father said. "It's not as high as it looks – six or seven hundred feet, maybe."

For the first time, the thought crossed Trina's mind that she might be going mad. Everything was confusion – the mountain; Cat; the crash. Yet from time to time, like a clear bell note, that strange name sounded in her ears: Mother Egg. It was a little like the dreams of the four friends, which still came now and again, though in very brief glimpses and snatches.

379

What was it Mother Egg had said she should be paying attention to? She was suffering from tell-evasion. It certainly wasn't news to her that she was suffering from television! She wondered if the thing she should be listening to was something on the television.

She wondered about the plane-crash on the news, but nothing more was being said about it, so she began to wonder if that had really happened. She didn't dare ask her mother if it had. But there was a lot of uneasy talk about "unrest in the inner cities", and Trina's mother told her father more than once that she didn't want him to be in town if there was going to be rioting again. That, certainly, worried Trina, but she couldn't understand what good she could do by listening to the reports about it.

The more she worried about it, the more tense and anxious she became. For the whole week after her meeting with

Mother Egg, it was as if there was something building up, building up in her, like water in a dam, ready to burst.

It finally burst on the Friday night in a terrible row with her mother.

The evening turned sour as soon as her father came home. He was back early, looking very glum. For about an hour he sat in the living-room, clutching a large glass of something. No one spoke until he had got to the end of the glass and then filled it up again. "There's no money for it," he said.

"What?" said Trina.

"You're joking," said her mother.

"Money for what?" Trina said.

"For his ship excavation," her mother said.

Her father took a long gulp of his drink and stared out of the window. "There was money for it," he said bitterly. "But the department's been asked to contribute to the new medieval village they're making at the museum. Once they've paid for the actors who'll stand about looking like medieval people in the medieval huts and paid for the machines that make medieval village smells, they'll have no money left for some serious research work on an ancient Burial Ship. I said we could reconstruct the ship – it's almost complete. They said that the medieval village would still be a better crowd-puller. In my day, children had to use their imaginations if they wondered what it was like to live in a medieval village."

"Children do love these things, Norman," Trina's mother said soothingly.

"Yes," he snorted, "and most of them are over forty."

He got up and started pacing round the room, picking up books and magazines and glancing at them and throwing them down again with a slap, rubbing at a small patch of grease on the windowpane, eventually striding out of the door, banging his shoulder against the doorpost.

Trina felt bewildered. Her father was always ranting and raving. ("It's because he cares," her mother had told her once, whatever that was supposed to mean.) But somehow, tonight, seeing him upset made her feel upset too.

The quarrel with her mother started so gradually that Trina didn't even notice it. First of all, she put the wrong supper-dishes on the table.

"I said dishes, not plates," her mother said. "It's stew and dumplings."

"Oh, what's the difference?" said Trina, who did not care for stew and dumplings.

"Don't be so stupid, Trina," her mother answered sharply. "You know very well what the difference is. Spoons too, it's a bit thin." *381*

"Watered down, you mean," Trina muttered.

"What's that supposed to mean?" Her mother was glaring at her, holding the stew-pot in both hands with the oven-gloves.

Trina didn't answer. She went round the table, thumping dishes and cutlery down in the three places.

"Mat in the middle," her mother said. Trina thumped down the mat. Her mother thumped down the pot. One of the dishes jumped off the table and smashed on the floor.

"Now look what you've done!" her mother yelled. "Oh, you are so clumsy!"

Trina was already down on the floor, gathering up the pieces. Her eyes had filled with hot tears. "Yes," she blurted, "I suppose you think I am clumsy. It was you that did it, but it's still my fault. And I'm clumsy – I'm always clumsy, or stupid, or slow, or – or – anyway whatever it is, it's just what you hate and I'm not good enough for you and you wish it was me that had been killed and Kitty was just everything that was wonderful – she probably wasn't that wonderful anyway, but you like to think she was because it gives you an excuse for hating me and – "

She paused for breath, but at that moment her mother stopped her altogether. "Trina," she said, in a quiet, strained voice, "who is this Kitty?"

Trina stared at her. Was her mother playing games? Perhaps she was deliberately trying to drive her mad? She felt drained and tired. Doubt crept into her mind. The worried frown on her mother's face looked very genuine.

"Come on, darling, tell me," her mother said gently.

"You know," Trina said, with a half-sob in her voice. Her mother said nothing, went on looking at her. "My sister," Trina said. "Your favourite."

"Trina dear," her mother said, her voice so quiet it was almost a whisper, "you never had a sister. We used to call you Kitty sometimes when you were a baby, though I can't think how you could possibly know that – I'd forgotten it myself. But you're the only child we've ever had."

the scroll cupboard

SHE DREAMED, STRONGLY AND VIVIDLY. SHE WAS WALKING along the cobbled street of an old village. She heard hens clucking and fussing from over a wall, and something that sounded like the rattle of a chain and the squeaking of wood from somewhere else. Then she was looking down a narrow path between bushes and the stone wall of a house, and sitting on a low bank of grass she saw the four friends. There were no ponies with them this time, only a small brown-and-white dog.

And this time she was able to recognize them. Not properly, because she couldn't see their faces from the front, but was looking at them from the side and behind. But she knew one of them was Kitty.

They were wearing the same rather worn, shabby kind of clothes Kitty and the boy had been wearing when she met them by the big waterfall; and she was certain that one of the boys was the same boy she had met that time with

Kitty, though he seemed to be wearing a patch over one eye now. The other boy had very short, brown hair, almost like moleskin; and the other girl had dark hair and rosy cheeks.

The dog must have heard her, because it immediately turned its head, peering, with its ears pricked. She started down the path towards them, but almost immediately everything started trembling and the scene in front of her eyes broke up like a reflection in water, and in the darkness behind the breaking picture she knew there was the brown tunnel and the gibbering voices, and she forced herself awake.

An owl hooted. Where was she? Everything was dark, and after the owl had fallen silent there was no other sound. She sat up. She was in her own bed but had lost track of the time. The owl hooted again – in the trees over on the other side of the park it must be. She couldn't remember having gone to bed. She looked at the clock at her bedside – it said twelve but it had stopped.

She got up, felt her way to the door, eased it open. The hallway was dark, but there was a line of light under the living-room door. She tiptoed to it and listened.

The first thing she heard was her mother's voice saying, "… must be, to be imagining things like that." They were speaking about her, then. Trina realized she must have been asleep for ages. She vaguely remembered now her mother helping her to bed, and giving her a pill with a glass of juice. Had they been talking about her ever since?

Her father said something which she couldn't make out, and then her mother said something about "the girl needs treatment". There was a long pause, and when her father spoke again Trina realized with a shock that he must have got up and walked over to the door. She meant to turn round there and then and run back to her room, but her father's words stopped her; froze her...

"She knows, Beth," he said; "knows what's happening. That's it."

There was an exclamation from her mother, and then her father went on in a firm, quiet, bleak voice. "She knows we're drifting apart – she may not *actually* know it, but she feels it. With other couples, they quarrel a lot and then one of them moves out, and that's that; or else they make things up properly. We don't do either of those things; we just carry on – we pretend everything's all right. She senses something's badly wrong, but she doesn't know what. She's probably terrified. She's imagining things. We're probably driving her crazy."

The handle of the door turned, and Trina fled back to her room. She just managed to get behind her door before her father came out into the hallway, but she didn't dare risk the extra noise of getting back into bed. She crouched in the dark...

385

Her father was only going out to the bathroom, and after a moment he went back into the living-room and shut the door. Still Trina crouched where she was.

So that was it. They were driving her mad. They weren't meaning to. They were doing something terrible to her because they were doing something terrible to themselves. "Drifting apart" – that's what it was. It was the sort of thing that happened to other people's parents, she knew – she had never thought it could happen to hers. For a moment, Trina seemed to go outside herself; she seemed to be standing over by the window, looking at herself crouched by the door. And a pain, like a jagged white line, seemed to be splitting her head in half. Then she was back in her body again, and jerked herself upright. There must be something she could do! Something to save them, something to make them interested in each other again, something to make them care again. In a flash, all the past months, the past years, came back to her, and Trina saw the truth of what her father had been saying; something had been going wrong, something had been draining out of their lives all that time – ever since...

Trina shook her head. It was no use. She only had one set of memories, and she couldn't make herself believe it wasn't true. The truth was, everything had been going wrong since Kitty was lost. She could think of no way of getting that memory out of her mind. She had had a sister, a sister who looked very like herself. She could see her – she had just seen her in her dream; an older sister, with fair, curly hair and misty blue eyes. Kitty. Her mother must have been mistaken about calling her that as a baby. Adults did sometimes get confused about that sort of thing. Kitty was her sister, and Cat was their cat, and...

The owl hooted again, and a beam of silver light wandered into the far corner of the room. Trina went to the window and looked out. A calm, round moon had appeared behind the roof of their neighbour's house. The night no longer seemed dark, but the shadows of the trees across the park were deep and mysterious. Still staring out into the night, Trina slipped her nightdress off and reached for her clothes. Five minutes later she was climbing down from her windowsill onto the moist, soft soil of a flowerbed.

She had never been out alone at night, in the wide countryside. She flitted, soft as a moth, amongst the shadows of the bushes on the old railway track. She was glad at least she didn't have to struggle through the pathless thickets as she had that first time. The moon sailed across the sky and came to rest on the bulky shoulder of the mountain. It was so bright in her eyes and on the small, shimmering trees on either side of the track that the track itself was like a river of darkness that she was wading in, chest-deep, hoping there was nothing to trip on. Yet she felt no fear – at least not till she came in sight of the old station. She was too busy with thoughts of her parents, thoughts of herself going mad, thoughts of the four friends – thoughts of escape.

The deserted station with its tumbledown hut was bathed in silvery light. It looked peaceful and quiet, but something made Trina suddenly stop and look ahead in doubt. In a moment she realized why – there was the quiet, distant, high-up sound of a jet. There was no doubt of it. It sounded different, but it was a clear, cloudless night, so everything would sound different. There was an aeroplane, somewhere high up and far away, and it was coming closer.

387

Trina took a few steps towards the moonlit station. "No," she muttered, "please don't do it again – please don't."

The sound grew rapidly louder. Would she be able to get to the shed before it came? The distant cry, the whining and screaming, the shrieking and grinding – the explosion? She had to get there. But would the shed door be locked again? Would Mother Egg be there?

The leaves were shifting round her, and still the noise grew. She forced herself forward, and tottered into the sea of moonlight that filled the old station area. The door of the shed looked very firmly shut. Trina covered her ears and took a few more steps towards it.

And there was the cry. It sounded different this time –

perhaps because there were no clouds – deeper, more menacing, more like a distant bellow than a shout. The note of the jet engine changed. Then the blast of wind came, and the trees bent under it and Trina was sent spinning round, staggering against the edge of the platform. The noise grew and grew and she found herself screaming through it, "No! No! Stop it! I can't stand it! Please! Help!"

And it stopped. It hadn't finished; it hadn't become as loud as it was going to. It wasn't the minute of quietness before the awful bang. It just stopped as though a radio had been switched off. Trina looked up. Mother Egg stood in the doorway of the shed with the moon transforming her tangled hair into a shining halo.

Trina scrambled onto the platform and went towards her. The old woman was smiling sweetly. Trina's throat felt tight. "What is it?" she whispered, gulping. "Why does it do that?"

"It is getting closer," Mother Egg said.

Trina was feeling shaky, but as before her fright was fading surprisingly quickly. She began to think again of the reason for her midnight visit.

"You've been listening, I see," Mother Egg remarked. "That's good. Now we can proceed."

Trina glanced around once more. Everything was peaceful, moonlit. "Please," she said in a small voice, "I don't know what to do – I'm so unhappy."

"Unhappy," Mother Egg repeated, as though she had never heard the word before. "My dear child, what do you want that you haven't got?"

Trina was finding it difficult to speak; "I want – I want – I want them to believe me – I want to know I'm not going mad," she blurted out. "I want Mum to like me. I want Kitty

– I want Mum and Dad to stay together – I don't want Dad going away…" Tears sprang to her eyes.

Mother Egg laid a bony hand on her head. "I wish I could give you what you wanted," she murmured. "But there are more important things, you see. And there is nothing you can ever be sure about. Not in your life nor in anyone else's. You can't even be sure that the name you have today will be the same one you have tomorrow – or even that it's the same you that has it."

Trina looked up at the old woman, who was gazing up at the moon. She felt a strange, silver quietness inside her, like moonlight, and she realized that she was waiting for something – something very important – to happen.

Mother Egg looked down at her. "If you're ready," she said, "I'll show you the Scroll Cupboard now, as I promised."

389

"All right," Trina said.

Mother Egg turned and went in through the dark doorway. Trina followed and the door immediately swung shut behind her. There came several minutes of blundering about in complete darkness, knocking into pieces of broken furniture, which seemed to be everywhere.

"Here are cobwebs," Mother Egg remarked unhelpfully, as Trina brushed the clingy strands away from her face for the fifth time.

"Don't you have any light in the Scroll Cupboard?" she asked.

"We aren't in the Scroll Cupboard," Mother Egg said. "There's plenty of light there – you just have to find it, that's all."

"That's the only light I can see," Trina said ruefully, looking at a thin blade of moonlight coming through a crack.

"Ah yes, of course," Mother Egg said. "I keep losing my bearings." She went over to the light and there was the creak of a door opening. Silver light streamed in, making the cobwebs glimmer like mist. "This way."

It was not moonlight. A dim, wide, empty hall – or perhaps it was a tunnel, for Trina could see no far end to it – stretched before her. Its low roof was slightly arched, pale in colour, and it seemed to be from here that the light was coming. The silvery light inside the Scroll Cupboard was dimmer and warmer than moonlight. That might have been because of the decorations all over the walls, which were of rather dull colours – cream, and brown, red and deep purple. Open-mouthed, Trina tiptoed over towards the part of the wall nearest her.

The decorations, which covered the walls from floor to ceiling, were all spirals of the same size: some tight-coiled, some looser, some no more than a short curl like a comma. Each one was framed in a brown square. There were thousands of them – millions… "Who painted them all?" Trina breathed.

"Tut, tut," came Mother Egg's voice from behind her. "You don't listen properly, and neither do you see properly." She reached over Trina, took hold of one of the spirals between finger and thumb – and drew it out of the wall. It was not a decoration at all, but a roll of something – no, of course, a scroll of something! Yet the Scroll Cupboard was not just the biggest cupboard Trina had seen, it was the biggest building of any kind; the arched tunnel stretched off into dimness in both directions. Its vastness, and its silence, overwhelmed her.

Mother Egg unrolled the scroll and turned it towards her. Trina was a little disappointed to see that it contained no writing, but was all taken up with a complicated pattern of interlacing lines, boldly drawn in bright, lively colours.

The disappointment lasted only a moment. As her eye followed the swirls and curls, the breaks and bridges, the arcs and angles of the patterned scroll, she began to realize it was very beautiful, and more than that, it began to give her a strange, uneasy, excited feeling – a feeling that there was something about the scroll that she knew … that belonged to her…

"What is it?" she whispered.

"Names," Mother Egg responded matter-of-factly. "Just names."

"I only see patterns," said Trina.

"That's because your eyes aren't good enough," Mother Egg said. "They're used to those great gross letters you have to learn, and can't see anything finer. These are names, but they're written in very small letters, that's all."

Trina bent forward till her nose was almost touching the scroll. Screwing up her eyes in the dim light, she could just make out that the lines of the pattern were slightly rough at the edges, and the colours had not been put on with smooth, even brush-strokes but were made up of countless tiny dots. Yes, although she couldn't see it, she could believe that the lines were in fact twisting, swirling, criss-crossed, staggered lists of tiny names.

"Whose names?" she said.

"The names of all the creatures."

Trina's eyes wandered off down the endless walls of the tunnel again. She tried to calculate, then gave up. "I didn't think there would be so many kinds," she said.

"Kinds? Who said anything about kinds? I know nothing of kinds. Here are the names of *every creature*, their connections, their places, the patterns of which they are a part."

Trina was silent, letting Mother Egg's words sink in. But the thought was too enormous. She did not even ask Mother Egg the question that occurred to her – how many names altogether? – because she knew the answer would be quite meaningless, even if Mother Egg knew it.

"No scroll is complete," Mother Egg went on. "Each shows only a part of the great pattern. On this are written the names of two trees, and the names of the creatures which lived in them, and the names of the creatures which lived off them, and those which burrowed among their roots, and the names of the stones among which their roots grew, and the names of the mountains from which those stones came and the names of the rivers and ice-sheets which washed and ground them down; here are the names of the things which were made of the trees' timber, and the names of the small creatures which were burned when the branches were cut up for firewood, and the name of a girl who sleeps in the bed that was made from their wood..." She raised the scroll as she spoke until she was looking at the bottom of it. "Also, the names of the plants which died back as the trees grew and spread their roots... That's it, more or less. It's not a very big scroll."

"The girl in the bed –" said Trina – "what's her name? Can you tell me?" She already guessed.

Mother Egg started rolling the scroll up again, smiling knowingly at Trina as she did so. "We've had enough of scrolls," she said, "for they don't concern us. Now, I shall turn you into a cat."

"What, me?" said Trina, backing away a little. "A cat? Well, I don't – I mean – I didn't think..."

"Don't you want to be turned into a cat?" Mother Egg

asked, in apparent surprise.

"No," said Trina. "I mean – well, I wouldn't mind – but only as long as I knew I'd be myself again when I wanted to be. I wouldn't want to be a cat for ever."

"No cat is for ever," said Mother Egg. "Cat is only Cat as long as the cat-form lasts. Just as Trina is only Trina as long as the Trina-form lasts. But have no fear; you will be able to come back when you wish."

"What kind of cat will I be like? Cat? He was a lovely cat."

"I will turn you into the only cat you can be," Mother Egg replied.

"When will you do it?" Trina asked.

"It's already done," said Mother Egg.

Trina looked down at herself. "I'm exactly the same as I was," she protested.

Mother Egg ignored her. "You will have to climb through the roof," she said. "There is a hole I shall have to lift you up to." She pushed the scroll back into its little frame on the wall and turned away down the long empty space of the Scroll Cupboard.

Together Trina and Mother Egg walked on between the endless scroll-lined walls of that mysterious place. The hall was quite empty and their footsteps made no echo on the sandy floor; and it suddenly seemed to Trina that she and Mother Egg were actually standing still, while the walls rolled past them like moving screens. Then Mother Egg stopped (or the walls did), and pointed up. "That's the place," she said.

"I'll never get through that," said Trina, looking at the small dark hole at the top of the pale arched ceiling above her. "And I don't think you could lift me up there anyway."

"Easy," Mother Egg said with a mischievous cackle – and she grabbed Trina round the waist and tossed her into the air.

Trina was too surprised even to cry out; and then she was too taken up with making a grab at the dark hole which appeared in front of her face. She clutched, dug in her nails and hung on, waiting for her body to stop swinging…

But strangely enough, her body didn't swing much, and before she knew what was happening, she found her legs were creeping up under her and grabbing the edge of the hole on either side of her hands. Except that they weren't her legs and hands at all, but paws equipped with strong, sharp claws, covered with the silkiest, finest black fur. Scrambling through the hole was quite gloriously easy.

One moment she looked down, and saw a pale blob which she took to be Mother Egg's face, though it looked more like the milky moon – or perhaps a saucer of milk… The next moment she was climbing upwards from the hole.

cat

TRINA PULLED HERSELF UP INTO DARKNESS, BUT THE
darkness was moving. It was hard to say exactly how. It was
something like swimming, and something like flying,
though she herself was still. She knew at once what it was
– the dark place of the gibbering voices and whirring
wings. But was she really here now? She felt more here than
the other times, and she liked it even less.

The feeling of movement stopped, and at the same time,
for a brief instant, she had a glimpse of the world outside
the tunnel: the blue sky, dotted now with white clouds, the
mountains, and then the scene she had dreamed of earlier
that same night: shadowed water, the smooth grey trunk of
a tree, a stretch of sunny grass, and a grassy bank with
people on it – three, she thought, not four… Then the
dark place again. The gibbering and wailing grew louder,
louder. She wanted to cover her ears, but she couldn't find
her hands. Then –

"Quiet," said an ordinary voice, a boy's voice, and the wailing died to a low, distant moaning.

The tunnel melted away. She was watching a boy walking into a dark, round room into which a beam of pale light fell from somewhere above.

There were stone walls, and a stone couch in the centre of the chamber, and a great shape of stone – a man sleeping – that lay on the couch; the shaft of light fell directly on a large-beaked bird perched on the chest of the stone man. Trina seemed to be looking up at all this from the floor.

For a moment the bird was grey stone also, then a ripple of black passed over it; the head and one wing moved; the beak opened in a gigantic yawn and snapped shut again. It was a crow. It shook itself, looked round, and its gleaming eye fixed on the boy.

396

"Herold?" the boy said.

The crow took a deep breath and its beak opened again as if the bird were about to let fly with a tremendous squawk. But the sound which came from it was the voice of a man, deep, quiet, and slow. It said one word: "Sparrow."

Yes! That was the name! The name of the boy who had come with Kitty. Not Robin – Sparrow! But the boy was speaking…

"Is everything all right?" he said.

"Perfectly," the crow replied in the man's voice. "But there are things you should know. The time is very close."

"I haven't seen Puckel," the boy said.

"No," the man's voice replied. "But you have seen the men of the five villages setting off to find if there's a way out of the mountains."

"We thought that was a bit of a joke," the boy said.

"It will certainly lead nowhere, but it is a sign of how near the time has come. And now there is a breath of air in the Scroll Cupboard. Perhaps that will be the bridge end. I thought it might have been here, in the Vault of the Bear, but it wouldn't have been safe."

"Why not?"

"There are reasons. The dead and the living come too close here. Only the living can come to the Scroll Cupboard."

Trina's head was in a spin – the Scroll Cupboard... The bridge end...

"I don't understand about the bridge," said the boy. (You can say that again, thought Trina.)

"You will. Very soon. You will see Puckel, and he'll explain," answered the crow with the man's voice.

"Puckel explain? Everything just gets complicated when he explains. Then he disappears and you don't see him for years."

397

"Everything will become clear. Puckel has to watch and wait. He has done that for years – more years than you can imagine. The moment must be just right; it may not come again."

The boy sighed. "You're almost as bad as him. I don't understand anything. What should I do?"

"Where are your friends?"

"Just now? They're at the Hollywell – well, Kittel and Ormand and Lissie are. Kittel and I are staying with them for a week. Gogs is working at home. Bull was taken with the men from the five villages when they went off into the mountains. He's their big hero now, ever since the Troubles. They ask him things and he asks me and then goes and tells them what I've said. They'd never think of just asking me – they wouldn't trust me."

"You're too peculiar. Don't worry about it. Be glad of him. Go back to your friends at the Hollywell now. Don't delay – something is happening."

"Goodbye, Father."

"Goodbye for now, Sparrow. All will be well."

"Goodbye, Herold."

The next time the crow opened its beak it was to let out an ear-splitting squawk. Its wings flapped furiously, but the bird didn't leave its perch on the stone man's chest. As it settled itself again, the grey of stone crept back over its black plumage, and then the round room faded and the voices began again, and horrible echoing laughter mixed with the sound of wings.

"Quiet," said the boy called Sparrow. The laughing stopped.

398

Again there were glimpses of mountains, blue sky, a village turning on the ground below as though they were viewing it from the eye of a circling bird. Trina was still a cat, yet she was somehow here, with the boy…

"Here," said Sparrow. The whirring stopped.

There was a glimpse of huge holly trees, their glossy leaves shining in the sun like polished leather. Then there was the low bank of grass again, only now Trina seemed to be seeing it from lower down. There were grass stems, and daisies, right in front of her eyes. Gradually she realized that a strange shifting, dragging feeling was because she was in water. Not swimming – her belly rested on mud – but all her body except her head was under water. Two feet came into her line of vision, walking away from her, then two legs attached to the feet. The boy Sparrow was walking over to the bank where the other friends were: the boy with the moleskin hair, the dark-haired girl, the dog and, lying now on her back with her arms behind her head – Kitty.

Except that the boy hadn't called her Kitty. He had mentioned someone called Kittel. It wasn't the same, but it was so close…

The small dog was sitting with one ear up and one ear down. Behind them were the bushes she had come down through, when she had dreamed before.

She heard the girl – the other girl, not Kitty – speak; but now something was happening, something was changing, fading. Yet the curious thing was that it seemed to Trina that it wasn't the four friends and their grassy bank that were fading, but herself – Trina. She was fading. She wasn't dreaming, she was the dream, and she was fading, while the life of the four friends went on; soon she wouldn't be there at all; none of her life would have existed… The only story was the story of the four friends and their mountains and their ponies and their old-fashioned village, where there was no electricity, and no booming television-voices, and no machines, and everything was quiet and green…

399

"Yes?" said the dark-haired girl, Lissie. She was looking straight at Sparrow.

"Yes what?" said Sparrow.

"What were you saying before you went behind that tree?"

Sparrow frowned. "Was I saying something?"

Kittel sat up, shaking grass and bits of twig from her pale curls. "You were moaning about how hard it is having magical powers," she said, with a yawn. "We were all feeling desperately sorry for you. And can't you take that patch off? You look like a pirate."

"It's sore just now," Sparrow mumbled. "My father – I had to go on the Secret Way… He had something important… It doesn't matter. Anyway – it's not magic powers… I don't mind them…"

He untied the strap that held the patch over his left eye and blinked a little. "It was simple when it was just magic powers," he said. "There's nothing wrong with them. I still like being able to fly, and shape-shift, and talk to the animals and that. Even the Secret Way is all right, though it's not as much fun – I mean, it's creepy…

"But that's not it. It's just that ever since they told me that all these things were *for* something … I don't know… I just can't seem to enjoy them properly any more. Ever since they told me I had to start learning about the Secret Way, and we all started waiting because we knew Something was going to happen. It's all become different."

"It's been a long wait, anyhow," said Kittel. "A year and nine months. We could wait for ever."

"I used to just live here," said the boy with the moleskin hair, Ormand. "Now I've been told I'm *supposed* to live here, and Lissie too, because we're the keepers of the well –" he waved his hand over towards the pool that lay under the shadow of five huge holly trees – "but how do you keep a well, for goodness' sake? The well's just there. It's like we're just waiting around too."

Everyone looked glum.

"My father said things have started to happen," Sparrow remarked thoughtfully.

"When?" Kittel asked.

"Just now. When I was away. It's what he said. He said we would see Puckel."

"Nice of you to tell us you were going."

"I didn't mean to. I was looking at the water and it just sort of – happened. It does sometimes. It was because my father wanted to speak to me."

There was a silence. Everyone felt a little awed about Sparrow's father. The people of the village had thought for years that he was dead, then Sparrow announced that he had found him and frequently went to speak with him. No one else ever saw him though.

"Anyway," Sparrow said, "he said that the men of the villages wouldn't find anything, but it was important they'd gone, or something."

"Huh," said Kittel. "It just means that next time the Council of the Five Villages meet, Plato Smithers will stand up and say there's no world beyond the mountains and I was just telling a pack of lies about it all – or else I'm nuts, which is what he's always thought anyway."

"Do any cats round here like swimming?" Lissie broke in. Everyone looked at her.

"Course not—" Ormand began.

"Because," she went on, "that's a cat that's been having a swim in the Hollywell and it can't have fallen in."

They turned to the water. The dog's other ear went up. A small black shape was dragging itself on to land, though to be sure it was quick of Lissie to have realized it was a cat. It was more like a wet mop with a lump at one end. It shook itself and then sat down and started to lick. Kittel reached over and grabbed the dog, just in time.

"The poor thing!" said Lissie, and jumped to her feet to go over to the cat.

But the cat was having none of it. It was across the grass and off among the bushes behind them in an instant.

"Oh!" Kittel exclaimed, holding onto the dog, which was now struggling and squeaking.

Peering through the bushes towards the house, Sparrow and Ormand saw the cat pause, look back, then disappear off round the side of it.

"It's not one of ours, anyway," said Lissie.

"It looks as though it knows where it's going," Sparrow commented. Then – "What's wrong?" he said to Kittel. "You're as white as a sheet."

Kittel was still holding onto the dog. "It wasn't a cat," she said slowly. "There was something hiding in it."

"You mean it was someone in cat's shape?" said Sparrow. Kittel nodded. "Who? Puckel?"

Kittel shook her head. She looked less pale now, but she was frowning hard – as if she'd just seen a pig flying or water flowing uphill and was trying to work out if she could believe what she'd seen.

"Well, if it wasn't Puckel and it wasn't Sparrow, who was it?" said Ormand. "They're the only ones who can shape-shift."

"It wasn't who, it was what," Kittel answered in a low voice. "It was the dragon."

There was a stunned silence.

"It can't have been," Sparrow said at last.

"You only saw it for a second," Lissie reminded her.

"It was the dragon," Kittel repeated, letting go of the dog, which immediately went nosing off after the cat's trail among the bushes.

"The dragon's under the ground," said Ormand. "We saw it going there, and Puckel said that's where it belonged and that's where it'd stay."

"I often pass the dragon on the Secret Way," said

Sparrow. "He's always asleep. He can't get out – and why would…" he tailed off.

"You don't have to believe me," Kittel said sulkily. "I'm just saying what I saw, that's all. It was a dragon in cat-shape."

"You're the only one who can see through shape-changes," Sparrow said doubtfully.

"Oh, so I'm just having you all on, am I?" Kittel flared at him.

"Follow the cat," said Ormand suddenly.

"Ever tried following a cat?" Sparrow said.

"Take Boffin's shape," Lissie suggested. "He'd follow it for a hundred miles."

Ormand whistled and shouted, and after a little the dog returned.

"Go on, don't hang around," Ormand told Sparrow.

"What'll I do if I catch it?" Sparrow said.

"Just go – see where it goes!" said three voices, all together.

Sparrow changed. He had been shape-changing now for over three years and could do it without thought or hesitation, as easily as diving into a pool of water. Sparrow's own shape was invisible now, but he was still there, his mind and his memory, except that his nose was down near the ground, his thoughts full of the scent of Strange Cat, his tail was waggling with excitement, his legs were tireless, his interest was endless – he was on the trail! He yapped once, twice, to the others, and was off.

the goats

404 SPARROW PAUSED, AND TOOK HIS OWN SHAPE AGAIN. Boffin looked bewildered for a moment – animals usually did when he had taken their shape for a while – then looked up at Sparrow and flopped down onto the stony ground. He was exhausted.

Now it was Sparrow's turn to feel confused. He had been in the dog's shape for several hours, thinking dog-thoughts and seeing with dog-vision. He had lost his bearings. He and Boffin were far up into the mountains, above the line of the trees, among rough grass and bog and stretches of grey shale, and there was already a promise of dusk about the light. The sky had become overcast, and low clouds rolled over the stony mountain peaks that stretched in every direction.

This was the most mysterious cat he had ever come across. He had seen no sign of it, but the trail was never in any doubt. This cat had done none of the usual things cats do – little detours to sniff or poke at something, little pauses to wash itself or stalk a bird or sit in the sun; this cat had gone straight as an arrow up out of the village of Villas, through the oak forests, up onto the moors, up into the mountains, due east all the time, without a hesitation.

It was no ordinary cat; but how could it be the dragon in cat-shape? What use would cat-shape be to the dragon? One use, possibly – to get away unseen from its great spiral den in the Star Wheel far off beneath the grass of the Valley of Murmuring Water. But if that was what the great beast was trying to do – and Sparrow didn't even know that it *could* do it – then why should it pop up right in front of Kittel, the only person who had the gift of seeing through shape-changes? The thing didn't make sense.

Ahead of them lay a rocky ridge. Sparrow rose into the air and hovered there effortlessly, while Boffin gazed up at him, panting, his head on one side, but without getting up. The ridge led onto a broad plateau of broken rock, and at the far end of it a mountain peak rose – a strange-looking mountain, steep-sided but flat on top, as though some tremendous knife had sliced off its true summit.

405

Sparrow knew only one mountain with that distinctive shape – he had first come to it, flying, just after he had received his magic gifts from old Puckel. He had come to it on the day the dragon broke free, long before the dragon had been brought to its proper place in the Star Wheel, the day when Kittel had arrived, crashing to earth on that very mountain peak in a burning aeroplane – an aeroplane burning because the dragon had attacked it. He supposed the wreck of the aeroplane still lay there, but he never went to see it, and it was one place Kittel had never asked to be taken to. She was the only one who had survived that crash.

The mountain top was a graveyard for two hundred unknown people.

There was something moving down the dark flank of the mountain. Not the cat; it would be impossible to make a cat out at this distance. Nor a waterfall. It was more like a grey-ish-white worm. Vast, it would have to be – dragon-sized, though it was nothing like the green-and-gold dragon that Sparrow knew.

He returned to the ground. "Come on, Boffin, good boy, show me," he said. Boffin got up and immediately started following the trail again. Sparrow didn't take his shape now. He wouldn't lose sight of him here, and he could easily catch up with him flying. Boffin could look after the cat; he wanted to keep an eye on the thing on the mountain. They left the bog-land behind and climbed the ridge onto the stony plateau. The thing was still moving down the mountainside. It looked more than ever like a colossal grey-white worm.

On Sparrow's right hand the plateau suddenly became the edge of a cliff; a deep valley of stone opened up below, and grey water foamed and churned in its distant depths. The cat's path led along the edge of the cliff, but held on in the direction of the flattened peak. The worm, or whatever it was, had come down to the further side of the plateau, and began to head in their direction. Sparrow kept close to Boffin, ready to lift him out of danger if need be.

When at last he made out what it was, he scarcely felt any relief, though he was surprised. It was a column of goats. What they were doing up in these barren parts he could not think – there must be hundreds of them, thousands! Shaggy, dirty-white creatures, heads held low, clashing their great curving horns as they jostled in a tight crowd.

They were coming straight towards them. Sparrow and Boffin stopped. The thin sweet billy-goat stench came to their nostrils. Sparrow snatched Boffin up and held him tightly under his arm, preparing to fly out of the goats' path.

But there was no need. At the last moment, just when they were within a stone's throw, the herd turned – and swerved off over the cliff. Sparrow's breath stopped in amazement as the silent, shaggy creatures, by tens and hundreds, flung themselves over the precipice. There was not a sound from them, not a bleat, not a whimper; no sound but the scuffling of hard-toed feet on the stony ground. Then even that noise stopped. Sparrow found he had closed his eyes. He opened them again. The goats were gone. He went to the edge of the cliff and looked over.

There was nothing to see. A sheer wall of rock fell to the river far below, but there was no pile of broken bodies. Not a single one. The goats had vanished without trace.

"I suppose you could call that tit for tat, really," a familiar voice said.

Sparrow almost lost his balance as he spun round to see Puckel standing behind him – Puckel, the same as ever, in his old tattered green-and-brown coat, with his nut-brown wrinkled face and the wild green eyes under their thatch of wild white hair. Puckel was never one for joyous greetings; when Sparrow met him, he always seemed to be continuing a conversation they had been having. "What's tit for tat?" Sparrow asked numbly.

"Not in any unfriendly way, of course," Puckel said. "She sends something this way, so I send something that way. Might as well make use of the channel while it's open."

"I don't understand what you mean," said Sparrow. It

was not the first time in his life he had said that to Puckel! "What's happened to the goats?"

"What goats?" The old man looked surprised.

"There was a huge herd of goats," Sparrow exclaimed. "You must have seen them!"

"No, no goats," the old man said flatly. "You don't get goats up here and that's a fact. What would they eat?"

"But—"

"Dreams, thoughts, a few good songs, a few good stories," Puckel went on vaguely. "No goats. Come on." He turned and started off towards the plateau and the mountainside where the goats had come from and where Boffin had now gone, running swiftly along their brown-stained trail. Sparrow followed. By the time he had caught up with the strange old man he had recovered from his shock over the goats, and a quiet, pleasantly familiar feeling had come over him. He was so used to being baffled and bewildered by Puckel that their brief conversation felt like coming home after a long absence.

"Why's it tit for tat?" he asked as he came level. "Where's your stick?" he added, noticing for the first time that both the old man's hands were free. And, before Puckel could possibly have a chance to reply, a third question: "Where have you been all this time? I can never find you."

"You've forgotten where you are, young Sparrow," Puckel retorted. "All this creeping through holes and secret ways, you haven't been flying over the mountains as you once did—"

"It was you told me I had to learn the Secret Way!" Sparrow broke in.

"Not me," Puckel said.

"Well, your stick then."

"Not *my* stick," Puckel returned. "She does what she likes, old brittle-bones. I just try to keep it all together, which is no easy task as things are. Anyway, she sends this way, I send that – tit for tat. It's quite simple."

Sparrow felt light beginning to dawn. "Do you mean the cat?" he exclaimed. "Did she send it? Where from? And why was it a drag—"

"Best just come and see," Puckel replied, pointing towards the summit of the mountain.

"Can we fly there? It's beginning to get dark."

"I wondered when you'd think about that," Puckel said, a little huffily. "Don't know why I bothered giving you the gift of flight, the amount of use you make of it."

Sparrow knew better than to argue. He rose into the air, and then turned to see if Puckel was following. But somehow he was unable to control his turning, and the whole world seemed to turn once, twice, three times round him. And the next moment he was standing, with Puckel, on the flat top of the mountain.

409

He noticed the twisted black wreck of the aeroplane, like the skeleton of a giant animal, but there was something else which more immediately took his attention.

They were in a circle of buildings – rather tall, narrow buildings, all exactly alike, joined to each other by a low wall the height of Sparrow's waist. They seemed to be made of wood, but they were covered from top to foot in glorious patterns, carved and painted in riotous colours, blue and green and gold and pink and blood-red. Sparrow had never seen anything like it. The only parts undecorated were the low triangular doorways. The roofs were steep and tower-like, and covered in gilded tiles. The buildings were so bright they gave Sparrow the feeling that the place stood in bright sun-light instead of the gloom of evening.

"Like it?" Puckel said.

Sparrow nodded, turning slowly round and round. "What is it?" he said.

"As for what it is, you should know that," old Puckel replied. "What do I call it? I call it a medieval village!" He wheezed with silent laughter for a couple of moments, before going on. "We wanted them bright and cheerful-looking for our little guest, since she's used to bright things where she comes from."

Sparrow was only half listening. He counted the build-ings – five of them, spaced regularly round an open, circu-lar area which took up nearly half the mountain top. "It's the Enclosure, isn't it?" he said. "It was at the Hollywell before, but it's been moved here…"

"Something like that," Puckel replied.

"I've been trying to learn about the Secret Way. But there's so much I don't understand. I can never find the Enclosure, and… And I'm not even sure about the five places of power. I know about the Star Wheel and the Vault of the Bear of course; and I know where the Scroll Cupboard is, it's under that place they call the Echoing Hall, over near Springing Wood; and Mother Egg is where the dead lake is, but I've never seen it, and it sounds more like a person than a place to me. And the other place is King Puck, and that sounds like a person too, but I've no idea where that is – I've searched and searched and I've shouted at the Polymorphs to take me there, but they just laugh and howl and make me feel stupid for even asking."

"You haven't done too badly, on the whole," Puckel said soothingly. "You've found your way about, haven't you?

410

The Polymorphs do what you tell them—"

"Apart from taking me to King Puck," Sparrow put in.

"They do what they can. There are some things they can't do, that's all. They're not going to let you know they can't do them. That's why they laugh. They just want to put one over on you. It's a good sign. It means you've got them under control."

"Where is King Puck, then?" Sparrow demanded.

"Ah, well," said Puckel slyly, "that would be telling now, wouldn't it? Everything in good time, that's the best way. Anyway, as I was saying, this is our medieval village, and I hope you like it."

"It's very bright."

"And in the right place, which is much more important. Tell me, young Sparrow, how did you reach the Enclosure before?"

411

"It was through the Hollywell. Your stick told me that's where the centre most often was."

"And what did you do when you were there?" Puckel was speaking in a soft, sing-song voice, as though he were playing a kind of guessing game.

"Well – I – I found the Vault of the Bear, and I found the Star Wheel and – oh, I should be able to find King Puck and Mother Egg from here now, shouldn't I? If I just go into one of the houses…"

"Never mind about that now," Puckel snapped, suddenly changing back to his usual grouchy tone. "All in due course." He closed his eyes, and the dreamy voice returned. "And what else did you do?"

"I don't – oh, yes. There was a sort of opening in the bottom of the Hollywell, and I had to throw my stone through and I saw it falling through the sky and—"

"And what stone was that?"

"It was the one that had been the top of a mountain, and you shrank it by mistake when you shrank the dragon. You said it had to be put back so it could grow back into a mountain top and…" Sparrow stopped. This was something he had never thought of before. What mountain had lost its summit? There was only one – only one flat-topped mountain, and that was this one…

But Puckel had shrunk the dragon, and the mountain top, *after* the dragon attacked the aeroplane; *after* the aeroplane had crashed down into the snow on the top of this same flat-topped mountain…

"I thought—" Sparrow began, but Puckel interrupted him brusquely. "Time to go," he said.

Sparrow was at a loss. "But … the mountain … the dragon … the cat … Boffin…" he mumbled.

At that moment Boffin appeared out of the triangular entrance of one of the buildings. He was panting, rolling his eyes, wagging his tail.

"Saw him off, did you?" said Puckel. "That's a good boy. What a tracker!" Boffin ran to the old man and bounced up at his leg, trying to lick his hand.

"What about the cat?" said Sparrow.

"What cat?" said Puckel.

"The cat that crawled out of the Hollywell!" Sparrow exclaimed, exasperated.

Puckel shrugged. "Still crawling out, I suppose," he said. "Like us."

And Sparrow blinked, for they were. He and Puckel were ankle-deep in water, facing Kittel, Ormand and Lissie, who were standing staring at them, too amazed to do anything but gape.

instructions

PUCKEL'S APPEARANCE AWED SPARROW'S FRIENDS INTO silence. The old man waded to the shore and then walked over to the grassy bank, where he turned and immediately started speaking in solemn, impressive tones.

"The time has come," he said. "The time for which we have been waiting so long. I have gathered you here, and now I am calling on you to give your help."

There was silence. A pale ray of the setting sun escaped the grey clouds and turned the great holly trees round the pool to towers of shimmering gold. No bird sang.

"First, your task," Puckel went on. "You have a gift to carry – to carry to a place where it's needed. What is this gift? You are sitting on it; you are breathing it; you are feeding on it, living in it. This country of mountains, as you may now know, was built – its valleys, its forests, its waters, its villages – to hide and protect a great doorway, a doorway into the centre of the earth. That is the gift.

"The giants' doorways – those that can still be found – always needed to be hidden. This one especially needed protection because of the dragon which long ago escaped from it and was out there in the world, wreaking havoc and destruction. And because the dragon was not here, the Polymorphs also threatened destruction from within. Partly thanks to you, these dangers have now been overcome.

"But the effects of the dragon's time in the world are still as bad as ever. There is madness and destruction, there is dragon-poison in the very air. It is time now to build a bridge between here and there – a bridge so that the power of the Giants' Door may again cross over. This will bring healing, first of all, and then many other unexpected results beside.

"A start has already been made, of course. The dragon has been returned to his true place and the Polymorphs have been controlled. As a result of this, the roads between the villages have become safe. That is why people have started travelling freely between the villages. You could say, bridges have begun to be made. Lissie lives here now, not in the village where she was born. And people have heard young Kittel's story about a world beyond the mountains. The men of the five villages have got a search party together to try and find a way to it. They are trying to build a bridge, too."

"Bull's gone with them," Lissie put in. "He's the guide for the search party."

"Well, that'll set the cat among the pigeons," Puckel replied, with a chuckle. "Listen. There are many ways of building a bridge, but this bridge has to be made with the right direction. Otherwise it will be all wrong. You will understand this eventually. The search party are trying to cross from this side. It is important that they find nothing.

There is a barrier. The bridge must be crossed from the other side. There is only one way to Kittel's place, and to find that way a bridge of dragon bones must be built to reach over the barrier."

"Dragon bones?" Sparrow and Kittel repeated together.

"Yes, dragon bones – bones from a dragon," Puckel snapped back at them. Speaking grandly always seemed to be too much of an effort for him, and now he sat down on the bank and rubbed his eyes as though he were tired.

"Where will we get dragon bones from?" said Sparrow. He was teetering on one foot, pouring water out of his boot.

"How does the dog find bones?" Puckel demanded, with a glance at Boffin.

"Dig for them?" said Ormand after a little pause.

"Now you're talking!" said Puckel. "There's a boy with some sense, for a change. Yes, you dig for them."

"But where?" Sparrow burst out, giving up trying to balance on one foot and squelching his sock down onto the grass. "The only buried dragon I know about isn't dead, and anyway you can't get to it because it's in the Star Wheel and you can't find it by digging, I know that."

"So?" said Puckel.

"So you need a dead dragon to find its bones, don't you?"

"What about the cat?" said Kittel.

Puckel sighed. "Questions, questions – you're always so full of questions." He stood up. "I haven't time for it. Ormand and Lissie must dig. Sparrow must take the bones and build the bridge. You must not do each other's jobs. Now it's up to you to get on with them. I wish you good luck, I wish you peaceful dreams, and I will give you a warning. This world where you live is built out of dreams.

The world which the bridge will cross to is built out of dreams. The bridge is not built of dreams. The bridge is built of the bones of the creature which dreams the dreams. When the building of the bridge is complete, then comes the moment of danger – that is when you must understand the nature of dreaming so that the bridge can be crossed the right way. If it is crossed the wrong way, it will lead to the loss of the Giants' Door, and a catastrophe beyond anything I can tell you." He fell silent, gazing sadly over at the golden holly trees.

"What about me?" Kittel asked at last, in a very small voice.

Puckel turned sharply towards her. "What about you?" he snapped.

"What's my job?" she said.

"Same as it's always been," Puckel said. "To keep this turnip-head in order." He nodded over towards Sparrow, who was standing with his boot hanging from his teeth by the laces while he wrung the water out of his sock.

"Oh," said Kittel. She had no chance to say anything else, because just at that moment there came a hullabaloo of yapping and yowling from among the bushes, and a second later a black something shot out into the open, across the grass and, without a pause, into the water of the Hollywell, where it disappeared with scarcely a ripple. A second after that Boffin appeared in hot pursuit, skidded to a halt at the water's edge, and began whining and yapping and running up and down. Boffin didn't like water.

Ormand, Kittel and Lissie ran to the pool, with Sparrow hopping along on one foot behind them. The last of the sunlight left as they got to it and peered in. The water under the trees was dark, but not too dark to see. There was no sign of the cat.

Sparrow turned back to Puckel. "That was…" he began, then stopped. The grassy bank, and the lawn between it and the pool, were deserted. Puckel had disappeared.

Sparrow looked round in dismay. Eventually he shrugged. "Was it the dragon-cat?" he asked Kittel.

"I don't know," she replied.

They went on peering, stupidly, into the pool. After a while Ormand looked up at the darkening sky, and then down at the dark water. "There's just one thing funny about those reflections," he said. "The sky's grey – dark grey. I mean our sky is. But those clouds in the pool are white."

It was true. As they went on looking, it gradually became clear that the clouds in the pool were not reflections of the clouds in the sky above them. Quite apart from their colour, they were moving, as if in a wind. The four friends became quite silent, watching intently, for the clouds were changing. They were not now like clouds blowing across a sky, but seemed more like clouds rushing towards them. Every now and then one of them came straight for them, and then for a moment or two the pool was full of grey mist, which soon faded into cloud-whiteness again and then vanished, leaving the clear greeny-blue of an evening sky.

This was no reflection. It was as if they were looking out of the window of something that was moving through the sky. And before long they realized that the darker thing just in front of their feet was ground – a flat plain, broken up into hundreds of small green and brown and yellow squares, small bumps here and there, irregular patches of dark green, strangely patterned brown things like uneven

417

starfish… "Towns," Kittel whispered; "like when you see them from an aeroplane."

The ground tilted, and began to rush closer, bit by bit filling the whole surface of the pool. Bumps became hills, squares and patches became fields and woods. They were rushing with incredible speed towards a strange, mountain-less landscape; yet they were standing on the ground of their own country. Almost they stopped breathing, standing tensed, waiting…

A small, conical green hill came into view – not below them but ahead of them. The steep crown of it was in the centre of their vision, rushing towards them. "Go on, Sparrow," Kittel whispered, and gave him a nudge which made him step forward into the pool…

There was no splash. The hill rushed into their faces, disappeared. But so did Sparrow. And a second later the reflection in the pool grew completely dark, and then all that was to be seen of it was their own three white faces gazing in.

crash

TRINA CREAKED OPEN THE DOOR OF THE OLD RAILWAY shed. It was still night, but an eerie red light was flickering on the abandoned station. It seemed to be coming from the mountain looming in front of her – somewhere behind the summit, because she could see the black crown of the mountain standing out sharp against it.

Quickly she turned away, making her way softly along the old railway track back towards Newborough. At least it was still night and she might have a chance of getting home before her parents realized she had gone. She thought now how stupid she was to have run off like that; it wouldn't solve anything. She would have to stand her ground, she would have to trust her mother and father, she would have to trust that she wasn't going mad, and she would have to trust that everything would come right in the end. Even if it didn't, she would have to go on trusting – trusting something – trusting Mother Egg if there was nothing else to trust.

Why being turned into a cat for a short while should have made her feel so different she didn't know, but it had certainly helped in some way. She could not really doubt that she had been turned into a cat, although it was already beginning to seem distant and dreamlike. One of the things that made her feel it must be true was that her body felt so stiff and stumpy, and that she kept wanting to ripple her back, sink her hands into the ground in front of her, and saunter along on all fours with her hips and her belly swinging.

I suppose cats have no memories, she thought, disappointed because the only thing she could remember was curling up for a nap. When she woke up again, she had been sitting, in her own form, beside the door of the railway shed. Her mind felt strangely calm, although whenever she looked back to the eerie, flickering light she felt a tug of uneasiness. Surely it was a fire burning up there on the hilltop? It was hard to make out in the dim moonlight, but now that she was further away from it, the hill seemed to have come down in size again – it was no longer a mountain, but the size it had been when her father told her it was called the Stack.

She frowned at the moon. She had never thought much about how the moon changed, but she was fairly sure it had been full, quite high in the sky on her left as she made her way to Mother Egg's hut. Now it was lower on the horizon on her right – and it was only a half moon.

Before she could think much about this, she was startled by a blue light flashing over across the fields – something moving on the Market Glass road probably, heading away from Newborough. Then there was a second blue light following it, and a third behind that. Police? Ambulance?

420

What was going on? It crossed her mind it could have something to do with the fire on the Stack.

When at length she reached the Square, everything was in uproar. People were standing in the street, some of them in dressing-gowns and pyjamas, all talking excitedly. Every now and then the din of a siren would blare out, and a fire engine, or an ambulance, or a police car would turn into the Square and go speeding off up the Market Glass road. It was obvious something awful had happened, and Trina shrank against the walls of the buildings as she made her way down towards the Union Bridge.

By the time she reached the door of Pats' house she found she had all gone to jelly and she felt her knees were going to buckle. She stopped, banged her fist against the door, then turned the handle and staggered in, slamming the door behind her and leaning against it as she shook and shivered in the dark hallway.

421

A door opened and a beam of light shone into the hall. Pats' father was standing there. He had on a dressing-gown, but he was still wearing his trousers, and his pipe in his mouth was wreathing his head in bluish smoke. He had probably been working on one of his books before he went to bed.

"Trina!" he exclaimed. "Thank God you're safe! Come in, come on in, I'll ring your parents right away."

"No," Trina gasped. "You can't go up there – there's something wrong." Pats' father refused to have a telephone in the house, and when he needed to he used the public call-box in the Square. "I don't think they know I've gone," she added. "They were asleep when I left."

Pats' father looked at her searchingly. "Perhaps you're not so safe after all," he said softly. "I'll get you a cup of tea first. I'll be all right up in the Square, don't worry. There's been a big accident – a plane-crash, I think – but there's nothing to stop me using the call-box. Just come in here and sit down. I don't like to leave Pats alone, or I'd run you home straight away. There's still tea in the pot, fine and strong, just the very thing. Pats is asleep – just you come and sit down and I'll be back in a few moments. Poor Trina, you're probably in shock. Did you know it's been a whole week since you disappeared? No, I see you didn't. The police have been looking for you up and down the country."

Trina gaped, and slumped into a chair. She hardly noticed when the mug was thrust into her hands, and it was only after she had been sipping at the hot, sweet liquid for a minute or two that she realized Pats' father had left the house and she was alone. But at that moment Pats appeared.

Pats was a strange sleeper. His nights were deep and long. His father said he doubted if anything would wake him – not even an earthquake. Yet here he was now, standing at the door in his pyjamas, looking at her, and showing no sign of sleep or bleariness. In fact he looked unusually alert…

In fact, Trina realized, with a shock that made her sit upright and slop some of the tea into her lap, there was something different about Pats, something completely new… Then it dawned on her – Pats was *looking at her*, looking directly into her eyes, not over her shoulder as he usually did. It flashed through her mind that he had lost his beautiful, faraway look and was much more like an ordinary boy now; and then Pats spoke.

"I know," he said simply, nodding as if to himself. "I

know what's happening. But some things are a bit confusing. What's your name?"

"Trina," Trina whispered hoarsely.

"Trina. That's right," Pats said. "Of course." Then, with a small frown, he announced, "You need to dream. So do I. I'm going back to sleep now." He turned and started out through the door again.

"Wait!" Trina cried. "Pats, wait a minute – I want to know..." She tailed off.

Pats turned again. "What did you call me?" he said.

"Pats," Trina answered. "Isn't that your name?"

"No, I don't think so," Pats said, frowning even harder.

"Then what is it?"

"Spa... Spat..." Pats shook his head. "I can't remember," he said. "It's something like that. I've got to get to bed." He turned again and this time was gone.

423

Trina's father arrived at the house, in his car, at the same moment as Pats' father got back from the Square, so Trina had no chance to tell him the incredible news about Pats. In fact, for the next fortnight, she had little chance to tell anyone anything sensible.

Her whole world seemed to be turned upside down, and the confusion in her own life that night got strangely mixed up with the confusion and panic over the accident out at the Stack. Her father drove her home, and one moment police cars and ambulances were racing past them with flashing lights and sirens whining; the next, the policemen and doctors and nurses seemed to have come crowding into her own room and questions, questions, questions kept coming at her from all directions. Where had she been? Who had taken her? Had she been hurt? What had she been given to eat? Had anyone given her pills of any kind? Injections? As the only things she could remember doing were going for a walk and being turned into a cat, Trina decided the only sensible thing she could do was to say nothing.

The next morning she was given an injection which made her feel very drowsy and faraway, and she was taken in an ambulance to the big city hospital and put in a bed by herself in a white room with a window that was just a little too high up to see anything out of. A young nurse who smiled a lot and an old nurse who never smiled kept coming in and out and feeling her forehead and taking her temperature and asking her if she was all right and if there was anything she wanted. Her mother and father were in and out as well, and occasionally another woman came in who looked at charts and asked the nurses things and never looked Trina in the eye. It was all extremely bewildering, and as days passed it soon became very boring. There was nothing to do except eat and sleep, and leaf listlessly through magazines and then eat and sleep again.

She dreamed a lot, but very little of what she wanted to dream. When had she last dreamed? Just before she woke up and wandered off into the night – or was it? Yes, that must have been it; the next time she had slept was when she was a cat. The dreams she had in the hospital were full of crashing aeroplanes and the barking of dogs, and Mother Egg walking slowly down endless corridors, and Pats continually appearing in doorways, and crowds of people milling about, and goats that kept turning up and wandering unconcernedly amongst the people.

If she tried to tell the nurses, or her mother, about this, they would just look sympathetic and stroke her head or plump up her pillows. The days of boredom lengthened, then shortened till she couldn't tell one from the next, and the only clear thought that formed in her mind was the thought that she would never go and visit Mother Egg again if it meant having to go through all this afterwards.

After a fortnight – though it seemed more like a year – Trina had a visit from Pats' father.

"Where's Pats?" Trina said. It was most unusual for Pats not to be wherever his father was.

"Wandering about in the grounds," he said with a shrug. "He wouldn't come in." Then: "I don't know what's happened," he said, "but he's suddenly started speaking. Not all the time – I mean, not every day – but, well, speaking perfectly; as though he's known how to all along. The little rascal must have been listening to everything we've been saying all these years. Do you know what he asked me? He asked me what the riddle of the Sphinx was. I vaguely remember talking about the riddle of the Sphinx – ages ago, months and months. He must have been listening..."

"I've heard of the Sphinx," Trina said. "It's that statue in the big concourse just down from the museum, isn't it?"

Pats' father laughed. "It was a lot worse than that in the original story," he said. "'A vast shape, with lion body and the head of a man, a gaze blank and pitiless as the sun...' You've heard of Oedipus? Well, the Sphinx asked Oedipus: 'What is the creature that goes upon four legs in the morning, and two legs at midday, and three legs in the evening?' And Oedipus had to answer it to save himself, because the Sphinx was going to kill him."

"What was the answer?" Trina asked, forgetting about Pats.

"Oedipus answered: 'A man, who in the morning of his

425

life crawls on hands and knees, and at noon goes on his two legs, and when he is old hobbles along with a stick.' And the Sphinx let him go."

"That's clever," Trina said.

"You think so?" Pats' father said. He got up and went over to the window. He was just tall enough to be able to see out of it, and he was silent a while as he gazed at the sunny day. Trina watched him. Pats' father wasn't like hers. He spoke a lot less and he never got agitated. "You may be able to save your life by answering a riddle like that," he said, "but then it becomes a question of whether the life you save is worth living. A child could have answered the riddle, really – but Oedipus thought he'd done all right. But he hadn't. He'd treated the Sphinx as if it were stupid. His city was destroyed by a plague. I suppose your father would say he was exactly like a modern man."

426

Trina grinned. Her father was always saying that modern people were stupid. "What was the answer?" she asked.

"There wasn't one. The Sphinx was asking: 'What is this creature, a man?' And Oedipus just answered, 'A man.' No wonder he came to a bad end. He should have turned it round. I think he should have asked the Sphinx: 'Who are you asking?' That might have blown its circuits!"

He came back over to Trina. "I'll speak to your dad," he said. His voice sank to a whisper. "It's time we got you out of here. It's summertime out there. I'll work on him, don't worry – if I can get any sense out of him, that is. Since they told him there'll be no money for that ship project, he's taken it into his head to do it all himself – rented a shed just down the road from here; it's got a little room on the end of it where he eats and sleeps, and he's been carting the timbers over to it every night in a van, and numbering them all so he knows the proper order to put them back together. Always thought he was a little cracked, but this just about does it."

"He did tell me something about it," Trina said. "That's probably why they don't want me out of here. Dad's all taken up with that, and Mum's – well, she's got her work, and … things…"

Pats' father said nothing; and Trina realized that she was just complaining because she was feeling sorry for herself. Of course they wanted her back home.

"Was it a plane-crash?" she said at last. She wasn't even sure if that had really happened or if it had all just been a confused dream-memory of that strange night.

He nodded. "A bomb, on the plane. The papers are still full of it. All those innocent people killed because somebody wanted to make a point." He turned as though he wanted to look out of the window again, but gazed at the wall instead, a dull, pained look on his face. "It's a terrible world," he said.

427

So it was no dream. And Pats talking wasn't a dream either.

After a short silence Pats' father said, "There's something else about this, though. In fact, everyone's completely baffled. The wreckage is still up on the Stack, most of it, and they've been up there sorting through it. They put the fire out a few hours after the thing happened, of course; but the strange thing is that every night it bursts into flames again, and they've got to put it out all over again. It doesn't look like ordinary fire to me, either. I've never been near it, of course, because they won't let anyone near, but you can see it from the town. It's a silvery sort of flame.

And every night it starts again, and has done for the last thirteen nights."

As Trina fell asleep later on, she thought of the silver fire that would be flaming up again in the darkness on her mountain. And when she slept she dreamed at last as she wanted to dream.

She dreamed of the boy – Sparrow he was called, not Robin; but how did she know that? – in the dark, gibbering tunnel. The boy was certainly the same one she had seen sitting on the bank, the boy she remembered from the waterfall. He wasn't wearing the eye-patch now.

As before, there were occasional glimpses of the world outside the darkness; but during one of these glimpses she suddenly felt herself caught up – and she was outside the tunnel, up in the air, circling above the mountains, above a small, circular-shaped green valley far below.

She was dropping as she circled, spiralling down towards the little valley. Very soon she could make out details: a small dark line cutting it through the middle was probably a stream; an area with a different shade of green was a wood… There were marks in the green grass on one side of the stream, like circles – huge circles taking up the whole of one side of the valley. She spiralled down towards them. Soon she was skimming low over the grass – very low; grass kept appearing right in front of her eyes, and she had seen something like that before, but where? She seemed to be travelling round the outermost circle.

And then she was through the ground – underground; in the darkness again, going through the ground as if it were no solider than mist. She was slowing, coming to rest… Voices moaned and wailed. Wings whirred.

428

The boy was there, beside her. There was a rough earth doorway in front of them, and a dim-lit tunnel beyond – a real tunnel this, with walls and a roof. And on the floor there was a gigantic head – the head of a sleeping beast. The eyes were on a level with her own, but they were shut. Clouds of mist drifted around the head – or was it smoke? It seemed to have a smell a bit like smoke. Breathing it, she began to feel dizzy. And then it came into Trina's mind that the sleeping beast was dreaming.

Something was happening. Something that had happened before, only she had forgotten about it; this time she would remember. She was no longer dreaming – *she was being dreamed*. The great beast was dreaming, and she was part of its dream. Or … no; Trina was part of its dream – but now she didn't seem to be Trina any more. It was more that she herself was the dreaming beast. And now it – or she – was starting to dream about something else, and Trina was fading away, Trina was no longer there…

dragon bones

"COPPERHILL AGAIN," LISSIE SIGHED, AS SHE ALWAYS DID when she came in sight of the village which had once been her home.

She, Kittel and Ormand were riding their ponies down the Old Road out of the mountains, and when they reached the place called the Cold Stone the valley opened out below them; and there, down amongst its green orchards and small, patchy fields, Copperhill nestled snugly in the warm sunshine under a haze of blue wood-smoke.

The Cold Stone was a tall standing stone, pierced through at the top, which stood beside the road. A little spring of clear water tumbled out into a trough at the foot of it, and here they stopped, as they always did, to let their ponies drink.

There were four ponies – small, fat, sturdy beasts, slow, inclined to be bad-tempered, but much loved by the children of the mountain villages who, now that the

Polymorphs had been controlled, made frequent long journeys on the old mountain highway. The fourth pony was Sparrow's, whose mother had insisted that he should have one and try a little to behave like the other young people, even though it was far easier and quicker for him to fly or go by the Secret Way.

It was three days now since Sparrow had disappeared into that other place they had glimpsed in the pool. The three friends were not greatly concerned about him – his life moved him on such strange paths anyway – but they did talk a lot about where he could be, and what he could be doing.

"Where was it? Was it your place?" Lissie and Ormand repeatedly asked Kittel, and Kittel could only shrug and say, "I don't know – it might have been."

"I didn't see any machines," Ormand said doubtfully.

"It's not just machines," Kittel said. "It's just ordinary country, really, just like here."

"I didn't see any mountains," Lissie said.

"There are mountains," Kittel said, "but not where I lived. Where I lived it was just houses and streets and shops and parks and gardens."

The last pony had barely raised its head, snorted the water from its nostrils and shaken its mane, when Sparrow suddenly appeared out of the hole at the top of the Cold Stone and plopped down in a heap beside the trough. "Phew," he said.

His friends were by now quite used to him popping out of nowhere, and didn't waste time being amazed over this sudden appearance. "Well? What happened?" they all burst out together.

Sparrow scratched his head and grinned up at them.

"There's not really anything to tell," he said.

"What!" Kittel exclaimed. "You've been gone three days, and there's nothing to tell. What happened? Where did you go? What did you do?"

Sparrow grimaced apologetically. "I don't really know," he said. "I think – I felt as though I was asleep and dreaming, really; that's what it was like."

"Well, what did you dream of?" said Kittel. "Was it the Modern World – I mean, my place? You must know."

"Probably," Sparrow said vaguely. "But it wasn't really like that. I saw your sister, though – I recognized her from that time before, by the waterfall."

"Trina? You saw her? Why didn't you say?"

"I just have. But it wasn't like that, really. It was all from funny angles, like in dreams…" He fell silent.

432 "And didn't you see – anything? Anything strange? Cars, trains, just … real towns or something? When you landed on that hill, what did you see? Where did you go?"

"Oh, yes," Sparrow exclaimed. "I'd forgotten about that hill. Yes, I remember landing on it. And then I looked up, and I saw the mountains. Our mountains here, I mean. That's right. Only – I was looking at them from underneath."

"Underneath? Do you mean from the bottom of the mountains?"

"No – no, from underneath. I was underneath them. And then they were just clouds. But I'd made them become clouds. I didn't want anyone to see them. That was like in dreams, when you want something to be something else, and it is. You can do that, using the Secret Way and the Polymorphs, only I haven't learned how to yet. Puckel can do it." He frowned. "But that's all I remember," he finished.

"Great," Kittel tutted. After a short silence, she went on. "Well, meanwhile, we're making our weary way home, to pick up some picks and shovels and stuff and then we're going on to the Valley of Murmuring Water to dig for dragon bones. Do you want to come, or do you want to go on dreaming?"

"I don't think there'll be any dragon bones to find," Sparrow said.

"Well, there's only one way to find out," said Ormand, swinging himself up onto his pony.

"I can tell you," said Sparrow, "that the dragon's there now. I've just been to the Star Wheel. But he isn't dead. He's asleep, just the same as he always is. I don't believe he was ever in the shape of that cat, and if he isn't dead there's no point in digging for his bones."

No one could doubt what Sparrow said; but then, no one knew of any buried dragons except the one under the Valley of Murmuring Water.

From Copperhill, the Valley of Murmuring Water lay some two days' journey, by pony, eastward into the mountains. It was a deserted, peaceful, mountain-ringed circle of bright grass, with a small birch wood on one side of the stream that cut it in two, and very little else except a large clump of nettles that grew in the middle of the grass on the other side. The four friends knew that where the nettles grew there had once been a little ruined house. Sparrow and Kittel had lived there, during the time everyone now called the Troubles.

Three more days went by before they arrived in the Valley, as Sparrow's mother had insisted on spending a whole day baking so that they didn't go hungry. Murie was an easy-going person in most respects, but she had grown up in the days when it was unsafe for the village people to travel, and she couldn't quite get used to the way the young people would go off for days at a time. So she always found something to worry about, even if it was only that they wouldn't have enough food.

On the evening of the third day, they halted under the seven gnarled and ancient trees on the low hill at the western end of the little valley. In the silvery light of evening the sunken marks of the great underground spiral of the Star Wheel showed clearly in the grass of the valley floor. "This is the way the search party went," Sparrow remarked. "I wonder where they are now."

"Most likely they're on their way home by now," said Lissie, "because Plato Smithers is missing his parsnip wine."

"Bull will soon sort them out, if they start grumbling," Sparrow laughed. Although Bull was by far the youngest person in the search party, even the grown-ups in Copperhill sometimes found him rather alarming.

"Where do we start digging?" Ormand wanted to know. "Tail end or head end?"

"Tail end, thank you," said Lissie. "I don't want to meet a live dragon face to face."

"That would mean starting amongst the nettles," Sparrow said.

"And the foundations of the cottage," Kittel put in. "It would be hard work digging."

There was a silence. The smooth whisper of the stream and the tiny hiss of a breeze amongst the trees were the only sounds to be heard. There was no place as quiet as the Valley of Murmuring Water.

"We'll dig at the head end," Ormand said. "And hope it's dead."

After their supper they wrapped themselves in their blankets on the dry, mossy ground of the birch wood and slept, while their ponies wandered on the sweet grass on the other side of the stream. It was so quiet that they could hear the beasts munching, while stars peeped out and disappeared amongst the fragrant birch leaves above them.

The next day the digging started. It was overcast and chilly, which was good from Ormand and Lissie's point of view, but not so welcome to Sparrow and Kittel, who had been told not to dig.

It was Sparrow's job to catch some fish for their lunch, while Kittel gathered dry wood for their cooking fire. Sparrow took half the morning to catch only four trout. He fidgeted too much to be a good fisher. Kittel said he should take the shape of the fish and jump into the net and then change back into his own shape in time to scoop his catch out, but he refused. Kittel got her fire going and fuelled up and then took over the fishing; within half an hour she had caught another four. Sparrow went over and gave Lissie and Ormand advice about digging their hole until they told him to go away. He poked about the place where the cottage had stood until Kittel called over to him to pick some nettle-tops for their trout stew, and then pointed out to him that the ponies had strayed to the edge of the valley.

The afternoon went by slowly. The pile of earth beside Lissie and Ormand's hole grew bigger and bigger. There was no sign of them now unless you stood right on the edge of the hole and looked in.

There was some argument about whether Sparrow should help by moving the soil away from the hole, as it was slipping back in because it was in such a big pile. "After all," said Lissie, whose face was furnace-red and beaded all over

435

with sweat, "Puckel only said you weren't to dig the hole; he didn't say anything about not moving earth." But Sparrow pointed out that to move the earth he would have to use a spade, and if you were using a spade you were digging. Kittel was never one to let Sparrow get away with anything, but she backed him up now. She had a clear – and unpleasant – memory of the sort of thing that could happen if you went against Puckel's instructions.

The soil was soft and crumbly, even at the depth Ormand and Lissie were digging, but there was no sign either of bones or of the underground passage of the Star Wheel. The last time an opening had been made in the Star Wheel everything had been too hectic and nightmarish for any of them to notice how deep under the ground it was. That opening had disappeared now, and it was not even certain that it was possible to get to the Star Wheel by digging. But at least they knew that, if it were possible, they were digging in the right place.

The weather had brightened again during the morning of the second day, and it was about noon that Lissie broke through. There was no doubt about the moment it happened. One moment there was only the sunny quietness of the small valley; the next, there was a sound that made your hair stand on end – a sound both quiet and huge, like a sigh that lasted as long as it takes to count to ten quite slowly; a long, moaning sigh that was like a sigh out of the depths of the earth.

"You've gone all white," Kittel remarked.

"So have you," said Sparrow.

"We're through!" came Lissie's voice, as her head appeared over the top of the mound of earth.

Sparrow and Kittel jumped up from the cooking fire and

hurried across to peer in. The pit tapered down to the small, cramped patch where Lissie and Ormand had been working, and where a small black hole was now visible just beside Ormand's foot. But whatever else might be in there, there was no coil of dragon smoke coming from the hole.

"Did that noise come from the hole?" Sparrow asked.

Lissie nodded. She looked white too.

Without another word, Sparrow slid down into the pit, bringing a small avalanche of loose earth with him. He squeezed past Ormand and struggled through the small opening, out of sight.

They almost expected another three-day disappearance, but it was only a few minutes before his head appeared again. He glanced up, looking pale and dirty. "You'll have to make the hole bigger," he said. "I think I might break this if I try to get it through."

"Out of the way, then," Ormand ordered, seizing his spade.

The hole grew bigger, and the patch of ground where Ormand was working grew smaller. At length Sparrow told him to stop and to get right out of the way. Ormand, Lissie and Kittel stood on top of the mound of earth and watched as Sparrow backed carefully out of the hole, holding onto something which none of them could make out. It looked most like a gigantic feather, bigger than Sparrow, and made of glass. "That's not a dragon bone, whatever it is," Kittel muttered.

Sparrow flew up out of the hole and landed on the grass some distance away from them. They ran over, but he shook his head warningly. "Don't come too close," he said. "I think it's very delicate."

"What is it?" Ormand said.

"It's a dragon bone," Sparrow said solemnly, holding onto the great, feathery thing, which shifted slightly as the breeze caught it, glinting with rainbow colours.

"That?" said Kittel. "Don't be silly, how could it be?"

"There's a whole line of them, down there in the tunnel," Sparrow answered. "Lying on the floor, one behind the other. There's no sign of the dragon. It's not really like the Star Wheel – it's just a tunnel through the earth – but that's got to be what it is, it's the same place and shape and everything. I just don't understand it."

the rainbow

TRINA'S FATHER DROVE HER HOME FROM HOSPITAL. THEN, after hovering around the house for a couple of hours he muttered, "Well, I'd better be getting off," and disappeared without a word of explanation. Her mother, who had been given some time off her work, was doing everything she could to make things appear normal, and said nothing about Trina's disappearance or about her time in hospital. Also, she wouldn't speak about the crashed aeroplane bursting into flames every night, however much Trina questioned her. It was almost as though she connected it with Trina's disappearance.

And Pats, it seemed, had gone back to his old, unspeaking self. "It's a downright disgrace," Trina's mother said. "That boy could probably be quite normal if he just had some proper care. They should take him away from his father and send him to a special school."

"I like Pats the way he is," Trina murmured. Yet she

couldn't forget the night he had talked; or what he had said
– about dreaming.

Trina had to stay indoors for a week, her mother said. It
was very galling, because she felt perfectly well, but her
mother had got it into her head that she "needed to get her
strength back". She felt like a caged animal. Her father
came home on two occasions, but he spoke little and
seemed ill at ease. Although he was there when Trina went
to bed, he was gone in the mornings.

It wouldn't have been so bad if she could have gone on
dreaming at night – even the confused dreams she had had
in hospital would have been all right, though she really
wanted to go back to the dream about the four friends. But
there was nothing; she had stopped dreaming altogether. It
nagged at her, because she kept feeling that there was one
dream she had forgotten – an important one, probably the
most important one of all. How did she know the boy was
called Sparrow? That must have been the dream she had
forgotten – but how could she get it back? She tried everything to make herself dream. She put books under her
under-blanket to make the bed uncomfortable; she tried
lying across the bed with her head and feet dangling over
the sides; on one occasion she slipped two large spoonfuls
of coffee into her bedtime cocoa, because she had once
heard someone say that it gave you amazing technicolour
dreams. She was almost sick at the taste of the disgusting
brew, and the only result of her tortures was that she
couldn't sleep for hours, and then when she did nod off she
sank into a black, dreamless pit from which she didn't wake
until eleven o'clock the next morning.

"What's Dad doing all the time?" she asked her mother.

"He's busy with that ship in the evenings," her mother

said. She was chopping vegetables and did not look up. "He has to do it in his own time, you know, because the university won't pay him to do it."

"Will he come back here when he's finished it?"

"Well of c—" her mother began, then stopped. She also stopped chopping, and stared at the bright pieces of chopped vegetable on the wooden board in front of her. At last she looked up, looked Trina directly in the eye. Her expression was a strange mixture of her normal, organized, bossy-mother expression and another expression which Trina remembered from Max – just about all she could remember now of their dog – an expression of endless woe. "No," she said at last. "No, I don't think he'll be coming back here to stay." Then she looked back down at her vegetables, and a moment later began chopping again.

"Will I be able to go and stay with him sometimes?" Trina asked, in a very small voice.

Her mother came over to her, and for the first time in she-couldn't-remember-how-long put her arms round her and held her close. "Of course you will," she said at last.

The week dragged to a close, and when her father appeared for a third time, at last Trina was allowed out. "Let's walk to the Stack," he said. "It's about time we saw what all the fuss is about. And then tomorrow we'll go up to the university and you can see my ship-building shed."

"I want Pats to come with us," Trina said firmly as they came down to the Union Bridge. She knew her mother would have objected if she had said it before they left the house.

Pats' father was only too happy to have his son go with them, especially as Pats seemed keen to be with Trina; and when Trina asked, he even said Pats could go with them the next day as well to stay the night at the shed where Trina's father was working on his Burial Ship. "Any day, he could start talking again," Pats' father said. "The more variety he gets, the more it's likely to happen."

The three of them left the Old Town square in bright sunshine, but by the time they had got halfway along the old railway track, thick dark clouds had come. At the same time it continued very warm, and soon numbers of flies were buzzing around them.

"Looks like thunder," Trina's father said. "We'll need somewhere to shelter."

Pats grunted cheerfully, though it was impossible to say why.

As they drew nearer to the Stack – Stack-size it seemed to be still, no mountain – Trina began to feel anxious. Would they hear the sound of the crashing plane again? Then a thought hit her. These things happen in threes. Twice she had heard it, and then there had been a real crash. That was three. There would be no more. Except –

"What was that?" she said suddenly.

"Lightning, I think," her father replied. "Be quiet a moment." They waited, and he counted slowly, "One – two – three – four – five." A long, menacing roll of thunder crossed over the sky and back again. "About a mile away," he said. "I wonder if we should turn back."

A small, whimpering sound came from Pats. But he was gazing along their path ahead and not back to the black sky.

"There's a shed across from the Stack, beside the railway – someone at school said so," Trina lied in desperation. "We could shelter there."

Her father glanced back. "All right," he said. "We'll give

it a chance."

They quickened their pace, every now and then glancing above their heads as the sky built up in great billows and towers. Intermittently the thunder grumbled, now and then shaking itself out of its grumble with a resounding crack, as if the very sky was starting to split open. On one occasion, Trina looked back just in time to see a jagged pink line running along the grey edge of one cloud with the menace of a pouncing cat.

"I think we'll make it," her father panted.

They did, but only just. At the very moment they climbed onto the flower-grown remains of the old station platform, a brilliant flash of light turned the colours and shadows of everything inside out, and at the same second a monstrous, slamming, tearing sound broke out above, below, and to all sides of them, as though giant hands were ripping up the earth like a carpet. A blast of wind followed the thunder and bent the trees over and sent Trina, her father and Pats hurtling forwards to the very door of the old shed. A moment later, without a drop to warn them, the rain was pouring down in torrents.

On finding the door locked, Trina's father did not pause. He stepped back and with a single kick sent it flying open, then bustled the two young people inside with the rain already dripping from their hair.

The noise was indescribable. It seemed the flimsy tin roof of the shed could not possibly hold back the cataract from the sky, while windows and doors rattled with the almost continual battering of the thunder. The darkness in the shed was shattered again and again by the terrible flickering light from outside.

In all the excitement of beating the storm, Trina had

clean forgotten to look at the Stack and see whether it was a mountain now or just a pyramid-shaped hill. Now, peering through the door from the depths of the shed, it was impossible to tell because of the curtains of rain and the sagging clouds.

Gradually the din lessened. She peered round the shed. All was empty, dust-covered, derelict. Slowly, she picked her way to an inside door. Was that the door to the Scroll Cupboard?

"Don't stand next to any windows," her father warned.

"I don't think there are any here," she said, going through the door. She was conscious of Pats behind her, peering into the gloom of the second room.

It was as dusty and empty as the first. Trina walked slowly round it, poking disconsolately at the walls, peering up at the cobwebby ceiling. There was nothing. If the Scroll Cupboard had really been here before it was certainly not here now. There was not so much as a hand-print in the dust. Dreams? She shrugged to herself.

A sudden light made her swing round. A shaft of silvery sunlight had shone through the door of the shed. Trina glanced at Pats, who had half turned too as she looked round. His face was only in silhouette, but somehow she could tell immediately that something had changed. His eyes, which slightly reflected the light, were seeing things properly again…

"Let's go out," she said. And Pats immediately went to the door between the two rooms and towards the outer door. Trina followed with her heart beating fast, certain that something was about to happen.

They went out into blinding sunlight, with every leaf and every bush sparkling. And then Trina found that she still couldn't answer the question about the Stack.

To be sure, there was a small, tree-covered hill just in front of them. But rising behind it there was a great mass of mountainside such as she had seen there before. Only now, that mountain was not the end of it; behind it, above it, one out-topping the other, other mountains rose, higher and higher towards the heights of the sky, while the grey of the lower ones merged into the pearl-colour of the middle ones, and those into the dazzling white of the highest.

Common sense told Trina they were not mountains at all, but only the clouds of the passing storm. And yet, and yet... She couldn't be sure. And as she stood there doubting, suddenly there was a rainbow.

It was not silently, serenely, there, in the way rainbows usually appear. They saw it leaping up and arching over from the high clouds like the path of a stone tossed down to them, like the trail of a diamond meteor. Like a shining mist amongst the trees it came to rest just inside the pink and white fence which had been put up all round the hill to warn people not to climb up.

Pats gazed at the towering column of the rainbow, and then exclaimed, in the sort of voice you use when you suddenly see the answer to a problem that's been nagging you for a week: "That's how it's done! As easy as that! Yes!" And with that he suddenly sprang into the air, clear off the old platform – and fell, with a sickening thud, on the stony track below.

"He's knocked himself out," Trina's father groaned. "Oh, Lord! What am I going to do?" They hurried down to Pats, who was lying without movement, and had turned a delicate shade of blue. Trina's father punched and pummelled him a bit, and at last Pats gasped, moved slightly, and then drew in a deep breath.

"Winded, I suppose," Trina's father murmured. "Am I imagining things, or did he speak back there?"

Trina nodded.

"We heard he'd been speaking a bit of course, then he stopped…"

Pats raised himself onto his elbow and reached for a stone lying on the track. He picked it up, turned it over and over in his hands, then brushed it gently backwards and forwards against his lips. His eyes were faraway.

"Well, he's back to his old self now, poor little chap," Trina's father said.

That night, all at once, Trina dreamed again.

That is, she supposed it was a dream, because her mother said nothing about it to her the next morning.

Somewhere in the darkness after midnight, she seemed to wake up – and with one idea in her mind. She had to watch television. Normally, she kept away from it. Now she knew she wouldn't get another wink of sleep unless she could watch it, just for a little.

She slipped out of bed and crept along the passageway to the living-room. She didn't put the light on for fear of alerting her mother, but fumbled about in the dark till she had found the plug, pushed it into the socket and switched on the set. Then she knelt in front of it and watched.

There was a black-and-white film on: two men making horrified faces while something black – presumably blood – trickled out of a wall. Trina was about to get up and switch channels when the picture faded and the screen went dark. She frowned and waited; this was peculiar. Perhaps the tuning was wrong…

446

And suddenly it was there – in full, living colour. It was the head of the sleeping beast in the tunnel, she knew that, but now it was head-on to her and somehow that made it look eerier. It was a golden head, very long, curving out at the foot of the screen into gracefully-flaring red nostrils. The top of the head was encrusted with green and golden scales, pointed and delicate as celandine flowers. The huge, black-edged eyelids were closed below grooved bones that were like the start of horns. The mouth was out of sight. It was like a mask, utterly still. Was it sleeping?

It was dreaming. This had happened before. And when it had happened before she had slipped into forgetfulness, because she had been in the creature's dream – or she had been the creature dreaming of herself – and then it had started dreaming about something else. But that wasn't happening now. Something different was happening. What?

Something about the mask-like face moved. Trina watched intently. There it was again – it was an eyelid twitching. The creature was about to wake up. Again she found she couldn't move. If it wakes up and looks at me, she thought, I'm going to be sick.

And then the scream came. An ear-shattering scream that Trina didn't at first realize was herself. It seemed too loud for her to have made alone. Within seconds, it seemed, the light was on, her mother was there, there were exclamations and soft, soothing words, and then bed, and a hand on her forehead and the cool pillows against her cheek, and the black tide of sleep. But before the tide quite overtook her, the memory burned through her mind like a burning coal on a carpet – the beast had woken; its eyelids had opened; she had looked into the red depths of its pit-like eyes, and seen her own reflection.

That was not quite the end of it. She had hardly dropped into sleep when she found herself standing in a small green valley with high mountains rising all around. The sun was shining, a sweet breeze was blowing, and everything seemed easy and kindly. Then there came a shout from one of the mountains and Trina, looking up, saw a boy and girl flying through the air down towards her.

It was Kitty, and the boy Sparrow. He was wearing his black eye-patch again. It was only the boy flying, she thought, but he was carrying Kitty, holding onto her by the waist.

"Kitty!" she called. "Is that you? Are you all right?"

Kitty waved and smiled, but it was the boy who answered. "She's fine," he called; "she's just fine. But what am I going to do with her? I can't put her down!"

And as Trina woke, she remembered; remembered the dream she had forgotten when she had woken up in the old railway shed – coming out of the water, the dash across the grass, the dog yapping at her heels, flight up the old village street, up the hillside, through the towering oak forests, the moors, up, up into the mountains. And then what? Goats… Something about goats… No, she didn't have the whole thing yet – but nearly, very nearly.

And with the memory of the dream there came a new thought – that when Pats had leaped off the railway platform, he had been trying to fly. No, not trying to fly – he had expected that he *would* fly.

bull

"WHAT AM I GOING TO DO WITH IT?" SAID SPARROW. "I
can't stand here forever, and there's all the others to fetch."

449

"Make a pile of them?" suggested Ormand. "You'll have
to have a pile of them before you can start building."

"But where's he going to build?" said Lissie.

"And how am I going to build?" said Sparrow. "I can't
pile them up – I can't even put them down; they'd break to
pieces."

"Well, you can't stand there like an idiot for the rest of
your life," Kittel said, "so we're going to have to decide."

It was well on into the afternoon. The others had eaten
the food Kittel and Sparrow had been preparing, but
Sparrow had had nothing. He had hardly dared to move
with the flimsy, feather-light bone of the dragon. Sitting
down with it, or holding onto it with just one hand, seemed
quite out of the question. They had talked through the
whole mystery over and over again – whether the dragon

was dead, whether it was the only dragon, what it was that Kittel had seen in the cat's shape. But always the conversation came back to the problem in the front of all of their minds: what were they going to do with this dragon bone, let alone possibly a hundred others?

Then the silence of the little valley was broken by a shout, and a swirl of birds flew up from the birch wood.

"Look!" Kittel exclaimed, pointing up towards the rocky ridge at the eastern end of the valley. "It's people – it's the search party. I'm sure that's Plato Smithers."

The others looked in silence for a moment. "What shall we do?" said Ormand.

There was a further shout. "I think they want us to go up to them," said Lissie.

"I'm off," said Sparrow. "I'm not going to hang around and let them see this thing." He set off, walking carefully up towards the clump of nettles, carrying the dragon bone slightly behind him as if dragging it through water.

"Where are you going?" Kittel said.

"To the Secret Way. I'll be back."

There was another shout. "They want us to bring a pony," Lissie announced.

"I don't know how you can make that out," Ormand grumbled as he went to fetch Sparrow's pony, which was the nearest. By the time he reached it and had coaxed it to him there was no sign of Sparrow or the dragon bone. "Come on," he said to the others. "We don't really want them coming down here and poking about yet."

It took them some while to get through the wood and up to the ridge. There seemed to be only two men there – one of them, Plato Smithers, easily recognizable by his huge size.

They watched the three children and the pony struggling up towards them but showed no sign of wanting to come down. The pony wasn't able to get up the last, steep stretch and Ormand stayed behind with it as Kittel and Lissie panted on up the incline. Plato Smithers and the other man, whom they didn't know, started down towards them.

"What are you youngsters doing here, anyway?" Plato Smithers enquired, with some concern. Smithers, who was the largest and strongest man any of them knew, was always concerned about people. He was a sort of policeman in Copperhill, and not always very quick on the uptake.

"We just came out here – for a ramble," said Kittel, smiling winningly.

"We thought we might meet the search party on their way back," put in Lissie.

"Did you now?" said Smithers with a guffaw. "Well, you're in luck, for we weren't going to be coming back this way, but there's been an accident."

"We're in luck too," remarked the other man, a small, foxy creature with red hair.

"We are, we are indeed, Bertie," Smithers agreed. "You couldn't have come for a – ramble – at a better time. Young Bull there, he's had a fall." He made a sign up towards the top of the ridge. "Broken his ankle, we think. He'll need to be got home. A pony'd be just the thing. We've had to carry him to here."

Bull was not the sort of boy who ever looked particularly pleased about anything. He certainly didn't look at all pleased now, though when he saw Kittel and Lissie his dark face broke into an expression of some relief, which immediately changed to one of pain because he had moved his leg. Plato Smithers heaved him up, as gently as he could, and carried him on his shoulders down to where Ormand was waiting with the pony.

"Well," Smithers said in a satisfied voice, when he had seen Bull safely settled, "we're not finished with our searching, so we'd best be getting back to the others. Young Bull will tell you what's been going on and you can take the message back to the villages. But it looks as though you were wrong about a way to another place beyond the mountains, missie." This was to Kittel.

"Couldn't you find it?" said Kittel.

"Well," said Smithers, removing his felt hat and scratching his head. "We found the edge, if you see what I mean."

Kittel shook her head.

"He means there isn't a way," the other man said drily. "There's just an edge, and then – nothing."

"Nothing?" Kittel echoed.

"Nothing," repeated the other man.

"Well," said Smithers, "there's clouds – blue sky, and great big clouds below you, when you look down. I don't really know where you got your story from, about another place, but I'm thinking you must have dreamed it. We're not giving up yet, though. What we're doing now is — " He broke off, peering down in some perplexity at the pile of bare earth on the valley floor. Then he scratched his head again. "Oh well," he finished, "best be getting back I suppose, eh, Bertie?"

Bertie said, "Don't hang around now," to the three friends, and then set off back towards the top of the ridge without another word. Plato Smithers repositioned his hat on his head and followed. Within five minutes they were out of sight.

Kittel stared after them, frowning hard. "Didn't it even seem strange to them?" she said to Bull.

"What?" Bull said.

"That the world just – ends like that? Do they really think they're the only people living in the world – that there's nowhere else except the five villages?"

Bull shrugged. "Can we get off this slope?"

Until they got back down to the birch wood and more level ground, their attention was taken up with trying to keep the pony, and Bull, steady. Bull's damaged ankle had been well bound up, but whether his foot was in the stirrup or out of it, each smallest jolt made him wince with pain. Once in the wood, things went a lot easier.

"What did he mean?" Kittel said. "What are they going to be doing now?"

Bull explained. "When we got here on the way out, there was an argument about which was the right way. I told them what you and Sparrow told me about that time when you tried to find the way back yourselves – how you'd followed the stream, then the long lake, then the river. But I told them it wasn't just as simple as that either – I was thinking of it all being a trick of the Polymorphs when you went before, though I didn't say that. I didn't think they'd be able to take that in.

"So anyway, I think they thought I just wasn't very sure. So some of them started saying that they should keep going due east – and that would mean climbing over from the long lake into the next valley. They reckoned that even if they couldn't find the old railway itself there'd be other ruined houses and stuff, like there was in this valley, and that would show them where the railway had been.

"Plato Smithers stuck by me, like he always does, and he

said that he was going to go my way even if none of the others did. So they stopped arguing and said they'd just go where he went.

"But then the river disappeared into a marsh, and we couldn't follow it any more. So we just wandered on, until we came to an edge, like he said, and there was nothing. We had to decide if we would keep on going along the edge and see if we came to a way that went down – though you couldn't see anything below – or if we would come back to the long lake and do what the others had said and try and find the old railway line."

"So how did you break your ankle – did you try to go over the edge?" Ormand asked.

"Me? No fear!" said Bull. "I wasn't going near that edge. No, I just got caught in a rockfall two days ago. It was really stupid. It was that Bertie's fault. He was the one that wanted to go the other way in the first place; I didn't like him."

When they emerged from the wood there was no sign of Sparrow. Not at the pit, nor up at the clump of nettles. But Lissie peered into the hole and said she thought another of the dragon bones had gone. That sounded hopeful; perhaps Sparrow had discovered what to do with them. They told Bull everything that had happened, and then decided that the best thing now was for Kittel to set off with Bull, and make a good start before nightfall. Ormand and Lissie in the meanwhile would continue to dig and make the hole bigger for Sparrow to get in and out.

"as easy as that!"

SPARROW HAD OFTEN TRIED TO EXPLAIN TO KITTEL AND his other friends what it was like going on the Secret Way of the Mountains. But what was there to explain? To them, it simply seemed like a way of getting from one part of the mountains to another without spending any time doing it, the limit being that it only worked inside the vast, five-sided frame which Puckel called the Giants' Door. East of the Valley of Murmuring Water, or west of the Dead Lake, there was no going on it. Kittel now thought of Sparrow's sinister conveyors on the Secret Way, the Polymorphs, as some sort of bad-tempered taxi-drivers, though she had encountered them more than a year before and knew they were far worse than that.

It was different for Sparrow. He never called for the Polymorphs to come and take him anywhere, and he never actually saw them. He could make them appear before his darkened left eye, though this was something he hardly ever did. He remembered well enough the horror of the sight of them – their grey, distant faces, their humped bodies, winged and armless, Bur with his two one-eyed heads… He had enough to remind him of what they were like when he travelled on the Secret Way and heard their gibbering voices and wailing laughter.

He didn't like the Secret Way, and used it mainly because Puckel had told him to. Entering it was for him a bit like having to swim through a pot of bubbling liquid. The bubbling was the voices of the Polymorphs, and the thoughts that kept bubbling up in his mind. You had to keep control of them, or they would take control of you; you had simply to concentrate all your attention on the other side of the bubbling pot – the place where you wanted to be; and when you did that, the place where you were suddenly fell away like mist and shadows; there would be a darkness, as though you were under the earth but the earth itself were misty and unreal; there were strange, twisting glimpses of the ordinary world, and then the place where you wanted to be took shape around you, grew solid, and you were back in the world of everyday.

So it was that the clump of nettles, the Valley of Murmuring Water and the mountains all around melted away, and the smooth grey-green pillars of the five holly trees took shape out of the darkness. Sparrow stood beside the Hollywell holding the great, delicate dragon bone under the spiked shadows of the trees, and wondered what to do. Was the bridge to be built from here? He looked into the pool through which he had gone into that other place – Kittel's place. He saw only water, and the swift shadow of a trout in its dark brown depths.

Then without warning the darkness rose up round him

out of the pool, and changed to light, and a gust of fresh wind lifted the feathery bone and almost pulled it out of his hand. He looked around him. He was on the flat-topped mountain with the wreck of the burned aeroplane lying within view. He was standing in the enclosure surrounded by the five bright-painted buildings which Puckel had called his medieval village.

"Puckel?" he called. "Are you there?"

There was no sound except the sharp-sifting wind. But Sparrow knew that if you found yourself in the Enclosure it meant that you were supposed to go into one of the five places of power that were hidden in the five angles of the Giants' Door. But which was which? And which did he want, anyway?

The Secret Way led past the places of power, but only by the Enclosure could you enter them for the first time. He had once been in the Star Wheel, before the dragon was returned to it, and had several times been in the Vault of the Bear to speak with his father. He knew where the companion-places of these two were – Mother Egg opposite the Star Wheel and the Scroll Cupboard opposite the Vault of the Bear; he knew that somewhere between the Star Wheel and Mother Egg was King Puck, though he had never found it; but that was all he knew.

Now he stood on the mountain top and felt sure only that it was not the Vault of the Bear or the Star Wheel he was to go to. And what had his father said? That there was a breath of air in the Scroll Cupboard – yes! And that was where his father believed the bridge was to be built from. He went towards the nearest of the low, triangle-shaped entrances, turned to go through it, stooping, backwards, so as not to risk damage to his strange burden.

Immediately, a dim, silvery light was all around him, and he found himself coming through a doorway into a place which he did not know.

It was utterly still. He tiptoed along beside an endless wall, gazing in wonder at the thousands upon thousands of little scroll-spirals which covered it. He was in no doubt that this was the Scroll Cupboard. Now that he was out of the sunlight in that dim place the dragon bone no longer flashed with rainbow lights but glowed like mother-of-pearl.

After a while, he realized he had been hearing a scuffling, scurrying sound without properly noticing it. He stopped, holding his breath. The sound came nearer, but it wasn't until the very last moment that he saw the movement at his feet. There was a small, jagged creature with four legs on each side of its reddish-brown body and an unpleasant-shaped tail that curved up over its back into a deadly-looking, pointed end. Sparrow had never seen a scorpion before, but he had heard descriptions of them and he stepped back hastily.

"If you go on gawping like that, mud-head, a bird's going to come and make a nest in your mouth," came a dry, rasping, very familiar voice. Sparrow shut his mouth immediately.

"I didn't know you turned into a scorpion as well," he said, as soon as he realized that the voice, which was the voice of Puckel's stick, was coming from the little creature at his feet.

"Don't be a fool," the scorpion returned without ceremony. "If you're here to dump that thing, then dump it and go and get on. You're not on a sight-seeing holiday."

Sparrow could never quite get used to the stick's rude-

458

ness, especially since he knew there was a connection between it and the old teacher they had had at the village school in Copperhill, in the days before Kittel came – gentle, mild, dottled old Ms Minn. He wasn't quite sure what the connection was; he had seen the stick turning into a snake, and a bowl of water, and a rainstorm, and a water-spout, but never – exactly – into the old teacher herself. Yet he was almost certain that they were one and the same. At any rate he knew better than to argue. "I'm afraid it might break if I put it down," he said.

"Don't be ridiculous," the scorpion snapped, rattling its tail. "You're just making excuses for being so slow. Why, a tortoise with a lead shell could do the job quicker than you're doing it. Just drop it there. Let go."

Sparrow hastily did as he was told. His arms were stiff from having held them in the same position for so long.

The bone of the dragon remained exactly where it was. It didn't drop; it simply floated, without movement.

"Well, go on, go on," came the scorpion's exasperated voice. "Or do I need to give you a prick in the heel?" It raised its tail menacingly.

"No," said Sparrow, and fled back the way he had come.

The bubbling of thoughts through his mind, which was the voices of the Polymorphs, was all mockery and deri-sion. The Polymorphs seemed to think it a very funny idea that he was slower than a tortoise with a lead shell. Sparrow's mind was full of pictures of giant, gasping tor-toises scrambling up endless slopes or labouring across endless stretches of dry, cracked mud. He endured it, and was soon standing among the nettles again in the Valley of Murmuring Water. There had been no glimpse either of the Enclosure or of the Hollywell. This didn't surprise him, and he was fairly sure that there would be no difficulty in getting back to the Scroll Cupboard with the next dragon bone.

He picked his way among the stones of the ruined cottage. There was no sign of any of the others in the valley, but he was more concerned about not getting into more trouble with the scorpion. He flew down into the pit, wriggled through the hole Ormand had made, scrambled along the small earth passage and carefully took hold of the second bone. This time he flew from the pit straight to the patch of nettles. The Polymorphs started up a mock-enraged howling like distant wolves as soon as he entered the Secret Way again, but he ignored it. And as he had expected, the Way now led directly to the doorway of the Scroll Cupboard. He had made a little bridge of his own!

There was no sign of the scorpion as he skimmed lightly down the endless tunnel of the Scroll Cupboard. In the silence of the place he could hear the great dragon bone humming softly as he dragged it through the air behind him. He came to the place where the first bone still floated, motionless, exactly as he had left it. He let go of the one he was carrying, and it hung floating beside the first.

Sparrow looked at the two great, feathery things and wondered about them. Even if they could be left floating in the air, would they make a bridge? Perhaps they would be more like stepping-stones – but from where, and to where? And who would walk on them?

Gently, he gave the second bone a push with his finger. It was an extremely light push; he simply wanted to see if it was fixed there in the air. The bone moved, swinging softly round towards its companion. They'll collide! Sparrow thought, frantically reaching out to stop the two bones

460

from knocking together.

A flash, like a rod of horizontal lightning, ran through the Scroll Cupboard. Blinded for a moment, Sparrow staggered back. When he could see again, there were the two dragon bones floating end to end, joined together by what looked like a small blue knot.

He stared at the two bones. There was something different about them – they hadn't exactly changed, but there was something about them which looked less fragile. Gently, he put out his hand again and touched one. The feathery end did not move; it felt hard, strong as steel. Amazement gave way to delight. "So that's how it's done!" he breathed. "As easy as that! Yes!" And he leaped into the air again, almost knocking his head against the arched roof of the Scroll Cupboard, and skimmed off back to the doorway.

461

Returning to the Valley of Murmuring Water, he saw Ormand and Lissie, but no sign of Kittel. The sun seemed to have disappeared behind the mountains. He wondered how long he had been away. There was no telling with the Secret Way – going from one place to another seemed to take no time at all, but in the Enclosure or the Scroll Cupboard any amount of time might have passed.

It turned out he had been gone about an hour. Bull had been collected and had set off with Kittel for Copperhill almost straight away.

"I've a better idea," Sparrow said as soon as he heard what had happened. "I'll go after them just now and fly home with Bull, then Kittel can come back here."

"I don't think you should," said Lissie firmly.

"Why?" asked Sparrow, who had already forgotten

what the scorpion had said.

"Because you're supposed to be making the bridge, and we're supposed to be digging for the bones, that's why," Lissie replied. "Kittel didn't have a job like that to do, and she'd just have to wait around for us anyway."

"It could take a long time to get all those bone things out," Ormand put in. "And we don't know when the search party will be coming back."

Sparrow hesitated. "Bull needs help," he said at last. "It'll be two days before he gets home if he goes with Kittel. But I could get him home tonight. I'll be back. You start digging again; it'd be a lot easier if the opening was made bigger. I'll be able to get more of the bones before it's dark."

"You'll be sorry," said Lissie. "You should do what Puckel said. We'll probably all be sorry." She stalked off back to the pit, followed by Ormand. Sparrow watched them slipping out of sight down the pile of soil. Then with a shrug he leaped into the air and flew off.

He flew low through the valleys. There was no path to follow, but he knew the way well, as did Kittel and Bull. There was only one way to go, so there was no risk of missing them.

"They must have been going at an amazing speed," he muttered to himself as quarter of an hour passed with no sign of them. Somehow, he felt uneasy.

A quarter of an hour after this, he could not fool himself any more. He had circled and searched, flown high to survey the land beneath, dropped to the ground to try and find tracks. But amongst rocks, bushes, moss, pools and heather, nothing moved. Kittel and Bull had disappeared.

It was going to be dark before long. Sparrow had a

sudden pang of conscience. Lissie had been right. He was going against what both Puckel and the scorpion had said. The only time he had disobeyed Puckel before it had nearly led to disaster. A cold sweat broke out on his forehead and in his armpits; a sweat of fear.

As swiftly as he could, he made his way back to the Valley of Murmuring Water. The sky had become overcast again, and low clouds were blotting out all but the feet of the mountains, bringing on the evening more quickly. He landed beside Lissie and Ormand, who were sitting on top of the pile of earth looking grey and disconsolate.

"You see?" said Lissie as soon as he landed. "That's what happens when you don't do what you're told. It's not our fault."

"What isn't?" said Sparrow, in fright. "What's happened? What's wrong?"

463

"We tried to move the next dragon bone," Ormand explained. "We were afraid the earth would fall on it and damage it."

"What happened?"

"Well, we broke it, didn't we?" said Lissie sulkily. "It wasn't our fault."

Sparrow thought about this for a moment. "It doesn't seem too bad to me," he said at length. "There's probably far more there than I need, anyway." He wasn't quite sure if he believed that himself, but it seemed too early to worry about it now. "Come on," he said, "I'm going to get the next one. Stand by; I shouldn't be too long."

Lissie and Ormand remained where they were as Sparrow eased the fourth bone over the third one, which lay shattered in a thousand pieces at the mouth of the small tunnel.

*   *   *

Ten times more he repeated his journey between the Star Wheel and the Scroll Cupboard, before it got too dark to see in the tunnel, and Lissie and Ormand went off to light the cooking-fire. Twelve dragon bones now floated, knotted end to end, glowing in the dim light of the Scroll Cupboard. It had not exactly been hard work for Sparrow, but by the time they had finished their supper by the light of their camp-fire, he felt tired beyond thinking. Even before Ormand and Lissie, exhausted as they were, had started to yawn, almost before he had had time to lie down, he was in deep sleep.

in the city

"WHAT A DAY!" TRINA'S FATHER GASPED, WIPING HIS FORE-
head with his handkerchief. The city streets had been sti-
flingly hot between the thunderstorms, and now, as
evening came on, it was only a little cooler. The breeze off
the sea would heave restlessly and then be still. The grey
clouds which covered the sky seemed to weigh down on
them, suffocating, as if they wanted to crush the tall buildings back into the ground. Worse than that, there was
another feeling in the air, connected with the heavy clouds
but not the same – an unpleasant, waiting feeling; as though
something were about to happen…

The really strange thing in all this was Pats. He remained
calm and good-humoured the whole day, despite the thunderstorms, and despite the crowds of people out on the
streets in the sunshine between the storms. That was not
what they had expected. Normally any kind of excitement
made him nervous. Certainly, he remained very close to

Trina and her father, preferring to walk between them if he could; but he seemed to be taking in everything with great interest.

Even stranger was what happened during the thunderstorms – Pats talked. His father had predicted that he would talk, but Trina was quick to notice that it was only during the storms that it happened. During the sunny spells he lapsed into his old silence. When he did talk, it wasn't at all like someone who had never talked before; everything he said was perfectly clear, although it didn't seem to connect with anything that was going on at the time. "I must hurry," he said on one occasion. On another, he said, "Well, it's not my fault either," in a distinctly sulky voice.

Trina realized that this happened only when the storm was directly above their heads; always just after the thunder and the lightning had come together. She whispered this discovery to her father, who muttered something about "electric shock treatment".

As evening came on, the storms stopped coming, and Pats returned to his familiar "absent" self, staring vacantly off into space, while one of his hands gently stroked the other.

They went back to the place where Trina's father was living. Trina noticed then that there seemed to be largish groups of young men standing at many of the street corners. They had an air of restless expectancy. "What are they waiting for?" Trina asked, as they crossed the road to avoid one especially large group.

"I don't know," her father said. "I don't know what's going on. I don't think I like the look of it though."

*   *   *

The place Trina's father had rented had once been a carpenter's workshop ("just the right place to rebuild a boat," he remarked), and at the back of the main part of the shed there were three rooms: a toilet, and two other rooms which had been offices but which were now a bedroom and a kitchen. It was all very bare and unhomely, with the wallpaper coming off the walls in places and dirty dishes stacked in the tiny sink, but at the same time it was quite exciting. Trina and Pats had brought sleeping-bags, and her father had managed to get a couple of camp-beds from someone at the university. They were going to be eating a take-away supper out of tinfoil dishes; and no one would expect them to get washed before they went to bed.

All three of them would be sleeping in the one room, but Trina's father said he would be working late on the Burial Ship, so she and Pats would be able to get to sleep without his disturbing them. It was a pity, she felt, that the thunderstorms seemed to have passed; she had been hoping for the chance of a private conversation with Pats.

Her father's Ship stood in the shed, already looking quite like a proper boat, sitting in a row of great U-shaped cradles he had borrowed from somewhere down at the docks. All the timbers he had been able to find had now been brought back to the shed, all numbered and ready to go into their place. But of course where the dragon-prow should have butted on to the massive keel, there was an empty space.

Trina helped her father a little after supper, while Pats wandered about the shed poking at pieces of wood. But it had been a long day, with visits to a funfair, journeys through endless shops that Trina wanted to see, and a trek through the harbour area to see the big ships. She was soon nodding off, standing on her feet as she was. For a while after wriggling into their sleeping-bags it seemed they wouldn't sleep, because of the strangeness of the place. Pats lay on his back staring at a brown patch on the ceiling. "I suppose everything's a bit strange for you, Pats," Trina said; and fell asleep.

She jerked awake again. She peered at her watch and saw it was past midnight, though her father was not in bed yet. Pats was still lying on his back, with his eyes closed now.

Dimly, somewhere behind the endless rumbling of the city – how long it seemed now since that had been a famil- iar, nightly noise! – Trina realized there was some sort of distant commotion. It was hard to make out exactly what it was. There was a queer jerkiness about the sound, but little more than that. She slipped out of her sleeping-bag and crawled over the creaking camp-bed to the door of the little room.

Her father was not by the boat, but was standing at the big double door of the shed, which was slightly open. She padded across the cold concrete floor and stood behind him. "What's happening?" she asked.

"I don't know," he said. He fell silent, looking grim. "It's this rioting," he went on at last. "It spreads, you see, from one city to another. And there are people too, who just go about from city to city and start riots."

"Why? Who?"

He sighed. "Angry people, I suppose. Just angry. We move out to Newborough to get away from all that, and what happens? The very first night you come back here, it all starts again."

Trina wondered if he was saying it was her fault.

"It's a sign of the times, that's all," he said.

"What do they do, when they riot?"

He shrugged. "Break. Burn. Make a lot of noise. Smash up shops and steal things out of them. Turn cars over and set light to them. If there's people they don't like the look of ... well..." He fell silent.

She shuddered. She was sure she wouldn't be able to sleep now. Was this really going on here, now?

She had just crawled back into her sleeping-bag when she heard the rustle of Pats' head turning in the bed next to her.

"Who are you?" Pats said.

"Trina," said Trina, and waited.

Pats sighed deeply. "Are you Kittel's sister?" he said at last.

"Whose sister?" said Trina, as her heart began to thump, fast.

"Kittel's," Pats repeated.

How could Pats possibly know about Kitty? "I had a sister called Kitty," Trina said unsteadily.

"It's because of the barrier," Pats whispered. "Puckel said there was a barrier. Like the wall of mist. It's because you don't hear things properly when you're dreaming. There's a game Kittel told me about—"

"Chinese whispers," Trina said. Of course, she and Kitty used to play it with their friends, years ago, by candlelight...

There was a long pause. At last Pats said, "There's a bridge being built."

"What sort of bridge?" Trina asked.

"A bridge so she can get home. No – more than that. I think it's a bridge for us all to get over; for something ...

from the Giants' Door … to get over."

"Where is she?" Trina breathed.

"She's lost at the moment," Pats said. "But I'm sure she's all right."

"When will the bridge be made?" Trina asked.

"Not long now, I don't think," Pats replied.

"Where does it go from?"

"The Scroll Cupboard, I think."

"I know where that is," said Trina. "I've been there."

"Have you?" Trina heard Pats sitting up in the darkness. "Do you know the Secret Way?"

"I – I'm not sure," Trina faltered. "I went along the old railway line—"

"The old railway line!" Pats burst out. "Oh! So it really did come here, all the way… It's buried at our end."

470   "I don't know what you mean," said Trina. "I met Mother Egg – perhaps you know her too? And she showed me the Scroll Cupboard."

"Is she a person?" Pats enquired.

"Yes, of course."

"What's she like?"

Trina described her.

Pats let out a soft whistle. "That's Ms Minn," he said. "I just know it is. She used to be our teacher. She is a person – in a way. But she's the place too – the place of power. And I bet it's the same with King Puck! I bet that's Puckel – that's where he's hiding when I can't find him."

Trina was silent. She was too amazed to speak.

Her father burst into the room at that moment. "You two," he said tensely, "I want you to get up and get dressed. It's certainly a riot. There are buildings burning. And I think it's coming this way. We're getting out of here."

As Trina and Pats hurriedly dressed, Trina, who scarcely noticed the excitement of what was going on outside because of the excitement she felt within herself, turned suddenly to Pats and said, "Pats – that's not your real name, is it?"

"I'm called Sparrow," said Pats.

"Can you fly?" Trina said, and giggled, despite herself, because what she had asked seemed so silly.

But Pats replied gravely, "Only at night, I think. I'm actually dreaming just now."

on the mountain top

KITTEL AND BULL WERE NEAR THE END OF THE LONG, gradual climb over the rock-strewn ground on the west side of the Valley of Murmuring Water. They were in sight of the forests which lay all around the skirts of the great, humped mountain which formed one end of the Copperhill valley. Kittel was hoping to get into the shelter of the forest before night came on, but there were still several miles to go, and the daylight was already failing.

"What's that funny light?" she said suddenly, pointing over to their left.

"Probably the sunset," Bull said. "I don't see anything special."

"It's not," Kittel said presently. "It's coming from those trees, down in that hollow."

Bull shrugged, and let his pony plod on.

"I'm going down to look," Kittel said. "Wait for me. It may be a good place to spend the night."

Bull tutted, but drew in his reins and waited, watching as Kittel climbed off her pony and led it down the rough slope towards the hollow. He saw her standing at the edge and then leaving her pony as she plunged into some bushes. He stared, at a loss. He couldn't follow her there, either on foot or on his pony.

Kittel had found where the light was coming from. It was a hawthorn tree, in full blossom, quite ordinary – except that it was haloed in a rose-white glow. As she approached it, its young, bright-green leaves began to rustle, even though there was no breeze. She stopped. There was something uncanny about the little tree. She glanced back and saw, between the leaves at the edge of the hollow, Bull waiting where she had left him on his pony.

"He must come too," came Puckel's voice. "You are the only two who have known this thing."

Kittel turned, and saw the old man sitting at the foot of the tree with his hands resting on his stick, which was upright in front of him. He had not been there a moment ago, she was perfectly sure.

"He can't walk," Kittel said hoarsely.

"Course he can," Puckel snorted, "he's just being a booby." He hauled himself to his feet, using the stick as a prop. "Come on down!" he roared up to Bull. "You can't stay there all night!"

Bull had very little option. The sound of Puckel's voice echoed against the mountains like thunder, and Bull's pony promptly reared up on its hind legs and threw him off. But before Kittel had even time to feel concerned, he had scrambled to his feet, cast a dirty glance at the wide-eyed pony, and come running down the slope towards them.

He burst through the bushes at the edge of the hollow. "It's better!" he exclaimed. "My ankle's mended! I…" Then he saw Puckel, turned white, and fell silent.

"Turn round, both of you," Puckel ordered. They obeyed, and the next moment they felt themselves gripped at the back of the neck, and were rocketing up into the air. Both shut their eyes and gritted their teeth and wished it would stop.

It did, quite soon. They landed on the top of a mountain. The freezing wind of evening, blowing off the heights, curled itself round them.

Kittel at once recognized the place, which Sparrow had described to her after his last visit there. Behind the low wall between two of the brightly-decorated buildings she saw the ruins of the aeroplane she herself had travelled in. She had never before been back here. She shivered.

"You, young Bull," Puckel said. "Do you know why I have brought you here?"

Bull shook his head.

"Well," Puckel went on, with a mysterious look on his wrinkled, unsmiling face, "there's a change to be made – a switch-over, you might call it."

Bull and Kittel watched as the old man turned and took a few steps, looking round at the dark triangle-entrances of the small buildings. He swung his stick and then, quite carelessly it seemed, sent it flying over and over to land inside one of them. He rubbed his face, as if tired. "Well," he said, "everything's ready. Now it's just a case of waiting for something to happen."

"What did you mean, only Bull and I have known something?" Kittel asked.

"Well," Puckel said, blowing out his cheeks in the rather

sly way he sometimes had. "Bull's in a bit of a unique position really, isn't he? Him and the dragon, you know."

Bull stirred, and looked uneasy. He and Kittel both knew what the old man was meaning – that disastrous week, three years ago, when Bull had had some of the magic powers that later passed to Sparrow. It had resulted in the dragon taking Bull's shape for a short time.

"Puckel," said Kittel. "You know the dragon's going about in the shape of a cat, and we couldn't work out how—"

"Yes, yes," Puckel interrupted her. "I was coming to that. One thing at a time."

Kittel fell silent. The air was growing darker now. Too quickly, it seemed, just to be the oncoming of night.

"It is time things were explained to you a little," Puckel said. "Explained to you, and through you on to Sparrow. I think you've all deserved it. You have, on the whole, done your work pretty well, and I'm moderately pleased with you."

"*You're* hardly one to talk," came a voice. Bull and Kittel looked sharply round, to see an old, frail-looking woman sitting in the triangle of the doorway where Puckel had thrown his stick.

Bull turned pale for a second time. "Ms – Ms Minn…" he stammered.

The old schoolteacher did not stir. "No need to be afraid of me now, Bull," came the dry, cracked voice. "What's past is past. The things you did wrong you had to do – there was no one else to do them."

The last time Bull had seen Ms Minn was when he had had magic powers and had foolishly tried to shift into her shape.

Puckel, who had actually looked a little embarrassed when the old woman first spoke, had collected himself again. "We waited many years," he said, "many, many years for one to waken up and understand that he was living in the dream of the dragon – the dragon, Ureychyoburenitho, who lay beneath the mountain and dreamed of all that was going on in the world. So many stupid, dough-brained folk, living their foolish lives and never thinking to look up and stop and wonder. Eventually one did; and that was Bull – Bull who woke up to the power that is sometimes called magic."

And now the night had gathered around them, and Kittel and Bull could see nothing of Puckel. But only a moment after she had realized it was completely dark, Kittel became aware of a growing light on the eastern horizon.

476

"As to that power," Puckel went on, "it is something people don't see; it comes from they don't know where. Magic is like the wind blowing – you see the trees bending and the leaves and dust flying, but you do not see the wind itself. This wind comes from the centre of the earth, from the Door – the Giants' Door."

Suddenly Kittel, who had been watching the light grow at unbelievable speed in the eastern sky, interrupted. "Puckel!" she exclaimed. "There's that cat!"

Sitting in the doorway where Ms Minn had been a moment before, and looking demure as anything, was the black cat from the Hollywell. Only now there was something different about it…

"It's not the dragon any more," Kittel whispered, peering hard at the creature in what was now the light of a grey morning. "It's – it's…"

"Yes?" Puckel prompted. "What do you see?"

"Nothing," said Kittel in a puzzled voice. "I mean, I know that something's there, something's taken the cat's shape, but I can't see what. It's a complete blank."

"Good," said Puckel. "You are one of the few who have seen something of the hidden powers of the Door. Let me introduce you to Mother Egg. Despite appearances, Mother Egg is not a cat; the cat, in his way, is just an ordinary mog – he happens to be one of a small group of slightly eccentric creatures who let themselves be used by the rest of us, when there's a need." He glanced at Bull. "So," he said, nodding, "switch-over completed."

"So where's the dragon?" said Kittel.

"Ah, now that's a bit of a complication," Puckel replied. "I think we'll leave the dragon for the moment – though as I've no doubt you've guessed, the dragon is the other hidden power. Where Mother Egg is nothing, the dragon Ureychyoburenitho is – or should I say the Star Wheel is, for along with the dragon you have the Polymorphs, as you know—"

"This is unnecessarily complicated," the dry voice of Ms Minn broke in. "You're simply trying to avoid telling the tale of your own foolishness."

Looking over in her direction, Kittel and Bull still saw only the black cat. But its little pink mouth was open when Ms Minn's voice spoke, and closed when it stopped. That could only mean that Ms Minn and the mysterious Mother Egg were one and the same, though Kittel couldn't understand why she wasn't able to see the old woman in the cat's shape.

Puckel gave a deep sigh, then pursed his lips, then made a dreadful grimace as if he were trying to come to a difficult decision. "All right," he said at length. "All right, I'll do it. I said I would."

For Kittel and Bull, who so far had heard only of Puckel's power and strength, a story of his foolishness was something quite new, and they listened agog. As the old man spoke, the sky darkened and paled, darkened and paled, as the light of a grey day was followed by the blackness of deep night, over and over again. Seven times the sky darkened and paled, though they didn't think to count it.

Far down in the Valley of Murmuring Water, Ormand and Lissie dug and waited, dug and waited; and Sparrow came and went, carefully removing the fragile, shimmering dragon bones from the tunnel beneath the valley floor. A vacant, faraway expression was on his face, as though his mind were somewhere else; and through the whole of that seven days, not a word did he speak to either of his friends.

And at the same time, but all in the one night, Trina and Pats shivered in the chill air of after-midnight and peered into the night of the city, where the sky was reddened with the burning of buildings. And all at once, Pats gave an exclamation. "The goats!" he said. "I have to find the goats!"

chaos

"ARE THEY COMING THIS WAY?" TRINA ASKED.

"Hard to say," her father answered. "But I don't want to be caught on the hop if they do."

"What'll we do?"

"Stay put," her father said, "and keep all the lights off. Don't do anything to attract attention. It's public property they'll attack first, or anything that looks valuable. So if we're not a hi-fi shop or a police station or a pub, they'll probably pass us by. But if things look bad, the van's out at the back, and there's enough small, quiet streets for us to make a getaway. If it comes to that, I want you to keep hold of Pats' hand and stay close to me."

Trina nodded. The braying and skirling of sirens were coming from all directions now. And over the rising tumult from the city a wind seemed to be getting up, swirling dust and pieces of rubbish along the pavement.

"We'd better shut the door now," her father said, "and

get to the other end of the shed."

"The goats!" Pats exclaimed suddenly. "I have to find the goats!"

Trina's father, who was just closing the door, stared at him. "Well, you do choose your moments—"

"He started speaking again just before you got us up," Trina said. "It's not really Pats at all, you know."

Her father ushered them down to the other end of the shed. Trina was about to explain what she had meant, when they heard the vibration of a heavy engine outside the door they had just closed, and saw lights through the small, grimy windows.

"Stay where you are," Trina's father said, and went back to the door to look. After a minute or two, they saw him hurriedly opening the door and speaking urgently with someone outside. A minute later, five or six strangers pushed through into the shed, including a man with a peaked cap carrying a small grey box under his arm.

It turned out to be the driver of the last bus of the night with a handful of scared-looking passengers. The road ahead was blocked, the driver said, and he had backed the bus into the entrance of the shed meaning to turn it round, but in his hurry he had got it stuck against the low wall just outside. Trina's father had signalled to him to come in and bring his passengers.

It seemed like a crowd to Trina. There was a woman of about her mother's age, with two small, bleary-looking children clutching her coat; a young man and two older men, all drunk; and an old woman who appeared to be very dirty and was clutching a snarling Pekinese under her arm. The driver was the only one among them who looked as though he would be any use in an emergency.

Trina's father was trying to assure the bemused visitors – who were gazing stupidly at the half-built ship – that they would be safe, when a roar came from outside. They started in alarm as something heavy struck the door of the shed, and a commotion of bangings, thumpings and yellings began. The two little children started whimpering.

"We have to go now," Pats said, with urgency in his voice. But no one moved.

"They're going for the bus," said the bus-driver at length.

He had hardly spoken when there was a roar that rattled the doors and windows, and a burst of orange light outside. Black smoke began to pour under the shed door.

"Just in time, mate – thanks," the bus-driver said.

Trina's father was not listening. With an exclamation he had started towards the double doors again. Trina quickly realized what was on his mind. The burning bus was against them, and piled next to them on the inside were the remaining timbers of the Ship. Trina sprang after her father, who was now frantically hauling at the tinder-dry planks and post. Already, yellow flames were licking greedily at the bottom edge of the doors.

The people from the bus, meanwhile, forgotten by Trina and her father, were shifting uneasily. "This way, please," Pats said suddenly, and walked through the midst of them, through the little kitchen and to the back door of the shed. There was a moment of confused shuffling, and then the people, led by the old woman with the Pekinese, followed him one by one. Pats opened the door at the back of the van.

It was soon obvious to Trina that it was no use. She could feel the heat of the fire through the doors. Her father's face was pouring with sweat in the red light. In a moment the doors were going to go up. Still he was heaving and hauling. One of the more badly-rotted planks cracked, and her father cursed, scrabbling at the long timber to try and hold it together.

"Where's Pats gone?" said Trina suddenly.

"What?" her father looked up, a savage expression on his face. "Where is he?"

"I don't know!" Trina wailed. "The people have gone as well!"

Woomph! The doors took fire, and flames enveloped them on the inside.

"Oh damn, damn, damn!" her father roared. "All that work! All that precious history!" Then after a moment's agonized hesitation he grabbed Trina's arm and rushed her through the shed to the open back door.

He was a little taken aback to see Pats and all the people from the bus piled into the back of the van. "A lot they could care," he muttered as he climbed into the driver's seat.

Trina wondered who had got them all organized. Not Pats, surely? She could see at a glance that he had once again become his old "absent" self. He sat gazing fixedly at a point in the middle of the old woman's chest, while her dog seemed to be trying to stretch out its squashed-up nose towards him. Not much chance of it smelling anything but its mistress, Trina thought to herself, as she wound down the window.

Her father was right about the streets at the back of the shed. In fact it seemed that, whoever the rioters were who had come up their road, they were not really at the centre of the trouble. Along at the ends of the streets they crossed there seemed to be crowds of people running, throwing things, milling together, dark figures against the lurid orange glow of burning.

They were heading towards the city centre, not out towards Newborough. It seemed that all the people from the bus lived on the other side of the city and were anxious to get back to their homes. Only the ragged old woman seemed to be unconcerned, and made growling noises into the Pekinese's ear.

But as they came nearer to the city centre, things began to get worse and worse.

"No use," Trina's father said, driving the van into a street off a large concourse, and then quickly reversing out again as a line of policemen appeared at the far end, facing away from them but retreating towards them.

"Go down that way," the bus-driver said, pointing to another street. All the streetlights were out here – Trina saw jagged edges of broken glass on one of them – but there were no fires and no people. The van's headlights swung into the sullen darkness. It was not until they had rounded a bend towards the far end that they found their way blocked by two cars lying upside down. By the time they had turned in the narrow street and driven back to the top end, the policemen and a crowd of stone-throwers were swarming in all directions over the concourse. Trina's father backed down the full length of the street again, grazing lampposts and parked cars in his haste.

"It's no use," he repeated, as they came to a stop before the two wrecked cars. "We'll have to get out of here and get indoors."

They decided they should all make a run for the bus-driver's sister's house, which was not far away. Unwillingly, everyone piled out into the dark street. One of the drunk men immediately set off in the direction of the trouble, and would pay no heed to the driver's warnings. The two little girls' whimpering had become a constant, low-pitched gibber. They, and all the others, obediently followed the bus-driver, but just as Trina turned to grab Pats' hand, she saw the old woman come up behind him and give him an almighty kick up the rear. What Pats would normally have done Trina didn't know, but what happened just now was that he sailed into the air and seemed to hover there for a second, before falling lightly down on his feet again in front of her. Pats grinned, and Trina knew that the boy, Sparrow – whatever he was – was back. "You must find your own way," he said quietly to her. "I have to find the goats."

"What?" said Trina. "What?" But Pats turned away from her and went to stand beside her father. She glanced round. No one else seemed to have noticed the old woman's extraordinary behaviour, or the fact that Pats had actually flown up into the air. They were filing between the two upended cars while her father counted them through. "Keep right behind me," he said to her as she came up. Cautiously, they set off after the bus-driver between the high, dark buildings.

Almost immediately, Trina heard the wail of "Leechee, where have you gone?" She turned, somehow knowing it was the voice of the dirty old woman. It was coming from behind the cars, although Trina had seen her going through the gap with the others. What was she up to? She was just the kind of old wretch who would be nothing but trouble. She seemed to be down on her hands and knees behind the car.

Of course, she *would* have to go and lose her dog! Trina

hesitated, looking after her father striding behind the bedraggled group from the bus, then ran back to the old woman. "Where did he go?" she said.

"I don't know, dash him," the crone bellowed in her ear. "He gave me the slip, the little garbage-can, the little flea-bag, he's always giving me the slip, and now look what he's gone and done!"

"You'll have to come," Trina said urgently. "He – he'll probably follow, he can't be far. Anyway, I'm sure he can look after himself better than we can, and we've got to get on." She was feeling she ought to get hold of her and drag her with her, but she didn't like the thought of touching the old creature.

"Oh, you don't understand – you don't understand!" the woman began to howl. "I can't leave him, he's everything to me, he's my only friend, he's – oh, there! Look, there he is! Quick, run and get him, dearie – oh, be quick, please!"

What was Trina to do? The others were already out of sight… But the street was so dark it was hard to make anything out except by the faint glow of the distant concourse; if they lost sight of the dog there was little chance of finding it again…

Trina made a dash for it. After all, it couldn't get far on those stumpy little legs, hidden under such a thick mat of hair…

a boot up the rear

SPARROW BLINKED. HOW LONG HAD HE BEEN SITTING here, looking at Ms Minn? There she sat, watching him fixedly, with a cold, distant look in her eyes. He frowned, shook himself, glanced around.

They were in the Scroll Cupboard; but there was something different about the light. It was no longer dim and silver-grey, but bright, with a special brightness like the sky before sunrise. He soon saw the reason – a part of the wall and a part of the low-arching roof had disappeared, and he could see a blue-green sky streaked with long, pale-yellow clouds.

And then he saw the bridge. In one clean, incredible arch it curved from the floor of the Scroll Cupboard into the sky – up, over and down, down out of sight. He scrambled to his feet and went over to the opening in the wall. And then he gasped.

There was a whole world down there – a world of

woods, fields, hills, rivers, towns. It wasn't spread out flat below him, but seemed to be tipped at an angle towards him – or else it was flat and he and the Scroll Cupboard were at an angle. It was all very still and quiet, shadowy-green. The great bridge of dragon bones arched like a rainbow from where he stood down to where a great pyramid-shaped mountain rose in the very centre of the wide land he saw. At the top of its curve the bridge must have caught the sunlight, for there it sparkled like a dazzling jewel.

"Did I do all that?" said Sparrow wonderingly. "While I was there, in the other place? How long have I been asleep?" For that was how it felt to him, even though the memory of the shed with the ancient boat, and the burning, and the frightened people in the van, was clearer than any dream could be.

"Don't be a fool," came the dry voice of Ms Minn behind him. "This is no time to congratulate yourself. Look at your feet."

But Sparrow, surprised, looked round. It was Ms Minn who was sitting there, sure enough, but the voice had been unmistakably the voice he had last heard coming from the scorpion – the voice of Puckel's stick. "Look at your feet," Ms Minn said again, with an edge of threat in her tone; and Sparrow did as he was told.

The first two dragon bones lay lightly on the sand and stones of the floor, just in front of his boots. But the next bone was not attached to them. There was a gap before the main part of the bridge started. Not a big gap; a gap of about one dragon bone's length.

"The bridge is not complete," Ms Minn remarked, "because of your tomfoolery."

"The third bone," said Sparrow in a low voice. "You mean there were just enough bones – not a single one more?"

"There was no room for error," Ms Minn confirmed. "Now only one creature can complete the bridge, and that is the one creature that must not be allowed to cross it."

"The dragon," said Sparrow dully. "But I still don't understand—"

"Nobody asked you to understand," Ms Minn said. "Only to do." There was a short silence before she went on again. "What you see below you is not the world as it is, but the world as it might have been if the dragon had not spoiled it. A green world, a world at peace with itself. A dream of the world, a possibility. If the dragon crosses the bridge again, it will be to complete the destruction it began."

488

"What can I do?" said Sparrow. "I'll do anything to put it right."

"You will not pay the price for your mistake," said Ms Minn.

"But I want to," said Sparrow. "I really do—"

"Silence," Ms Minn said sharply. "That's not for you to choose. Look at me, boy – look at me closely."

Sparrow, who had been gazing out of the opening in the wall, turned to look at Ms Minn again. It seemed that his old teacher was just as he remembered her; but as he looked now, he saw that there was something different. At first he thought she was fading – as he had seen her do once before – but she was still perfectly visible. Yet as he looked it seemed to him more and more as if she had turned to glass; not completely clear glass, but glass that was just clear enough to look through, if you put your mind to it.

And Sparrow saw what seemed to be a pool of water, with ripples in circles out from its centre – except that the ripples were the coils of a red-and-brown snake; and the coils of the snake were the hard, brittle twists of the wood of Puckel's stick. And there was the scorpion too, deep in the centre of the pool, with its evil sting poised above its back; and in the midst of the scorpion was a tiny egg; and inside the egg a darkness that Sparrow presently realized was the night-sky full of its countless stars.

"Yes," Ms Minn said. "You have seen correctly. That old gas-bag that you called Ms Minn is no more – and no less – than the outer shell of Mother Egg. And I have no choice either. You must do what it's your job to do, and others must suffer to put right your mistakes."

Sparrow bowed his head. It seemed such a small mistake – made for what seemed good reasons at the time – yet it seemed it could have such enormous consequences.

"In this last week you have been able to come and go as you please," said Mother Egg. "Now, for the bridge to be completed in the right way, you must cross it from where you do not belong to where you do belong. There is only one way for you to come back to the mountains of the Giants' Door – across the completed bridge. If the bridge is completed in the wrong way – through being crossed from this side – you will not be able to return. You will wither away inside the shell of the boy you are down in that place. So you are a hostage of our success. So is the girl. She will remain here until you have completed the bridge. Tell her she must find her own way. And tell the man who makes a boat out of the splinters of my spinning-wheel that there is one piece missing which must be found. You have the Secret Way with you, and the Masters of the Dragon's

Dreaming are stirring up nightmare in the dark pit they call a city. And that is all as it should be. Now go."

"I don't know if I can find the way back," said Sparrow humbly.

"You must follow the goats," said Mother Egg. "Turn round again. I shall send you."

Sparrow had barely turned back to the opening in the wall when he felt the force of Ms Minn's leather boot lifting him off his feet and high, high, impossibly high into the air.

the nightmare statue

"BACK UP TO THE CONCOURSE," TRINA'S FATHER YELLED. "It's the only way she can have gone."

Sparrow ran with him, up the dark street, between the toppled cars.

"Here, into the van," Trina's father gasped. "We'll take it as long as we can get through."

The concourse was complete pandemonium. There were people everywhere, yelling, running, rolling about fighting, throwing things, waving things, breaking things. There were no buildings burning here, but somewhere behind they could see a great spout of spark-lit smoke rising and billowing wildly in the hot wind. Could Trina possibly be here? Surely not.

Her father climbed onto the roof of the van and gazed about feverishly. At that moment Sparrow saw the statue of the Sphinx – a great stone lion-shape, paws outstretched and head erect, the stone mane cropped in the shape of a bell, and the human face with faraway eyes and faintly-smiling mouth.

But it was not a statue. It was a Polymorph. That is to say, it was a Polymorph hiding in the statue. Sparrow had long ago received a wound in his left eye, which was how he could see the things of the Secret Way if he wanted to. This Polymorph was hiding in the stone Sphinx, but it couldn't hide from his seeing eye. The stone shape was like a shadow enclosing the humped, vulture-like form of the creature; its small dark eyes gloated from behind the unseeing stone ones.

The Polymorphs had not been allowed out of the Secret Way and the Star Wheel for well over a year now. There was something crazy about seeing one of them here in the city – and yet … perhaps it wasn't crazy at all. What were those words of Mother Egg's – about the Secret Way and the Masters of the Dreaming being with him? Was it possible he could have brought the creatures with him – that somehow the Secret Way had opened out into this strange place, and they could create madness here, stir up nightmare, just as they had done once before, in the mountains?

Trina's father was looking away. Sparrow skipped into the air and rose effortlessly up to stand on the ledge beside the Sphinx's mane.

The stone eye seemed to roll round at him. "You're the Polymorph Eni," Sparrow said coldly. "You're doing all this to the people – you're the cause of it all."

The Polymorph seemed quite untroubled. "You want my head?" it said in its dull, sneering voice. "Take it. See what happens."

Sparrow hesitated. He knew that the huge stone head of the sphinx was only the dreaming, and the real thing was the Polymorph's tall, domed head, which he could easily remove. He had done so, once before. That would certainly put the Polymorph out of action, though he didn't know if he would be able to return the head to the Star Wheel. Possibly he could seek out all the Polymorphs here, and take their heads, and everything would immediately calm down in this city. But Mother Egg had said that what they were doing here was "all as it should be".

Sparrow decided he couldn't dare to interfere or again do something he had not been told to do. Whatever trouble the Polymorphs were causing here, it was all part of what was happening – it might even be a part of the finishing of the bridge.

"No," he said. "No, I don't want your head. But I want goats. I'm looking for goats. Where are they?"

"All sheep here," said the smiling Sphinx-mouth. "No goats, just sheep. Look."

Sparrow looked down at the seething crowd. They were a bit like sheep – sheep scrambling madly to get through a gate, sheep caught in a hopeless tangle of brambles, struggling endlessly, uselessly, stupidly...

"Pats! What in heaven's name are you doing up there?" came the voice of Trina's father. "Will you come down! At once!"

Sparrow turned, and jumped from the ledge to the ground below. "Sorry," he said.

"Things are bad enough as they are without you getting yourself into trouble," his companion scolded. "Now keep by me."

Sparrow did as he was told, though he was aware that the Polymorph Eni was jeering at him from the statue. He ignored it. He decided that if Trina's father was searching

493

for Trina, and he himself was searching for goats, and neither of them had any idea how to find what they were searching for, they might as well search together.

They searched. Through the roaring streets, through the hot wind with its cargo of dust and ash and sparks and fearful smells of burning, through the orange glare and the dark eerie shadows, through the screams and the sudden silences, through the surging crowds and the empty streets. Sometimes they went in the van, sometimes on foot. The van was never touched, even though they left it unlocked when they got out to hunt among the streets they couldn't drive into. And they came to no harm, either from the rioters or from the scores and hundreds of police who were now appearing from every side. The recklessness of despair seemed to protect Trina's father. It was obvious from the start that they had little chance of finding Trina; but finding Trina was the thing he had set out to do, and he didn't seem to care about anything else. He took risks, and no harm came to them. On one occasion something hard hit him on the side of the head. He scarcely noticed. He brushed the blood away with his hand and strode on, while Sparrow trotted beside him.

When Sparrow had been in the city earlier in the day, and glimpsed through Pats' eyes the ordinary traffic and crowds, he had been fascinated, but terrified, by all its strangeness. Now, in some strange way, with the Polymorphs here with him in the city, he felt comforted. He didn't like them or trust them, but he was used to their madness – it belonged to his world; it was a link with the Mountains, and Mother Egg, and Puckel.

the old riddle

PUCKEL TOOK A DEEP BREATH. "VERY WELL," HE SAID, "I shall tell the tale of my foolishness." He gazed out over Kittel's and Bull's heads to the darkening and brightening sky.

"Long, long ago," he began, "years and years and more time than even I care to think of, I was a young lad, curious and not very wise. And one day when my master, Obyr, was away, I was wandering about in my loafish way, peering and poking into things that didn't concern me and generally trying to find out more than a young fellow should.

"And so I came to Mother Egg, and stood on the edge of the great abyss that has no bottom, and wondered if it could be crossed, and what would lie on the far side if it were crossed.

"And as I stood and wondered, up came the dragon, Ureychyoburenitho, slithering and steaming. 'Would you like to build a bridge across, little Puka?' he asked. 'How can I do that?' I said. 'Easy,' said Ureychyoburenitho. 'You must let me ask you a question which you cannot answer.' 'That should be easy enough,' I agreed. 'What's the question?' 'The question is this,' said Ureychyoburenitho: 'Are the things of the world there because I dream them, or do I dream them because they are there?' 'I don't know,' said I, without thinking. 'Not good enough,' said he. 'You must try to find the answer.' For three days and nights I sat and tried to think of the answer, and I knew I shouldn't, because Obyr had told me I should engage in no conversations with the dragon. But as the three days passed, I became more and more curious to know what the answer was to his riddle, and I forgot about the bridge over the abyss.

"But at the end of the three days Ureychyoburenitho came back and asked me: 'Have you found the answer?' 'No,' I said. 'What is the answer?' 'I never said I would tell you it,' said he, 'but thanks for the bridge.' And with that he arched over the abyss like a rainbow. And as his nose touched the far side, I had a vision of a world that was spoiled with ash and smoke, where the plants withered and the animals died and the people went mad. And I knew that Ureychyoburenitho had cheated me and broken the balance of the Giants' Door.

"When Obyr returned, he was very angry. But when he had finished being angry he was distressed, and for three days he sat and wept. And when he had finished weeping he sat for three days more and thought. And when he had finished thinking he put out all of his power, and made certain changes to the Giants' Door that would one day lead to the recapturing of Ureychyoburenitho. But at the same time he said that the bridge Ureychyoburenitho had made could never be unmade, and that the power of the Door would always pass across a bridge of dragon bones.

"So Obyr exhausted all his strength, and he left us, and I took his place in King Puck at the head of the Door, and my sister was in the place of Mother Egg. And from seven scales which Ureychyoburenitho had left behind in the Star Wheel there came the Masters of the Dragon's Dreaming – the Polymorphs. And when I had grown older and a little wiser, I saw that we still had time to act, because the power of the loosened dragon was growing only slowly. So then we – I, my sister and the Masters of the Dreaming – shaped the mountain-country as a shell in which to hide the Giants' Door, and in the course of time brought people from the world to live among the mountains, to live simply and without change, free of the madness of the dragon. Though many thoughts of the dragon slipped over the bridge, none of them had any power—"

497

Bull was unable to contain himself. "That's not what Ms Minn told us!" he burst in. "She said there was a railway line, and the mountains were just an ordinary part of the world, and—"

"Well?" Puckel said, turning towards the black cat, with one bushy eyebrow raised. Kittel thought he looked rather delighted, and at the same time she was sure that the expression on the cat's face was, in its turn, rather embarrassed – if a cat ever can look embarrassed. At any rate, it suddenly started vigorously washing its face with its paw. "It was as true as it needed to be," Ms Minn's voice said at length, sounding slightly sulky.

"Huh," Puckel snorted, turning from the cat back to Bull and Kittel. "The railway line was no railway line at all – it was the bridge of dragon bones."

"What?" Bull burst in again. "It can't be! I know that railway line! I – we've walked on it! They've taken bits of it and melted it down and made things. My gran says our kitchen stove was made from the railway line—"

"That's right," Kittel interrupted him. "It's all like the dragon and the dragon bones – it doesn't make sense. One moment you say the dragon needs a bridge to cross over, and the next you say the dragon *is* the bridge; and Ormand and Lissie dug up the dragon bones, and yet the dragon was still running about in the shape of that cat – I don't get it."

Puckel raised his hand, and Kittel fell silent. "You can't think of the dragon like an ordinary animal," he said. "Not like a fat old cow or an elephant, or anything like that. You can't exactly say, 'Here is a dragon', or, 'There goes a dragon', or, 'I've got a dragon in my garage'. You can't say, 'The dragon is dead', or, 'The dragon is alive and kicking and getting up to all sorts of mischief'. You can't say that kind of thing. The dragon is here, and there, and everywhere. His bones lie in the earth at the same time as he's flying through the air. He's a thousand little dragons and at the same time one whopping big dragon. You can't hold him down. And now everything that he has touched, every little drop of air that he has breathed, every little thought he has had, can turn into a dragon. Even your kitchen stove will spout flames when the wind tickles it the wrong way! But the world down there, beyond the mountains, where he breathed and sent all the people mad – it's full of dragons now, little ones and big ones, and they are all the one dragon.

"One thing holds the dragon back; one thing can check him, and that is Mother Egg. Little abysses for little dragons, big ones for big dragons. That was how it was all those years ago, when the trap we set for the dragon was Mother

Egg herself in the form of a great lake – the same that you now call the Dead Lake. At the end of the dragon's freedom in the world, he devoured his own tail; in the frenzy of the madness he had stirred up he plunged into the abyss. After that, he could be trapped on the bridge of his own bones, which I then hid under the mountains."

Kittel and Bull still felt confused. Puckel's story was quite different from the story they knew – and yet, in some odd way, they could see it was the same story. "I suppose the dragon's just a confusing thing," Kittel said.

"You get used to him," Puckel said. "We've had longer than you to do that. If you can see he's confusing then you're off to a better start than I was. You'll do well. Even stupidity has its value. We've waited many years, trusting the day would come when out of these simple, stupid mountain-people one should appear who could put right what I had done wrong, rebuild the dragon bridge in a different form, and undo the madness and destruction which the dragon had brought."

499

"Sparrow," said Bull, a little bitterly. Puckel nodded.

"I never realized he was so special," Kittel murmured.

"He's not," said Puckel sharply. "And don't you go trying to let him think he is. Without Bull, for example, where would he be? Still digging for pretty stones to give his mother, probably. Where would he be without his mother – or without you? Sparrow's only the seed; and you need a whole plant before you can have a seed.

"And now," he said, suddenly becoming brisk and businesslike, "it is time we had some action." He flung his tattered green coat on the ground. What was underneath was not much better, as clothes go. It was a brown tunic that showed his great, bare arms, brown and knotted with muscle, like oak branches. He swung round towards the doorway where the black cat still sat regarding him unblinkingly. "What you are about to see," he went on, "is the arrival here of the first little dragon from down yonder. It has come all the way just to disappear inside Mother Egg. Things are nearing completion."

Peering at the cat in the grey morning light, Kittel saw that in the nothingness inside it – the nothingness that was taking the cat's form – a tiny speck had appeared. The speck grew, and became a distant figure. Kittel narrowed her eyes. Bigger and more distinct the figure grew, until it seemed to be filling the whole shape of the cat. And then the outlines of the cat seemed to blur and fall apart – until at last, where the cat had been, head lowered to creep out of the small triangular doorway, there came a girl.

foundations

LITTLE BY LITTLE, THE CROWDS SEEMED TO BE THINNING. Buildings were still burning here and there, sirens were still wailing, but there was a definite feeling that the excitement was beginning to die down.

Now for the message, Sparrow thought – perhaps he'll pay attention now. They were in the van again, driving through almost deserted streets, swerving now and again to avoid piles of masonry or shattered glass or car wheels lying in their way. "There was a bit missing, from the boat," he said.

"The prow," Trina's father said shortly. "Probably shaped like a dragon's head."

"Ah," said Sparrow. Then: "You have to find it, you know."

Trina's father grunted. "Not much point now," he said. "Everything burned."

"You have to find it tonight," Sparrow said, very firmly.

Trina's father glanced briefly, strangely, across at Pats. "That's where it should be," he said, indicating a huge, dark area just beyond the pavement they were driving alongside.

There were the remains of a fence on the inside edge of the pavement, but the boards which had lined it were ripped away. In the half-darkness of the building site beyond, they could make out the criss-crossing lines of concrete foundations. At one end was a large mound of rubble and clay. "Somewhere in that pile of rubbish," Trina's father said.

Sparrow leaned across and put his hand on the steering wheel of the van. He had some vague idea he could slow the thing down if he touched the wheel. "You won't find Trina this way," he said. "You've got to find the missing part of the boat."

502

"Pats, get your hand off—" Trina's father was just beginning, when the van coughed, stuttered, and then jolted them forward in their seats. At the same moment, the headlights went off. They coasted forwards for a little, and came to a stop.

"Petrol? Electrics?" Trina's father muttered, running his hands through his already wild-looking hair.

Sparrow clambered out of the passenger door. "Come on," he said, and hopped across the pavement and over the edge of the drop down to the floor of the building site.

"Wait! Pats! Don't you dare go off! Come back here at once!" Trina's father spluttered. When he saw Pats taking no notice, he followed.

Sparrow waited for him at the last of the low foundation walls, near the mountain of rubble and clay. Trina's father seemed to have got over his angry outburst. He came and sat down on the wall near Sparrow. For a while he sat with his hands flopped between his knees, staring bleakly over the desolate site. Then he put his head down and hid his face in his hands. After a while he started shaking, as if with sobs.

"The very first time," he groaned. "The very first time she's left with me – and I go and lose her. I can't do anything right – I just can't do anything right. My whole life – I mess everything up. I lose Beth – now I've lost Kitty. What's wrong with me?

"Even the Ship," he went on. "What's become of it? A pile of ashes, that's what. Nothing left. That's what my life is – a pile of ashes."

Sparrow lifted his head and sniffed. There was a faintly familiar smell blowing towards him on the now lessening wind. He flared his nostrils, trying to get more of it, to make it out… A sweet, faintly sickly smell that made you wrinkle your nose and want to blow it out again…

That's what it was – billy-goat!

And round a corner of the street, into the light of the two street-lamps at the further end of the building site, the goats came trotting in a line.

There were nothing like as many as there had been on the mountain – twenty or thirty, maybe – but they looked outlandish enough in this strange, square, city-world. They were just as he had seen them before, heads down, jostling, clashing horns together, intent. They crossed the street, tripped onto the pavement, and without a pause jumped down onto the building site, where they came towards Sparrow and Trina's father, jumping over the low foundation walls in ones and twos, an undulating column. They looked dull orange in the weary light.

Trina's father let his hands fall and raised his head. But he wasn't looking towards the goats. He was staring off in the other direction, into the featureless city sky.

Just before they reached them, the goats stopped. Then the leader raised its head, shook its horns, looked directly at Sparrow, and bleated. Trina's father appeared not to notice. Suddenly the goat vanished.

Sparrow didn't feel at all surprised. He had seen something like this before, long ago. Far more important was the thought that came into his head at that moment. "What was your life, anyway?" he asked Trina's father. "What did you do? Were you a weaver?" (He was a little confused in his mind by what Mother Egg had said about the man making a boat out of her spinning-wheel.)

Trina's father frowned at him. "A weaver?" he said. "How do you work that out? I was an archaeologist. I don't think I'm anything now. I dug things up – old things – and examined them and tried to find out about the past – how people used to live, what they did…"

"Why?" said Sparrow.

"Why? Because the past's important, that's why. Because it tells us where we've come from. And perhaps that tells us a bit about where we're going to." He grunted. "Not that it makes much difference. I could have told you years ago where we're all going to. That's why I became an archaeologist. No one listens to you."

"Where are we all going?" asked Sparrow.

"Here," Trina's father said. "To places like this, in cities like this. Tonight. To destruction. To burning, looting…"

The two goats now at the front of the column raised their heads and bleated, then they too disappeared. Sparrow suddenly had another thought. He had been thinking of

504

this strange man up to now as Trina's father – now he realized he was Kittel's father too. That seemed very queer. Then the thought struck him that apart from Kittel, this was the first person from this other world whom he'd had very much to do with. Ms Minn had told him ages ago that they were all mad in Kittel's place. He had never thought that Kittel was mad, but he was beginning to be fairly sure her father was.

Two more goats bleated, disappeared.

"I don't know who you are," Kittel's father said, looking straight at Sparrow. "I don't know what kind of world you've been living in all these years. 'In a world of his own' – that's what we said about you. Do you know what kind of world this is – the real world, I mean? It's a world where people put bombs on planes and kill everyone on board just so that other people in the world take some notice of them. They don't know the people they've killed. Never see them. They're just numbers. They're not people, to them. In the old days, the days of the Vikings, they were bad then too of course; but at least they killed people with their own hands – they looked into their eyes – they knew who they were killing…"

505

The wind was rising again. Bits of paper were buffeting across the low walls towards them. Shaggy goat-hair was stirring. Sparrow was not sure what was happening with the goats. They seemed to be bleating all the time now, raising their heads and disappearing, but there was always another in the place of the one which had just gone.

Suddenly Kittel's father gave a great howl, as if in rage or pain. He leaped to his feet and seized his hair in his hands, tugging at it violently. "It's gone far enough!" he yelled. "This is the end! It can't go on! Why can no one see it can't go on? They're all crazy – the whole world's gone mad! The whole world spoiled with ash and smoke – withering, dying! Freedom – they talk about freedom; what's freedom all about? They've let loose a dragon in the world – that's what their freedom's all about – a dragon that will destroy us all, destroy everything, until in the last frenzy of our madness it turns and devours its own tail!"

There was foam round his mouth, but as quickly as he had started raving he grew calm again. "And then," he said, in a quiet, but shaking voice, "then, if there's anything left, we'll have peace. At the end of everything."

There was one goat left. All the rest had disappeared.

Ideas, thoughts, a few good songs, a few good stories – no goats. That was what Puckel had said, and now Sparrow understood. Once, long before, when he had first been learning the Secret Way of the Mountains, Sparrow had sent a messenger to Bull without even knowing he was doing it. It had taken the form of a small Puckel-man. Even longer ago, he had seen Puckel himself turn into a whole menagerie of animals, and one of them – a goat – had given him a sort of message without words. It occurred to Sparrow that Puckel must be doing something like this the whole time. This strange, raving man in front of him was saying something important – something which came from thoughts which Puckel had sent to him. Somewhere out in the darkness of this city – or perhaps in the deeper darkness around the city – all those other goats would be going, taking thoughts, new songs, new stories, to people who were waiting to hear them. If this was what Puckel could do before the bridge had even been made, what could be done if they managed to complete it…?

The last goat was standing waggling its head in a foolish

fashion, but it didn't bleat, and it didn't disappear.

"That's my goat," said Sparrow.

The goat disappeared.

Sparrow was watching Trina's father steadily. His hair was pulled all over the place by what his hands had been doing as he ranted and raved. But it wasn't just that; his hair was actually rising up from his scalp. And his eyes were staring upwards. He looked as though he had seen a ghost.

Sparrow suddenly realized he had risen off the ground and was floating in the air above the man. He wondered how that had happened. He grinned, and came lightly down to the ground again. "Sorry," he said. "I didn't mean to startle you."

Trina's father collapsed onto his knees. "Who are you?" he whispered.

"I'm called Sparrow," Sparrow answered. "I – I don't come from here. I come from somewhere else. I'm stuck here till I can get the bridge finished. If I don't, the dragon will come back. He's trying to. That may be why the Polymorphs are here, I don't know. They make people go mad – not just dangerous; they do silly things as well. You probably don't know what I mean."

"Oh, don't I?" Trina's father answered huskily. "No, I know exactly what you mean. But I think I'm going mad. I thought I saw you flying just now."

"I was," said Sparrow. "I can. All the time in my own place – I don't know if I can fly all the time here, though."

"And you need to find the dragon-prow to get back to your own place? Is that what you're saying?"

"I don't know if that is it exactly," Sparrow said. "It's just what Mother Egg said you had to do. I think it'll help, but I think there's something else that needs to be done at the other end, too."

Trina's father scrambled to his feet and dusted his knees with his hands. He shook his head. "It's impossible," he said. "It's lost. Gone. No idea where it could be. I've looked – believe me, I've looked."

"You've got to look again," Sparrow said.

"I've got to find Trina," her father said despairingly.

"She's all right," Sparrow said. "I've sent her off. She'll find her own way."

"Where?" breathed Trina's father.

"To my place. You'll see her again, but only if the bridge is finished."

"Are you threatening me?"

"No!" Sparrow chuckled. "No, I can't help it. She wanted to go – to find her sister."

"She doesn't have a sister."

"Doesn't she? Well, I know her sister. I met Trina once before, too – it was all a bit mixed up though. Anyway, we've got to get on. Are you coming?"

"I don't know if I'm coming or going," Trina's father muttered. "I'll show you the only place the prow might be."

They picked their way over to the mound of stones and clay. Dark, high, hopelessly huge, it loomed above them. "There," Trina's father said, flapping his hand towards it. "That's where it'll be. Can you burrow as well as fly?"

"It doesn't look much use," Sparrow agreed despondently. Then he took a jump towards the mound, flew up into the air and landed on top of it. The glow of a distant streetlight caught the side of his face as he gazed down over the shadowy building site.

"Incredible," Trina's father murmured. "Absolutely incredible. Perhaps Trina wasn't imagining things after all.

If boys can fly, there can be mountains that… Perhaps there is a change. Perhaps the world can change. Perhaps…" He tailed off. Then he said, in the same murmuring voice, "You're standing on its head. I'm not dreaming. You're standing on its head!" His voice rose.

"What?" the boy called down to him.

"Your foot! Look at your foot!" the man cried, starting to scramble up the slippery clay.

Sparrow looked down at his feet and saw something round. Bending down and peering, he found that it was a carved eye staring up at him from a strange-shaped, carved face. He saw a snarling mouth of spiky wooden teeth. He was standing on the neck. He stepped off and noticed the ground moving. The whole length of the lost prow lay there on the surface, buried under no more than a skim of clay.

509

Trina's father was scrabbling on the steep slope, and at last managed to crawl his way to the top just as Sparrow was clearing the mud from the head. "What a beauty," he murmured. "What a beauty."

The prow of the Burial Ship looked very dragon-like. It was not particularly the same shape as the head of the dragon which Sparrow had had dealings with, but there was something about its fearsome, intent expression that was just like the living dragon – it was a creature with a clear sense of direction.

Trina's father rocked the prow up and down a little with his foot. It seemed quite loose in the sticky soil and stones. "It's a miracle," he muttered. "I looked everywhere for it. And the digger must have dragged it to the top here when they were piling everything up. Can you give me a hand with it? I must get it to the van." He took hold of the neck and wiggled the prow slightly towards the edge of the mound.

Sparrow went to the other end and heaved, but he couldn't lift it. He could only rock it while Trina's father wiggled.

With a low groan of timber on stony earth, a yelp from Trina's father, and a skittering and clattering of slipping rubble, the prow slipped over the edge of the mound. Sparrow managed to jump clear; but Trina's father, heaving at the head, was knocked sideways and fetched up on his back halfway down the slope. The prow slipped round and down and ended wedged upright by the small landslide it had caused. Rearing up in the faint light from the street, it looked as though it had suddenly sprung to life.

"I've jiggered my arm," Trina's father said. "I can't move it."

"I'll take the prow. Where do you want it to go?"

"Goodness knows," Trina's father said. He was clutching his shoulder and his face was drawn with pain. "The shed's gone. You couldn't manage it alone anyway."

"I could though," Sparrow replied. "Things aren't heavy when I fly."

"I believe you could," Trina's father gasped, as he tried to struggle into a sitting position. He closed his eyes. "Rainbow lights," he muttered. "Rainbow lights before my eyes." His forehead was beaded with sweat.

"Do you remember the rainbow?" said Sparrow. "Before I was properly here, and I tried to fly? The shed and the mountain?"

Trina's father seemed barely conscious. "Take it there," he murmured. "Yes. Good place."

"I think that's the answer," said Sparrow seriously. "But

510

would you be all right here, if I left you?"

Trina's father didn't answer.

Sparrow hesitated. Which was more important, the injured man, or the dragon-prow? Trina's father seemed to have fainted, which must mean that his injured arm was bad. On the other hand, all Mother Egg had said to do was to find the missing piece of the boat. But she hadn't said he was to do anything *with* it. He rose into the air and flew to the prow, then worked it loose and pulled. It came free easily, and Sparrow hovered there holding it as if it were no heavier than one of the feathery dragon bones, though it hung below him to three times his height. He didn't even know the way to the mountain from here.

At that moment, people came round the corner of the buildings on the far side of the street. There were three or four of them. Sparrow didn't think they looked dangerous. "Over here!" he called. "There's a man hurt! Help! Please!"

He remembered Kittel once telling him that people in the city didn't always help you if you were in trouble, but these people started to come towards the building site as soon as Sparrow shouted to them. He wasted no more time. "I hope I'll see you again," he said to Trina's father, and rose swiftly up into the black air. He heard shouts below him, but he paid no heed, and the city with its necklaces of lights and great scabs of burning buildings fell away beneath him.

As soon as he was high enough to be clear of the lights, Sparrow found himself under a paling sky scattered with a few stars. The deep roar of the city, the smell of burning, faded.

Almost straight away he saw the mountain. Or, rather, he saw where the mountain was. There was never a moment's doubt about it. There was a light, like the light that filled the Scroll Cupboard, only brighter, which drew his attention – a pale silver fire that burned far, far off in the dark west, yet which drew him like a beacon. He flew slowly towards it, hampered by the bulky timber wrapped in his arms.

The swift dawn was coming up behind him, and gradually the beacon fire ahead seemed to be getting paler. Before long he could see the grey outline of the pyramid-shaped mountain he had seen from the Scroll Cupboard. Closer and closer he flew, while the pale fire faded, until he was circling over it. And then he saw the wreck of the aeroplane, and understood.

512 Had Puckel planned all this? How had things actually happened? Puckel had removed and shrunk a mountain top; an aeroplane had crashed onto the flat-topped remains of the mountain; Sparrow had thrown the shrunken mountain top through a hole in the Hollywell; it had grown back to its original size; an aeroplane had crashed onto it.

As he circled downwards, the mountain below him seemed to get smaller, greener. It was no longer the great mountain he had seen from the Scroll Cupboard, but the small green hill he had landed on when he first came through from the Hollywell. There was a white line, like a thread, disappearing and reappearing among the trees on the slopes of the hill; and there were people, walking up and down near to the white line. Where should the dragon-prow go? He could see the old railway shed now, just across the dark line of a small river at the foot of the hill. Would he be seen if he flew down there just now?

Then he understood that he could land nowhere else but on the top of the hill. The light had guided him there. The proud dragon-prow didn't belong in a dusty old shed. It should stand on the hilltop. He stooped down the morning-wind towards it.

And as he came closer, the pale fire, which had almost disappeared, suddenly blazed up towards him in a sheet of flame. He cried out, and threw his arms across his eyes, dropping the prow as he did so. It fell out of sight into the dazzling silver light. He rose again, but as he rose the silver fire chased upwards until he seemed to be held, like the point of a candle-flame, at the tip of the light. And at that moment the sun rose.

through the barrier

TRINA RAN. THE DOG WAS FORGOTTEN AND THE OLD woman was forgotten. For a short while, the thought had passed through her mind that the whole business with the dog had just been a miserable trick by the old crone – a trick to land her in deep trouble. Now, that and every other thought was gone, and she ran for her life.

Of course, she couldn't be sure that anyone was actually chasing her. She knew that the people howling and yelling, and the people wielding knives and bottles and stones and sticks, the people running away and the people running after them, were nothing to do with her; but did *they* know that?

She ran, and occasionally she whimpered, "Dad," or sometimes even, "Mum," as she dodged in and out, keeping her eyes peeled for dark streets, dark corners, quiet places – the very places she would have avoided on a normal night. She had no idea where she was or where she was going, and still less idea where the others had got to. She ran.

There seemed to be a lull in the uproar. Trina slipped into a doorway and leaned against a tall plate-glass window, her heart hammering, her breath rough and salty. There were the remains of a glass door next to her, hanging off its hinges, shattered all over the floor. Was it safe to go on? She peered out.

No! People were surging down the street in her direction, leaping in the air, some of them banging on what looked like dustbin lids. She stepped out of the doorway to begin running again – and stopped, and gaped, despite herself, despite the danger.

The street was blocked at the other end by a flock of goats. They weren't very distinct, but she could see beards wagging and tall horns sweeping. They were goats, just like in her dreams in the hospital.

Bang – bang – bang! came from behind her. The leaping people were coming closer. Were they going to fight with the goats? *Beh – beh!* the goats answered. Heads were lowered, horns were tossed, the leader reared up on its hind legs and curvetted. Trina turned.

There was only the doorway. She slipped inside, stepping gingerly under the jagged glass that still hung from the steel frame, crunched over more broken glass in the dark interior, and crouched in the shadows.

For a long while nothing happened. She relaxed a bit and her breathing calmed down. She glanced round her. There was something familiar about the great empty hall she was in; she had been here before. The Scroll Cupboard? No – no, of course not. That door there… Then she remembered – she was in the museum.

A crash, the sound of falling glass, sudden yells, and Trina was running again, running inwards now, into the depths of the building, running blindly, not pausing to look back. There was a dim gleam of glass cases. Jagged outlines here and there where some of them were broken. Her feet crunched. It wouldn't do to fall here. She must find somewhere among all these rows of glass cabinets, somewhere to crouch and be safe till the morning came. There was a sound of running feet – of scuffling, hard feet. Was it people? There was a sound of voices – not words; voices, voices crying, wailing, gibbering, moaning. She had heard that before, in some brown nightmare darkness... She halted. Faint light had caught something ahead of her – a gleaming post, and a pale rope, about the level of her waist. Darkness beyond. A picture that had appeared before, in front of her closed eyes, appeared again in that darkness, the stooping brown mummy-figure sitting examining its empty insides. The back of her neck prickled.

She looked back. There were faint lights bobbing, like will-o'-the-wisps among the glass cases. There were whisperings, and a faint *bleh!*

At least the mummy was dark. It reflected no light. But it was dead – a dead thing – a dead person! She couldn't do it. Yet even as she told herself she couldn't do it, Trina was slipping under the rope. Her head felt as if it were full of spikes, there was a buzzing in her ears like a swarm of bees, cold sweat was running down her back, but her shaking legs were carrying her step by step into the darkness. Her hands touched the cold bony hands clasped round the bony knees. She crouched, wormed her head and shoulders under, in, up, into the huge emptiness of the ribcage...

*   *   *

Darkness fell; complete darkness, without a hint of light, without the shadow of a shadow. There was no feeling of being anywhere; she could as well have been floating, or flying, or falling. She closed her eyes to keep out the darkness.

Then she felt she was being held. Was it the mummy? It felt bony, whoever it was, but maybe not quite hard and bony enough... A moment later she realized that the faint shaking she could feel was herself sobbing. Who was holding her? She opened her eyes.

Somebody was hugging her, but she was looking over the somebody's shoulder at a blue triangle. She blinked, and sobbed; blinked and sobbed.

The blue triangle was a sort of doorway, and the blue was pale blue sky... Two hands took hold of her shoulders, she was pushed backwards a step. She was looking into the face of Mother Egg, thin, solemn, and faraway as ever.

517

"Come," said Mother Egg, and stooping she turned and passed through the triangle-shaped doorway.

"*Miaow*," said a voice from the shadows. She peered round. She seemed to be inside a very small hut. Then, near the doorway, she made out the bushy ruff and erect tail that had once been so familiar to her. "Hello, Cat," she murmured, going down on her hands and knees...

"Is that your sister?" Bull whispered, his voice hoarse and loud in the silence of the mountain top.

But Kittel went on staring at the girl who had crawled through the doorway of the bright-painted building and was standing blinking stupidly in the pale light. There had been few days, over the last three years, when Kittel had not thought a little about her young sister. Especially at night, just before she went to sleep, she would imagine the faces of her family swimming before her eyes – Mum, Dad, Trina… Now, suddenly, everything seemed to have changed. She shook her head. "I – I don't know," she said. "I don't think I ever had a sister."

"Not quite true," Mother Egg remarked. "You have many sisters, as you would see if you could read some of the more complex scrolls. The souls of the earth are joined by many invisible threads. Human sisters, animal sisters, plant sisters, and a whole crowd of sisters in the unseen world – ghosts, sprites, angels. Brothers too. Do not underestimate the size of your family!"

"I don't know what you mean," Kittel murmured.

"You look different," Bull suddenly said to her.

"I feel different," she said, a little crossly.

"No – I mean, you look different," Bull persisted. "Your hair's darker or something. More like…" He turned towards the other girl.

The other girl was no longer there. Apart from the four of them – Puckel and Mother Egg, now sitting in the entrances of two buildings next door to each other, and Kittel and Bull – the Enclosure was quite empty.

"I've had a split personality," Kittel said. "I must have been a bit mad, after all."

"Don't be foolish," said Mother Egg sharply. "You have been engaged in a work of great precision."

"A bridge has one foot in each of the two places it joins, that's all," Puckel put in, nodding with satisfaction.

"The mountain is in two places," Mother Egg said, "but it is one mountain. The flying ship – " she glanced briefly over towards the wrecked aeroplane – "is in two places, but it is all the one machine. This is the place where you entered the door, both now and three years ago. Now I will tell you what has been, and what will come."

"But not you, my lad," Puckel butted in, looking at Bull, who was still gaping at Kittel. "You've got a job to do. Go on, through that door – " he indicated the empty doorway of the building next to his – "and we'll meet up with you directly. Don't worry. You're a dragon-holder again, just as you were once before, and just as this one here has been –" he nodded towards Kittel – "but you'll come through, no fear of that."

Bull immediately did as he was told, crouching to go through the low entrance. The sky was beginning to shine with gold over the north-eastern mountains. Sunrise was very close. The decorated fronts of the five wooden buildings already looked as bright as if they were standing in full sunlight.

"Now I will tell you," Mother Egg began. "Many years ago—"

"Five," Puckel interrupted her.

"Five hundred, more like," she retorted.

"Split the difference," Puckel said with a shrug. "Call it fifty."

"As you wish," Mother Egg said stiffly. "Many years ago, a group of children were brought here to safety. You've heard that story."

"The children on the train – during the air raids?" Kittel asked.

"Those ones," Mother Egg nodded. "But it was not the fire from the sky that was the greatest threat. They were brought to be safe from the poison of the dragon's breath. The dragon's breath had poisoned half the peoples of the world. They were hopelessly mad. Those children were brought here, and looked after until they were old enough to look after themselves. There was nothing special about them; they were not particularly clever, or strong, or talented, or virtuous. They were children of the earth such as there have always been. They lived, and they did one thing which was of great value – they learned not to ask questions. Sometimes that can be a good thing.

"Meanwhile, life in the world they had left went on. Thoughts were thought, and things were made. Some of those thoughts and things came here, though their use was not known. Time went by, and we waited while the ones ripened who would take part in the building of the bridge.

"But this little dragon – " Mother Egg smiled mysteriously at Kittel – "has been the bridge itself. Where Sparrow could only hop like a bird from one side to the other, this little dragon was split in two, and had to be made whole."

520

She was silent, but as she said the word "whole", a thousand little memories seemed to fall into place, all together, in Kittel's mind – Kittel, who understood at last that she was also Trina. She thought with amazement, and a little sorrow, of the years she had spent wishing she could see her father and mother and Trina again; of Trina's longing to be one of the four friends of her dreams. All that time she had been longing for what she already had. Little thoughts and memories drifted past – the growing hill on the Market Glass road, the stone in Sparrow's hand…

"If you two are quite finished now," Puckel's voice broke in, "sunrise has come and it's time we were on our way."

"Don't you think she deserved an explanation?" Mother Egg asked him sharply.

"She certainly never stops asking questions," Puckel

humphed. "Just as well she wasn't one of the ones we brought here in the first place. Between her and that Bull the whole scheme would have been wrecked before we'd even had time to think it up."

"We will go," said Mother Egg, and rising from her doorway she crossed to the one next to it, the one nearly opposite Puckel's. Puckel got up and followed her, ushering on Kittel-Trina – who was trying to think which name she liked best, or whether she should just content herself with her full name of Katrina.

Following Mother Egg into the dark entrance of the doorway, she felt the sudden burst of light behind her as the sun rose; and the next moment they were standing in a place which the Kittel part of her had never seen before but which the Trina part immediately recognized – the Scroll Cupboard, lit now not by its usual dim silver light but made radiant, rich-coloured as the five painted buildings on the mountain top, by the full light of day.

the wrong direction

LISSIE AND ORMAND HAD NOT FINISHED FILLING UP THE PIT again when the search party returned, straggling tiredly down the ridge at the eastern end of the valley.

"I don't want to be around when they come through here," Ormand said. "I can't be bothered with all their questions."

"We won't be able to pack up and get away in time. And, anyway, we haven't finished," Lissie pointed out. "We could hide in the wood, but they'd easily find us if they wanted to."

It was very early in the morning. Their cooking-fire had been got going and was boiling up the water for their breakfast of biscuit-porridge. They were doing a little gentle filling-in to get the chill from their limbs while they waited for it. The ponies had just started on their early graze. It would certainly not be easy to disappear.

As they stood there, indecisive, a shout came – not from

the men, but from the opposite direction, the west – a shout that was sudden, and echoing, and that grew in strength as it echoed. The branches of the birch wood across the stream suddenly bent as if a gust of wind had hit them. Ormand and Lissie turned, and saw a small dark figure among the trees. "That's Bull," said Lissie.

There was another great shout: "This way! Make haste! Make haste!" The echoes rolled around the valley like a rumble of stones on a dry hillside.

"That can't be Bull," Ormand said. "He could never shout like that." Yet even he had to admit that it looked like Bull coming towards them. "Let's go and see," he said.

"I don't think I want to," Lissie muttered, following him slowly.

Lissie saw Ormand reach Bull just as Plato Smithers and the others at the head of the search party came out from among the trees. The men were running. Bull stopped, as if waiting. He seemed to be ignoring Ormand. Lissie felt more and more reluctant to go up to him, yet her feet kept moving her forwards.

Bull was gazing past Ormand towards the eastern end of the valley. Lissie wasn't even sure he was looking towards the men of the villages. "What's wrong with him?" she whispered to Ormand as she came up.

"I don't know," Ormand whispered back. "Something. He won't speak to me."

"Bull?" Lissie said hesitantly.

"Make haste!" the great voice boomed out again from Bull, and the force of it sent Ormand and Lissie staggering back. Bull started to walk straight towards the clump of nettles in the middle of the valley.

"His ankle's better," Ormand remarked.

"I wish Sparrow was here," Lissie said.

"Haste!" Bull called. "I have found it!"

Now the men of the villages were coming up from the stream towards the nettle-patch. They were walking rapidly, heads down, packed together shoulder to shoulder. Like a flock of sheep, Lissie thought. But she too, although she would have liked to hang back, was following Bull. She couldn't seem to help it. Ormand was walking beside her, looking pale and tense. They came together, Ormand and Lissie facing the men of the villages across the nettles while Bull walked straight into the tall plants as if they weren't there and stood still. He was peering intently at something at his feet.

"You found it then, young Bull," said Plato Smithers, in a strained voice, as though he were trying hard to act as if everything was normal. "Leg's better too, I'm glad to see."

Then Bull raised his head and gazed round at them all. Lissie's heart missed a beat, and she almost choked on her breath. His eyes were rolled upwards, with only the whites showing. His dark face was quite expressionless.

And suddenly, with a bellow that shook loose the rocks high in the mountain crags and sent everyone staggering to their knees, the dragon came. Out of nowhere it seemed to come. One moment Bull was standing there with his blank white eyes; the next, there was no sign of him, but the huge head of the dragon was where he had been, with the vast, green-golden bulk of its body stretching back towards the western end of the valley.

They had just got to their feet when they were toppled again – this time by a small earthquake. The dragon had dug its smoking snout into the ground – deep in, as if the ground were no more solid than water. And then, as if the dragon had simply peeled back a layer of the world to reveal another, in place of the Valley of Murmuring Water they were standing on the short turf by the huge, still trees of the Hollywell in Ormand's own garden.

Ormand and Lissie blinked. Everything was as they had left it two weeks before. And everything else was as it had been two minutes before – the dragon, the bewildered men of the five villages – but for no more than a second. Again the dragon bellowed, and the glossy spiked leaves shivered down in a shower out of the holly trees. Again the snout plunged into the earth, and the ground that was Lissie and Ormand's home was ripped apart.

And they were in a wild, rocky place, surrounded on three sides by a towering cliff. Ormand and Lissie quickly recognized it as the place called the Echoing Hall just outside the village of Springing Wood.

Again a roar – and this time the blast of the dragon's voice rebounded from all sides of the cliff so that they were deafened and dizzied by the din, and everything went black before their eyes – and a third time the terrible head plunged into the rock. And as it did so, the sun rose into a cleft in the rock face and shone through on them.

the moment of danger

BECAUSE EVERYTHING HAPPENED SO QUICKLY, KITTEL found it impossible to say whether she and Puckel and Mother Egg had arrived before the dragon, or whether the dragon had arrived before them, or whether they had all arrived together. At any rate, there the dragon was, lying across the floor of the Scroll Cupboard while its tail snaked away down one wall. Its head and shoulders lay in an arch-shaped opening in the opposite wall, and right in front of its nose stood Ormand and Lissie – Ormand nearer to it, pale and terrified, Lissie huddling behind him – with their backs to a glorious, shining thing that Kittel knew must be Sparrow's bridge. Clustered round the dragon's tail were twenty bewildered-looking village men, while crawling on hands and knees on the sandy ground beside its immense flank was Bull, looking very sick and shaky.

No one moved. Two long wisps of smoke issued from the dragon's nostrils and bent in a slight breeze that came from the wide sky and the distant world outside. Kittel wondered how long it took for the dragon's breath to send you mad.

"Aren't you going to do something?" she whispered to Puckel. Puckel ignored her. She could see no sign of Mother Egg.

Then the dragon spoke – a soft, hissing sound quite unlike the thunderous bellow which was the only sound Kittel had heard from it before. It was almost a sweet sound, thin, vague, a little like the sound of wind in trees. "Son of a slug," it said, "daughter of earthworms, you are standing between me and my bridge. What have you to say?"

Its great jaws scarcely moved, but at each word a thick puff of smoke shot upwards from its nostrils. It was almost as if it were speaking through its nose. Kittel saw Ormand's mouth working. Lissie was staring back at the dragon over Ormand's shoulder, her normally ruddy face pale as a toadstool. Then Ormand gave several great gulps, and spoke.

"I don't think it's really your bridge," he stammered. "Sparrow made it, you see … it was out of the bones of another dragon … we dug them up."

There was a small explosion of smoke from the dragon's jaws, and a broad, indistinct noise, like a gale getting up in the distance. It occurred to Kittel that the dragon was laughing.

"What do you know of bones?" the great beast said. "You understand nothing. Step aside."

Kittel noticed now that, although the narrow end of the shining bridge rested on the floor of the Scroll Cupboard, just behind Lissie's feet there was a gap in it where it began its huge, impossible arch into empty air. She could see nothing below the bridge, which scarcely looked solid and had no parapet or rail, and she could only pray that Lissie wouldn't step back.

But now Lissie was mumbling something into Ormand's ear. "No," Ormand said after she had finished, his voice scarcely louder than a whisper. "No, I think we've just got to stay here." Ormand looked both determined and uncertain. Kittel realized he had not noticed her and Puckel.

"You have strayed into my dream, slug-son," the dragon said. "Yet I am awake. When you dug your impudent blade into the soil of my resting place, you strayed in then. Now you are trapped, like these sheep at my tail. Look – "

And suddenly the whole scene was reversed. Ormand and Lissie stood inside the Scroll Cupboard, while the dragon lay facing them with its tail stretched across the bridge, its neck bridging the gap. "What do you say now, little ones?" it hissed.

Again, Lissie murmured into Ormand's ear. "I say – " Ormand brought the words out with a struggle – "that dragons can't go backwards!"

"Ha!" the dragon's voice was for a moment like an echo of its terrifying bellow, while an even bigger gout of brown smoke burst upwards. A second later the scene was as it had been before – Ormand and Lissie with their backs to the bridge, the dragon stretched across the floor of the Scroll Cupboard.

"Give me back something of what you've taken," came the dragon's soft hiss, "and I'll let you go free."

"I don't think we can," said Ormand. "I was only doing what I was told, and we weren't supposed to touch the bones. It was an accident, and I think that's why the bridge—"

The dragon cut him short. "What have you in your hand?" it hissed.

"Nothing," Ormand replied.

"Let me see this nothing," the dragon said.

Bewildered, Ormand opened his hand, palm toward the dragon.

"It is, indeed, a very small nothing," the dragon hissed agreeably. "Hold it closer, so that I may see it better."

Ormand obediently stretched his hand further out towards the dragon.

"Closer still," the dragon sighed. "The nothing is almost invisible."

Ormand stepped towards the dragon, holding his hand out at full stretch.

Snap! A sound like cracking rock split the air. The dragon lunged forward. A second later there was a piercing scream from Lissie. "Ormand! Your arm! Oh no, your arm!"

Ormand dropped to his knees, clutching at his right shoulder. But there was nothing to clutch; his arm was clean away, chopped off just below the shoulder. There was no blood, no mess – just the stump of an arm that looked as though it might have healed years ago.

At that moment, Bull staggered to his feet, lurched forward, and supporting himself against the dragon's crooked foreleg, then its huge jaw, stumbled to the edge of the bridge, almost brushing the dragon's nose. He seized Ormand by his remaining arm and dragged him clear, back towards Puckel. It was perhaps the bravest thing he had ever done, though in fact the dragon paid no attention. Lissie, both hands clapped over her mouth as if to stop herself screaming again, tottered after them. Whether or not they had been able to see Puckel before, they could clearly see him now.

"Why didn't you stop it?" Kittel found herself sobbing, shaking Puckel by the arm as she sobbed. "I asked you to do something." She felt weak and sick.

"A price had to be paid," the old man said, taking hold of Ormand's shoulders and steadying him on his feet. He was now holding his stick in his hand. "Well done," he said. And then, "Look – here comes the young one."

Kittel was so used to Sparrow flying that the first thing she did was glance up into the air. But Sparrow was not flying; he was walking slowly towards them over the glittering bridge.

In fact, it was only the long curve of the bridge's arch that made him look as though he was coming slowly; he was actually walking quite quickly, with a light, confident step and a strange air about him as if he had just discovered everything that there was to know about anything. He was dressed in the old, shabby, patched clothes that boys in the mountain villages always wore. Kittel and Trina compared notes about him: Trina told Kittel that this was not Pats; Kittel told Trina that this was Sparrow; Trina and Kittel agreed that Sparrow and Pats looked very alike but were not exactly alike; both of them wondered who, or what, Pats had been, all those years when Sparrow was living his life in the mountains. "Sparrow ought to be in Pats' clothes," Trina told Kittel. "Illusion," Kittel told Trina. "Clothes are just an illusion – Sparrow can make mountains look like clouds…"

Sparrow came without hesitation to the edge of the bridge, and stood with the toes of his boots just poking over into the gap between him and the first two dragon bones. The dragon crouched, eyeing him intently. He faced it straight-on and said, "Here I am."

"I know," said the dragon, in a smooth, long-drawn whisper like a wind in the keyhole of a door. "And can you come any further?"

"Not while you're there," Sparrow answered promptly. He was looking into its orange-smouldering eyes without any sign of fear.

The dragon spoke again. "Would you like to have the bridge completed, little Puka?" it said softly.

"Yes, I would," said Sparrow.

"I could make it complete, but you must step out of my way."

"Then it would be finished for you, but not for me," Sparrow said carefully.

531

"That is true," the dragon answered, with a low laugh like the echo of an owl's wings amongst rocks. There was a long silence.

"Will Sparrow be safe?" Kittel whispered anxiously to Puckel. "The dragon could just frazzle him up, couldn't it?"

"Not here," Puckel replied. "Not in the Scroll Cupboard, where the names of all living things are kept – here nothing can kill. The dragon can't move forward across the bridge if a living soul stands in his way. Watch, and listen."

"I will make a bargain with you," the dragon said to Sparrow.

"All right," said Sparrow warily.

"Let me ask you a question," the dragon hissed. "If you cannot answer it, the bridge is for me to use; if you answer it correctly, it is for you to use – a living bridge, or a bridge of bones."

Sparrow glanced over at Puckel. But Puckel's face was as set as a statue's. "All right," Sparrow said at last.

"How are things, in the scrumptious little world down there?" the dragon asked.

"Is that the question?" said Sparrow.

"No," said the dragon, "I was merely being conversational."

"There's burning. There's fighting. I think they're all crazy there."

"Still!" the dragon exclaimed, with another of its long, husky laughs. "Then all is ripe for my return, and my eager little flock –" the monster's eyes rolled back towards the men of the five villages – "will be the first to cross and see what they've been missing for so long."

"You didn't like it much last time you were there."

"Ha!" said the dragon, as a gout of black smoke shot up from it like an umbrella. "This is the question, little Puka. Listen. This will put the grin on the back of your head."

Sparrow, who had not been grinning at all, began to look extremely serious.

"It is this," said the dragon. "Are the things in the world there because I dream them; or do I dream them because they are there?"

"That's the question it asked you!" Kittel whispered frantically to Puckel. "Do you know the answer now?"

"I do," said Puckel, never taking his eyes off Sparrow.

"Can't you tell Sparrow?" Kittel asked.

"No, I can't," Puckel answered curtly.

"Why not? It's life or death – it might be the end of the world!"

"I can't tell him," Puckel retorted, "because the question has no answer."

Kittel looked round desperately. There must be something they could do! She looked at the stick in Puckel's hand. Couldn't she grab it, and throw it over to Sparrow, or something? But the stick looked back at her very woodenly. I am nothing but a stick, it seemed to be saying, there's no point in looking at me. Then she looked over at Sparrow again, in sudden doubt. A memory – Trina's memory – flitted through her mind. The riddle ... the riddle that had no answer...

Sparrow had not been grinning before, but he was now. A broad smile of self-satisfaction was on his face. He rocked himself gently backwards and forwards at the edge of the awesome abyss.

"You must tell me something before you hear the answer to that, Ureychyoburenitho," he said.

"What must I tell you?" the dragon hissed.

"You must tell me who you're asking," Sparrow said calmly.

"Why you, boy – you! Who else?" the dragon growled.

"Not so fast," said Sparrow. "I've been in and out of so many shapes, I just don't know who I am any more. Are you asking a boy you're dreaming of because he's there – or a boy who's there because you're dreaming of him?"

There was an awful silence. The smoke that seeped from the dragon's jaws grew slowly thicker. Yet as it grew thicker, it also became paler. From black to brown it turned, and from brown to gold, and from gold to white. Sparrow's form could only dimly be seen now, swathed in the drifting cloud. And then from white, the smoke turned to colours – yellow and green and blue, and then a luminous violet like cranesbill flowers. And still Sparrow was there, upright in front of the dragon.

Slowly the smoke cleared, until only two thin wisps were rising from the beast's nostrils.

"I have bones in my mouth, little Puka," the dragon said.

"Let's have them then," said Sparrow. "It's time we were off for our breakfast."

The massive, tooth-spiked jaws of the dragon opened, its black tongue flicked, something shot into the air which Sparrow caught in his hand. For a moment, Kittel, Bull, Ormand and Lissie glimpsed a white bone, with a joint in the middle and a small fan-shape at the end, which must once have been Ormand's arm and hand – and then Sparrow bent and placed it under his toes.

The Scroll Cupboard, the abyss of sky, the rainbow bridge and the world at its foot, the dragon and the men of the five villages – all vanished without a sound and without a trace. The young people were standing in the sunlight under a blue sky alive with huge white clouds. Their ears were filled with an endless, musical, booming roar. They were on a mountain, flat-topped but empty, scattered with outcrops of gleaming white-and-gold rock. The largest of these, just beside them, reared up like stone clouds, and on the top sat Puckel, cross-legged and still, with Mother Egg behind him.

Then they looked down and saw the waterfall. It poured from a gap under the rocks where Puckel sat, foamed wildly over the broken ground at the mountain's edge, and fell, thousands of feet it seemed, gathering in strength and power as it fell, deep blue-green, bearded with white foam, casting rainbow shadows over the whole mountainside. They had never seen a waterfall so huge or so beautiful, not even Kittel and Sparrow, who had once seen something like a copy of this one. From the cliff-top, they could see the whole of their mountain-country stretching below in its humped and jagged and pinnacled glory, green valleys and the grey bones of mountainsides, deep-cleft rivers and snow-gleaming peaks.

"King Puck," said Sparrow in awe. "We've come to King Puck. It doesn't seem like a hidden place, but I could never find it."

"Now you will be able to find it at all times," Puckel said. "For I am going to have a well-earned rest, but you'll be needing my advice pretty soon, I expect, and I shall be here to give it. You'll have your work cut out with that bridge. You must learn how to come and go across it, and you will have to teach your whole troop how to do the same."

"What troop?" said Sparrow.

"Well, what do you think that school's for? The men of the five villages? Not likely! You need younger fools, tender ones, still able to bend. You didn't think this was the end of it all and you could just go back to fishing and pony-trekking, did you? There's work to be done – serious work, grim work. The Polymorphs have kicked up a rare old rumpus for you down there; that'll cause you problems, though it's to help you in the long run. A smoke screen to work behind.

"So, listen, all of you. You are the first. You are the teachers, you are the leaders. All have your places, all have your tasks. You are a seed, just as the top of this mountain is a seed, planted by Sparrow on the other side of the bridge. Don't expect to see results, mind. Healing will take a long time, and there's only so much you can do in one lifetime. We have made a chink in the armour of the sorry world beyond the bridge, and it will be for you to pour the first of the power of the Giants' Door through that chink. No more goats now; things can be more direct – you will be little goats yourselves. Many goats – and a Sparrow, and a Cat, and a Bull."

He turned to Bull. "Bulls are too big to cross," he said. "You must learn to grow smaller, boy. It will be a long task. You will be needed to direct and govern things among the people of the five villages. No more wild-goose chases off into the mountains! But when you do cross, you will go as the representative of the dragon – as Kittel came here as the representative of the dragon. Through Bull the dragon will cross the bridge, but will no longer be able to break out of Bull's form."

Bull looked doubtful.

536 "Don't worry, boy," Puckel said. "You will have great power. That's what you've always wanted. It's not always a bad thing. But Sparrow will have you in the palm of his hand, and that's the best place for you to be. Together you'll do great things, take my word for it. And now, old spindle-shanks – "

Suddenly he turned round and seized Mother Egg by the ankle. Dumbfounded, they watched the old lady being lifted off the ground and turned unceremoniously upside down by Puckel, until her head was on the ground beside them. She didn't protest and she seemed to have gone quite rigid. Puckel put both hands on the soles of her feet and then vaulted off his perch on the rock to land beside them himself, and where she had been, Puckel's old stick was in his hands again.

"And now," he said briskly, "breakfast, and then a send-off. You, my dear – " he turned to Kittel – "are expected, over across the bridge, but we won't make you cross *that* on an empty stomach."

Kittel's mouth seemed to have gone dry. "You mean…" she mumbled, but couldn't bring any more words out. It was one thing, thinking of a bridge to cross to get back home, but quite another to think of that narrow shining thing, with nothing to hang on to, nothing to support her, spanning a horror of empty air…

Puckel nodded. "You'll manage," he said briefly, giving her a wink. "There's nothing worth getting that isn't worth a bit of a struggle. You'll get used to it."

"You've fallen off a cliff before," Sparrow put in with a grin. "And you're still here."

And Kittel had to be content with that.

epilogue

"I DIDN'T GET A LIFT HOME WITH A STRANGER," TRINA told her father. "I walked."

"You must admit it's a bit hard to believe," he said.

"Well, Mum certainly thinks I'm a liar." She fell silent. The monotonous hum of the engine, the buzz-buzz of the windscreen wipers and the hiss of tyres on wet road were the only sounds. They drove slowly, because Trina's father had his arm in a sling and it was hard for him to steer properly.

They had been to collect his things from the university. The university had been closed down because of all the damage. Its library had been burned to the ground, and now no one knew what was going to happen.

For the three days since the riot there had been almost constant, driving rain. The city was unutterably dreary – blackened buildings, streaks of soot and ash washed across walls and pavements by the rain, piles of rubble, holes in the road, burned-out cars. Everywhere there were soldiers. Dark-painted army lorries and armoured cars stood in every street. There was hardly any of the normal city traffic, and no crowds. It seemed that if more than four or five people met together, they were quickly surrounded by soldiers with guns who searched them and told them to go away home.

Trina's father seemed very depressed. "A lot of things are going to change – for the worse," he said. "It's been coming for a long time. I just hate to think what kind of world you'll be growing up in."

"'Vexed to nightmare,'" Trina said, with a small smile. It was a relief to be out of the house, away from her mother's accusing glances. And she felt light at heart.

"What's that?" her father demanded.

"'Vexed to nightmare,'" she repeated. "It's in a poem Pats' dad keeps saying."

"He's off with the fairies," her father muttered. "Always has been."

"It's not really a nightmare though," Trina said. "Whatever it looks like. It's a smokescreen."

"I don't know what you're talking about," he said crossly.

They were coming home by the Market Glass road. "Dad," she said suddenly. "You know when I went off – I mean the other time, for that whole week?"

"Yes?"

"I know where I was now."

"Where?"

"The same place as when I got lost in the riot."

Her father sighed. "Where was that?"

"I don't know."

"What's the point in telling me, then?"

Trina sighed. *Buzz-buzz*, *buzz-buzz*, went the windscreen wipers. Then *squeak-squeak*, *squeak-squeak*; the rain had stopped. "Dad?" she said.

"What?"

"You've not to worry."

"How can I not worry about you?"

"There's things happening," she said. "I won't be here all the time. I've work to do."

"You'll have exams before very long."

"Oh – exams," she said. She shook her head. "It won't be like that."

"If you don't do well in your exams, it'll spoil your chances in life, you know."

540   The conversation wasn't going the way she wanted it to go. She would never be able to talk to her parents, to tell them… But all of a sudden her father laughed. "Listen to me! I'm like an old cracked record. You'd never think half the university had just been burned down. I don't know where we're going, Kit. I don't know what things are going to be like. There's no point in coming to me for fatherly advice – about exams, or anything else."

"I know," she said. "You've just got to trust me."

The clouds were starting to break up, rolling back over the dark hills in streamers and flags. By the time they came in sight of the Stack, pale sunlight was falling in shafts on the green country. All of a sudden – "Look!" Trina said. "The rainbow!"

Out of the side of the Stack the great arch sprang, rising, shining with almost painful brightness to the height of the pewter-coloured sky, disappearing into the white sides of mountainous clouds.

"It always makes you feel better, a rainbow," her father said. "It almost looks solid, doesn't it."

"Yes, it does," Trina agreed.

Charles Ashton is a highly respected author whose books include the Dragon Fire trilogy: *Jet Smoke and Dragon Fire* (shortlisted for both the Guardian Children's Fiction Prize and the WH Smith Mindboggling Books Award), *Into the Spiral* and *The Shining Bridge*, as well as the novels *Time Ghost* and *Billy's Drift*. His stories for younger readers include *Ruth and the Blue Horse*, *The Giant's Boot* (shortlisted for the Smarties Book Prize), *The Boy Who Wasn't a Bear* and *The Snow Door*.

The landscape and characters of his home in Scotland play a huge part in his work.